A VISION OF SHADOWS

WARRIORS

THUNDER AND SHADOW

WARRIORS

THE PROPHECIES BEGIN

THE NEW PROPHECY

POWER OF THREE

OMEN OF THE STARS

EXPLORE THE WARRIORS WORLD

MANGA

The Lost Warrior

Warrior's Refuge

Warrior's Return

The Rise of Scourge

Tigerstar and Sasha #1: Into the Woods

Tigerstar and Sasha #2: Escape from the Forest

Tigerstar and Sasha #3: Return to the Clans

Ravenpaw's Path #1: Shattered Peace

Ravenpaw's Path #2: A Clan in Need

Ravenpaw's Path #3: The Heart of a Warrior

SkyClan and the Stranger #1: The Rescue

SkyClan and the Stranger #2: Beyond the Code

SkyClan and the Stranger #3: After the Flood

NOVELLAS

Hollyleaf's Story

Mistystar's Omen

Cloudstar's Journey

Tigerclaw's Fury

Leafpool's Wish

Dovewing's Silence

Mapleshade's Vengeance

Goosefeather's Curse

Ravenpaw's Farewell

SURVIVORS

A VISION OF SHADOWS

WARRIORS

THUNDER AND SHADOW

ERIN
HUNTER

HARPER

An Imprint of HarperCollinsPublishers

Special thanks to Kate Cary

ISBN 978-0-06-238641-0 (trade bdg.) — ISBN 978-0-06-238642-7 (lib. bdg.)
ISBN 978-0-06-257415-2 (special ed.)

Typography by Ellice M. Lee
16 17 18 19 20   CG/RRDH   10 9 8 7 6 5 4 3 2
❖
First Edition

ALLEGIANGES

THUNDERCLAN

LEADER   **BRAMBLESTAR**—dark brown tabby tom with amber eyes

DEPUTY   **SQUIRRELFLIGHT**—dark ginger she-cat with green eyes and one white paw

MEDIGINE GATS   **LEAFPOOL**—light brown tabby she-cat with amber eyes, white paws and chest

JAYFEATHER—gray tabby tom with blind blue eyes

     APPRENTICE, ALDERPAW (dark ginger tom with amber eyes)

WARRIORS   (toms and she-cats without kits):

BRACKENFUR—golden-brown tabby tom

CLOUDTAIL—long-haired white tom with blue eyes

BRIGHTHEART—white she-cat with ginger patches

THORNCLAW—golden-brown tabby tom

WHITEWING—white she-cat with green eyes

BIRCHFALL—light brown tabby tom

BERRYNOSE—cream-colored tom with a stump for a tail

MOUSEWHISKER—gray-and-white tom

POPPYFROST—pale tortoiseshell-and-white she-cat

CINDERHEART—gray tabby she-cat

LIONBLAZE—golden tabby tom with amber eyes

ROSEPETAL—dark cream she-cat

BRIARLIGHT—dark brown she-cat, paralyzed in her hindquarters

BLOSSOMFALL—tortoiseshell-and-white she-cat with petal-shaped white patches

BUMBLESTRIPE—very pale gray tom with black stripes

IVYPOOL—silver-and-white tabby she-cat with dark blue eyes

DOVEWING—pale gray she-cat with blue eyes

CHERRYFALL—ginger she-cat
APPRENTICE, SPARKPAW (orange tabby she-cat)

MOLEWHISKER—brown-and-cream tom

SNOWBUSH—white, fluffy tom

AMBERMOON—pale ginger she-cat

DEWNOSE—gray-and-white tom

STORMCLOUD—(formerly Frankie); gray tabby tom

HOLLYTUFT—black she-cat

FERNSONG—yellow tabby tom

SORRELSTRIPE—dark brown she-cat

QUEENS   (she-cats expecting or nursing kits)

DAISY—cream long-furred cat from the horseplace

LILYHEART—small, dark tabby she-cat with white patches, and blue eyes (mother to Leafkit, a tortoiseshell she-kit; Larkkit, a black tom-kit; and Honeykit, a white she-kit with yellow splotches; fostering Twigkit, a gray she-kit with green eyes)

ELDERS (former warriors and queens, now retired):

PURDY—plump tabby former loner with a gray muzzle

GRAYSTRIPE—long-haired gray tom

MILLIE—striped silver tabby she-cat with blue eyes

SHADOWCLAN

LEADER   **ROWANSTAR**—ginger tom

DEPUTY   **CROWFROST**—black-and-white tom

MEDICINE CAT   **LITTLECLOUD**—very small tabby tom

WARRIORS   **TAWNYPELT**—tortoiseshell she-cat with green eyes

        APPRENTICE, NEEDLEPAW

TIGERHEART—dark brown tabby tom

        APPRENTICE, SLEEKPAW

STONETOOTH—white tom

        APPRENTICE, JUNIPERPAW

SPIKEFUR—dark brown tom with tufty fur on his head

        APPRENTICE, YARROWPAW

WASPTAIL—yellow tabby she-cat with green eyes

        APPRENTICE, STRIKEPAW

DAWNPELT—cream-furred she-cat

        APPRENTICE, BEEPAW

SNOWBIRD—sleek, lithe, well-muscled, pure white she-cat with green eyes

SCORCHFUR—dark gray tom with slashed ears, one of which is torn

BERRYHEART—black-and-white she-cat

CLOVERFOOT—gray tabby she-cat

RIPPLETAIL—white tom

SPARROWTAIL—large tabby tom

MISTCLOUD—spiky-furred, pale gray she-cat

QUEENS   **GRASSHEART**—pale brown tabby she-cat

PINENOSE—black she-cat (mother to Birchkit, a beige tom-kit; Lionkit, a yellow she-kit with amber eyes; Puddlekit, a brown tom-kit with white splotches; and Slatekit, a sleek, gray tom-kit; fostering Violetkit, a black-and-white she-kit)

ELDERS   **OAKFUR**—small brown tom

KINKFUR—tabby she-cat, with long fur that sticks out at all angles

RATSCAR—scarred tom

WINDCLAN

LEADER   **ONESTAR**—brown tabby tom

DEPUTY   **HARESPRING**—brown-and-white tom

MEDICINE CAT   **KESTRELFLIGHT**—mottled gray tom with white splotches like kestrel feathers

WARRIORS   **NIGHTCLOUD**—black she-cat

GORSETAIL—very pale gray-and-white she-cat with blue eyes

CROWFEATHER—dark gray tom
APPRENTICE, FERNPAW (gray tabby she-cat)

LEAFTAIL—dark tabby tom with amber eyes

EMBERFOOT—gray tom with two dark paws

BREEZEPELT—black tom with amber eyes

FURZEPELT—gray-and-white she-cat
APPRENTICE, LARKPAW (pale brown tabby she-cat)

SEDGEWHISKER—light brown tabby she-cat

SLIGHTFOOT—black tom with white flash on his chest

OATCLAW—pale brown tabby tom

FEATHERPELT—gray tabby she-cat

HOOTWHISKER—dark gray tom

QUEENS **HEATHERTAIL**—light brown tabby she-cat with blue eyes (mother to Smokekit, a gray she-kit, and Brindlekit, a mottled brown she-kit)

ELDERS **WHITETAIL**—small white she-cat

RIVERCLAN

LEADER **MISTYSTAR**—gray she-cat with blue eyes

DEPUTY **REEDWHISKER**—black tom

MEDICINE CATS **MOTHWING**—dappled golden she-cat

WILLOWSHINE—gray tabby she-cat

WARRIORS **MINTFUR**—light gray tabby tom

DUSKFUR—brown tabby she-cat
APPRENTICE, SHADEPAW (dark brown she-cat)

MINNOWTAIL—dark gray she-cat

MALLOWNOSE—light brown tabby tom

PETALFUR—gray-and-white she-cat

BEETLEWHISKER—brown-and-white tabby tom

CURLFEATHER—pale brown she-cat

PODLIGHT—gray-and-white tom

HERONWING—dark gray-and-black tom

SHIMMERPELT—silver she-cat

LIZARDTAIL—light brown tom
APPRENTICE, FOXPAW (russet tabby tom)

HAVENPELT—black-and-white she-cat

PERCHWING—gray-and-white she-cat

SNEEZECLOUD—gray-and-white tom

BRACKENPELT—tortoiseshell she-cat

JAYCLAW—gray tom

OWLNOSE—brown tabby tom

QUEENS **LAKEHEART**—gray tabby she-cat (mother to Harekit, Dapplekit, Gorsekit, and Softkit)

ICEWING—white she-cat with blue eyes (mother to Nightkit and Breezekit)

ELDERS **MOSSPELT**—tortoiseshell-and-white she-cat

A VISION OF SHADOWS

WARRIORS

THUNDER AND SHADOW

CAT VIEW

GREENLEAF
TWOLEGPLACE

TWOLEG NEST

TWOLEG PATH

TWOLEG PATH

CLEARING

SHADOWCLAN
CAMP

HALFBRIDGE

SMALL
THUNDERPATH

GREENLEAF
TWOLEGPLACE

HALFBRIDGE

ISLAND

STREAM

RIVERCLAN
CAMP

HORSEPLACE

HAREVIEW
CAMPSITE

SANCTUARY
COTTAGE

SADLER WOODS

LITTLEPINE ROAD

LITTLEPINE
SAILING
CENTER

TWOLEG VI

LITTLEPINE
ISLAND

RIVER ALBA

WHITECHURCH ROAD

KNIGHT'S
COPSE

PROLOGUE

Sun split the branches above Echosong's head and sliced through the shadows dappling the forest floor. Echosong relished the rays as they warmed her back. She swished her tail happily as a soft, warm wind rustled the leaves. Overhead, birds chattered, and she licked her lips hungrily. She would hunt before the sun set.

She paused.

Before the sun sets?

Hadn't it set already today? And hadn't rain been lashing the juniper bush where she'd made her solitary nest?

Yes! She'd fallen asleep to its thrumming, wondering where her scattered Clanmates were sheltering as the storm swept the forest.

This is a dream.

Yet it felt too real to be a dream. *A vision?* Her heart lifted. It had been so long since she'd had a vision. She was beginning to think that StarClan had forgotten SkyClan, just like the other Clans had forgotten them countless moons ago.

Ahead she heard fur brush the undergrowth. Paw steps were stalking toward her. *Danger?* Echosong froze, fear clutching her belly. *No.* She calmed herself. *This is a vision. I'm safe here.* And yet she didn't move. Instead she waited, her paws pricking with expectation.

A broad-shouldered tom slid from between the ferns and stopped a few tail-lengths ahead. Stars sparkled in his pelt, and his blue eyes shone like the sky.

"Who are you?" Recognition itched in Echosong's paws. His thick gray pelt was familiar, and he blinked at her softly, as though they were old friends. She'd seen him before in a vision!

"Embrace what you find in the shadows, for only they can clear the sky," the tom murmured.

Her thoughts quickened. "What shadows? Who are *they*?"

He gazed at her, not speaking.

"And what does *clear the sky* mean?" Frustration tightened her chest. This cat had brought her a prophecy before: *What remains when the fire has burned out?* It had baffled her. Why couldn't he ever say what he meant? "Just tell me." Was he trying to give her a clue about what had happened to her Clan? The cats she'd known her whole life had scattered when the rogues had driven them from the gorge. She didn't even know if any of them were still alive.

The gray tom lifted his gaze and stared into the oak canopy. As he did, a sharp wind whisked through the branches. She followed his gaze. He was watching a flurry of leaves as they fluttered toward the ground. Dancing, the leaves twirled between them for a moment before drifting onto the forest floor.

Echosong blinked at the leaves. They were not oak leaves. They were bigger and didn't have softly curved edges. Each of them had five points, more like maple than oak.

"Now you're scattered like leaves, blown by the wind." The tom's mew broke into her thoughts. He reached out a paw and swept the fallen leaves, piling a small heap in front of him. Another five-pointed leaf was falling, larger than the rest. It fluttered toward him like a moth. Deftly he reached up and hooked it from the air. He laid it on top of the pile. "Look."

Echosong leaned forward, excitement tingling through her pelt. What did the leaves mean? Why were they maple and not oak? As she gazed at them, trying desperately to understand their meaning, she saw them fade.

"No!"

The vision was blurring. Darkness clouded her sight. It mustn't disappear yet. She didn't understand!

"Tell me more!" Her own panicked mew woke her, and she lifted her head sharply. She blinked into darkness, disappointment swamping her. She was back in her makeshift nest, rain beating the juniper branches above her. Cold water dripped through the leaves and soaked into her pelt. Shivering, she closed her eyes and tried to remember every detail of the vision. Her heart pounded. What had StarClan been trying to tell her? *I have to understand!* If only she could figure it out, she might finally find her way home.

CHAPTER 1

Alderpaw's gaze drifted toward the trailing brambles at the entrance of the medicine den. Outside, leaves would be drifting into the hollow. Leaf-fall had come so soon! Less than a moon ago he'd been trekking back from his quest beneath sunny blue skies.

"Alderpaw!"

Jayfeather's sharp mew snapped him from his thoughts. He turned his attention back to the herbs piled in front of him.

"You're meant to be separating the yarrow from the colts-foot." Jayfeather glared at him with sightless blue eyes.

"Sorry," Alderpaw mumbled. Nothing he did seemed to please Jayfeather. Hurriedly he began to peel the wide, limp yarrow leaves away from the brittle coltsfoot.

Beside him, Leafpool reached deeper into the crevice at the back of the cave. She hauled out another pawful of leaves. "I think that's the last of them. Once we've sorted these, we can decide what we need to gather before leaf-bare."

"We'll need catmint," Jayfeather mewed. "If we'd gathered more last year, we might not have lost Spiderleg."

At the far side of the medicine den, Briarlight pushed

herself upright in her nest. "I can help with the sorting."

"Thanks," Jayfeather told her without turning. "But we have enough cats here already." His ears twitched irritably as he added, "And kits."

Alderpaw glanced guiltily at Twigkit. The young cat was playing with a leaf just inside the entrance. She stood on her hind legs, reaching up to bat the leaf into the air, then ducked as it drifted down, to catch it on her back. As it landed between her shoulder blades, she gave a *mrrow* of delight. "I had to bring her with me," Alderpaw explained. "She didn't have anyone to play with."

"What about Lilyheart's kits?" Jayfeather snapped. "They're her nestmates, aren't they?"

Leafpool pushed a pile of thyme to one side. "Lilyheart's kits are nearly five moons old," she reminded Jayfeather gently. "They're far too boisterous for Twigkit."

And they're not interested in having a young kit tag along. Alderpaw was grateful that Lilyheart had agreed to raise Twigkit along with her own kits, Leafkit, Larkkit, and Honeykit, but he wished the older kits had more patience with their foster littermate. Still, he knew they would be apprentices soon; they were more interested in pretending to hunt and fight than in playing nursery games with Twigkit.

If only her sister, Violetkit, had been allowed to stay with her in ThunderClan. Alderpaw remembered with a spark of disgust how callously the ShadowClan cats had carried Twigkit's sister away from the Gathering. They hadn't cared that they were separating orphaned littermates. All they cared about was that Needlepaw—a ShadowClan apprentice—had helped find them. And since the kits might be part of a prophecy sent from StarClan, Rowanstar was determined to claim one of them for his Clan.

Anger surged through Alderpaw. *It was* my *prophecy! I led the quest that found them.* And yet that wasn't why he resented losing Violetkit so much. He felt sorry for Twigkit. And for Violetkit. Was ShadowClan taking care of her? Did she have a foster mother as kind as Lilyheart? Memories of his own kithood with his sister, Sparkpaw, and his mother, Squirrelflight, warmed his heart. *How would I have felt if I had been separated from them?*

Twigkit batted the leaf into the air once again, then leaped, her short fluffy tail whipping to balance her as she spun in the air. Nimbly she caught the leaf between her forepaws.

"She's agile." Leafpool watched approvingly.

"She should be playing outside," Jayfeather huffed. "A medicine den is no place for kits."

"She could play with Briarlight," Alderpaw suggested.

Because of her crippled hind legs, it was important for Briarlight to keep her forelegs strong and active and her lungs clear. Chasing a leaf with Twigkit would be good exercise.

Jayfeather frowned, but Leafpool spoke before he could object. "That's a great idea, Alderpaw." She called to Twigkit. "Would you like to play catch with Briarlight?"

Twigkit blinked at Leafpool, her eyes sparkling with delight. "Can I?"

"Of course," Briarlight purred. "You can play with me anytime you like."

Jayfeather huffed and began untangling the pile of thyme. "Does this mean she's going to be in here even more?"

"Don't be so grouchy," Leafpool chided. "She's not doing any harm."

"I guess I only trip over her three or four times a day," Jayfeather snorted.

Alderpaw's pelt pricked with irritation. It was almost as though Jayfeather *enjoyed* being the grumpiest cat in the Clan. At least Twigkit didn't seem to have heard him. She was happily crossing the den, hurrying toward Briarlight with her leaf.

"Get on with your work!" Jayfeather's ears twitched crossly. Not for the first time, Alderpaw wondered if the blind medicine cat could read his thoughts. Guiltily he turned his attention back to the yarrow and coltsfoot.

The trailing brambles at the entrance rustled, distracting him again. Graystripe popped his head through and blinked at Jayfeather. "Jayfeather, Bramblestar wants to see you, Leafpool, and Alderpaw."

Alderpaw's heart quickened. *Why?*

He waited for Jayfeather to speak, but Graystripe went on. "Can I take some comfrey back to the elders' den?" The gray elder glanced at the herb piles hopefully.

Leafpool tipped her head. "Are your joints aching again?"

"Not mine," Graystripe huffed. "Millie's."

"Should I come and check on her?" Leafpool was already rolling up a wad of leaves.

"There's no need. Unless you know a cure for aging." Graystripe pushed his way into the den. "Besides, I don't think you should keep Bramblestar waiting. Rowanstar's with him."

Jayfeather pricked his ears. "Why didn't you tell us?"

"I just did."

As Graystripe grasped the comfrey between his jaws, Jayfeather brushed past him and headed for the entrance.

Alderpaw glanced at Twigkit. Had something happened to Violetkit? Was that why the ShadowClan leader had come? "Stay here with Briarlight, okay?"

She nodded.

Alderpaw's heart was racing. He nosed his way through the brambles after Jayfeather, the sharp sunshine stinging his eyes.

Outside the nursery, Lilyheart stretched beside Daisy, soaking up the meager warmth. There was a chill in the air, but the cliff sheltered the camp from the blustery breeze that was stirring the branches at the top of the hollow. Leafkit, Larkkit, and Honeykit were nosing around the fallen beech, poking their noses through the gaps in the woven walls of the apprentices' den.

"There's so much room inside!" Leafkit gasped.

"I want a nest in the middle," Larkkit mewed.

"Sparkpaw's and Alderpaw's nests are there already," Honeykit sighed. "I can see them."

Leafpool's mew distracted Alderpaw from their chatter. "I hope the patrols come back soon," she mewed. "The fresh-kill pile is empty."

Alderpaw glanced at the bare patch of earth. Brightheart,

Whitewing, and Cloudtail paced beside it. Hadn't they brought prey back from their patrol? Perhaps they'd met Rowanstar before they had a chance to hunt. They gazed through narrowed eyes at the muscular ginger tom as he stood beside Bramblestar on the Highledge.

Jayfeather was already beside him, fur pricking along his spine.

Alderpaw followed Leafpool up the tumble of rocks and stopped.

Bramblestar's expression was grave. "Littlecloud is dying." He dipped his head to Leafpool. The two medicine cats had known each other a long time.

Leafpool's eyes darkened. "Is he suffering?"

"Dawnpelt is with him now," Rowanstar told her. "She's giving him poppy seeds to ease his pain, but she doesn't know what else to do."

Leafpool flicked her tail. "If only you'd chosen a medicine-cat apprentice moons ago," she fretted. "Littlecloud would have someone to care for him properly."

"And ShadowClan wouldn't be left without a medicine cat," Jayfeather growled.

Rowanstar's pelt ruffled. "I didn't come here to be lectured!"

Bramblestar stepped forward. "He came here for our help, Jayfeather," he said in a warning tone.

Alderpaw watched his father, impressed by his authority. Bramblestar clearly understood that it would do no good to rub mouse bile into ShadowClan's wound. A gentler approach was needed. Alderpaw stepped forward hesitantly. "Can I help?" he asked softly.

Jayfeather flicked him away with his tail. "You're not borrowing our apprentice," he told Rowanstar tetchily.

Alderpaw bristled. *Why not? You're always complaining I get under your paws.*

Rowanstar scowled. "I don't want an *apprentice*. Littlecloud needs proper care."

Alderpaw twitched his tail indignantly.

"I'll go," Leafpool offered.

"Thank you." Rowanstar leaned forward. "Grassheart's kits are due any day. Tawnypelt, Snowbird, and Dawnpelt will be able to help at her kitting, but it's Grassheart's first litter, and I'd prefer to have a medicine cat close by to help if there are problems."

Alderpaw shifted his paws. It sounded strange to hear the ShadowClan leader talk with such concern about his Clanmates. After Rowanstar had snatched Violetkit from the Gathering, Alderpaw had decided the ginger tom must have no heart. Hope flickered through his fur. Had he been wrong? Perhaps Violetkit was as safe and loved in ShadowClan as Twigkit was in ThunderClan.

"I'll fetch herbs and come as soon as I can." Leafpool turned toward the rock tumble. She paused at the top and called over her shoulder, "Alderpaw, travel with me. I'll need help carrying the herbs."

"To ShadowClan's camp?" Alderpaw blinked in surprise.

"Of course!" Leafpool whisked her tail.

Jayfeather's pelt twitched. "Are you going to leave me to take care of the whole Clan myself?" he asked crossly.

Leafpool glanced at him, amused. "I'm sure you can handle it. But don't worry. I'll send Alderpaw straight home."

Jayfeather nosed his way past Alderpaw and followed Leafpool down the rocks. "I'd better help you choose the herbs. I don't want you leaving me with nothing but a pile of stale tansy."

Alderpaw began to follow, but he felt Bramblestar's tail flick against his spine. "Wait."

Alderpaw glanced back in surprise as Bramblestar dipped his head to Rowanstar. "You should leave now. Your Clan must need you at this time. Leafpool will travel to your camp as soon as she can."

Rowanstar nodded. "Thank you for your help," he meowed formally. Alderpaw wondered what it had cost him to come to ThunderClan for assistance. ShadowClan cats were not known for swallowing their pride. Chin high, Rowanstar padded past Alderpaw and leaped down the tumble of rocks. He crossed the clearing, avoiding the curious gazes of Whitewing, Brightheart, and Cloudtail, and disappeared through the thorn tunnel.

Alderpaw faced Bramblestar expectantly. Why had he asked him to wait? Did he have news of Violetkit after all?

"I'm sending a patrol." Bramblestar's mew was soft, his gaze flicking past Alderpaw as though checking for twitching ears among the cats in the clearing below. But Whitewing and

Brightheart were talking to each other, heads close. Cloudtail had followed Rowanstar out of camp, and Lilyheart and Daisy were dozing while the kits clambered along the fallen beech. Bramblestar went on: "To search for SkyClan."

Alderpaw's heart leaped. *Thank StarClan!* His quest to find SkyClan had failed. Vicious rogues had driven the long-lost Clan from their home in the gorge. He'd found one SkyClan survivor, but Darktail, the rogues' leader, had killed him, and there was no sign of his Clanmates.

StarClan's prophecy had been hard to understand from the beginning: *Embrace what you find in the shadows, for only they can clear the sky.* But it had led to the quest: Bramblestar and Sandstorm had been convinced that they must find SkyClan. Instead Alderpaw and Needlepaw had found Twigkit and Violetkit, abandoned in a shadowy tunnel. Everyone believed now that the two motherless kits would "clear the sky," but Alderpaw couldn't help wondering if they needed to find SkyClan after all. He wanted to finish the quest he had started. "Can I go?"

"I'm sending Squirrelflight, Lionblaze, and Cinderheart," Bramblestar told him. "We need you here."

"But *they* don't even know SkyClan exists," Alderpaw pointed out.

Only Firestar and Sandstorm had known the truth. Ashamed that the Clans had driven SkyClan from the forest long ago, Firestar had shared the secret only with the cat he had trusted most. But Sandstorm had told Bramblestar, and now Alderpaw, Sparkpaw, Cherryfall, and Molewhisker knew too. Surely Firestar wouldn't want the secret spread any further?

"I told them," Bramblestar confided. "They couldn't search for a Clan they'd never heard of. But they're under strict orders to keep it to themselves. As far as the rest of the Clan will know, they are going to search for Twigkit's mother."

Alderpaw tensed. "Then Twigkit mustn't hear about it. I don't want her getting her hopes up." When he'd found Twigkit and Violetkit, they were only a few days old. No queen would abandon kits so young and helpless unless she had no choice, or was dead.

Bramblestar shifted his paws. "The Clan will be as worried as you about getting Twigkit's hopes up unnecessarily. No cat will want to tell her anything. All Twigkit will know is that a patrol is out . . . patrolling."

Alderpaw glanced at the top of the hollow, remembering the long journey to the gorge. "Do you think they'll find Sky-Clan?"

"Only StarClan knows." Bramblestar blinked at Alderpaw. "You'd better get back to your duties. It looks like some cat is waiting for you."

Alderpaw glanced over his shoulder, following Bramblestar's gaze. He expected to see Jayfeather beckoning him impatiently. Instead he saw Twigkit, shifting her paws impatiently at the edge of the clearing, her eyes fixed on him. How long had she been there? Had she overheard their conversation?

As Bramblestar turned toward his den, Alderpaw scrambled down the tumble of rocks.

Twigkit scampered across the clearing to meet him. "Leafpool says you're going to ShadowClan." Her eyes were bright with excitement. "Can I come?"

Alderpaw blinked at her, wishing she could. She hadn't seen her sister since they'd been separated, half a moon ago. He wondered for a moment whether to ask Leafpool or Bramblestar for permission. Then he imagined Jayfeather scowling. *Take a kit to treat a dying cat? What nonsense!* He would never allow it.

"Can I?" Twigkit asked again, lifting her front paws hopefully.

"No," Alderpaw told her regretfully. "You're too young to leave camp."

Sadness glistened in Twigkit's green eyes.

"I'm sorry—" Alderpaw began. But before he could finish, Twigkit hared toward the nursery.

"Wait there!" she called to him. "I won't be long!"

He watched her go, wondering what she was up to.

Beside the honeysuckle wall of the elders' den, in a dip that caught the morning sun, Graystripe was washing comfrey pulp into Millie's fur. Millie's eyes were half-closed, pleasure showing in the slits as he worked the herb into her spine. Alderpaw dipped his head as he caught Graystripe's eye.

Graystripe lifted his muzzle, green pulp staining his jaws. "Let me know if you need help gathering more comfrey before the frosts come," he meowed. "I may not be fast enough for mice these days, but I can stalk herbs."

Millie purred. "You can hunt mice as well as any warrior," she told him.

"Why bother," Graystripe asked, "when I can let the young-sters catch them for me?"

Twigkit squeezed out of the narrow entrance of the bramble nursery. Alderpaw could see that she was carrying a red feather between her jaws.

She trotted toward him and laid it carefully at his paws. "Will you give this to Violetkit?"

"A feather?" Alderpaw looked at it, a pang in his heart. It seemed a small offering, but Twigkit was staring at it excitedly.

"Violetkit found one before they took her away," she told Alderpaw. "She kept it in our nest because she thought it was so pretty. This isn't the same one. Lilyheart threw the other one away when she was clearing out the old bedding. But I found this one at the edge of the camp the other day, and I knew Violetkit would like it." She stared at Alderpaw eagerly. "You'll take it to her, won't you? And tell her it's from me?"

Guilt prickled through Alderpaw's pelt. If it weren't for the prophecy StarClan had shared with him, the Clans wouldn't have squabbled over the kits. They'd still be together, not in different Clans. They could play together instead of sending feathers by messenger. *At least they're alive.* Alderpaw shook out his pelt. If it weren't for the prophecy, he and Needlepaw might never have found them, and they'd have died, alone in the wild.

He licked Twigkit fondly on the head. "Of course I'll give it to her. And I'll tell her that you're thinking of her." As Twigkit nuzzled his cheek, purring, he picked up the feather and headed toward the medicine den.

ShadowClan scent, tinged with the sharp smell of pinesap, filled Alderpaw's nose. The bundle of herbs between his jaws was making his tongue tingle.

A ShadowClan patrol, led by Tawnypelt, met them as he and Leafpool crossed the border. Alderpaw recognized his father's coloring among the splotches in the tortoiseshell's mottled pelt. She was Bramblestar's sister, and for the first time Alderpaw realized how strange it felt to have kin in another Clan. He thought of Twigkit. How much stranger it must feel when that kin was a littermate.

Tawnypelt greeted them warmly. "Thank you for coming," she meowed, signaling with her tail to a white tom at her side. "Help carry their herbs, Stonewing."

Leafpool laid down the parcel of herbs she had been carrying and let him take it. "Thank you."

Alderpaw recognized Sleekpaw standing beside them. He remembered the feisty she-cat from his first Gathering. Twigkit's feather was tickling his nose, sticking out from the wad of rolled leaves he was carrying between his jaws, and he looked hopefully at the yellow apprentice, wondering if she might offer to help carry his bundle.

Sleekpaw glanced at him haughtily and headed away between the pines.

Alderpaw sneezed.

"Let me help." Tawnypelt took the leaves from him gently, tugging them with her teeth. The feather fluttered to the ground, and Alderpaw snatched it up quickly.

Tawnypelt and Stonewing followed Sleekpaw between the trunks. Alderpaw hesitated, glancing at the straight, evenly spaced pines. This was the first time he'd been in Shadow-Clan territory, and he was surprised how different it was from ThunderClan's forest, where twisting trunks and low branches covered dips and rises, their leaves already browning and falling. In ShadowClan, the forest floor was smooth, dotted here and there with brambles and rutted occasionally with ditches, and there seemed to be no leaf-fall at all. Pines stretched into the distance, their thick canopy blocking out the sun. Countless moons' worth of fallen needles made the ground feel springy beneath his paws.

Leafpool nudged him. "Stop staring and keep up," she whispered. "I don't want you getting lost."

Alderpaw hurried forward, following Stonewing as he leaped over a fallen tree. He scrambled over the rough bark, landing clumsily as Leafpool dropped lightly beside him.

"I don't see why we need to ask ThunderClan for help," Sleekpaw meowed loudly.

Tawnypelt flicked her tail but didn't reply. Stonewing continued walking. Alderpaw guessed that the herb parcels between their jaws were keeping them silent. But he wondered if they felt the same way about leading ThunderClan cats to their camp.

Leafpool sniffed. "*Someone* needs to take care of Little-cloud."

"I don't see why," Sleekpaw retorted. "It's not like you can cure him. He's so old he should have joined StarClan moons ago."

Tawnypelt halted with a growl and dropped her herb parcel. "Carry this, Sleekpaw," she mewed sharply. "It'll help you hold your tongue."

Sleekpaw glowered at the ShadowClan deputy, but she took the parcel and, lifting her tail, marched on through the woods.

Tawnypelt looked apologetically at Leafpool. "Young cats don't seem to have any respect these days."

Young ShadowClan *cats,* Alderpaw thought crossly. He resented being lumped in with arrogant furballs like Sleekpaw. He remembered being shocked by how she and Needlepaw had mocked their elders at the Gathering. Perhaps that was just the way ShadowClan cats were. Needlepaw had always enjoyed breaking rules. That was why she'd left her Clan to follow him on his quest. *Needlepaw.* Thinking about the young she-cat made his fur tingle. He couldn't help admiring her carefree self-assurance. Would he see her in camp? His belly tightened. He'd been sure that they had become friends on the quest, but she'd been pretty hostile at the last Gathering. What if she was as unfriendly as Sleekpaw now?

He realized the others were pulling ahead, and he broke into a run, catching up as they neared a towering wall of bramble. Tawnypelt was already disappearing through a tunnel,

Stonewing at her heels. Sleekpaw pushed past Leafpool and ducked in next. Alderpaw followed Leafpool, unnerved by the heavy stench of ShadowClan.

The tunnel opened onto a clearing surrounded by thick bramble. Low branches hung over the camp, and a large rock stood at one end. He scanned the camp, wondering where the medicine den was and hoping to see Needlepaw or Violet- kit. He spotted neither, but warriors moved around the edges, where scrubby grass sprouted beneath the trailing brambles. They watched him, their eyes sharp with distrust. Only one cat hurried forward to greet them. The cream-furred she-cat looked pleased to see them. "Thank StarClan you're here," she meowed with relief.

"Dawnpelt." Leafpool met her gaze. "How's Littlecloud?"

"He's in pain, and I've run out of poppy seeds," the she-cat told her.

"Don't worry," Leafpool told her. "We've brought plenty of herbs. I will ease his suffering the best I can."

"This way." Dawnpelt headed toward an opening in the brambles. Stonewing reached it first and dropped his bundle of herbs at the entrance.

Sleekpaw spat hers out with a snort. "These taste foul."

Leafpool nudged her away and sniffed at the herbs, as though making sure none had been damaged. "It doesn't mat- ter what they taste like; it's what they do that counts."

"Leafpool!" A deep mew called across the clearing.

Alderpaw turned to see Crowfrost hurrying toward them, his black-and-white pelt rippling in the breeze.

Rowanstar followed more slowly, his eyes dark with worry. "We need to talk to you."

Leafpool dipped her head respectfully to the ShadowClan leader and his deputy. "I must check on Littlecloud first."

The ShadowClan leader halted. "Of course." He sat down and curled his tail over his paws. "We will be waiting when you're done."

Leafpool nodded to Alderpaw. "Come with me." She picked up an herb bundle and disappeared inside.

Relieved to escape the stares of ShadowClan, Alderpaw followed her into the den, wrinkling his nose as the stench of sickness rolled over him.

Leafpool crouched beside Littlecloud.

Alderpaw stared at the sick medicine cat, shock pricking his paws. Littlecloud's fur was matted, and he looked so small, curled in a nest that looked as though the bedding hadn't been changed in a moon. His nose was pale and dry, his eyes half-closed and cloudy. He wheezed with every breath.

Carefully Alderpaw laid the feather he'd been carrying on the needle-strewn floor of the den.

As he did so, Dawnpelt padded in, her eyes shimmering with worry.

"Who's been looking after him?" Leafpool turned on her. "His nest is filthy, and he needs water."

Dawnpelt flinched. "I've been doing my best."

"Couldn't you have sent an apprentice for clean bedding or wet moss?" Leafpool demanded.

Dawnpelt dropped her gaze. "I'm sorry."

Alderpaw felt a wave of sympathy for the she-cat. She looked weary and anxious. He wouldn't have liked to have to ask an apprentice like Sleekpaw to help with mundane duties like moss gathering.

Leafpool's gaze softened. "I'm sure you've done your best. But we need to get him more comfortable."

"Should I fetch moss now?" Dawnpelt offered.

"Not yet." Leafpool straightened. "I need to speak with Rowanstar and Crowfrost, then check on Grassheart." She looked worried, as though she feared the queen might be as poorly cared for as Littlecloud. "Stay here until I get back." Deftly she unwrapped the bundle of herbs and pulled out a few stalks of tansy. "Chew this into a pulp and try to get Littlecloud to swallow it. It should ease his breathing." She shoved the tansy toward Dawnpelt, then hurried out of the den.

Alderpaw paused, uncertain what to do.

"Alderpaw!" Leafpool's call made him jump. He hurried after her, catching up as she reached Rowanstar and Crowfrost. He tried to ignore the gazes of the other ShadowClan cats, who were still watching from the edge of the clearing. Tawnypelt stood, looking anxious, beside Stonewing. A dark gray warrior with a torn ear was whispering to a lithe white she-cat. Two young toms were crouching beside the fresh-kill pile, a half-eaten thrush lying between them.

"Make it quick." Leafpool's mew was brisk as she addressed the ShadowClan leader. Alderpaw's ears twitched hotly. Were medicine cats allowed to speak to Clan leaders that way?

Rowanstar seemed unruffled. His solemn gaze rested on Leafpool. "I have something important to ask you."

"Then ask," Leafpool told him. "I need to check on Grass-heart."

Rowanstar exchanged glances with Crowfrost before speaking. "We were hoping you would agree to stay with us for a while."

"I'll stay for as long as Littlecloud and Grassheart need me."

Rowanstar leaned closer. "We were hoping you'd stay long enough to train our apprentice medicine cat."

"You have an apprentice?" Leafpool's ears pricked with surprise. "About time! Where is he? Or have you chosen a she-cat this time?" She scanned the camp eagerly.

"Puddlekit's a tom, and he hasn't been apprenticed yet," Crowfrost explained.

"Puddle*kit*!" Leafpool stared at the deputy in disbelief. "You want to put a *kit* in charge of your Clan's medicine den?"

"Puddlekit is six moons and will be made an apprentice any day now, along with his littermates," Rowanstar told her sharply.

"Did Littlecloud choose him?" Leafpool asked.

"No." Rowanstar shifted his paws.

"Then you've had a sign from StarClan?" Leafpool pressed. "Or has Puddlekit had a vision?"

Crowfrost's fur rippled along his spine. "We don't know."

"You don't know?" Leafpool's eyes widened. "Does this kit have any connection with StarClan at all?"

Rowanstar lifted his chin, his gaze hardening. "Shadow-Clan must have a medicine cat. We have decided Puddlekit will be the one. I am asking if you would be willing to train him."

Alderpaw stared at Leafpool. He understood her shock. It seemed like madness to choose a random kit to take care of a whole Clan. Would she agree to help?

Leafpool closed her eyes for a moment as though gathering her thoughts. "I suppose a starving cat can't choose its prey," she growled. "How long would you need me to stay?"

Crowfrost answered. "We thought a couple of moons would be enough."

"You think it's that easy?" Leafpool stared at him. In ThunderClan, medicine cats stayed apprentices for many more moons than warriors. "I'm not training him to stalk birds. There's a lot to learn. And even then a medicine cat needs experience—more experience than you can get in a couple of moons."

Rowanstar held her gaze. "As you said, a starving cat can't choose its prey."

Leafpool glanced up to the canopy, as though trying to glimpse Silverpelt sparkling above. "StarClan help you." With a sigh, she faced Rowanstar. "Very well. I will stay and help for a couple of moons. But I can't promise it will be enough."

"It will be plenty," Rowanstar growled softly. "Puddlekit is a ShadowClan cat. He will learn quickly and perform his duties well."

Leafpool stared at him. Alderpaw could sense the tension between them and wondered how Leafpool would react.

"Alderpaw." Leafpool looked at him. "While I check on Grassheart, find some moss and soak it in water. Littlecloud will be thirsty." She glanced at Rowanstar. "Is there an apprentice who can help?"

Rowanstar turned his head, scanning the shadows beneath the bramble wall. "Needlepaw!"

Alderpaw's heart quickened. Two bright green eyes flashed beneath the trailing branches. Slowly a sleek, silver she-cat with white chest fur slid out. Alderpaw straightened, forcing his ruffled fur to smooth along his spine.

Needlepaw caught his eye and nodded a curt greeting before padding toward her leader. "What do you want?"

"Go with this ThunderClan apprentice and gather wet moss for Littlecloud to drink from," Rowanstar told her.

Needlepaw glanced toward the medicine den. "Wouldn't it be easier to carry Littlecloud to a ditch and let him drink there? He weighs hardly more than a mouse."

Rowanstar showed his teeth, his eyes flashing with anger. "Do as I tell you."

Tawnypelt hurried toward them. "Are you being insolent again, Needlepaw?" She glared crossly at her apprentice.

Needlepaw's eyes rounded innocently. "I was just making a suggestion."

Leafpool shook out her fur and headed across the clearing. "I assume the nursery is still where it's always been?"

"Yes." Tawnypelt followed her. "Grassheart is resting. But

she's eating well and hasn't complained of any pain."

"Good."

As the two she-cats walked away, Alderpaw glanced at Needlepaw. "Where's the best place to collect moss?"

"The whole forest is practically one big moss garden." Needlepaw sighed and padded toward the camp entrance. "Hi, by the way."

"H-hi." Alderpaw followed, his pelt hot. *Is she pleased to see me?* She was acting so casual it was hard to tell. He searched for something interesting to say, but Needlepaw beat him to it. "Every cat around here is really impressed with me," she told him. Her voice echoed around the trees as they emerged from the bramble tunnel. "I brought back a special kit for the Clan. Now we're part of the prophecy too."

Alderpaw ignored her boasting. "How is Violetkit? Is she okay? Has she settled in?"

"How should I know?" Needlepaw mewed. "She's in the nursery most of the time with Pinenose and her kits."

Anxiety prickled in Alderpaw's belly. "But she comes out to play, right?"

"Of course she comes out to play." Needlepaw stopped at a large pine and began scraping moss from between the roots. "She's a kit. What else do kits do?"

"Do you play with her?" Alderpaw thought of the games he played with Twigkit: moss-ball, cat and mouse, hunt the acorn . . .

"She's a kit." Needlepaw pulled off a long strip of moss and flung it toward Alderpaw. "I don't play kit games."

"But you helped find her," Alderpaw reminded her. "Doesn't that make her special to you?"

Needlepaw glanced at him. "Do you play with Twigkit?"

"When I'm not busy with my apprentice duties," Alderpaw told her.

Needlepaw sat back and looked at the pile of moss she'd collected. "I'm training to be a warrior, not a medicine cat. It takes up all my time. Are you going to help with the moss or what?"

"I think you've gathered enough," Alderpaw told her. "We just need to soak it in water now."

"There's a pool over there." Needlepaw nodded past the camp wall. "Follow me."

As she marched away, Alderpaw grabbed the moss between his jaws and followed.

When they reached a small pool filled with rainwater, he dunked the moss. The cold made his nose ache. As he lifted it out, water dripped onto his chest.

Needlepaw stared at him, her bold green eyes sparkling with amusement. "You look like an otter."

Alderpaw's fur ruffled along his spine. He turned, self-conscious, and headed toward the camp entrance.

As he carried the sodden moss into the medicine den, Dawnpelt stood to greet him. Her jaws were green with tansy pulp; Alderpaw could smell the sharp tang of it even over the musty scent of the dripping moss. Needlepaw padded in and stopped beside the entrance, looking curiously at the sick medicine cat. "He looks so small," she commented.

"His fur needs washing." Alderpaw piled the moss beside Littlecloud's nest and lifted a clump of it to the sick tom's mouth.

Littlecloud's nose twitched, but he didn't open his eyes. Turning his head, he lapped helplessly at the moss. Alderpaw pressed the soaked leaves closer so that the moisture ran into his mouth.

Littlecloud swallowed with a gasp.

Alderpaw turned to Dawnpelt. "You need to make sure he has water all the time."

Dawnpelt nodded, looking guilty. "Okay."

As she spoke, Leafpool padded into the den. "Grassheart seems well. She's close to kitting." She stopped beside Alderpaw and pressed her ear to Littlecloud's chest. "The tansy has eased his breathing," she commented. "I'll mix some herbs that will help his fever."

"Can I help?" Alderpaw reached for the herb pile.

"You can fetch clean bedding with Needlepaw," Leafpool told him.

Alderpaw felt a stab of disappointment. He wanted to show Needlepaw how much he'd learned about being a medicine cat. But he didn't argue. He should be focusing on helping Littlecloud, not showing off to Needlepaw. Nodding, he headed for the entrance. "Do you know where there's any dry bracken?" he asked as he brushed past her.

She followed him out of the den, ignoring his question. "Don't you get bored of being bossed around?"

"I want to help my Clanmates."

"Littlecloud isn't your Clanmate; he's mine."

Alderpaw stopped and faced her. "Don't *you* want to help him?"

Needlepaw shrugged. "I guess, but I thought that was why Leafpool came here."

"She can't do everything by herself," Alderpaw meowed, feeling a prickle of irritation.

Needlepaw gazed at him for a moment, then flicked her tail. "Do you want to see Violetkit?"

Alderpaw's heart lifted. "Yes, please!"

"She's in the nursery." Needlepaw's mew was suddenly bright. "Come on—I'll take you there."

"Wait!" Alderpaw suddenly remembered Twigkit's feather. He turned back toward the medicine den and darted inside, snatching it from the ground and speeding out again before Leafpool could speak. He raced back to Needlepaw, the feather fluttering against his nose.

Needlepaw purred and headed across the clearing. "This way." As she reached a bulge in the bramble wall, she ducked.

Alderpaw watched Needlepaw squeeze through a narrow entrance among the prickles. He climbed after her, ignoring the thorns scraping his pelt.

Inside, he was surprised to see the entrance open into a warm, spacious den. A black she-cat lay in one nest, a pale brown tabby in another. The pale tabby was round with unborn kits. Alderpaw dropped his feather and stared at her. "Grassheart?" He'd never seen such a pregnant cat. He was amazed at her size and wondered how big her litter would be.

Grassheart lifted her head wearily. "Who are you?"

The black she-cat hissed, "Yes! Who are you?"

"It's okay," Needlepaw soothed. "He's a medicine cat. He came with Leafpool."

Alderpaw felt hot with embarrassment. "I'm just an apprentice," he corrected. "I was hoping to see Violetkit." He gazed hopefully at the black queen, guessing that she must be the cat who was nursing Violetkit.

"Oh, *her*." Pinenose sighed and relaxed back into her nest. "She's a funny little thing. I keep trying to persuade her to go out and play with my kits, but she insists on staying indoors and amusing herself."

Alderpaw followed Pinenose's exasperated gaze and saw a small black-and-white kit sitting on her haunches at the edge of the den, pawing at a tendril sticking out from the wall.

"Violetkit?" he called softly. Would she remember him? She'd been so young when Rowanstar had taken her away.

She turned her head and blinked at him, her eyes showing no emotion.

Alderpaw's heart tightened. She looked even lonelier than Twigkit, playing by herself. "It's me, Alderpaw. I've brought you a present from your sister."

"My sister?" Violetkit blinked at him, confused. "You mean Lionkit?"

"Lionkit's not your sister," Pinenose corrected.

"It's from Twigkit." Alderpaw pushed the feather slowly toward her.

Violetkit stared at it, her fluffy pelt spiking. "It's a feather," she mewed slowly.

"Yes." Alderpaw nudged it closer. "A red one, like the one you used to play with when you shared a nest with her."

Violetkit's eyes suddenly lit up. "I remember!" She pricked her ears and bounded forward. "Is it the same one?"

Alderpaw shook his head, then softened the story a bit for the young kit. "The old one got dirty, so Twigkit found you a new one."

"Especially for me?" The kit's mew cracked before she broke into a loud purr. She pounced on the feather, trapping the quill between her paws and washing the fluffy tendrils until they were limp and soggy. "I love it!" Violetkit lifted her face and stared at Alderpaw. "Tell Twigkit I love it!" She sat up suddenly. "How is Twigkit? What's she like? Has she got a feather too? Is her tail fluffy yet? She always wanted the fluffiest tail. Has she tasted vole yet? I want to taste vole but Pinenose says I'm not ready."

Her words tumbled out excitedly, leaving Alderpaw breathless. Which question should he answer first?

Suddenly he thought of Sparkpaw. She'd been a lively kit too. His heart ached to imagine how he could have grown up without her endless questions and ideas for new games.

"Twigkit's tail is getting fluffier every day, and she tasted her first vole two sunrises ago. She helps me out in the medicine den a lot and—"

"Is she going to be a medicine cat?" Violetkit asked excitedly.

Alderpaw purred. "I don't know."

"Violetkit," Pinenose called to her. "It's time for your nap."

"But I'm not tired," Violetkit glared at the black she-cat.

"Yes, but Grassheart is," Pinenose answered. "And she doesn't want to listen to your chatter."

Alderpaw swallowed back frustration. Violetkit was so young. Surely the queens could be kinder to her? "Perhaps she could play with her feather."

Pinenose crossed her paws irritably. "It's time for her nap," she insisted.

Alderpaw could see that it was pointless arguing with the queen. He looked sadly at Violetkit. "You'd better rest," he murmured. He glanced at Pinenose. The ShadowClan queen was scowling at him. "Besides, I have to go home."

"Already?" Disappointment sparked in Violetkit's wide amber eyes.

"My Clanmates will be expecting me."

Violetkit stared at him hopefully. "Will you come and visit again soon?"

Pity welled in Alderpaw's throat. She should be in ThunderClan, playing with her sister. Not here, in this unfriendly den. He longed to help her. "I'll try."

Violetkit gazed at him bleakly, as though she didn't believe he meant it. "I'd better go for my nap." Tail drooping, she turned and climbed into the nest to settle in beside Pinenose.

Alderpaw lifted the feather between his teeth and set it

down beside her. "Sleep well, Violetkit. I'll tell Twigkit all about you."

"Tell her I'm going to be the best warrior ever!"

"I will." Regret filled Alderpaw's belly. Trying not to show it, he headed for the entrance. "We'd better go find some bedding for Littlecloud," he told Needlepaw.

"I guess." Needlepaw squeezed out after him. "I never realized Violetkit was so talkative."

"Perhaps you should try spending more time with her." *After all, you did find and name her.* Alderpaw padded across the camp.

"Maybe." Needlepaw sounded thoughtful. "It could be cool to have a kit following me around."

Alderpaw hardly heard her. He was lost in his own thoughts. Violetkit seemed so lonely. If only there were something he could do to help her. He pricked his ears as a thought struck him. At the camp entrance, he halted and stared at Needlepaw. "I have an idea."

Needlepaw met his gaze eagerly. "What?"

Alderpaw lowered his voice. "Why don't we let the kits meet?"

"You mean Violetkit and Twigkit?" Needlepaw look puzzled. "But how?"

"We can decide on a meeting place, then sneak them out one night and take them there."

"You mean in secret?" Needlepaw's eyes shone. "While everyone's sleeping?"

Alderpaw nodded, ignoring the guilt worming through his belly. Surely Violetkit's happiness was more important than

Clan rules? Besides, Alderpaw couldn't help feeling that the Clans should never have separated the kits. He pushed away the thought that this would also be a chance to see Needlepaw again. This wasn't for him. It was for the kits.

Needlepaw was pacing. "There's a great spot near the border. I can show you while we're collecting bracken. It'll be perfect. No one would ever know but us." She flicked an ear toward her unseeing Clanmates, pleasure warming her gaze. Then she turned back to Alderpaw. "Don't you just love secrets?"

CHAPTER 2

Violetkit shifted and snuggled closer to Pinenose, but she couldn't get comfortable. Ratscar's words ran around in her head.

But she's not really one of us, is she?

It was late and the Clan was sleeping now, except for the cats sitting vigil beside Littlecloud's body. He had died as the sun had set, two days after Leafpool had arrived. The ThunderClan medicine cat had been at his side, and the Clan had crouched at the edges of the clearing, avoiding one another's eyes as they listened to the weakening moans of their medicine cat.

I should be sad that Littlecloud is dead. She knew that she was *supposed* to be sad, but she'd hardly met Littlecloud. He'd checked her over when she'd first arrived in the Clan, but he'd already been sickly-looking then, and she had shuddered at his sour breath.

Besides, Ratscar's words were still gnawing at Violetkit too sharply to allow her to concentrate on Littlecloud. *She's not really one of us, is she?* She'd heard the skinny, dark brown elder's meow as she passed the elders' den that morning. *He was talking about me.*

Kinkfur had protested. "She must be one of us. StarClan sent Needlepaw to find her."

Violetkit had paused, pricking her ears, hoping Oakfur would agree with the old she-cat. But he had remained silent, and his silence had jabbed Violetkit's heart like a thorn.

"Pinenose?" She pressed Pinenose's belly with her paw. The queen's older kits had moved into their own nests in the nursery, arguing that they were nearly apprentices and far too old to share their mother's nest. Grassheart was asleep, her round belly moving in the dappled moonlight. From time to time she moaned, as though bad dreams kept waking her.

Pinenose was snoring softly. "Pinenose!" She poked the queen again.

"What is it?" Pinenose snorted as she woke. She looked blearily at Violetkit. "Are you ill?"

"No." Violetkit blinked at the queen through the darkness, wondering suddenly if she'd ever seen her real mother's face. She couldn't remember it. "I need to ask you something."

Pinenose yawned. "Can't it wait until morning?"

No. "Do I really belong in ShadowClan?"

"Of course you do, dear." Pinenose shifted, pushing Violetkit closer to the edge of the nest. "You wouldn't rather be with ThunderClan, would you? They're such a bunch of know-it-alls."

"But I heard Ratscar say—"

Pinenose interrupted her. "Don't listen to Clan gossip. Especially not gossip you hear in the elders' den. Those cats have nothing to do but talk."

Violetkit longed for Pinenose to pull her closer as Lilyheart used to do and lap her head until she felt calmer. But Pinenose rolled over with a grunt and, within moments, was snoring again.

Violetkit hung her chin over the edge of the nest, feeling Pinenose's flank fall and rise against hers. Across the nursery, Grassheart was still fidgeting and moaning. Birchkit was curled into a tight bundle, his muzzle buried under his paw. His limbs were quivering, as though he was dreaming of hunting. Puddlekit's head lolled; his mouth was open slightly. Slatekit stirred, but the gray tomkit didn't wake. Violetkit wondered if *they* thought she didn't belong, too. Perhaps every cat in ShadowClan thought she shouldn't be here. *Then why did Rowanstar take me?*

She tried not to remember the night of the Gathering when, without warning, the ShadowClan leader had plucked her by her scruff and carried her away from Twigkit. It had felt like an awful dream, but it hadn't been; the next morning she'd woken up here and not in Lilyheart's nest.

Suddenly she remembered her feather. She dug into the moss and pulled it out from where she'd hidden it for safekeeping. She buried her nose in its soft fringes and shut her eyes. Was that Twigkit's scent she could smell? She breathed in deeply, feeling herself relax. Tiredness began to seep into her pelt. Imagining Twigkit beside her, Violetkit let herself drift into sleep.

"Puddlekit!" Pinenose's alarmed mew woke her. "Go and fetch Leafpool! Grassheart is kitting!"

Violetkit blinked open her eyes, her heart pounding. Pinenose was crouching beside Grassheart, who was writhing in her nest. The pale tabby's breath was fast and hard, a growl deep in her throat.

Puddlekit darted from the den.

"We'll go with him." Birchkit leaped from his nest, Lionkit at his heels. They disappeared through the entrance.

Violetkit blinked at Pinenose and Grassheart. *What should I do?* Grassheart's growl turned into a wail. Trembling, Violetkit squashed herself deeper into her nest, flattening her ears. A moment later, Leafpool burst into the den. In the moonlight filtering through the bramble walls, Violetkit watched her run a paw over Grassheart's heaving belly.

"Everything's just as it should be," the ThunderClan medicine cat meowed calmly. "For now she only needs some wet moss to drink."

"Violetkit can fetch some," Pinenose meowed briskly.

"Violetkit?" Leafpool turned and blinked through the shadows. "Are you there?"

Violetkit peeked over the edge of the nest and nodded.

"Go to the apprentices' den," Leafpool told her. "You can sleep there tonight."

"But what about the moss for Grassheart?" Violetkit stared at her, round-eyed.

"I've already sent Puddlekit to fetch some," Leafpool told her. "He's going to help me deliver these kits."

Pinenose bristled. "He's not an apprentice yet!"

"He will be soon, and the quicker he starts training, the

better," Leafpool meowed firmly. She flicked her tail toward Violetkit. "Go."

Violetkit scrambled from her nest and headed for the entrance, relieved to get away from Grassheart's frightening moans. She nosed her way out and froze.

Rowanstar, Crowfrost, Tawnypelt, and Stonewing were still sitting vigil beside Littlecloud's body. It lay like a stone in the center of the camp. Ratscar, Oakfur, and Kinkfur crouched nearby.

Her heart pounded and she swerved to avoid the vigil, but as she moved closer to the apprentices' den, new worries invaded her mind. What would Sleekpaw and the other apprentices say when she told them that Leafpool had sent her to sleep with them? They weren't exactly friendly.

A soft mew sounded behind her. "Violetkit. I was just coming to find you." Needlepaw padded from the shadows at the edge of the camp.

"Find me?" Violetkit spun around, alarmed. Had she done something wrong? Needlepaw had spoken to her a few times since Alderpaw's visit, but before that she'd hardly paid her any attention.

"We have to go somewhere." Needlepaw halted, her green eyes shining in the moonlight.

"But Leafpool told me to go to the apprentices' den," Violetkit told her. "Grassheart is having her kits."

"So?" Needlepaw shrugged. "You can do that later."

Beside Littlecloud's body, Tawnypelt turned. Her eyes flashed with worry as she caught sight of Violetkit and

Needlepaw. The tortoiseshell hurried toward them. "Violet-kit, why are you out of the nursery? It's late."

Needlepaw answered for her. "Grassheart is kitting." She jerked her nose toward the nursery. "I'm supposed to take care of Violetkit."

That's a lie. Violetkit blinked at the apprentice, surprised.

"Make sure she gets a warm nest and some sleep." Tawny-pelt turned back toward the nursery.

Violetkit was impressed. Tawnypelt hadn't doubted Nee-dlepaw for a moment. *I wish I were like Needlepaw. She's so sure of herself.*

Needlepaw glanced at her. "Are you ready?"

Ready for what? Violetkit stared at her. Tongue-tied, she could only nod.

"Then follow me and keep quiet." Needlepaw headed for the camp wall, slipping into the shadows where the brambles swallowed the moonlight. "We mustn't be seen."

"Why not?" Violetkit whispered. Butterflies fluttered in her belly.

"We're going on an adventure."

"Where?"

"Outside the camp."

Violetkit hesitated. *"Outside?"*

Needlepaw turned and thrust her muzzle close. "You're not scared, are you?"

"No," Violetkit lied. She didn't want Needlepaw to think she was a scaredy-mouse. "But I might get into trouble if I leave the camp."

"Not if you're with me." Needlepaw blinked at her.

Violetkit shifted her paws. Was that true? Was she allowed to leave the camp if she was with Needlepaw? Perhaps it was a special mission. Something to do with Littlecloud dying, or Grassheart having kits. Everything had been strange all day. Perhaps leaving camp was okay now.

Needlepaw ran her tail along Violetkit's spine. "Just stay close to me and you will be safe."

Needlepaw's tail felt soothing. *I will be safe.* It sounded reassuring. Violetkit lifted her chin. "Okay. Let's go."

Needlepaw purred as she headed deeper into the shadows. As Violetkit trotted after her, she wondered where they were going. Then she smelled the familiar scent of the dirtplace and realized they were heading for the narrow tunnel that led out of the back of the camp.

She ducked through it after Needlepaw, blinking as darkness pressed in with the brambles. A moment later she was outside.

Needlepaw tasted the air. "Come on." Her silver pelt shone as she padded through a strip of moonlight. "Follow me."

Violetkit tried to stay close behind Needlepaw, peering up at the trees. Their great trunks disappeared into shadow overhead, and specks of starlight glinted through gaps in the thick canopy. She tripped over a root and landed on her chin. "Oof!"

"Be careful." Needlepaw turned to look at her, her eyes shining in the dark.

"I wasn't watching where I was going," Violetkit confessed.

"You'd better start. The forest is a dangerous place at night. There could be foxes anywhere."

Foxes? Fear sparked in Violetkit's chest. She didn't even know what a fox looked like, but from the nursery tales she'd heard, she knew they were fierce. She strained to see into the shadows. Sniffing for strange smells, she hurried to catch up to Needlepaw. She was used to the warm cat scents of the camp. Out here countless odors filled her nose, and everything was dank and strange. How would she know if a fox was nearby? She padded closer to Needlepaw, brushing her flank.

"Give me some space!" Needlepaw nudged her aside. "I don't want to be tripping over you all the way there."

"All the way *where?*" Violetkit glanced at her anxiously.

"It's a surprise." Needlepaw ducked beneath a low-hanging branch and jumped across a ditch.

Violetkit halted at the edge, wondering if she could clear the deep rut in the forest floor. She could see water glimmering at the bottom. It smelled rank. She didn't want to fall in. Bunching up her muscles, she crouched and wiggled her haunches. Fixing her gaze on the far side, she leaped.

Her front paws reached the far side, but her back paws fell short. She hooked her claws into the needle-strewn earth and scrabbled desperately with her hind legs. Alarm flashing through her, she struggled to haul herself up.

Teeth clamped down on her scruff, and she felt herself being swung through the air. Needlepaw dropped her onto the ground. "This journey will take forever if you can't jump a simple ditch."

An owl screeched. Violetkit ducked, her heart pounding. "What was that?"

Needlepaw snorted with amusement. "An owl, toad-brain! Haven't you heard one before?"

"Yes, but I didn't know they could fly!" She'd heard Lionkit and Birchkit talking about owls that stole kits in the night. She'd thought they were like foxes. She fought the urge to duck under Needlepaw's belly. What if it came back? It could scoop her up and take her to its nest like fresh-kill.

"Don't worry," Needlepaw told her, as though reading her thoughts. "I can fight off an owl. Here." She crouched beside Violetkit. "Climb onto my back or we'll never get there in time."

"In time for what?" What was this mysterious adventure about?

"Stop asking questions."

Burning with curiosity, Violetkit forgot the owl and scrambled onto Needlepaw's back. Clinging to the slender apprentice's shoulders, she flattened herself against her spine. Needlepaw broke into a trot. "Is Pinenose feeding you enough?" Needlepaw teased. "A mouse would be heavier."

"She feeds me plenty," Violetkit told her, but she was worrying that she was too small. What if she never grew as big as the Clan cats? Then they'd always think she didn't belong.

Needlepaw was moving quickly now. Violetkit had to grip on hard as the apprentice leaped a fallen tree, picked up speed as she ran down a slope, then cleared three ditches in a row. Watching the forest flash past, lit by strips of moonlight, made Violetkit dizzy. She closed her eyes and clung on like a tick. Where were they going?

Needlepaw was heading farther and farther from camp. What if someone noticed they were gone? What if they got lost? As Violetkit's thoughts whirled, the scents around her started to change. She opened her eyes and saw that the pines had been replaced by gnarled oaks and slender birch trees. The forest floor was littered with leaves, and their musty scent filled Violetkit's nose. "Where are we?" she breathed.

"Can't you tell by the stink?" Needlepaw slowed to a halt and sat down.

Violetkit slid from her shoulders, the leaves crunching beneath her paws as she landed. She took a deep breath. There was cat scent here, but it didn't smell like ShadowClan scent. It was still familiar, though. She blinked, remembering. *Thunderclan scent!* "Are we on ThunderClan land?" She glanced around nervously. "What if a patrol finds us? What if a Shadowclan cat sees us here? What if—"

Needlepaw cuffed her gently around the ear. "You and your *what-ifs*! No one's going to see us. ThunderClan will be asleep, and our Clanmates are too busy mourning Littlecloud and worrying about Grassheart to patrol."

"Why are *we* here?" Violetkit gazed at Needlepaw, her ears twitching nervously.

Needlepaw was staring at a clump of ferns. Moonlight pooled around them. Leaves fluttered down as a breeze stirred the sleeping forest.

"Why—" Violetkit began to ask again but Needlepaw cut her off.

"Hush! They're coming."

"Who?"

"Quick! Hide!"

Violetkit felt like her heart was going to burst as Needlepaw darted behind the arching roots of an oak. She scampered quickly after her, panting as she ducked down beside the apprentice. She could hear paw steps. *You said they'd all be sleeping.* Violetkit didn't dare speak out loud. Blood roared in her ears. She wanted desperately to peer over the root, but she knew she mustn't be seen.

"Needlepaw." A soft mew sounded a few tail-lengths ahead. "Are you here?"

Violetkit frowned. She'd heard that mew before. She opened her mouth and let scent wash over her tongue. It was a tom—a tom she'd met only a few days ago. "It's Alderpaw!" she hissed at Needlepaw, less alarmed now. "What's he doing here?"

"He's brought someone to see you." Needlepaw leaped onto the root and swished her tail. "Hi, Alderpaw." Her eyes shone with amusement as Alderpaw backed away, alarm spiking his pelt.

"You made me jump!" he mewed reproachfully.

"Did I?" Needlepaw tipped her head innocently to one side. "Did you bring her?"

"Bring who?" Pelt prickling with anxiety, Violetkit scrambled up beside Needlepaw and stared at Alderpaw.

A small shape moved behind him. Two ears poked out beside him, then a muzzle.

"Violetkit?" A tiny mew sounded through the darkness.

Violetkit froze, her thoughts racing. Could it be? She jumped down from the root and sniffed the air. A strange scent touched her nose, familiar and not familiar. "Twigkit?"

Green eyes blinked beside Alderpaw. Then a gray kit darted forward and slammed into Violetkit. Unbalanced, Violetkit tumbled backward.

"It's you! It's really you!" Twigkit thrust her nose against Violetkit's cheek, purring loudly.

Surprised, Violetkit shook her off and leaped to her paws. She stared at Twigkit.

Twigkit stared back. "You remember me, right?"

"Of course I do!" Violetkit blinked at her, too overwhelmed to move.

Worry sparked in Twigkit's gaze. "You *are* pleased to see me, aren't you?"

Violetkit hesitated, emotions swirling through her like storm clouds. She was more pleased than she could say. But what did Twigpaw expect? How should she act? "Of c-course!" she stammered.

"You look different and not different all at the same time," Twigkit blurted. She leaned forward and sniffed Violetkit. "And you smell weird."

"So do you." Violetkit was surprised that the smell of ThunderClan seemed so strange to her now. "You smell like cobwebs."

"You smell like pine needles." Twigkit padded around her, purring loudly and rubbing against her. "It's so good to see you again. I've been learning how to be a medicine cat. I want to be a medicine apprentice when I'm old enough. Just like Alderpaw. Alderpaw's my friend." She glanced at Needlepaw. "Is *she* your friend?"

Violetkit followed her sister's gaze nervously. Would Needlepaw mind if she said yes? She didn't want Twigkit to think she hadn't made friends in ShadowClan. Twigkit was clearly close to Alderpaw. She probably had lot of friends in Thunder-Clan. "I guess," Violetkit mewed softly.

"What's her name?" Twigkit blinked at Needlepaw.

"I'm Needlepaw." The sleek, silver she-cat jumped down from the root and padded around Alderpaw. "Did you manage to sneak out of camp without being seen?" Violetkit saw a glint in Needlepaw's eyes. She sounded like she was teasing Alderpaw. She frowned. Were *they* friends?

"Let's play!" Twigkit's mew took Violetkit by surprise. A paw thumped her flank. "Got you! You're the warrior now and I'm the mouse." Twigkit raced toward the root and scrambled over it.

Violetkit watched her go, wondering what to do.

"It's a game, toad-brain," Needlepaw told her. "Go and chase her. Alderpaw and I can talk. Don't go far though. There are owls here too."

Owls? Violetkit's heart lurched.

The tips of two small ears showed behind the root. "Come

on, Violetkit! Chase me!" Twigkit called. Her ear tips twitched enticingly.

Excitement tugged at Violetkit's paws. In a moment she forgot owls and, with a squeak of delight, leaped over the root and bowled into Twigkit, rolling them both through the leaf litter.

Twigkit struggled away. "Now *you're* the mouse!" She raced for a patch of blackberry bushes.

Violetkit darted away, leaves brushing her face as she pushed through the blackberries. Ferns rustled behind her as Twigkit dived into a clump.

"I'm going to catch you!" Twigkit called happily. Violetkit plunged through the ferns, squirming between the fronds until she felt soft paws touch the tip of her tail. Twigkit tugged. "I'm the mouse now!" she cried. Turning, she squeezed her way out and hared across a stretch of open ground.

As Violetkit ran after Twigkit, her heart leaped. She'd been so lonely in ShadowClan. Now she was with her littermate again. And they were playing like she hadn't played since they'd been parted. She felt like she might burst with joy.

They played until they were both out of breath and scrambled to a halt in front of Alderpaw and Needlepaw. The apprentices were talking, Alderpaw watching Needlepaw with wide, beseeching eyes, while Needlepaw paced back and forth, her tail high.

"I bet Tawnypelt is a grumpier mentor than Jayfeather."

"No cat is grumpier than Jayfeather."

Violetkit interrupted them. "Why don't *you* play?"

Alderpaw blinked at her. "I've been training all day," he told her. "I don't want to play."

Needlepaw rolled her eyes. "ThunderClan cats are so dull."

"That's not true." Alderpaw nudged her shoulder teasingly with his nose.

Needlepaw stepped away. "Come on." She nodded at Violetkit. "We'd better head home."

"Home?" Grief jabbed Violetkit's heart. Weren't she and Twigkit meant to be together now? Wasn't that why Needlepaw had brought her here? She blinked desperately at the ShadowClan she-cat. "Is Twigkit coming with us?"

"Twigkit can't come to ShadowClan." Needlepaw sounded surprised.

"Then why did you bring me here?" Violetkit asked. She wanted to wail.

"To visit your sister." Needlepaw shrugged. "You've had fun, haven't you? Now it's time to go."

Sorrow threatened to knock Violetkit off her paws as Alderpaw glanced up through the branches. "Dawn will be coming soon. We should get home before the camps start to wake up."

"Ours is already awake," Needlepaw sniffed. "Littlecloud died yesterday. The old cats are sitting vigil."

Alderpaw's gaze darkened with sorrow. "I'm sad to hear that."

Needlepaw shrugged. "It's not exactly a surprise. He was,

like, the oldest cat in the forest." Needlepaw headed upslope toward the pines. "Come on, Violetkit."

Violetkit stared at her numbly, struggling to understand. Why would Needlepaw bring her here and then just take her away?

Needlepaw flicked her tail. "We need to get back before Pinenose notices you're gone."

Violetkit's throat tightened. She stared desperately at Twigkit. "Did you know we were just visiting?"

"Alderpaw explained." Her sister touched her muzzle gently to her cheek. "He and Needlepaw wanted to cheer us up. This was the best way he could think of." Her warm, sweet breath tickled Violetkit's ear. Violetkit pressed against her, trembling. Suddenly she remembered what it felt like to sleep beside her sister, curled tight against her soft fur.

"We'll see each other again soon," Twigkit promised.

Violetkit wasn't convinced. "How do you know that?"

"Because we have to." Twigkit pulled away, her eyes round. "We're kin."

Alderpaw dipped his head toward Twigkit. "Come on. We'd better hurry." Gently he nosed her away, up a leaf-strewn bank.

Violetkit's belly grew hollow as she watched him guide her over the top. Leaves swished as they disappeared into the shadow of the woods.

"No!" The wail escaped her before she could swallow it back. Sadness pressed around her like freezing water. She had to go back to ShadowClan, where no one wanted to play with her; where she couldn't smell her sister's warm scent. She'd be alone again.

A warm muzzle touched the top of her head. Violetkit's heart lurched. She looked up, surprised to see Needlepaw gazing at her with soft, sympathetic eyes.

"Don't worry, toad-brain," Needlepaw mewed gently.

"But I belong with *her*! Not with ShadowClan." Anger surged through Violetkit's chest. "ShadowClan doesn't want me. No one cares about me there. I'm so lonely!"

Needlepaw's eyes glistened kindly. "I know how that feels, kit." She ran her tail softly along Violetkit's spine. Then she puffed out her chest as though she'd made an important decision. "But that's going to change. From now on, I'm going to look out for you. You're going to be fine."

Violetkit blinked at her, a flicker of hope piercing her sorrow. It still hurt terribly that she didn't have her sister in ShadowClan, and that so many of the cats there barely seemed to notice her. But she saw sincerity in Needlepaw's eyes. Maybe now all that would change.

Maybe now she finally had a friend.

CHAPTER 3

❧

A half-moon after Alderpaw brought Twigkit to play with her litter-mate, he was surprised when Dovewing nosed her way into the medicine den and asked him to report to the Highledge. Squirrelflight had returned with Lionblaze and Cinderheart.

He followed her excitedly and left her at the foot of the rock tumble to join Bramblestar, Squirrelflight, Lionblaze, and Cinderheart at the top.

"Did you find anything?" he asked as soon as he reached them.

Squirrelflight met his gaze darkly.

Bramblestar looked worried. "The gorge was empty."

"Empty?" Alderpaw could hardly believe his ears. "What about the rogues we met on our quest?" He knew that Bramblestar had warned the patrol that they might find cats pretending to be SkyClan at the gorge.

"There was no one there," Lionblaze confirmed.

"A few stragglers," Cinderheart chipped in. "But they were just loners passing through. There was no sign of fresh nests in the gorge. The dens were deserted."

Alderpaw's thoughts swam. "But if the rogues are gone,

SkyClan might return to the gorge. They might not have any-place else to go." *We might find what is in the shadows after all.* "We should send the patrol back to search again."

"There's no point," Squirrelflight told him. "We checked the whole area. If there are any SkyClan cats left, they're nowhere near the gorge."

"They'd be mouse-brained to go back there," Lionblaze meowed bluntly. "The gorge is far too open to attack. It's clear they can't defend it."

Bramblestar was frowning. "I wonder where they've gone."

"Who?" Alderpaw blinked at him. "SkyClan?"

"The *rogues.*" Bramblestar's expression was serious.

"Don't you care about SkyClan?" Alderpaw glared at him.

"Keep your voice down!" Squirrelflight glanced nervously at Dovewing at the bottom of the rocks. She was staring up at them with a wide, curious gaze. Thornclaw and Poppyfrost were washing nearby, while Purdy, Millie, and Graystripe lounged outside the elders' den.

Bramblestar turned his gaze toward Alderpaw. "What can we do?" He looked distressed. "SkyClan is lost to us."

Squirrelflight eyed their Clanmates below. Lionblaze and Cinderheart glanced at each other in surprise.

"So you're giving up on the prophecy?" Alderpaw demanded.

"We still have the kits, remember?" Cinderheart shifted her paws. "They were found in shadow. They might still have a part to play."

Alderpaw wished he could believe her. The kits were spe-cial, he was sure. They had been found in shadow. But they couldn't be all there was to StarClan's prophecy. What about clearing the skies? Even though he felt a twinge of disloyalty toward Twigkit for thinking it, the prophecy *had* to be about SkyClan. They were Clan cats, after all, and he couldn't believe StarClan would let them disappear without doing *something*.

He eyed his father curiously before departing, but Bramblestar wouldn't meet his gaze. Frustration surged through Alderpaw's limbs as he excused himself and made his way back to the medicine-cat den.

He had to believe SkyClan was still out there. But he knew Bramblestar wasn't about to change his mind.

"Excuse me." Alderpaw nudged past Fernsong. The yellow tabby tom was blocking his view of Honeykit.

"Lilyheart asked me to bring her to you," Fernsong explained again.

"I know. She has a bellyache." Jayfeather flicked his tail at Fernsong. "You already told us."

Fernsong paced around the white-and-yellow kit, his pelt prickling with worry. "Lilyheart was busy with the other kits, and Honeykit has been miserable all morning. I was going to go hunting with Ivypool, but Lilyheart asked me—"

"To bring her here. Yes! We *know*." Jayfeather touched his nose to Honeykit's head. "Alderpaw, come and check whether she has a fever."

Alderpaw squeezed past Fernsong again, wishing the tom would give them more room.

As though reading his mind, Briarlight called from her nest. "Come over here, Fernsong, and let them examine her properly."

Distractedly Fernsong padded to her side. "I just want to make sure she's okay."

"She's a kit with bellyache," Jayfeather grunted. "She'll be fine."

"But it hurts," Honeykit whimpered as Alderpaw sniffed the top of her head.

Jayfeather ignored her. "So?" he quizzed Alderpaw. "Does she have a fever?"

"No." Alderpaw sniffed again, feeling the warmth of her fur. Was it normal? Was he right? Perhaps she did have a fever and he was being mouse-brained.

"Good." Jayfeather mewed. "A bellyache without a fever means that she probably ate something that disagreed with her, or too much of something she liked." He ran his paw over Honeykit's belly. "What have you eaten today?"

"I shared a rabbit with Leafkit and Larkkit," Honeykit told him.

"Did Twigkit eat any?" Alderpaw asked. What if she had the same bellyache and was afraid to bother anyone?

"She had a vole."

Jayfeather huffed. "Stop fretting about Twigkit and concentrate on the patient," he snapped to Alderpaw. "Feel her belly. Is it swollen?"

Alderpaw touched his paw to the kit's round flank, wondering if the tightness there was normal. "It feels a bit swollen?" he guessed hesitantly.

Jayfeather's ears twitched irritably. "Yes. How should we treat her bellyache?"

Alderpaw's thoughts froze. He felt Briarlight and Fern-song's eyes on him. Honeykit blinked at him hopefully, pain flashing in her green eyes.

Jayfeather's blind stare was burning into his pelt. "Well?"

Alderpaw wished again that Jayfeather were less cranky. *I'd remember more if he didn't make me so nervous.* "Chervil," he blurted.

"Good." Jayfeather sounded satisfied. "Fetch some."

"Will it help?" Honeykit asked eagerly.

"Of course it will," Jayfeather told her.

Alderpaw reached into the crack at the back of the den. It was well stocked. In the half-moon since he'd taken Twigkit to meet her sister, he and Leafpool had gathered all the herbs they could find. Each morning brought heavier dew and a colder chill in the air. It wouldn't be long before the first frost would scorch the precious leaves they'd need through the long days of leaf-bare. His paw tips touched the soft leaves of the chervil bundle, and he hauled it out.

He began to untangle a few sprigs, his thoughts wandering to the morning he'd gathered it. The orange sun had shimmered above the horizon, its pale warmth hardly chasing the chill from his pelt. The forest had smelled heady. The scent of wilting ferns and decaying leaves had filled his nose.

"Hurry up!" Jayfeather's tail flicked impatiently. "I don't know what's wrong with you. You've been distracted ever since Squirrelflight returned."

Squirrelflight. Alderpaw looked up in surprise. He hadn't realized his concerns about what his mother hadn't found were so obvious.

"Alderpaw!" Jayfeather's sharp mew jerked him back to the present. The medicine cat's eats were pricked toward him. "What in StarClan are you doing?"

"I'm ripping up leaves for Honeykit." Alderpaw stared at him, confused. "Chervil is for bellyaches."

"The *roots*, not the leaves." Jayfeather snatched the bundle of chervil away and snapped off a root. He rolled it toward Honeykit. "Eat this."

Honeykit looked at it nervously. "What does it taste like?"

"It doesn't matter what it tastes like," Jayfeather snapped. "It will make your bellyache go away."

Fur ruffled, Honeykit picked up the root between her teeth and began to chew. Alderpaw felt a wave of sympathy as she screwed up her face at the acrid tang. But she kept chewing, peeking at Jayfeather as though she was scared of what he might say if she stopped. At last she swallowed.

"Well done." Alderpaw hurried to her side and ran his tail along her spine. "You'll feel better in no time."

Paw steps pattered outside, and the brambles swished. Twigkit burst through, a mouse dangling from her jaws.

Jayfeather frowned as the kit hurried across the medicine den and dropped the mouse beside Briarlight's nest. "I brought you prey."

Briarlight purred. "Thank you. But you didn't need to. You know I can get to the fresh-kill pile by myself."

"I know," Twigkit squeaked happily. "But the hunting patrol just got back. It's still warm."

Fernsong sniffed. "That reminds me. Ivypool is waiting for me." He blinked at Honeykit. "Are you feeling better?"

Honeykit was washing her paws, licking them fiercely as though trying to clean the taste of the chervil from her tongue. She paused and looked at Fernsong. Then she burped.

"Yes, I think so."

Twigkit bounded toward her. "Larkkit and Leafkit are going to explore the ferns behind the fallen birch. They said you should hurry up." She looked hopefully at Honeykit, who was three moons older and nearly twice as big as Twigkit. "Can I come too?"

"It's not a game for kits. We're going to practice hunting," Honeykit told her. "Leafkit caught a frog there yesterday. If you come, you'll frighten the prey away."

"No I won't!" Twigkit's eyes rounded with indignation.

Alderpaw felt a surge of sympathy. "I'm sure she'll be quiet, Honeykit."

Jayfeather snorted. "Twigkit's never quiet, and she's always getting under some cat's paws."

"That's not true!" Twigkit glared at him. "I'm very helpful."

As she defended herself, the brambles rustled at the den entrance. Ivypool padded in. "Are you ready to hunt, Fernsong?"

Fernsong blinked at her, his eyes shining. "Yes," he meowed happily.

"Great." Jayfeather began to sweep the sprigs of chervil

together with sharp jabs of his paws. Alderpaw could see irritation rippling though his pelt. "Go hunting. And take these kits out of the den with you."

"Twigkit is not coming with me!" Honeykit objected. "She's too noisy. You always say that, Jayfeather."

Twigkit's pelt spiked with indignation, but the blind medicine cat simply looked away.

Briarlight heaved herself onto her front paws. "Come with me, Twigkit," she meowed. "We can take this mouse outside and choose some prey for you."

Fernsong stood aside as Briarlight hauled herself out of her nest and began to drag her limp hind legs toward the den entrance.

Alderpaw called after Twigkit as she followed. "Perhaps you can come back and help us later."

"No!" Jayfeather glared at him, his blind blue gaze flashing. "We have work to do."

Alderpaw flexed his claws, angry at the medicine cat, as Twigkit shot Jayfeather a resentful look and followed Briarlight from the den.

Ivypool glanced sympathetically at Alderpaw. "Come on, Fernsong. The prey won't catch itself, and I've promised Graystripe I'll find him a shrew."

Alderpaw hardly heard her. He was fuming. As the two warriors left, he turned on the medicine cat, too furious to tiptoe around him this time. "You don't have to be so mean to Twigkit," he snapped. "Can't you see that she doesn't have anyone to play with?"

Jayfeather froze, his eyes narrowing.

Alderpaw tensed as he saw Jayfeather's ears flatten. He knew this look too well. But he didn't care. He'd had to say something.

"Don't tell me how to behave!" Jayfeather hissed. "*I* already know my herbs. I can cure my Clanmates. You should spend less time worrying about that kit and more time concentrating on your training."

Frustration jabbed at Alderpaw's belly. Why hadn't he remembered the root was for bellyaches, not the leaves? He whisked his tail crossly. He wouldn't have forgotten if Jayfeather hadn't been breathing on his tail like an angry fox. "I'll try harder," he growled through gritted teeth. "But I'm doing okay, aren't I? No one else in the Clan doubts me. *They* value me. After all, it was *me* who received StarClan's prophecy."

"There's more to being a medicine cat than passing on messages from StarClan," Jayfeather hissed. "StarClan won't tell you how to heal a wound or cure a chest infection. You have to learn that yourself. It takes hard work. And it's the most important thing you can do for your Clan. It may help you save a life one day."

Jayfeather's words seared through Alderpaw's heart. Memories of Sandstorm flashed in his mind. Could he have done more to help her when she got sick? Sandstorm had visited him in a dream and told him her death wasn't his fault. But what if she was just being kind? Perhaps she hadn't needed to die.

He was holding back a shudder, remembering how it had felt to wake up beside her stiff, cold body, when paws thundered into camp.

"Bramblestar!" Mousewhisker's yowl cracked the air.

Jayfeather shot out of the den. Alderpaw raced after, his heart pounding. What had happened?

Mousewhisker and Cloudtail stood in the clearing, their pelts bushed as their Clanmates gathered around them. Sparkpaw left the mouse she'd been eating and hurried closer. Brackenfur and Birchfall leaped to their paws, and Lionblaze, Poppyfrost, and Rosepetal darted from the warriors' den.

"What's wrong?" Bramblestar leaped down from the Highledge. Fur spiked along his spine.

"There's a fight inside our border!" Mousewhisker puffed.

"WindClan!" Cloudtail added, his flanks heaving.

Graystripe leaped to his paws, ears flat. "An invasion?"

"No!" Mousewhisker swung his muzzle toward the elder. "WindClan cats are fighting rogues."

Rogues? Alderpaw stiffened. *What rogues?*

Thornclaw lashed his tail. "If WindClan wants to fight rogues, they can do it on their own territory!"

Bramblestar stared at Cloudtail. "Couldn't you have driven them off?"

Cloudtail shook his head. "There were too many of them. The rogues look vicious. I think WindClan needs help."

Alarm prickled through Alderpaw's pelt. If there was a fight, there'd be wounds. What herbs would they need? Quickly he began running through the list in his head:

marigold, oak leaf, goldenrod, comfrey.

Bramblestar nodded. "Cloudtail, Birchfall, Lionblaze, and Rosepetal. Come with me."

"I'm coming too." Squirrelflight stepped forward.

"And me!" Sparkpaw hurried to stand beside her mother.

"You two can guard the camp with the others," Bramblestar told them. "Until we know what's going on, keep the kits in the nursery." He shot a look at Graystripe. "The elders too. It's the easiest den to protect."

Alderpaw's thoughts whirled in confusion. Why was the fighting on *their* territory? Was WindClan attacking? Were the rogues invading?

"Alderpaw and I will come with you." Jayfeather stared steadily at Bramblestar, his blind blue eyes calm. "There will be injuries."

Alderpaw's heart was racing. This was his first battle. Had he learned enough to help properly? Would the wounds be bad? Fear and excitement fizzed in his belly. "Should I fetch herbs?"

Jayfeather shook his head. "We can use what we find in the area and bring any injured cats back to camp."

Bramblestar nodded curtly and raced for the thorn barrier. He disappeared through the tunnel, and Cloudtail chased after him, Birchfall, Lionblaze, and Rosepetal at his heels.

Alderpaw started after them, surprised as Jayfeather dodged past him and into the tunnel. He couldn't imagine running blind, but Jayfeather burst from the camp without missing a paw step. The patrol streaked up the rise. Jayfeather raced after them, his nose to Rosepetal's tail. As though he could sense the forest, he leaped over roots and swerved around brambles. Alderpaw raced to keep up.

Ahead, shrieks and yowls rang through the trees.

Alderpaw's chest burned as they reached the top of a rise near the edge of the forest. Mousewhisker pulled up first, scrambling to a halt and looking downslope. Bramblestar stopped beside him and followed his gaze.

As Alderpaw caught up to them, he saw the fight below. His pelt bristled with shock as he took in Oatclaw, Emberfoot, Furzepelt, and Onestar clearly fighting for their lives. Screeches ripped through the air and fur flew like thistledown in the slanting sunshine. The scent of blood and fear soured the breeze.

"WindClan is outnumbered," Birchfall gasped.

"By *rogues*?" Rosepetal sounded shocked.

Sometimes a loner or two passed through the forest, but it had been moons since a gang of rogues had dared cross Clan territory.

"Help them!" Yowling the order, Bramblestar charged downslope.

His Clanmates followed, fanning out as they neared the fighting cats. Bramblestar reached the rogues first. Their pelts were tattered, their tails bushed, but they twisted as nimbly as weasels as they fought. Their musky stench reached Alderpaw's nose as their malicious snarls echoed among the trees. Bramblestar flung his paws out and hooked his claws into the pelt of a rogue. With a yowl he hauled the tom away from Oatclaw.

Cloudtail threw himself between a tabby and Furzepelt. The rogue turned on him, hissing, and lunged, knocking Cloudtail's legs from beneath him. Rearing, the tabby slammed his paws onto Cloudtail's spine.

"Get off him!" Birchfall clamped his jaws around the rogue's scruff. Grunting with effort, he flung the tabby aside while Cloudtail flipped himself back onto his paws.

Rosepetal grappled with a mangy white she-cat while Birchfall aimed sharp blows at a black she-cat. Lionblaze fell, hissing, onto a silver-gray tom.

Alderpaw watched, his claws itching to join in. But he had never learned battle moves. He'd be no help. Guilt twisted in his belly.

Emberfoot reared up beside Bramblestar and began batting a muscular white tom back through the trampled ferns at the borderline.

Oatclaw found his paws and dived to help Rosepetal pin the white she-cat to the ground.

"Stop!" The white tom ducked away from a blow and glared at Bramblestar. At his command, the other rogues fell still.

Alderpaw froze. These were no ordinary rogues. His heart seemed to jump into his throat. *Darktail!* He recognized the leader of the gang of cats that had driven SkyClan from the gorge.

Bramblestar lashed his tail, his sharp gaze flitting from cat to cat. "Let them go," he growled to his Clanmates.

Cloudtail released the tabby, and Rosepetal and Oatclaw backed away from the she-cat. Lionblaze and Birchfall stood protectively in front of Emberfoot and Furzepelt. They stared at the rogues, who huddled together, their eyes glittering with hate.

Now that he could see them better, some of the others looked familiar to Alderpaw, too. Rain, a long-furred gray tom; Raven, a black she-cat. Beside them were a silver-gray tom and a shabby white she-cat. Beside them crouched a tabby, its ears flat. His hackles lifted. Where were the rest of the cats? There had been more in the gorge than this. He scanned the undergrowth anxiously. Had the rest of their group traveled to the lake too? Were they waiting to join in the fight?

"What is it?" Jayfeather jerked his muzzle toward Alderpaw. "Do you know them?"

Alderpaw blinked at the medicine cat. "I-I've seen some of them before," he stammered. "On the quest." As he spoke, Darktail caught his eye. The rogue leader glared at him, eyes flashing with malice.

Alderpaw felt sick. *He recognizes me.* He fought the urge to back away as Darktail's gaze bored into his.

"Jayfeather!" Bramblestar called up the slope. "We need help here. Some WindClan cats are wounded."

Jayfeather raced down the slope. Urgency tugging at his paws, Alderpaw broke away from Darktail's glittering gaze and bounded after his mentor.

"Leave." Bramblestar stepped toward the huddled rogues. "Before we rip the pelts from your backs."

Alderpaw watched Darktail turn his gaze on the Thunder-Clan leader. Would he give in so easily?

The rogue leader snarled, his teeth showing blood as he spoke. "This won't be the last you see of us. We have a mission here, and we know more about your so-called *Clans* than you think."

Fear ran along Alderpaw's spine like icy water as the rogue leader turned and headed away through the ferns. Growling, his campmates followed. *Is he talking about what I told him at the gorge?* Alderpaw shivered as he wondered whether the rogue gang had followed them back to the lake.

Bramblestar glanced around his warriors. "Who's hurt?"

"I'm fine." Cloudtail ran a paw over his bloody ear tip.

"Just a scratch or two," Rosepetal reported.

Lionblaze was licking a few wounds of his own, but Alder-paw could see from where he stood that they were no more than shallow scratches.

"Alderpaw, find some cobwebs."

At Jayfeather's order, he hurried to the roots of a tree where cobwebs crowded the gaps. His paws were trembling as he pulled long strips out and carried them back to Jayfeather.

The ThunderClan medicine cat was crouched over Oat-claw. The WindClan tom lay limp, blood oozing from deep cuts along his flank. "Cover them and stop the bleeding," Jayfeather ordered, taking a clump of cobweb from Alderpaw and heading toward Emberfoot.

Alderpaw spread the remaining cobwebs over Oatclaw's

wounds, packing them in where the cuts were deepest, as Jay-feather had taught him.

"Onestar is badly hurt," Birchfall meowed, leaning over the brown tabby tom.

As Jayfeather hurried to look, Alderpaw glanced at the WindClan leader. He was on his side, his fur matted with blood.

Alderpaw quickly finished dressing Oatclaw's cuts. "Stay still until the bleeding eases," he told him before turning to help Jayfeather.

Onestar lay as still as fresh-kill, a bloody wound opening the pale brown pelt below his neck. "I'll fetch more cobwebs." Alderpaw gasped. "He's blee—"

Before he could finish, a groan sounded behind him. He turned to see Furzepelt stagger, then collapse.

"Furzepelt!" Alderpaw darted toward her, his throat tight-ening as he saw her flanks shudder, then fall still. He sniffed her, shivering. His heart sank to see her sagging limbs. "She's dead!"

"Dead?" Bramblestar darted to his side, his pelt spiking.

Birchfall and Rosepetal approached slowly. Oatclaw lifted his head, his eyes round with shock as he stared at his fallen Clanmate.

Emberfoot limped closer. "They *killed* her?" Disbelief edged his mew.

Alderpaw looked for wounds, finding bitemarks on Furze-pelt's spine and scratches along her flank. Then he saw the ugly lump at the back of her head. "She must have hit her head." He scanned the ground and noticed, for the first time, the sharp points of deeply buried rocks jutting from the forest floor. Blood and fur clung to one nearby. He glanced toward Jayfeather.

The medicine cat hadn't moved. His blind eyes had turned to Onestar. Blood was pulsing from the WindClan leader's throat.

Alderpaw touched Furzepelt's lifeless body with his paw. There was nothing he could do for this cat, but perhaps he could help Onestar. "I'll get cobwebs." He headed for the tree roots.

"No." Jayfeather's mew was grave.

"But the bleeding!" Alderpaw darted to his mentor's side.

The ground beneath Onestar was stained ruby red. The fur at his throat was scarlet and glistening.

Why wasn't Jayfeather doing something? Alderpaw's throat tightened with dread. "We must help him!"

"There's nothing we can do," Jayfeather murmured softly.

Alderpaw looked up. Cloudtail and Rosepetal had backed away, their eyes wide. Bramblestar hadn't moved. He was staring at the WindClan leader, his amber eyes as dark as night. Birchfall and Lionblaze exchanged glances as Oatclaw staggered to his paws and padded closer to his leader. Alderpaw could see him trembling.

Then Onestar gasped, as though taking his first breath after a near drowning. Shuddering, he gulped in air and opened his eyes.

Alderpaw blinked in surprise as he saw that the leader's

wound had disappeared. Blood still stained his fur, but the gash had closed as though it had never been there.

Understanding washed through him. "He lost a life," he whispered to Jayfeather.

Jayfeather nodded.

Alderpaw swallowed. He knew that leaders had nine lives, but he'd never imagined what it must be like to lose one. Did dying hurt? How did it feel to come back to life?

Lionblaze looked questioningly at Oatclaw. "Has he many more?"

Oatclaw shrugged. "Only Onestar knows that."

The WindClan leader flashed Oatclaw an angry look. Growling, he pushed himself to his paws. Oatclaw dipped his head.

Alderpaw frowned. Surely Onestar's Clan knew. They must count each passing life. And yet a casual observer could never know how many lives a leader had left. Alderpaw searched the leader's gaze, wondering what he would see.

Onestar lifted his chin, his gaze murderous. Staring between the trees, he flattened his ears. "Where have the rogues gone?"

"Away," Bramblestar told him. "For now."

"We must follow them."

Bramblestar's gaze flicked around the WindClan cats. "Furzepelt is dead," he told Onestar softly. "Oatclaw and Emberfoot are injured. Come back to our camp, where Jayfeather and Alderpaw can treat their wounds properly."

Onestar glanced back toward the edge of the trees, as

though he hadn't heard the ThunderClan leader. "We should go home."

"Oatclaw and Emberfoot are in no state to travel that far right now," Jayfeather put in.

Onestar narrowed his eyes, glancing at the injured warriors. Oatclaw was leaning against Birchfall, blood welling on his flank. Emberfoot was staring at their fallen Clanmate, his eyes shimmering with grief. "What about Furzepelt's body?"

Alderpaw was surprised to see coldness in the WindClan leader's gaze. Had losing a life robbed him of feelings? Perhaps he was numb with shock.

Bramblestar nodded to Cloudtail. "You and Rosepetal, sit with her. Make sure nothing disturbs her body until a patrol can fetch her." He turned to Onestar, softening his mew. "Come home with us. We can take care of you."

"We can take care of ourselves," Onestar snapped.

Jayfeather snorted. "If Oatclaw doesn't bleed to death first."

The WindClan leader looked to where the moor rose toward a darkening sky. A storm was moving in. He nodded briefly. "Very well."

"Chew up more horsetail and marigold," Jayfeather ordered.

Alderpaw was helping treat the injured WindClan cats in the shelter of the medicine den while the rain thrummed outside. He'd already made enough pulp to put on Oatclaw's and Emberfoot's wounds, and his Clanmates' scratches, and his tongue was numb from the herbs. He wished Leafpool were here to help. *Should someone warn her that dangerous rogues are in the forest?*

Alderpaw had seen Darktail kill the only SkyClan cat he'd found near the gorge. Now he'd brought his rogues here and had killed again. *We have a mission here, and we know more about your so-called Clans than you think.* He remembered Darktail's words with a shudder. What in StarClan did they want? "They are so vicious," he muttered to himself.

Jayfeather's ears twitched. "I haven't seen cats like them since the Dark Forest."

Alderpaw blinked at the medicine cat. Every kit had heard nursery tales about the Dark Forest. His father and many of his Clanmates had fought in a battle against the evil cats who lurked there. "Do you think that's where they're from?" he asked.

Jayfeather shook his head. "No. Only Clan cats find their way to the Place of No Stars, and these rogues have clearly never belonged to any Clan."

Oatclaw was sleeping now, in a makeshift nest beside Briarlight's, drowsy from the poppy seeds Jayfeather had given him. Emberfoot moaned softly as Jayfeather licked pulp into his wound.

Sparkpaw pushed through the trailing brambles. Her rain-soaked pelt dripped water onto the medicine-den floor. "Are they hungry?" She glanced at Oatclaw and lowered her voice. "The hunting patrol is back. There's plenty of prey on the fresh-kill pile."

"I want to make sure there's no infection in these wounds

before they eat," Jayfeather told her.

"Those rogues sound hateful," Sparkpaw commented. "The whole Clan is talking about them."

Alderpaw glanced at her. Should he tell her they were the same rogues who'd driven SkyClan from their home? That they might have followed them back to the lake? *No.* He must say nothing to Sparkpaw yet. He needed to tell Bramblestar first. He wondered if his father had already guessed where the rogues had come from. After all, it had only been a few days since Squirrelflight had reported that they had abandoned the gorge. Alderpaw had never imagined they'd show up by the lake. He spat the herbs he'd been chewing onto a waxy leaf and carried it to Jayfeather. "Can Sparkpaw help you for a bit?"

Jayfeather stared at him, eyes narrowed, but said nothing.

Sparkpaw sniffed. "*I'm* not a medicine cat."

"You can chew, can't you?" Jayfeather grunted.

"I guess." Sparkpaw looked bemused.

"So I can go?" Alderpaw stared at Jayfeather. "It's important. I won't be long. I need to speak to Bramblestar."

"What about?" Sparkpaw pricked her ears.

Alderpaw ignored her and kept his gaze fixed on Jayfeather.

Jayfeather nodded. "Don't be long."

"But if it's something important, I want to know," Sparkpaw fluffed out her wet fur.

Jayfeather pawed a pile of marigold leaves toward her. "When you're Clan leader, you can be the first to hear everything. Until then, you can help by chewing these leaves."

Muttering crossly, Sparkpaw crouched beside the medicine cat and grabbed a mouthful of herbs. "Ewww!" she gasped. "How do you stand this?"

"You get used to it." Alderpaw nosed his way through the trailing brambles. Rain battered his face. Outside, his Clanmates were sheltering beneath the ferns edging the camp. Alderpaw could sense tension in the air. Graystripe looked out from the elders' den. Snowbush and Ambermoon huddled beneath the thorn barrier. Cinderheart sat in the downpour, guarding the entrance to the nursery.

Bramblestar sheltered with Onestar, Lionblaze, and Birchfall beneath a jutting branch of the fallen beech. Alderpaw hurried toward them, slowing as he neared.

"Did you chase them onto ThunderClan territory?" Bramblestar asked Onestar.

"They were already on your territory." The WindClan leader's eyes were still dark with fury. "They were scouting for something. I'm not sure what. We crossed the border to warn them off. I was planning to come and tell you once they were gone."

Lionblaze narrowed his eyes. "But they attacked you."

"Did you provoke them?" Birchfall asked.

Onestar growled. "If you mean did we ask them why they were nosing around Clan territory, then yes."

Alderpaw caught Bramblestar's eye. "Can I speak to you alone?" He was aware that he was interrupting. But this was important.

Bramblestar's ears twitched.

Onestar scowled at him. "What is it?"

"I need to speak with my father." Alderpaw met the Wind-Clan leader's gaze.

Onestar growled and looked away.

Bramblestar frowned, his fur rippling uneasily. "What is it?" He guided Alderpaw quickly to a clump of ferns sprouting near the camp entrance. They ducked beneath the browning fronds.

Alderpaw shivered as rain dripped onto his spine. "The rogues who attacked WindClan are the same rogues we found in the gorge."

Bramblestar closed his eyes, sighing. "I feared as much. It was too much of a coincidence for a band of rogues to show up now."

"Do you think they followed us home?" Guilt wormed beneath Alderpaw's pelt.

"Probably." Bramblestar met his gaze. "But you can't blame yourself for what other cats choose to do."

Alderpaw shifted his paws, wishing it were that simple. "Why do you think they've come here?" The question had been niggling in Alderpaw's thoughts since he'd recognized Darktail. "Darktail said he had a reason."

Bramblestar looked away. "Who can say why rogues act like rogues? All we can do is protect our Clan." He leaned closer to Alderpaw. "How many of them were there in the gorge?"

"I don't know." Alderpaw tried to remember. "But it was definitely a bigger group than the one that attacked the WindClan patrol."

Bramblestar's gaze darkened. "So there might be more of them in the forest."

"Yes. Squirrelflight said that there were none left in the gorge." Alderpaw shifted uneasily. Was the forest full of rogues? Why had they come here? "We should warn Leafpool," he whispered.

"We should warn all the Clans." Bramblestar padded from the ferns and called to his Clanmates. "Let all cats old enough to catch their own prey join here beneath the Highledge for a Clan meeting."

Alderpaw watched as his father leaped onto the Highledge.

Brackenfur, Cloudtail, Brightheart, and Thornclaw padded from the warriors' den. Whitewing, Berrynose, and Poppyfrost slunk out from beneath the juniper. Squirrelflight slid from Bramblestar's den on the Highledge and jumped down to stand with her Clanmates. As Jayfeather and Sparkpaw emerged from the medicine den, Dovewing and Cherryfall padded from the shelter of the fallen beech.

Dovewing glanced around. "Has anyone seen Ivypool?" Her blue eyes brimmed with worry.

"She's hunting with Fernsong." Alderpaw padded to her side.

Dovewing's pelt spiked anxiously. "I hope they don't bump into those rogues."

Cherryfall pressed closer to her friend. "Ivypool survived the Dark Forest. She can handle a few rogues."

"I hope so." Dovewing huddled against the rain.

Onestar wove through the crowd and stood at the front.

Water streamed down his whiskers as he lifted his face to the Highledge. "I want to take Furzepelt back to our camp so we can sit vigil."

Jayfeather stepped forward. "Oatclaw and Emberfoot are too wounded to help carry her. Movement will reopen their wounds. They should stay here for a few days."

Onestar glared at him. "They are warriors. They are strong. They will travel with me."

Unseeing, Jayfeather held the WindClan leader's gaze. "I have an apprentice; Kestrelflight has none. Let him save his herbs and his energy for his Clanmates on the moor. We can take care of Oatclaw and Emberfoot until they are fit to travel."

Onestar glared at Bramblestar, whose manner turned gentle and coaxing. "I will send a patrol home with you, Onestar. They can help carry Furzepelt's body."

Onestar's tail flicked angrily.

Jayfeather held his ground. "You've lost one Clanmate today," he meowed steadily. "Don't risk another."

Onestar snorted. "Very well."

"You decide wisely, Onestar." Bramblestar's gaze flicked around the Clan. "Snowbush, Blossomfall, and Berrynose. Escort Onestar home. Carry Furzepelt's body as though she were your Clanmate."

The three warriors nodded as Bramblestar went on.

"Dangerous rogues are in the forest. We don't know how many there are. They have shown that they are willing to fight to the death. Until we know why they are here and what they intend to do next, we must be on our guard. And we must warn ShadowClan and RiverClan of the danger." Again he scanned the cats gathered below the Highledge. "Lionblaze. Take Cinderheart, Birchfall, Sparkpaw, and Poppyfrost. Travel to RiverClan's camp and warn Mistystar about the rogues. I will take Cherryfall, Bumblestripe, Dovewing, and Stormcloud to ShadowClan to warn Rowanstar."

"I want to come!" A tiny squeak sounded from the nursery.

Alderpaw turned as he recognized Twigkit's mew. She was struggling out of the nursery entrance.

Cinderheart stared at the kit as she splattered onto the muddy ground and stared up at Bramblestar.

"Please let me come with you to ShadowClan. I want to see my sister!"

"Don't be mouse-brained!" Poppyfrost stared at her from the clearing.

Thornclaw snorted. "This is a patrol, not a nursery!"

Disapproving murmurs rippled through the gathered cats.

Alderpaw pushed past his Clanmates and stopped beside Twigkit. "You're too young to travel to ShadowClan," he told her gently. "Especially with rogues in the forest."

She stared up at him, her eyes as wide as an owl's. "That's why I *have* to go. I have to make sure Violetkit is safe." She was trembling.

Cinderheart moved closer to the kit and wrapped her tail around her. Rain was soaking Twigkit's pelt. "Alderpaw is right," she murmured. "You're too young to be out in the forest. Especially in weather like this and with rogues around."

Twigkit pulled away. "But Violetkit's my sister! What if they've hurt her? She should be with me, where it's safe."

Alderpaw's heart twisted. How would he feel if Sparkpaw were in danger? He looked up at his father. "Let *me* come with you," he meowed. "I can check on Violetkit and speak to Leafpool while I'm there." He glanced at Jayfeather hopefully, relieved when he saw Jayfeather nodding.

"It would be good to know how much longer Leafpool will be away," Jayfeather agreed.

Bramblestar bowed his head. "Okay, you can come."

Alderpaw bent down and touched his nose to Twigkit's wet pelt. "I can't bring Violetkit back with me, but I can make sure she will be safe."

Twigkit looked up at Alderpaw with wide, serious eyes. After a moment she leaned up to nuzzle his cheek. "Okay," she murmured. "I trust you, Alderpaw."

Alderpaw closed his eyes, feeling the soft fluff of Twigkit's cheek against his own. *I hope I'm worthy of your trust, Twigkit.* He heaved in a breath. *I hope I can make sure we will all be safe.*

CHAPTER 4

"Come back, Alderpaw!"

Alderpaw halted and turned. He'd gotten too far ahead of the group again, and Bramblestar was calling him back. Frustration rippled through his pelt. *You're all too slow!* What if the rogues *had* hurt Violetkit? He had to find out. "Can't we move any faster?" he yowled to Bramblestar.

"We need to be wary." Bramblestar caught him up. "The rogues could be anywhere. And ShadowClan won't thank us for charging across their border."

Pacing restlessly, Alderpaw waited with Bramblestar as Cherryfall, Bumblestripe, Dovewing, and Stormcloud scanned the bushes along the trail. He could see the ShadowClan border ahead, where the oaks turned to pines. The scent of their sap tasted sharp on his tongue.

The rain was easing. Bumblestripe shook out his pelt as he stopped beside Alderpaw. His fur stood on end, spiked and wet.

Cherryfall purred with amusement and nudged his shoulder with her nose. "You look like a hedgehog."

"And you look like a RiverClan cat," Bumblestripe teased,

flicking raindrops from her whiskers with his nose.

Bramblestar paced around them, mouth open as he tasted the air. "Concentrate!" he ordered. "There could be rogues anywhere."

"We've been checking for their scent all the way and smelled nothing," Stormcloud pointed out.

Dovewing pricked her ears. "They've probably run away."

Bramblestar scanned the forest. "I don't think these rogues scare that easily." He glanced at Alderpaw, and Alderpaw guessed what he was thinking. They knew that the rogues were not afraid of Clan cats—not after what they'd done to Sky-Clan. "We should still check for their scent along the border before we cross it. They may have come the long way around."

"But we need to get to ShadowClan's camp and warn them." Alderpaw plucked at the ground impatiently. *And check on Violetkit.*

"Knowing where the rogues went is more important." Bramblestar padded past, following a trail that shadowed the border.

Stormcloud followed, with Bumblestripe, Dovewing, and Cherryfall at his heels. Impatiently Alderpaw trotted after them.

Bramblestar stopped suddenly and lifted his muzzle. He didn't need to speak. The others had smelled the scent too.

"They've passed this way." Stormcloud sniffed a thornbush, his nose wrinkling.

"Were they the same ones you fought earlier?" Dovewing asked.

Bramblestar narrowed his eyes thoughtfully. "It's the same scent."

Bumblestripe sniffed. "All rogues smell the same to me."

Bramblestar looked at him sharply. "You'd better learn to tell the difference. We might be dealing with more of them than we know."

Dovewing's eyes widened. "Is it an invasion?"

Cherryfall was sniffing the thornbush now, her pelt rippling with fear. "It's them, isn't it?" she gasped. "The ones who drove—"

Alderpaw's heart lurched. Cherryfall had been on the quest with him. She'd met the rogues. And she knew about SkyClan. Before she could betray the secret to Stormcloud, Bumblestripe, and Dovewing, he interrupted. "They're the ones we met on our quest," he confirmed, glaring at her meaningfully.

She shifted her paws self-consciously. "Oh," she mumbled.

Dovewing was still staring at Bramblestar. "Do you know who they are?"

"Alderpaw and the others encountered the same rogues on their quest," Bramblestar admitted.

Stormcloud was frowning. "Why have they come here?"

Bramblestar padded to a bramble and sniffed it. "I don't know. Let's hope they are just passing through."

We have a mission here.

Alderpaw felt his pelt twitch. He was uncomfortable keeping secrets from his Clanmates.

Paws thrummed over the forest floor nearby.

Alderpaw stiffened, his heart quickening. Hackles lifting, he backed closer to Bumblestripe as the patrol bunched together.

Bumblestripe tasted the air. "Is it the rogues?"

Stormcloud jerked his muzzle toward the pines. Shapes moved between the trunks.

"No!" Dovewing suddenly hurried toward the border. She looked back at the patrol. "It's ShadowClan." Her eyes were bright.

Alderpaw glimpsed familiar pelts between the trees. Tigerheart was trotting toward them, Stonewing and Juniperpaw beside him. His heart quickened with hope as he saw Tawnypelt at the rear. She was Needlepaw's mentor. Was Needlepaw with them?

The ShadowClan patrol spread out as they neared the scent line and glared at the ThunderClan cats. Disappointment pricked Alderpaw's belly as he saw that Needlepaw wasn't one of them.

"What are you doing here?" Tigerheart demanded.

Dovewing padded toward him. "Tigerheart!" She sounded pleased to see him. "We have news."

Tigerheart showed his teeth as she stepped over the border. She stopped, her ears twitching with surprise.

Tawnypelt padded forward and looked at Bramblestar. "What news?" Her nose was twitching. Distractedly, she sniffed the brambles that straddled the border. "What's that scent? We've been smelling it ever since we left camp."

"Rogues," Bramblestar told her. "That's why we've come.

We need to speak to Rowanstar."

"Rogues? On our land?" Tawnypelt's tail twitched.

Alderpaw felt a glimmer of relief. Violetkit must be safe if ShadowClan wasn't even aware of the rogues' presence.

"I must speak to Rowanstar," Bramblestar insisted.

Tawnypelt nodded. "Tigerheart, escort them to the camp. I'll follow this scent trail with Stonewing and Juniperpaw."

"Be careful," Bramblestar warned. "These rogues aren't strays or loners. They're dangerous. If you find them, send for help." He looked at Juniperpaw. He was lithe, his black pelt showing muscles beneath, but he was small. "Two warriors and an apprentice won't be enough to fight them."

Juniperpaw puffed out his pelt. "I'm strong."

"These rogues are stronger," Bramblestar told her darkly. He crossed the border, meeting Tigerheart's gaze. "Lead the way. Rowanstar must be informed as soon as possible."

Tigerheart glanced at Tawnypelt, then nodded. "Follow me."

Alderpaw padded beside Bumblestripe as Bramblestar fell into step behind Tigerheart. As leaves turned to pine needles beneath his paws, he glanced back at Tawnypelt, Stonewing, and Juniperpaw. "Should Bramblestar have warned them that the rogues killed Furzepelt and stole one of Onestar's lives?" he whispered.

Bumblestripe shook his head. "Onestar won't want the news that he's lost a life to spread around. Leaders don't like to appear vulnerable."

Alderpaw suddenly wondered if his father had ever lost a

life. He padded between the pines, recognizing the trail to the camp as they neared.

As Tigerheart led the patrol inside, surprised faces turned to glare at them.

Snowbird showed her teeth. "ThunderClan *again?*"

Beside her, Scorchfur grunted. "It's bad enough that one of them has to live with us. The others don't have to visit."

Bramblestar kept his gaze on Tigerheart. Alderpaw scanned the camp. Was Needlepaw here? What about Violetkit? He searched for a glimpse of the kit's black-and-white pelt. There was no sign. Perhaps she was with Needlepaw. His eye wandered further across the camp as he thought of the silver she-cat. Beepaw and Strikepaw were practicing battle moves at the edge of the clearing, concentrating so hard that they didn't notice the ThunderClan patrol. Needlepaw wasn't with them. She wasn't at the fresh-kill pile either. Where was she?

"Bramblestar." Rowanstar's deep mew snapped Alderpaw's attention back. He almost bumped into Cherryfall, who had stopped beside Bramblestar.

The ShadowClan leader stood at the head of the clearing, his eyes narrow with suspicion. "Have you come to fetch your medicine cat? She's out gathering herbs."

Crowfrost padded from a den in the camp wall as Tigerheart peeled away from the patrol and stood squarely beside Rowanstar.

"They say they have news," Tigerheart meowed.

"What news?" Rowanstar fixed his gaze on Bramblestar.

"Onestar and his patrol challenged a gang of rogues that was nosing around our territory. The rogues attacked. Furze-pelt was killed and Onestar . . ." Bramblestar hesitated. "Onestar was badly injured. So were the other two members of his patrol."

Alderpaw exchanged glances with Bumblestripe. The young warrior had been right. Bramblestar wanted to protect Onestar.

"How many rogues were there?" Rowanstar asked.

"Six."

Rowanstar's gaze sharpened with surprise. "Is that all?"

"They might have killed more WindClan warriors if we hadn't sent a patrol to help," Bramblestar told him steadily.

"So you say." Rowanstar sounded unconvinced. "Does ThunderClan have to believe no other Clan can survive without them?"

Bramblestar dipped his head. "I'm just reporting the truth. The safety of your Clan may depend on it."

Dovewing stepped forward. "Their scent is already on your territory!"

Bramblestar shot her a warning glance. "We don't know how many rogues might be in the woods."

"What makes you think there might be more?" Rowanstar narrowed his eyes suspiciously.

"They are from a large gang of rogues our patrol met on their quest. We can't presume that only a few of them came to the lake." Bramblestar turned his head and glanced around the camp. "We picked up a rogue scent trail leading from our land to yours. I'd like your permission to follow it. I want to see if the rogues have left our territories."

Rowanstar flexed his claws. "You want to search Shadow-Clan territory?"

"That's not why we came," Bramblestar met the Shadow-Clan leader's gaze. "But now that we know they've been here, I'd like to find out where they've gone."

"No." Rowanstar's refusal was instant. "ShadowClan can guard its own territory. It doesn't need help from Thunder-Clan."

Bramblestar dipped his head. "I understand your concerns, Rowanstar. But we know the scent. I still have rogue blood beneath my claws. Let's at least send a joint patrol—ShadowClan and ThunderClan—to track their trail. We'd be stronger together, and this threatens every Clan. Don't forget the prophecy: *Embrace what you find in the shadows, for only they can clear the sky.* Perhaps these rogues are connected. We have not seen such cruel cats since the battle with the Dark Forest. They might be the danger that StarClan is warning us about."

Tigerheart's eyes flashed. "The prophecy meant the *kits*!"

Crowfrost shifted his paws. "Bramblestar may have a point."

Rowanstar jerked his gaze to his deputy.

Crowfrost held his ground. "What if the rogues are linked with the prophecy? Perhaps we *should* track them together."

Tigerheart growled. "Why don't we track them alone and report what we find at the next Gathering?"

Rowanstar frowned thoughtfully. "You said Onestar was badly wounded?" He spoke to Bramblestar. "*How* badly?"

Bramblestar returned his gaze steadily. "Badly enough."

Rowanstar's eyes sparked with interest. "So," he growled. "These rogues truly are dangerous."

Bumblestripe leaned closer to Alderpaw. "He's worried he might be the next leader to lose a life."

"Fine," Rowanstar agreed. "We will send a patrol to track these rogues with you. Crowfrost, you will lead it. Take Tigerheart, Scorchfur, and Spikefur with you."

A dark brown tom with a tuft of fur sticking up between his ears crossed the clearing toward them. "Did you say my name?"

"You're going with these cats." Rowanstar threw a scornful look at the ThunderClan patrol. Alderpaw heard Bumblestripe swallow back a growl. "There are rogues on our land. You will track them and find where they've gone."

"Should I take Yarrowpaw?" Spikefur asked.

"Of course," Rowanstar meowed. "It will be good training for her."

The trail headed away from the sun, drawing the two patrols deeper into the pinewoods. Alderpaw's pelt twitched nervously as they made their way through ShadowClan territory. The needle-strewn ground turned muddy beneath his paws as the trees clustered tighter and the shadows became so dark that it felt like night.

The dank smell of a stagnant stream rose ahead. Alderpaw

strained to see through the darkness.

Tigerheart was already pacing the bank of a narrow ditch.

As Bramblestar caught up to him, Crowfrost sniffed the earth.

"The trail ends here," the ShadowClan deputy announced.

"I smell rabbit blood." Dovewing circled the patrols.

Crowfrost sniffed. "They must have hunted here before they left the territory." He nodded beyond the ditch. "This is the ShadowClan border. It is no-Clan's-land beyond here. If the rogues went that way, as it appears, then they are gone."

"Shouldn't we cross the ditch and check?" Bramblestar pressed.

Dovewing leaped over the foul-smelling stream and began sniffing the earth ahead.

Tigerheart jumped after her, nudging her aside to press his own nose to the ground. "Nothing here."

"Perhaps they waded along the stream to disguise their scent," Dovewing suggested.

Tigerheart snorted. "Rogues aren't that clever. Besides . . ." He peered into the ditch. Stinking black water lay at the bottom. "What cat would get their paws wet in there?"

Dovewing glared at him challengingly. "A cat that wants to hide its trail?"

Tigerheart held her gaze for a moment, then growled. "You still have to be the smartest cat in the Clan."

Dovewing's blue eyes flashed in the gloom. "And you still have to be the most arrogant."

"Come back, you two." Bramblestar flicked his tail. "It

looks like the rogues have left the territory. We might as well go home."

Alderpaw wondered if Bramblestar truly believed they were gone. He tried to catch Bramblestar's eye for reassurance, but the ThunderClan leader was looking at Crowfrost.

"Thank you for letting us help search your territory." The ThunderClan leader meowed.

Crowfrost dipped his head formally. "Let us escort you to your border."

Alderpaw stiffened. He'd promised Twigkit he'd check on Violetkit. "I need to go back to your camp!" he blurted to the ShadowClan deputy.

Crowfrost blinked at him in surprise.

Stammering, Alderpaw struggled to gain his composure. "Jayfeather wants me to speak with Leafpool. He needs to know when she'll be returning to her own Clan."

Crowfrost rolled his eyes. "Very well," he grunted crossly. "You can go back with Yarrowpaw. Tigerheart, Spikefur, and I will take your Clanmates to the border."

Bramblestar blinked reassuringly at Alderpaw. "We'll wait for you there."

Alderpaw nodded. As the warrior patrol moved away, he followed Yarrowpaw back to ShadowClan's camp.

"Where's Needlepaw today?" he asked, trying to sound casual.

Yarrowpaw glanced suspiciously over her shoulder. "Why do you want to know?"

"She wasn't with Tawnypelt," Alderpaw meowed. "Or in

camp. I was just wondering where she was."

"It's none of your business," Yarrowpaw snapped. "Do I ask where your denmates are?"

"I was just trying to make conversation," Alderpaw meowed.

Yarrowpaw flicked her tail. "Silence is fine with me."

They padded back to camp without another word. At the camp entrance, she led the way through the tunnel, stopping as he emerged, then nodded toward the medicine den. "She'll be in there if she's back from gathering herbs. If not, you'll have to wait. I'm not escorting you all over the territory looking for her."

"Thanks." Alderpaw made a face at the ShadowClan apprentice as she stalked away, then crossed the clearing to the medicine den.

He could smell the warm, familiar scent of Leafpool as he approached. And the scent of freshly picked herbs. She must be back. "Leafpool?" He stuck his head inside the den and saw her crouched beside Puddlepaw.

"This is tansy and this is horsetail," she told the young apprentice. "Tansy is good for coughs. Horsetail is good for infected wounds."

Surprise flashed beneath Alderpaw's pelt. Was she still teaching him simple facts like that?

She looked up, purring as she saw him. "Alderpaw! I thought I'd missed you. Grassheart said a ThunderClan patrol stopped by while I was out."

"They're waiting for me at the border," Alderpaw explained.

"I came back because Jayfeather wanted me to speak with you before we left." He glanced at Puddlepaw. He wanted a few words alone with Leafpool without the apprentice overhearing.

Leafpool seemed to guess. "Let's go outside," she told him, then turned to Puddlepaw. "I want you to split all the herbs we gathered today into separate piles."

Puddlepaw stared wide-eyed at the heap in front of him. Alderpaw felt a wave of sympathy, suddenly remembering his first days in the medicine den. He'd thought he'd never learn the name of every herb.

Leafpool shooed Alderpaw backward and slid out of the den. She stood close to him in the easing rain. "I know it was foolish to gather herbs on a day like this." She shook out her wet pelt. "They'll take forever to dry. But I smell cold weather on the way. I want to get ShadowClan's stores as full as possible before leaf-bare." Worry darkened her gaze, "StarClan knows how they'll make it through."

"Is Puddlepaw a quick learner?" Alderpaw asked hopefully.

Leafpool sighed. "He tries his best, but half the time he still can't tell an herb from a weed."

"But you've been training him for half a moon!" How much longer would she have to stay?

"He's young, and I'm not sure he was ever cut out to be a medicine cat. He has no dreams or visions. He says he wanted to be a warrior like his littermates until Rowanstar told him he would be a medicine cat."

Worry tightened Alderpaw's belly. "Do you think Shadow-Clan has chosen the wrong cat to be their medicine cat?"

"I don't know if there's a *right* cat in the whole of Shadow-Clan," Leafpool fretted. "No wonder Littlecloud never chose an apprentice. The whole lot of them are only interested in hunting and fighting." She shook her head wearily. "It seems so unfair. StarClan has given us three medicine cats, and ShadowClan only has Puddlepaw."

Alderpaw gazed at her anxiously. "Will you be coming home soon?"

"Of course." Leafpool glanced back toward the medicine den as though she was worrying how Puddlepaw was managing without her. "I don't want to spend leaf-bare in this gloomy place."

"They're treating you okay, though, aren't they?"

"They're treating me fine." Leafpool blinked at him reassuringly. "I always have first pick of the fresh-kill pile. Everyone is very polite. And I get along fine with Grassheart. Her kits are adorable."

"What about Violetkit?" Alderpaw knew she was safe from the rogues, but he remembered how upset she'd been when she'd had to leave her sister in the woods. Was she happier now? "Is she okay? Can I go and visit her before I leave? I promised Twigkit I'd check on her."

Leafpool glanced distractedly toward the medicine den. "I don't see why not. But I can't come with you. I have to help Puddlepaw. He's probably put the nettles and watermint in the same pile again."

Pelt ruffling, she turned to go. As she headed toward the den, she turned. "Thanks for coming. Please tell Jayfeather

I'm fine and I'll be back as soon as I can."

Alderpaw blinked at her fondly as she disappeared into the den. Then he padded toward the nursery. Beepaw and Strikepaw had finished practicing battle moves and were watching him through narrowed eyes. Would they question where he was going?

"Alderpaw!" A familiar mew sounded from the camp entrance. Needlepaw's scent reached his nose.

"Hi." He turned to meet her, purring.

She was bounding across the clearing.

"Where were you?" Alderpaw asked as she slid to a halt beside him.

She stared at him. "What do you mean?"

Does she realize she's shifting back and forth on her paws, like she's feeling restless . . . or guilty? "You weren't with Tawnypelt, or in camp when we got here." Alderpaw felt suddenly awkward, as though he was prying. "I just wondered where you were."

"I was in Twolegplace," she told him quickly. "You know how I like a taste of kittypet food sometimes."

Alderpaw blinked at her. *Yes. But you're usually not so quick to admit it.* Besides, she smelled of freshly killed prey. He narrowed his eyes. Why was she acting so strange?

Needlepaw changed the subject. "Yarrowpaw says you came with your Clanmates to hunt for rogues. Did you find any?"

"No." Alderpaw looked at her. She didn't seem to be herself. Something had ruffled her fur. He wondered with a purr which part of the warrior code she'd been breaking this time.

He leaned closer and nudged her teasingly. "What have you been up to?"

Needlepaw bristled. "Nothing!" she snapped. "What's with all the questions?"

"I'm s-sorry." Her sudden temper startled Alderpaw. Shame surged though him. Had he tried to be too familiar? But they were friends, weren't they? Had she forgotten their journey together, or finding the kits? Perhaps she didn't see him as anything more than a cat from another Clan. And yet she had raced over to meet him. Confused, he glanced toward the nursery. "Can I speak to Violetkit?"

"If you want to." Needlepaw shrugged and headed toward the prickly entrance.

Alderpaw followed, still not sure what to make of Needlepaw's mood.

"Violetkit!" Needlepaw called through the opening. "Someone wants to see you."

The brambles rustled and Violetkit scrambled out. Her eyes lit up as she saw Alderpaw, then scanned around him. "Is Twigkit with you?" she asked excitedly.

"She's not allowed out of camp yet," Alderpaw reminded her gently.

"But she came—"

Needlepaw nudged the kit playfully. "That's our secret, remember?"

Violetkit blinked at her guiltily. "Oh, yes! I'm sorry." She clamped her jaws shut.

Needlepaw nudged her again with her nose. "You're such a toad-brain."

Violetkit nudged her back. "*You're* such a toad-brain. You remember when we played hide the pinecone and you took a whole day to find it?"

"How could I? You hid it under Kinkfur's nest!" Needlepaw purred. "That old fleabag was sitting on it like *forever!*"

Alderpaw swallowed back a purr. He was happy to see the closeness between the two cats. Violetkit wasn't alone in ShadowClan after all. And it was good to see Needlepaw behaving more like the friendly cat who'd traveled with him on his quest.

Violetkit turned to him, her eyes round. "How's Twigkit?"

"She's fine," he told her. "She sends her love and wanted me to check that you're okay."

"I'm great." Violetkit looked fondly at Needlepaw. "I really like ShadowClan now. Needlepaw's teaching me how to hunt. I caught a moth yesterday."

Needlepaw purred.

"I still miss Twigkit, though," Violetkit added.

"She misses you too," Alderpaw told her.

"Violetkit!" Pinenose's stern mew sounded from inside the nursery. "Come in out of the rain. I don't want you catching cold. You might spread it to Grassheart's kits."

Violetkit's shoulders drooped. "I have to go." She turned toward the entrance. "Tell Twigkit I've kept her feather safe. I sleep with it every night."

Alderpaw purred and touched his muzzle to her head

before she climbed into the nursery.

As she disappeared, Alderpaw blinked at Needlepaw. "Perhaps we can get them together again soon. Twigkit keeps asking." Another nighttime meeting would do both kits good. And it would be nice to see Needlepaw without the gaze of the other ShadowClan apprentices scorching his pelt.

"I guess." Needlepaw sounded distracted. Her thoughts were clearly elsewhere.

"I'm sure Violetkit would appreciate it," Alderpaw pressed.

"Yeah." Needlepaw's gaze met his. And yet he felt she wasn't really seeing him. "Let's do that." She nodded and turned to leave.

"Soon?" Alderpaw called after her.

"Soon," she answered without turning back.

Alderpaw frowned and headed for the camp entrance. Bramblestar and the others would be waiting for him. It would be good to get back to camp and into a dry den. But he couldn't shake his unease. *Soon.* Why hadn't Needlepaw said when? Didn't she care if the kits met? *She must!* Needlepaw seemed genuinely fond of Violetkit. *Perhaps she doesn't want to see me anymore.* Disappointment weighted his paws like stone as he trudged through the pine forest toward his Clanmates. Perhaps the friendship they'd forged on their journey was over now that they were back with their Clans.

CHAPTER 5

❧

Violetkit gazed across the den. *Moonlight* showed through the gaps
in the brambles and dappled the fluffy pelts of Grassheart's
kits. Snakekit, Flowerkit, and Whorlkit—still too tiny to play
with—were snuggled together, a tangle of paws and tails,
beside Grassheart's belly. Violetkit sighed, her heart aching.
She and Twigkit used to sleep like that. Now she was alone
beside Pinenose, who was snoring. *Am I the only one awake?* She'd
heard the night patrol come in not long ago and whisper a
report to Crowfrost before retiring to their dens.

She wondered if they'd found any sign of the rogues. In the
days since Bramblestar's visit, rumors had spread through the
Clan. Dawnpelt had declared that they were just a pack of kittypets looking for trouble. "They'll get bored and go back to
their cozy Twoleg dens before long," she'd predicted. Violetkit hoped she was right. The thought of strange cats roaming
the forest made her nervous.

No cat had stirred since the patrol had gone to bed. A fox
had screeched in the distance and Whorlkit had lifted his
head sleepily, but he'd only yawned and tucked himself deeper
among his littermates before falling asleep again.

Violetkit longed to cross the den and curl up beside them, but she didn't want to upset Pinenose. She knew that the queen did her best and was as patient and caring as she could be. But she suspected that Pinenose's paws itched to be out in the forest again, hunting with the other warriors, now that her own kits had moved to the apprentices' den.

Why can't I move to the apprentices' den? She guessed the other cats wouldn't approve. She was barely three moons old. But Needlepaw, her only real friend, was in the apprentices' den. She imagined with a purr how much fun it would be to curl up in the nest beside Needlepaw. They could talk all night if they wanted or play moss-ball or share a mouse while everyone else slept. It would be great.

A pair of eyes shone through the nursery entrance. Violetkit lifted her head sharply, her hackles lifting. Then she smelled the familiar scent of Needlepaw. Had her friend been thinking about her too? Excitement tingled in her paws, and she wriggled forward and slithered, quiet as a snake, out of the nest.

"Needlepaw?" she hissed.

"Quick! Come outside," Needlepaw whispered back.

Violetkit pricked her ears happily. Were they going to go on another nighttime adventure? Her breath caught in her throat. Were they going to meet Twigkit?

She nosed her way through the entrance, the well-trodden brambles smooth beneath her paws, and dropped onto the ground outside. Stars sparkled in the wide black sky like dew on a soft pelt. The moon shone, blanching the clearing with crisp light. A chill cut through Violetkit's fur, but she hardly felt it.

"Are we going out of the camp?" she whispered to Needlepaw.

Needlepaw swished her tail along Violetkit's spine. "Yes."

Violetkit watched Needlepaw's green gaze flick past her. She followed it, stiffening as she saw another she-cat standing in the shadows. Her yellow fur shimmered, ghostlike, in the gloom.

"I still don't see why we have to take *her.*"

Sleekpaw! Violetkit shivered as she recognized the apprentice's mew. There was scorn in it.

Sleekpaw had never even looked at Violetkit before, stalking past her as though walking past stale fresh-kill when she passed her in camp. She stared at her now, and Violetkit fought the urge to back away. Spite glittered in the older cat's gaze. Confused, Violetkit looked back at Needlepaw. "I don't understand. Is Sleekpaw coming to meet Twigkit too?"

Sleekpaw tipped her head sideways. "Is that what you usually do?" She stared questioningly at Needlepaw.

Needlepaw flicked her tail. "Maybe."

"Really?"

Violetkit felt a shiver of unease as Sleekpaw spoke. The yellow apprentice made the word sound like a threat.

Needlepaw lashed her tail. "Don't be such a fox-heart, Sleekpaw. I asked you to come with me tonight because I trusted you."

Sleekpaw's expression changed, like dawn breaking through

darkness. "Of course you can trust me. I love sharing secrets."
She glanced at Violetkit. "But can you trust *her*?"

Violetkit lifted her tail indignantly. "Of course she can! I'm
her *friend.*"

Sleekpaw's whiskers twitched with amusement. She thrust
her muzzle close to Violetkit's. "Then you'd better keep your
mew quiet. Unless you're *trying* to wake the whole camp."

"Come on!" Needlepaw padded toward the narrow tunnel
that led to the dirtplace.

Violetkit scampered after her. She wanted to ask again
why Sleekpaw was coming with them, but Sleekpaw was close
behind her. *Needlepaw knows best,* she reasoned. *Perhaps it's in
case we run into the rogues.* Suddenly she felt reassured. *Of course!*
Sleekpaw was coming to protect them.

She ducked through the tunnel after Needlepaw, her nose
wrinkling as she smelled the dirtplace. Outside, they veered
away from it, following the track they'd used last time.

Excitement twitched through Violetkit's pelt. She was
going to meet Twigkit again. They could play cat and mouse.
And she could show Twigkit how much she'd grown. *Perhaps
she's grown too.*

Needlepaw padded past a bramble and kept going straight.

Violetkit frowned. They'd traced the curve of the brambles last time and crossed the ditches. "Are we going the right
way?" she ventured uneasily.

"'Are we going the right way?'" Sleekpaw mimicked her,
squeaking like a kit.

Embarrassment flashed hot through Violetkit's fur.

Needlepaw glanced over her shoulder, exchanging a look with Sleekpaw.

Worry twisted in Violetkit's belly. Was this a safer route to the ThunderClan border? She didn't dare ask in case Sleekpaw made fun of her again.

They trekked on, Violetkit's paws growing tired. She half hoped that Needlepaw would offer her another lift on her shoulders, but pushed the hope away. Sleekpaw would mock her if she let Needlepaw carry her like a weak kit.

Before long the needles began to grow squishy beneath her paws, turning to mud as they headed farther from the camp. Brambles turned to bracken beside the trail. The trees crowded closer, blocking out the moonlight so that Violetkit had to open her eyes wide to see where she was going. Had Alderpaw had suggested a new meeting place?

Tiny paws skittered over the path ahead. Needlepaw pricked her ears, her tail twitching. She bounded forward, and the bracken swished as she dived through it.

Violetkit halted, her nose twitching as she smelled mouse.

Sleekpaw stopped beside her and licked her lips as she stared at the bracken.

Needlepaw nosed her way out, a dead mouse dangling from her jaws.

"Nice catch." Sleekpaw padded toward her. She sniffed the mouse.

Needlepaw dropped it. "Do you want first bite?" she asked the yellow apprentice.

Violetkit blinked at them in surprise. "I thought apprentices were only meant to hunt for the Clan."

Sleekpaw snorted. "Don't be such a cleanpaw."

"The rest of the Clan is asleep," Needlepaw pointed out. "I don't think they'd want us to wake them up for a morsel of fresh-kill."

Sleekpaw batted the mouse toward Violetkit. "Let's pretend Needlepaw caught it for you. You're *Clan*, aren't you?" Her eyes narrowed. "Oh, no. I forgot. You weren't even born here." She hooked the mouse back with a claw and took a bite. "I guess I should eat it."

Needlepaw bristled. "Don't be mean." She tugged the mouse from Sleekpaw. "Are you hungry?" she asked Violetkit, dangling the mouse from her claw.

"No, thanks." Violetkit shook her head. Her throat was too tight to swallow. She just wanted to get to Twigkit and Alderpaw. Sleekpaw was making her nervous. "Are we nearly there?"

Needlepaw glanced around. "Nearly."

Violetkit opened her mouth to taste the air. "I can't smell Alderpaw or Twigkit."

Sleekpaw padded across a stretch of muddy earth and peered between the shadowy trees. The fur rippled along her spine. "I smell them."

Needlepaw pricked her ears. As she turned her head to follow Sleekpaw's gaze, the bracken rustled and a long-furred gray tom leaped out.

Fear shrilled through Violetkit. *Rogue!* She backed away, her heart pounding in her ears. Paw steps sounded behind her. She jerked her head around and saw a she-cat slide from the bracken, her dirty white pelt glowing in the dim moonlight. Beside her walked a long-furred black she-cat. They were under attack!

A silver tom emerged and stopped beside the gray tom. "I thought she wouldn't come." He eyed Needlepaw distrustfully.

"Of course she did." The gray tom brushed past the silver one and stopped in front of Needlepaw. "She's brave, for a Clan cat."

Violetkit froze. Panic gripped her chest. She glanced at Sleekpaw. Was there going to be a fight? But Sleekpaw watched the rogue calmly, her pelt smooth.

"Needlepaw." The gray tom's eyes sparkled as he spoke.

How does he know her name?

Needlepaw dropped her gaze. "Hi, Rain."

She's acting shy! As shock washed over Violetkit like cold water, needles showered from the pine above. She looked up. A shape moved along a branch, then slithered down the trunk and landed on the ground.

It was a white tom.

"Hi, Darktail." Needlepaw nodded to him.

Violetkit saw the muscles rippling beneath his pelt. She began to tremble. *Why have Needlepaw and Sleekpaw come here? How does Needlepaw know these cats?* "Are these the rogues who attacked WindClan?" The words tumbled out before she could stop them.

Behind her the tom purred with amusement.

"WindClan attacked *us*," Darktail growled.

Violetkit wanted to race to Needlepaw's side, but her paws felt rooted to the earth. She gazed at Darktail, fighting back terror.

"Of course they did." Needlepaw swished her tail. "Clan cats are so defensive."

Needlepaw was acting like they were friends. Suddenly Violetkit understood, and disappointment swamped her. *We didn't come here to meet Twigkit! We came to meet them!*

Sleekpaw hooked up a leaf idly. "Clan cats don't like to share their land with anyone."

"They want all the prey for themselves," Rain sneered.

Violetkit realized that all the cats were staring at her. Did they expect her to say something bad about the Clans too?

"Is this the kit you told us about?" The silver tom padded toward Violetkit, his eyes flashing with curiosity.

"Yes." Needlepaw strode past him and stood beside Violetkit, her chin high. "This is Violetkit."

The silver tom sniffed Violetkit. "She smells like a Clan cat. I thought you said she wasn't one of you."

Violetkit stared at Needlepaw in disbelief. *Did she really say that?*

"She's been living with us," Needlepaw told him. She glanced at Violetkit. "This is Roach," she said, nodding to the silver tom. "That's Rain and Darktail."

Violetkit followed her gaze to the gray tom and the white one.

"And that's Silt and Raven." Needlepaw introduced the she-cats.

Violetkit swallowed. "Why are they here?"

Darktail sat down. "We have to live somewhere."

"Pinenose says you don't belong by the lake," Violetkit whispered.

Darktail snorted. "Pinenose sounds like a greedy cat who wants all the prey to herself."

"She's not!" Violetkit mewed defensively.

Darktail ignored her and looked at Needlepaw. "You were right. There *is* lots of prey here. We're going to grow fat."

"Are you going to stay here?" Violetkit could hardly believe her ears.

Roach narrowed her eyes. "Is there any reason we shouldn't?"

Violetkit's fur prickled with fear. The she-cat was staring at her as though she were prey. "This is Clan territory," she whispered hoarsely.

Needlepaw flicked her tail irritably. "Why shouldn't we share it? Why do Clan cats behave like they're so special? They're just cats, like these cats."

Violetkit looked at the dark-eyed rogues. *You're nothing like Clan cats.*

Sleekpaw stepped forward. "No kit can help where she's born. Why should the Clans deprive other cats of good hunting just because they weren't born in a Clan?"

Darktail's gaze flicked over Sleekpaw. "Who's this?"

Needlepaw dipped her head. "Sleekpaw. I told her about you and she wanted to meet you."

"Can we trust her?" Rain padded closer, pelt prickling.

Sleekpaw raised her muzzle. "Of course you can!" she declared. "I think the Clans are wrong too. All their borders and rules just make more battles." She nudged Violetkit.

Violetkit stared at her, surprised.

"You weren't born in a Clan," Sleekpaw told her. "Don't you think it's weird having so many rules?"

Before Violetkit could answer, Silt leaned forward. "If you weren't born in the Clan, why do they let you live with them?"

Violetkit blinked at her. "I don't know."

Darktail stared at her. "What's it like living with Clan cats when you know you're an outsider?"

Unease tugged at Violetkit's belly. She wanted to be loyal to ShadowClan. She thought of Tawnypelt and Puddlepaw. What would Rowanstar say if he knew she was here? He was stern and distant, but she wanted to earn his respect. "I guess it's okay." She tried not to remember how lonely she felt in the Clan. How Pinenose's kits ignored her. How she wasn't allowed near Grassheart's kits in case she passed on an infection. "They try to make me feel welcome." Her breath caught in her throat. *Don't they?*

Darktail leaned closer. "And yet you don't."

Violetkit backed away. *How does he know?*

Needlepaw padded around Darktail, her chest puffed out.

"Rowanstar makes rules about who's allowed in the Clan and who isn't. But he's old and set in his ways. He needs to learn that we're all just cats. We all want the same thing—to hunt and live in peace. But he's so busy defending his borders, he's forgotten that."

Violetkit's thoughts whirled. Needlepaw sounded so certain. Was she right? They *were* all just cats. Perhaps the Clans *were* wrong. They acted like rogues were no better than foxes just because they came from outside the Clan.

But she's not really one of us, is she? As she remembered Ratscar's words, a thought flashed through her mind, chilling her to the bone. *Is that how they all see me?* She stared at the rogues. *Does ShadowClan think I'm like them?*

CHAPTER 6

Twigkit swallowed the last morsel of vole and licked her lips. She was bored, and even though the sun was high, it was chilly in camp. Did Alderpaw need some help? She knew Jayfeather would be irritated to see her again, but she'd given up worrying about his grumbling. She guessed he enjoyed it. She got to her paws, skirted the clearing, and headed toward the medicine den. As she passed the camp entrance, she could still smell the scent of WindClan around the thorn tunnel. Emberfoot and Oatclaw had left at dawn. In the days since the fight, Jayfeather and Alderpaw had cared for them as though they were Clanmates. Twigkit had been proud to help, fetching moss for their nests and bringing fresh-kill from the pile. Alderpaw had even let her mix herbs once when Jayfeather was out of the den.

As soon as the WindClan warriors' wounds were healed enough for them to travel, they'd returned to their camp. Twigkit had guessed by the prickling of their fur as they talked of going home that they were worried about their Clanmates. The fight with the rogues had unsettled them. It had unsettled everyone. Bramblestar had been sending out larger patrols to hunt and insisted the borders be checked day and night.

"Twigkit!" Lilyheart called from outside the nursery. She had settled in a patch of weak sunlight. "Aren't you sleepy? You were up before dawn. Come and have a nap."

Twigkit flicked her tail. "No, thanks," she mewed back. "I'm fine." She didn't feel at all tired. She'd done nothing all morning apart from wander around the camp: nosing through ferns in hope of catching a frog, and practicing balancing on the fallen beech.

Larkkit, Leafkit, and Honeykit were outside the nursery too, dozing lazily beside their mother, the cool leaf-fall wind ruffling their fur. Twigkit felt a pang of frustration. She knew from experience that it was pointless asking them to play with her. Even when they agreed, they ran so fast and got bored so quickly that she always felt disappointed. She preferred hanging out with Alderpaw. At least she felt she was useful in the medicine den, despite Jayfeather's scowling at her like she was an unwanted flea. Briarlight loved playing moss-ball with her, and it was good exercise for the crippled she-cat. Perhaps she could play with her now.

She padded past the warriors' den, scanning the camp for a good-sized scrap of moss.

"Do you really think she's the cat that StarClan was trying to tell us about—the one who will clear the sky?"

Rosepetal's mew drifted through the prickly wall of the den and made Twigkit stop. Who was Rosepetal talking about?

Mousewhisker answered her, a yawn in his mew. "For a

special cat, she's pretty ordinary."

"I guess she *is* young," Rosepetal conceded. "But nothing has changed since she arrived. Nothing's gotten better. In fact, things have gotten worse, with the rogues coming."

"You're right. Besides, if she *was* special, wouldn't StarClan have sent more of a sign?" Mousewhisker's nest rustled. "I know they were found 'in shadow,' but that doesn't seem like enough."

Twigkit leaned closer to the den wall and pricked her ears. *They're talking about me and Violetkit!*

"Perhaps the prophecy was about something else," Rosepetal meowed thoughtfully.

"And finding Twigkit and Violetkit was a coincidence," Mousewhisker concluded.

"Like you say, Twigkit does seem pretty ordinary. And until she learns to hunt, she's another belly for the Clan to fill." Rosepetal sighed. "Let's just hope leaf-bare is mild. Heavy snows mean scarce prey. There may not be enough to get us through to newleaf."

Another belly to fill? Anxiety pricked through Twigkit's pelt. And what did they mean by *ordinary*? Had the Clan only taken her in because they believed she was part of a prophecy? Her breath caught in her throat. What if she wasn't special? Would they ask her to leave? If there wasn't enough prey during leaf-bare, they might! She imagined wandering alone through the forest, thick snows piling between the trees, a cold wind slicing through her fur. She could picture foxes watching from the undergrowth, their hungry gazes sharpening as they saw her. *How would I survive alone?*

Outside the nursery, Larkkit rolled over sleepily and stretched.

If only I were Clanborn. They couldn't throw me out. She lifted her chin determinedly. *I have to prove that I'm special!*

Pelt twitching nervously, Twigkit hurried toward the medicine den. She pushed through the brambles.

Alderpaw turned. His eyes rounded with worry as he saw her. "Is something wrong?"

Twigkit forced her fur to smooth and blinked at him innocently. "No." She wanted to run to his side and feel his comforting warmth against her. She wanted to ask him if she was special and hear him tell her that of course she was. But he was standing beside Jayfeather.

"Look at this, Alderpaw," Jayfeather mewed curtly, ignoring Twigpaw's arrival. "Can you see any signs of infection?"

The medicine cat was inspecting a cut on Birchfall's paw, and Twigkit knew that he wouldn't be pleased if she interrupted.

Alderpaw peered closely at the warrior's pad. "It looks like a clean cut."

"How should we treat it?" Jayfeather asked.

"Cobweb," Alderpaw replied.

Jayfeather lifted his gaze sharply toward his apprentice. "*Just* cobweb?" Irritation edged his mew.

Alderpaw shifted his paws, his eyes flitting nervously toward the herb store.

"Just because there's no infection now doesn't mean one

won't develop," Jayfeather meowed.

"We could wash in some marigold pulp before we dress it," Alderpaw suggested hopefully.

"Go and fetch some, then!" Jayfeather turned his attention back to Birchfall's paw, turning it gently with his own to closer examine the warrior's pad.

As Birchfall winced, the brambles swished beside Twigkit.

Whitewing limped in, pain darkening her gaze. "I have an ache in my side," she murmured.

Jayfeather dropped Birchfall's paw and hurried toward her.

"When did it start?" He sniffed the white she-cat's breath, then ran his muzzle along her flank.

"Around dawn. After I'd eaten a mouse."

"Did it come on suddenly?" Jayfeather asked.

"Quite sharply, but it's been getting worse all morning."

"Have you vomited?" Jayfeather pressed his paw into Whitewing's flank.

She gasped with pain.

"Well?" He padded around Whitewing and pressed her flank on the other side.

"No," she rasped. "I don't feel sick."

"Come here, Alderpaw." Jayfeather flicked his tail.

Alderpaw stared across the medicine den, a bundle of marigold in his mouth.

"Hurry up!" Jayfeather snapped.

Alderpaw dropped the marigold and hurried toward his mentor.

"Press here." Jayfeather pointed to Whitewing's flank.

Alderpaw lifted his paw slowly and pressed gently against her pelt.

"Harder!" Jayfeather ordered. "She won't even feel that."

Twigkit saw Alderpaw's eyes flash with trepidation as he pushed harder into Whitewing's side.

Whitewing winced.

"Sorry," Alderpaw mewed quickly.

Jayfeather huffed. "If you apologize to a patient every time you hurt them, you'll never get anything done. Now, what did you feel?"

"It feels hard beneath her pelt," Alderpaw answered.

"Trapped wind." Jayfeather turned back to Birchfall. "She ate her mouse too quickly. How should you treat it?"

I know! Twigkit leaned forward excitedly. She remembered Honeykit's bellyache. She willed Alderpaw to remember.

But Alderpaw stared helplessly at Jayfeather.

"Chervil root!" Twigkit blurted. *See! I am special!*

Jayfeather's whiskers twitched irritably. "Chervil is for nausea," he snapped. "Trapped wind needs *watermint*. And no one was asking you. If you must hang around the den, keep quiet!"

Twigkit shriveled beneath her pelt, hot with shame.

Alderpaw brushed past her as he hurried toward the medicine store. "Don't listen to him," he whispered.

Twigkit hardly heard him. *Why is Jayfeather so mean to me?* She stiffened as a thought flashed in her mind. *He talks to StarClan. Have they told him I'm not special?*

"There are only a few leaves left." Alderpaw reached deep into the crack and hooked out a pawful of dusty stems.

"Then we'll have to collect more," Jayfeather meowed briskly. "But not today. It's too far to the lake. Give Whitewing all the watermint we have; then chew up some pulp for Birchfall's cut while I gather fresh cobweb."

As Jayfeather padded from the den, Twigkit watched Alderpaw drop the dusty leaves beside Whitewing. They were large and pale. She tried to imagine what they'd look like when they were fresh. A thought struck her. *I know how to prove I'm special! I'll fetch more watermint from the lake. Then the Clan will see how clever and useful I am, and they won't want to get rid of me.* Her heart lifted like an escaping butterfly.

"I'll see you later," she called to Alderpaw.

"You don't have to leave." Alderpaw looked at her apologetically. "Jayfeather doesn't mean half the things he says."

Twigkit lifted her tail happily. "That's okay. I have something important to do."

"What?" Alderpaw blinked at her curiously.

Twigkit hesitated. "Ummm . . . I have to find a new feather for Violetkit. In case you visit Leafpool again," she mewed hurriedly.

Alderpaw scooped up a mouthful of marigold and began chewing. "Good luck." His mew was muffled.

"Thanks." Twigkit nodded politely to Whitewing and Birchfall and backed out of the den. She bumped into something soft.

"Look where you're going!" Jayfeather's hiss made her jump as she got tangled in his paws.

Brushing her away, he ducked into the medicine den.

Twigkit stared after him crossly. *Next time you're going to be happy to see me!*

She crossed the clearing, scanning the camp nervously. Graystripe was dozing outside the elders' den. Honeykit was crouched beside the ferns nearby, clearly watching for frogs. Lilyheart had disappeared. *She must be resting in the nursery.* Bramblestar and Squirrelflight were sharing a mouse on the Highledge, while Leafkit and Larkkit were inventing battle moves in the clearing. Poppyfrost, Ambermoon, and Snowbush were watching them. *The other cats must be in their dens or out on patrol,* Twigkit decided as she padded toward the thorn barrier. She avoided the camp entrance. It was too risky. Instead she ducked behind the warriors' den. Out of sight of the clearing, she searched the bottom of the thorn barrier for a gap. She could see a patch where the branches didn't twine so thickly on the ground. She squeezed through, wincing as thorns scraped her pelt. Eyes screwed tight shut, she pushed forward until she burst free.

I made it! Quickly she checked the leafy rise outside camp. *I'm outside!* The trail was clear, and she hurried along it, her ears pricked for patrols. She veered off, then ducked between the bracken stems crowding the slope. Excitement fizzed in her paws. Ordinary kits weren't meant to leave camp. But she was special, and everyone would know it when she returned with a huge bundle of watermint. Jayfeather was going to be *so* grateful. He'd never be mean to her again! And Rosepetal and Mousewhisker would be embarrassed that they'd ever suggested she wasn't special.

She nosed her way out of the bracken and stared across a wide glade where the forest dipped down toward a dried streambed before rising toward a wall of brambles. Which way *was* the lake? She paused, opening her mouth and letting forest scents wash over her tongue. Fear clutched her heart as unfamiliar smells crowded in. What was that sharp stench? Fox? Owl? Rogue? She glanced around, her heart thundering in her ears. Something small skittered across the streambed. Above, leaves fluttered in the chilly breeze, and branches creaked as they swayed.

Twigkit lifted her chin. *I'm special,* she reminded herself, feeling a little less special than she had in camp. *I have to prove it, or they'll make me leave.* Her belly tightened. *I have to find the lake.* Ignoring the fear fluttering in her chest, she padded down the slope and hopped over the dry streambed. She felt sure she'd be able to see if she was going the right way if she could make it past the brambles. She climbed the rise and squeezed through a gap in the prickly branches. As she emerged on the other side, the scent of water streamed over her muzzle. The breeze carried lake scent. It *must* be lake scent. She could smell wet stone and earth and imagined a large pool, water lapping at its edges. In front of her, the forest sloped downward. Were those ripples sparkling in the distance? She broke into a run, zigzagging between trees and scrambling over roots. Her paws slipped on the fallen leaves, and she tumbled clumsily into a patch of nettles. Stings sparked through her nose and she leaped backward, blinking away the pain. Running again, she raced toward the sunshine, which glinted between the tree trunks.

Suddenly she burst from the forest. Wind tugged at her fur, and a wide grassy slope plunged away from her. She gasped. The lake! It stretched out as big as the sky in front of her. Glittering like Silverpelt, it rippled in the breeze. She strained to see the far shore, amazed at how tiny the trees looked from here. Farther along, the land rose to heather-pelted hilltops, and beyond that an island rose from the water.

There must be watermint here! The shore stretched so far, Twig-kit felt sure she'd find the pale green leaves somewhere at the water's edge. She hurried down the slope, her paws slithering on the dewy grass. As she reached the pebbly shore, she slowed, picking her way over the stones and wincing where they jabbed into her soft pads.

She scanned the shore. Tiny waves lapped the pebbles, but there was no sign of plants. She followed the waterline, keeping her paws clear of the rippling water. Straining to see ahead, she spotted greenery sprouting around a mass of boulders jutting out into the lake. Her heart leaped.

Watermint? She glanced at the sky, between the white puffy clouds. *Oh, StarClan. Let it be watermint!*

Excitement surged in her belly as she neared and recognized the wide, pale leaves she'd seen in the medicine den. They weren't dusty or dry, but she could already detect the same sharp scent she'd smelled on the leaves Jayfeather had given to Whitewing. *StarClan answered my prayer!* Joy surged through Twigkit. *I must be special.*

She climbed onto the first boulder, unsheathing her claws to grip the smooth stone. The watermint was growing in clumps between the rocks that jutted into deeper water. She scrambled toward them, clambering over boulder after boulder until she was right at the edge where thick leaves sprouted.

I'll take back the biggest bundle ever! Twigkit imagined the surprised look on her Clanmates' faces as she walked into camp, a great wad of watermint in her jaws. Larkkit, Leafkit, and Honeykit would be amazed. They might even let her join in their frog hunts. Everyone would congratulate her. Jayfeather would come out of his den to see what the fuss was about. Then he'd smell the mint and *have* to thank her.

Happily, Twigkit hooked her claws into the biggest leaf and tugged. To her surprise, it didn't tear free of the clump. The force of her tug unbalanced her, and she jerked clumsily. Her paws slid from beneath her. Her heart lurched as her rump hit the rock. She let go of the leaves, scrabbling to find her paws, but they slithered on the smooth stone. *Help!* She felt herself falling. With a yelp of horror, she plunged into the lake.

The chill of the water stole her breath. Terror scorched through her as she sank. She flailed desperately, opening her mouth to mew, choking on the water that rushed in. Bubbles streamed around her as the water washed through her fur. It stung her eyes and filled her ears. She struggled, tumbling as currents caught her and dragged her deeper. *StarClan, help me!* She struck out, trying to pull herself to the surface, but light seemed to glimmer on every side. *Which way is up?* Her panic spiraled. *I can't find my way out!* Her lungs ached for air. *I'm dying!* How could this happen? *I'm a special kit!*

Suddenly a voice sounded through the roaring of blood

in her ears. *Twigkit.* She stopped struggling, letting the water swirl her like a leaf. *Twigkit!* The voice sounded again, and she recognized it with a flicker of hope.

Is that my mother? She had forgotten that gentle, familiar purr. She'd only been with her mother for a few days, and since Alderpaw had carried her back to ThunderClan, she'd been unable to remember even the touch of her fur. Now her mother's scent surrounded her.

Swim, my special kit, swim!

At her mother's command, Twigkit flailed once more, trying to fight her way to the surface. Her lungs bursting, she fought the water as it dragged her down. *I'm not strong enough! Help me!*

Teeth sank into her scruff, biting into her fur and jerking her upward. *Mother?* Limp with shock, she felt herself being pulled. The water around her grew lighter and lighter until, like prey escaping the jaws of a fox, she burst into fresh air.

She gulped it down, struggling to fill her lungs and coughing helplessly. The teeth held onto her scruff, dragging her until she felt pebbles brush her paws. She let herself be hauled, helpless, onto the shore. "You saved me," she mewed weakly. Her mother had come back! *She rescued me!* Dazed, Twigkit coughed up water from her lungs and belched it from her belly.

"Twigkit?" A ginger she-cat was leaning over her, eyes flashing with fear. "Are you okay?"

Twigkit blinked in surprise. "Sparkpaw?" Disappointment jabbed her chest. *It wasn't my mother.* Fighting grief, she let her thoughts clear. Of course it wasn't her mother. *I'm a mouse-brain!*

What would her mother be doing here, beside the lake? She struggled to her paws, forcing a purr. "You saved me, Sparkpaw! Thank you!" Coughing, she collapsed.

Sparkpaw sat down, her wet pelt streaming. "What in StarClan are you doing here? Did you want to see what it's like being a RiverClan cat?"

Twigkit blinked at her, shame sweeping over her so hotly it drove the chill of the water from her pelt. "I came to fetch watermint," she mewed weakly.

Sparkpaw's eyes widened. "Did Alderpaw send you?"

Twigkit shook her head. "It was my idea. I wanted to help the Clan."

"I'm not sure drowning yourself is very helpful." Sparkpaw shook out her pelt, spraying Twigkit with water.

Paws thrummed toward them and pebbles cracked as another cat leaped onto the shore. Twigkit looked up and saw Cherryfall.

The warrior stared at Twigkit. "You were right, Sparkpaw," she meowed in surprise. "It *was* a kit on the shore. I was sure it was an otter."

"*Otters* can swim." Sparkpaw butted Twigkit playfully with her muzzle.

Twigkit blinked at her helplessly. She was cold, embarrassed, and exhausted.

Cherryfall slid past her apprentice. "I won't ask what you were doing by the lake, Twigkit. We need to get you home and warm as soon as possible." She crouched. "Climb onto my back. I'll carry you back to camp."

Twigkit reached up and tried to haul herself onto the warrior's shoulders, but her paws weren't strong enough. She felt Sparkpaw's muzzle beneath her haunches as, with a grunt, the apprentice boosted her up.

Twigkit clung on, relishing the warmth pulsing from Cherryfall's pelt. Closing her eyes, she let the warrior carry her home.

"Why did you even leave the camp?" Jayfeather scolded as he tucked her deep into Emberfoot's discarded nest.

"I was trying to help," Twigkit rasped sadly. She glanced toward the entrance, hoping Alderpaw would arrive. Would he be cross with her too? She couldn't bear not knowing.

"Kits should not try to help. They cause nothing but trouble!" He folded dry moss around her. "Briarlight, wrap yourself around her. We need to get her warm."

Briarlight slid gently into the nest beside Twigkit and curled close. Twigkit was still shivering, her throat sore from coughing up water. She could hear the Clan murmuring outside. They'd gathered around as Cherryfall had carried her into camp.

"Where did you find her?"

"Did the rogues kidnap her?"

"What was she doing out of camp?"

"How did she get so wet?"

Anxious voices had surrounded her, and she had buried her muzzle deep into Cherryfall's fur and closed her eyes. This wasn't the heroic return she had planned. She hadn't even brought back any watermint.

Now, in Emberfoot's nest, she heard Lilyheart's mew.

"Where is she?" The queen pushed her way through the brambles.

Twigkit peeped at her from the moss.

"Cherryfall said you'd gone to the lake." Lilyheart sounded as cross as Jayfeather. "How could you leave the camp? I'm ashamed of you. What will the Clan think?"

Twigkit shrank deeper into the nest.

Jayfeather stepped in front of the queen. "She needs rest," he told Lilyheart. "You can growl at her when she's recovered."

Lilyheart fluffed out her pelt indignantly. "I'm supposed to be looking after her."

"Then you shouldn't have let her wander out of camp." Jayfeather steered Lilyheart firmly toward the entrance. "Especially when there are rogues in the forest."

Lilyheart grunted and stalked from the medicine den.

Twigkit blinked at Jayfeather. Had he actually defended her?

He headed for the back of the den. "I'll mix you some herbs for the shock," he mewed over his shoulder. "And don't complain if they taste bad. You deserve everything you get."

As he spoke, Alderpaw raced through the brambles and skidded to a halt beside Twigkit's nest. "I was out gathering oak leaves." He was panting. "Cherryfall told me when I got back. Twigkit! What happened? What were you doing by the lake?"

Twigkit blinked at him, bracing herself for another

scolding, but Alderpaw was staring at her, his eyes wide with fear. "Are you okay?"

"She'll be fine." Jayfeather growled from the back of the den. "Briarlight's warming her up and I'm mixing some thyme and poppy seeds for her."

Alderpaw leaned forward and nudged Briarlight with his nose. "Let me take your place," he mewed softly. As Briarlight moved away, he slid into the nest and wrapped himself around Twigkit. His familiar scent soothed her.

"Sparkpaw said you were trying to help," he murmured softly. "How could you help by going to the lake?"

"I wanted to get watermint," Twigkit whispered, her throat tightening. "You'd run out, and I wanted to prove I was special." Her heart seemed to crack as the words tumbled out. "Mousewhisker and Rosepetal said they thought I wasn't special. They said there was a prophecy. The Clan thought I was part of it but I'm not. They said I was just an ordinary cat. But if I'm just an ordinary cat, the Clan won't want me anymore. So I had to prove I was special."

Alderpaw squeezed tighter around her and for the first time, Twigkit stopped shivering. "Of course you're special! StarClan led Needlepaw and me to you. And the Clan will always want you. You're one of us now, and nothing will ever change that."

You're one of us now. His words soothed her. Twigkit relaxed against him and began to purr.

"Alderpaw!"

Sparkpaw's mew made her jump. The flame-colored

apprentice burst through the brambles. Her eyes were shining. "Cherryfall told Bramblestar that I rescued Twigkit, and he says it's time for my assessment. You know what that means? I'm going to be a warrior!"

Twigkit felt Alderpaw stiffen beside her.

"A warrior already?" His mew was tight. "That's great, Sparkpaw. That's really great."

"I know!" Sparkpaw paced. "I can't wait for my ceremony. That's if I pass my assessment. I will pass, won't I?" She glanced anxiously at Alderpaw but didn't give him a chance to answer. "Of course I will. I've been training so hard for this moment. I wonder where the hunting assessment will be. I hope they choose the glade beside the stream. There are always squirrels there. . . ."

Twigkit's attention slid away. The warmth of Alderpaw and the nest was making her drowsy. Her eyelids felt heavy. As she closed them and sleep began to pull at her pelt, she wondered why Alderpaw had felt so tense when Sparkpaw had told him about her naming ceremony. He was happy for his sister, wasn't he? Of course he was. Darkness swirled around her. Why shouldn't he be?

CHAPTER 7

"Sparkpelt! Sparkpelt!"

Pride surged through Alderpaw's pelt as he called his sister's new warrior name. His Clanmates cheered around him.

Graystripe's mew sounded farther around the clearing. The elder was murmuring to Millie. "I thought they'd choose Sparkfire for her warrior name. She looks more like Firestar than any cat I ever saw. It would be a good way to remember him." He sighed. "But I suppose Bramblestar is leader. He must know what he's doing."

Sparkpelt stood beside Bramblestar in the center of the clearing, her chin and tail high. Joy shone in her bright green gaze. The bright half-moon shone in a clear black sky, lighting the camp and striping the Highledge with shadow.

Bramblestar brushed his muzzle along Sparkpelt's chin. Squirrelflight hurried forward and touched noses with her. Alderpaw shifted uneasily. He was trying to ignore the envy pricking in his paws. Sparkpelt deserved her warrior name. She'd been a great apprentice from her first day of training. Cherryfall and Brackenfur had announced that she had performed brilliantly during her assessment, catching a pigeon and two mice and outwitting Cherryfall in a mock fight with a battle move she'd thought up herself. And yet Alderpaw couldn't help wishing that he were standing in the clearing beside her instead of watching.

He glanced at the moon. Would StarClan speak to him at tonight's meeting at the Moonpool? Perhaps they would tell him that his apprenticeship was nearing its end. Longingly he imagined Jayfeather giving him his medicine-cat name while his Clanmates looked on. Would Jayfeather finally stop telling him what to do?

"Alderpaw!" Sparkpelt's mew called him from his thoughts. Their Clanmates were drifting to the edges of the camp, back to the prey they had left so they could witness the naming ceremony.

He hurried to meet her. "Congratulations!"

She looked as happy as a kit. "Thanks." She touched her muzzle to his cheek. "It'll be you next," she promised softly.

"I hope so," he sighed.

Jayfeather stomped past them, his tail flicking. "Stop wishing and hurry up, Alderpaw. We don't want to be the last cats to arrive."

Sparkpelt's gaze followed the medicine cat toward the camp entrance. "I think you're great," she whispered to Alderpaw. "The way you put up with him. I'd have thrown all his dumb herbs into the lake by now."

Alderpaw swallowed back a purr. "I've been tempted."

Sparkpelt nudged him away. "You'd better go." Jayfeather was already disappearing through the entrance tunnel. "I'll see you when you get back!" she called as Alderpaw turned to follow him. Sparkpelt would be sitting vigil in the clearing until dawn, to honor her new name.

At least Alderpaw didn't envy her *that*. The clear sky meant a chilly night. There was probably frost on the moor. "Don't get cold!" he called over his shoulder.

"My new name will keep me warm!"

Alderpaw purred as he ducked through the tunnel.

Jayfeather was already halfway up the rise. Alderpaw hurried to catch up with him.

They met Mothwing and Willowshine at the border and followed the stream as it cut between moor and forest, tracing it back toward the hills where it rose.

Alderpaw scrambled up a boulder after Jayfeather. The stream tumbled over rocks beside them. "Should we wait for Leafpool and Puddlepaw?"

"They're already there," Jayfeather answered without pausing. "Can't you smell their scent?"

Alderpaw opened his mouth, tasting the faint trace of Leafpool among the tang of water, stone, and heather.

"I wonder how Puddlepaw's training is going," Mothwing called out behind them.

"What's the point in wondering?" Jayfeather answered gruffly. "We'll find out when we get there."

"We'd probably get there quicker if a blind cat weren't leading the way," Mothwing mewed fondly. She hurried to catch up to Jayfeather. "He's as grumpy as an elder," she breathed, rolling her eyes as she bounded past Alderpaw.

"I heard that," Jayfeather huffed. "And you know I can follow this trail as well as any sighted cat."

"Sorry, Jayfeather," Mothwing purred. "I forgot you have the hearing of a bat."

Willowshine fell in beside Alderpaw as the older cats chatted. "How's your training going?"

"I think I'm doing okay," Alderpaw whispered. "I'm not sure if Jayfeather agrees."

"I don't think Jayfeather's agreed with anything his whole life," Willowshine purred. "You'll be a great medicine cat, though. You're being trained by one of the best."

Alderpaw swallowed back a sigh. Jayfeather might be one of the best, but there were days when being trained by a badger might be easier.

He was out of breath by the time they'd climbed the last rocky ridge. He hauled himself over the edge, his heart lifting as he saw the Moonpool below. It lay at the bottom of the shallow hollow, ringed by smooth cliffs. Tonight the water was so still that the moon reflected in it without a shimmer. He let Willowshine lead him down the slope, dimpled by countless paw steps. At the bottom he saw Leafpool.

She was hurrying to meet Jayfeather as he reached the water's edge. "How's the Clan? Are they well?" Leafpool's eyes glittered eagerly.

"A few bellyaches and thorn pricks," Jayfeather told her. "Nothing to worry about."

Alderpaw joined them, happy as he smelled Leafpool's familiar scent. "Everyone misses you," he told her.

Leafpool's eyes rounded with longing. "I miss you too." She glanced toward Puddlepaw, who was staring into the moonlit water blankly.

"How's the training going?" Jayfeather asked.

"We're making progress," Leafpool told him.

Alderpaw searched her gaze. Did that mean Puddlepaw was doing better than when he'd visited her in camp? Before he could ask, three shapes appeared at the edge of the hollow.

In the moonlight Alderpaw could make out Kestrelflight. He was flanked by two WindClan warriors. Gorsetail and Sedgewhisker followed him stiffly down the paw-worn path.

Jayfeather and Leafpool exchanged glances.

"Why'd he bring them?" Leafpool hissed.

Mothwing called out. "This meeting is for medicine cats!"

"We're not staying." Gorsetail halted as Kestrelflight reached the water's edge.

Leafpool blinked at Kestrelflight. "Is everything okay?" She nodded toward his Clanmates. "You don't usually bring company."

"Onestar's orders." The WindClan medicine cat sounded apologetic. He nodded to Gorsetail and Sedgewhisker. "I'll be fine now. You'd better go."

"We'll wait outside the hollow until you've finished," Sedgewhisker growled. She turned and climbed up the slope. Gorsetail followed.

Alderpaw's pelt prickled uneasily. The warriors seemed edgy. Kestrelflight's fur was ruffled.

"What's happened?" Mothwing padded closer, her eyes round with curiosity.

"Onestar is worried about the rogues," Kestrelflight explained. "He's ordered every cat to have an escort if they leave camp."

Jayfeather's ears twitched. "Doesn't he trust StarClan to watch over you?"

Kestrelflight shifted his paws. "Since the fight with the rogues, he doesn't seem to trust anyone." He frowned. "If only I'd been there when he was hurt. I might have helped him."

"There was nothing you could have done," Jayfeather told him gruffly.

Alderpaw blinked sympathetically at the WindClan medicine cat, remembering his own guilt over Sandstorm's death. *Is this what it means to be a medicine cat? To always regret the lives you couldn't save?*

"Poor Onestar," Mothwing murmured. "Losing a life must be hard."

Alderpaw blinked at her. How did a RiverClan cat hear about Onestar losing a life? Bramblestar had hinted at it in his conversation with Rowanstar, but no more. Had some cat in Lionblaze's patrol spoken out of turn?

Jayfeather snorted. "At least he had more than one life to lose. Furzepelt probably found dying harder."

Leafpool leaned closer to Kestrelflight. "Why were Gorsetail and Sedgewhisker so prickly?"

Kestrelflight lowered his voice. "Onestar's acting strangely.

He sends scouts ahead when he goes on patrol. He's set a permanent guard at the camp entrance. He's enforcing every rule. Half the Clan is on punishment duty for breaking one code or another." He glanced over his shoulder. "Everyone's scared they'll be reported. The warriors are so tense they hardly speak to one another, and the apprentices act like they're walking on quails' eggs."

Jayfeather flicked his tail impatiently. "The sooner Onestar pulls himself together, the better. Have you thought of slipping a few poppy seeds into his prey? It would give the Clan a break while he slept them off."

Kestrelflight's whiskers twitched with amusement. "I might try it." His shoulders softened for the first time since he'd arrived.

Leafpool still looked worried. "Has there been any sign of the rogues on the moor?"

"Not so far," Kestrelflight answered.

Mothwing sniffed. "They must have moved on by now. Why would they stay in territory that's already been claimed?"

Willowshine nodded. "Fighting us for every morsel of prey will be way too much trouble. They're bound to have left."

"Let's hope so," Leafpool agreed. "Rogues are usually happy to travel. It's what makes them rogues."

Alderpaw's belly tightened. She didn't know *these* rogues. They'd driven SkyClan from their territory and made their home in the gorge. And Darktail had vowed they'd see more of him. Should he warn the others? He glanced at Jayfeather.

His mentor had overheard the rogue leader's threat too. But the blind medicine cat was padding around Puddlepaw, sniffing the apprentice's pelt.

"You smell of herbs," Jayfeather grunted. "Leafpool must be teaching you *something*."

Leafpool hurried forward. "Puddlepaw is a fast learner."

"Good," Jayfeather mewed. "Because we need you back in ThunderClan. Is he ready to become a full medicine cat yet?"

Already? Alderpaw's pelt prickled with indignation. *I'll be training until I'm an elder if Jayfeather gets his way.*

"A full medicine cat?" Leafpool looked at Jayfeather in horror. "After one moon's training?"

Mothwing whisked her tail over the stone. "I'm sure you and Alderpaw can manage to take care of ThunderClan without Leafpool for a while longer. If you ever need help, send for me or Willowshine."

Jayfeather snorted dismissively. "We won't need help." His blind gaze fixed on Puddlepaw. "But it would be good to know how long you will be wasting your talents on ShadowClan."

Leafpool's ears twitched crossly. "Shared knowledge is never wasted."

Anxiety sparked in Puddlepaw's eyes. "I appreciate everything Leafpool has taught me, and I'm learning as fast as I can."

Alderpaw felt a sudden surge of pity for the young cat. Perhaps training too quickly was worse than training too slowly. In another moon Puddlepaw would be expected to take responsibility for the welfare of every cat in his Clan. "I'm sure you will be a great medicine cat," he assured him. "It just takes patience."

Jayfeather snapped his head around. "And the ability to tell the difference between chervil root and leaves."

Anger pricked through Alderpaw's pelt. "That's not fair—"

Leafpool interrupted him. "At least we know that Alderpaw has plenty of patience." She stared meaningfully at Jayfeather.

As though he could see her fierce gaze, Jayfeather turned away and padded to the edge of the pool. "Since there's little else to say, let's share with StarClan." Crouching, he touched his nose to the water's smooth surface.

Alderpaw pulled his nose tip from the chilly water, disappointed.

"Did StarClan speak to you?" Leafpool was looking at him hopefully.

He shook his head, straightening. He'd seen nothing but his own thoughts. Jayfeather, Kestrelflight, and Willowshine glanced at each other. Puddlepaw stared at the ground.

"Didn't anyone speak with them?" Leafpool pressed.

Jayfeather shook out his pelt. "I guess there was nothing to share."

"What about the rogues?" Leafpool looked worried.

"They must be no threat," Willowshine guessed.

"I told you," Mothwing jerked her head up. She lay by the water, but she hadn't dipped her nose to it like the other medicine cats. How could she share with a Clan she didn't seem to believe in? Even though she'd witnessed the great battle with the Dark Forest, she'd never truly believed that those cats were their own ancestors, but simply thought of them as rogues from beyond Clan territory. "They'll have moved on by now."

Alderpaw wished he could believe her. But that wasn't the worry that wormed in his belly. He'd been hoping for StarClan to give him a clue about SkyClan. The more he thought about it, the more convinced Alderpaw felt that the *sky* that would clear in the prophecy referred to SkyClan. And surely StarClan knew where the lost Clan had gone. Why couldn't their ancestors send word? Or at least give a clue about whether Twigkit and Violetkit were part of their prophecy? With a twinge of pity, he thought of Twigkit snuggling in beside him, shivering after her fall in the lake. *If I am an ordinary cat, the Clan won't want me anymore.* He pushed the thought away with a shiver. Of course the Clan would want her, whether she was special or not.

"Are you ready to return?" Sedgewhisker's mew sounded from the rim of the hollow. She stood silhouetted in the moonlight.

Kestrelflight hurried toward her. "I'm coming." He glanced back at the others. "May StarClan light your paths," he called as he joined his Clanmate.

Mothwing and Willowshine followed him up the slope. "See you at the Gathering," Mothwing mewed over her shoulder.

Willowshine dipped her head as she passed. "Take care."

Jayfeather was inspecting Puddlepaw again. "Tell me what herbs you know," he quizzed the young cat.

"Watermint, horsetail, marigold . . ."

As Puddlepaw began to list them, Alderpaw noticed Leafpool gazing anxiously at the moon's reflection in the water.

"Were you hoping that StarClan would tell you if Rowanstar has made the right choice in Puddlepaw?" he asked softly, padding to her side.

"I know he has," Leafpool answered quietly. "Puddlepaw is quick to learn and has sympathy for his patients. He's going to make a fine medicine cat."

"Then why do you look so worried?" Alderpaw recognized the dark shadows in Leafpool's eyes.

"I'm worried about ShadowClan," she murmured.

"Is something wrong?" Alderpaw leaned closer.

"Not exactly wrong," Leafpool meowed hesitantly. "Not yet, anyway. But it's so chaotic."

"Perhaps ShadowClan is just like that. Not all Clans are the same."

"ShadowClan has always had its own sense of the warrior code, but at least they respected it." Leafpool met Alderpaw's gaze anxiously. "These days, the younger cats show their elders no respect. They ignore some rules completely. I had to hunt for Grassheart yesterday. The apprentices aren't bringing her enough food to keep her milk flowing. Flowerkit, Whorlkit, and Snakekit are growing fast. Grassheart needs all the prey she can eat."

"Why don't the *warriors* send their apprentices out hunting?" Alderpaw was confused.

"Mentors don't seem to be able to tell their apprentices *anything*. Sleekpaw talks back to everyone, even Rowanstar. And Needlepaw's not much better."

Alderpaw's hackles pricked as Leafpool criticized the young she-cat. "She's still looking after Violetkit, though, isn't she?"

Leafpool blinked at him. "If you mean does she have Violetkit trailing everywhere after her, yes. She takes her out of camp to StarClan knows where."

"Out of camp?" Guilt warmed Alderpaw's pelt. *Is that my fault? It was me who encouraged her in the first place.* "Doesn't Rowanstar punish her?"

"I don't think he even knows," Leafpool sighed. "There are simply more apprentices than the Clan can handle. Beepaw and Yarrowpaw have been saying that we shouldn't bother with StarClan. They ask why should they believe in a bunch of cats they've never even seen."

Alderpaw interrupted, shocked. "They mustn't reject StarClan!"

Leafpool went on anxiously. "Sleekpaw says dead cats are dumb. She says StarClan can't possibly understand the forest anymore. They've been living in their own hunting grounds too long."

Alderpaw leaned forward. "Can't you tell them they're wrong—what you've seen with your own eyes?"

"I'm a ThunderClan cat." Leafpool stared at him helplessly.

"Anything I say will just make it worse. And the warriors have stopped arguing with them. It's like they don't see the point anymore."

Alderpaw's heart quickened with fear. "Perhaps that's why StarClan didn't share with us tonight. They might be angry about ShadowClan."

Leafpool closed her eyes. "Or maybe StarClan doesn't know what to do." She blinked them open, as though pushing away worry. "Perhaps it'll pass. These are young cats. They'll grow out of this nonsense." She fluffed out her pelt against the chilly night air. "I'm probably worrying over nothing. Like you say, ShadowClan has always been different. It could be that every new set of apprentices is the same and the warriors are doing the right thing by quietly waiting it out." Before Alderpaw could comment, she padded toward Puddlepaw, interrupting Jayfeather, who was questioning Puddlepaw about how to treat an infected claw. "Come on. It's time we were going."

Puddlepaw looked relieved. He nodded to Leafpool and headed for the top of the hollow.

"I'll be home in a moon or two," Leafpool told Jayfeather as she followed him.

"I wish it were sooner," Jayfeather huffed.

"So do I." Leafpool caught Alderpaw's eye as she went on. "Be patient with Alderpaw. Cats learn far more from kindness than anger."

Alderpaw glanced nervously at Jayfeather, wishing Leafpool hadn't said anything. *Never poke your claw into a bees' nest.*

Jayfeather's whiskers twitched with amusement. "If I start being gentle with him now, he'll worry I'm getting soft in my old age." He followed Leafpool up the slope. "It sounds like you're doing a good job with Puddlepaw. At least *he* seems to know what chervil is for."

Alderpaw hardly heard his mentor's jibe. He was worrying about ShadowClan. What if Leafpool was wrong? What if the bad behavior of the apprentices didn't pass? What would happen to Needlepaw? His heart lurched. How could Violetkit learn to be a true warrior in a place like that?

CHAPTER 8

Violetkit narrowed her eyes as she glanced at the setting sun blazing between the treetops. Her paws ached. She was getting used to the walk back from the rogues' camp. Needlepaw usually helped her over fallen trees and ditches, but it still felt like a long way. She was relieved to see the bramble wall of the camp ahead.

"Come on," Needlepaw whispered, guiding her toward the dirtplace tunnel.

Violetkit stumbled wearily as a mew took her by surprise.

"Where have you been?" Tawnypelt strode from between the trees and blocked their path. Her angry gaze fell on Needlepaw.

Needlepaw blinked back at her, unfazed. "I was showing Violetkit the best spot for squirrel hunting."

Tawnypelt glared. "Violetkit is too young to hunt squirrels. She shouldn't even be out of camp."

Needlepaw rounded her eyes imploringly. "But she gets so bored. Pinenose's kits are apprentices now."

"What about Grassheart's kits?" Tawnypelt stood her ground. "She could be helping to entertain them."

Violetkit stepped forward. "Pinenose says they're too young for me to play with." At least that was true. The kits were so cute, but Pinenose always had a reason why Violetkit should stay away from them.

"Nonsense," Tawnypelt snapped. "When I was a kit, I played with my denmates the moment I opened my eyes, no matter how old they were."

But you were Clanborn. Violetkit swallowed back resentment. She didn't want to appear ungrateful. Pinenose and Grassheart were kind to her. They were just overprotective, that's all. "I'd play with them if I was allowed to," she mewed defensively.

Tawnypelt narrowed her eyes. "I'll speak with Pinenose and Grassheart." Then she switched her gaze sharply back to Needlepaw. "If Violetkit is having problems in the nursery, you won't solve them by breaking rules. You should have come to me straight away." Her tail twitched irritably. "That's an afternoon's training wasted. I'd planned to teach you how to track scent trails. It's the most important warrior skill you can learn."

Violetkit stiffened. *What if Tawnypelt tracked our scent to the rogues' camp?*

But the tortoiseshell went on. "I went hunting with Snowbird and Stonewing instead." She looked Needlepaw up and down. "Did you catch any squirrels?"

"They were too fast," Needlepaw mewed quickly.

"So you've got nothing for the fresh-kill pile at all?" Tawnypelt looked exasperated. "The Clan comes first!"

"I was taking care of Violetkit," Needlepaw protested.

"You were teaching her how to break rules." Tawnypelt's mew deepened to a growl. "Come with me. This must be reported to Rowanstar."

She turned away, tail twitching ominously.

Needlepaw glanced at Violetkit. "Don't worry," she murmured. "I won't let you get into trouble."

Violetkit's heart was pounding. *Rowanstar!* The Shadow-Clan leader occasionally paused while crossing the camp to say hello and ask her how she was settling into Clan life, but she'd never managed more than a squeak in reply. Now she was going to be reported to him for breaking Clan rules.

As Needlepaw padded after Tawnypelt—shoulders loose, tail flicking breezily—Violetkit pressed back the panic rising in her chest. Forcing her pelt to smooth, she followed them, pretending to be calm.

The sun had dipped behind the trees and the Clan had settled around the clearing to eat. Violetkit glanced at the fresh-kill pile, almost empty now. Beepaw was rooting through it. Violetkit's belly churned as the apprentice sniffed at a thrush. She felt too sick to be hungry.

Rowanstar looked up from the mouse he was eating beside Crowfrost. "Tawnypelt." He got to his paws, greeting the she-cat with a worried look. "What's happened?" Clearly, he could see anger in her rippling pelt.

"Needlepaw took Violetkit out of camp." Tawnypelt stepped aside and let Needlepaw face Rowanstar.

Violetkit halted. Her paws felt shaky as she sensed the eyes of the other cats lifting from their fresh-kill and fixing on her. She glanced nervously at Needlepaw. Was her friend in serious trouble? *And what about me?* Did ShadowClan punish kits?

Rowanstar glared at Needlepaw. "Kits don't leave camp," he meowed sternly. "What were you thinking? There may be rogues in the forest. There are certainly foxes, and Spikefur said he saw an adder yesterday. A *warrior* would be lucky to survive an adder bite. A kit would die."

Needlepaw blinked at him coolly. "I look out for adders and foxes. I wouldn't let anything hurt her."

Rowanstar's hackles lifted as though he was surprised to hear her talk back. "Kits do *not* leave camp," he repeated.

Needlepaw glanced calmly at Beepaw beside the fresh-kill pile. "It's a dumb rule."

Beepaw leaned closer, her eyes sparking with interest.

Violetkit stared at Needlepaw, shock fizzing through her fur. Had she really said that? And why had she shot a sly glance at Beepaw? Had they been planning to challenge Rowanstar like this?

Crowfrost stood up. His tail twitched angrily as Needlepaw went on.

"Like I told Tawnypelt, Violetkit was bored in camp." She flicked her muzzle dismissively toward the clearing. "There's nothing to learn here except how to grow old."

Sleekpaw, Juniperpaw, Yarrowpaw, and Strikepaw were padding closer, their eyes flashing with interest. Birchpaw and

Lionpaw hung back, eyeing each other nervously, but Beepaw pricked her ears excitedly, as though willing Needlepaw to say more.

Rowanstar's gaze flicked toward them, then back to Needlepaw. It was blazing with anger. "There is plenty to learn in camp," he hissed. "The *warrior code*, for a start. Too many rules are being ignored."

"It's impossible to remember all your rules." Needlepaw flicked her tail irritably. "Perhaps if we had fewer rules, we'd obey more of them."

Crowfrost flattened his ears. "Perhaps if we had smarter apprentices, they wouldn't have such a hard time remembering."

Sleekpaw and Strikepaw, Crowfrost's kits, hissed at the ShadowClan deputy. "Are you calling us dumb?"

Strikepaw glared at his father. "If you treated us better, we might try harder," he snarled. "Don't forget there are nearly as many of us as there are of you. You'd be wise to give us a little more respect."

Was that a threat? Violetkit stared at him, her mouth open. She shifted her paws uneasily. The apprentices were edging nearer to Needlepaw, as though gaining confidence with every complaint. Had they planned this rebellion, or had Needlepaw's boldness sparked resentments that had been simmering for moons?

Yarrowpaw and Juniperpaw flicked their tails irritably. Beepaw padded from the fresh-kill pile to join them.

"*Respect!*" Rowanstar narrowed his eyes. "Respect has to

be *earned*." His growl was hard.

Beepaw tipped her head. "I don't see the older cats earning any respect. All they do is hunt and sleep."

Snowbird padded forward quickly, her pelt ruffled. "Beepaw!" She blinked at her daughter anxiously. "You mustn't speak about your elders like that."

"Why not?" Beepaw moved closer to Yarrowpaw. "*You* taught us that ShadowClan cats can say what they like."

Alarm sparked in Snowbird's gaze as her kits stared at her petulantly. "Where has all this come from?"

Beepaw stared at her mother. "If you ever *listened* instead of just talking, you'd know."

Crowfrost fluffed out his fur, his nervous gaze on his own kits. Sleekpaw, Juniperpaw, and Strikepaw were bunched close, staring questioningly at Rowanstar.

Sleekpaw lashed her tail. "The elders used to tell stories about how ShadowClan was feared by the other Clans," she meowed. "Now we only try to make peace."

Strikepaw snorted. "We hide behind our borders like kitty-pets."

"It's true!" Juniperpaw agreed. "Not even WindClan respects us anymore. At the last Gathering, Fernpaw called us a bunch of frog-eaters. In the old days, apprentices from other Clans didn't even dare speak to us. Ratscar told us that ThunderClan used to tell nursery stories about how terrifying we were. I bet their nursery stories aren't so scary now."

Rowanstar shifted his paws. "Peace brings prey," he

meowed. "Why fight over borders when we have enough prey to feed every cat?"

Ratscar got to his paws. The brown tom's eyes were narrow. "The apprentices have a point. ShadowClan used to rule the forest. Now we live like a bunch of ThunderClan cats. All we want is peace and food. We're hardly better than kittypets."

Kinkfur growled. "What nonsense! ShadowClan will always be feared and respected by the other Clans."

"Even if we're not feared and respected by our own kits," Ratscar rasped dryly.

Oakfur crossed the clearing and faced Rowanstar. "Why can't the mentors keep their apprentices under control? In my day, we did what we were told."

Stonewing shouldered his way through the gathered cats and glared at Juniperpaw. "How could you embarrass me like this? Haven't I been a good mentor to you? I've taught you everything you know."

Juniperpaw curled his lip. "Cats are born knowing how to hunt and fight. Why do I need *you* telling me what I already know?"

Stonewing swung his muzzle accusingly toward Rowanstar. "I warned you the apprentices were getting too big for their pelts."

Rowanstar glared back at him, pelt spiking. "I shouldn't have to control your apprentice for you."

Dawnpelt hurried forward and gazed imploringly at Sleekpaw and her denmates. "I don't understand why you're so angry. When I was your age, I was proud to be an apprentice," she mewed. "We all were. We *wanted* to learn the warrior code."

"Only because you wanted to be like ThunderClan," Needlepaw scoffed.

Dawnpelt bristled. "That's not true!"

Tawnypelt hissed at Needlepaw. "Respect your elders!"

"Not until they respect us!" Sleekpaw butted in.

Angry yowls echoed around the camp. Violetkit shrank against Needlepaw's flank as the Clan argued around her. Perhaps the warrior code *was* too restrictive. She'd heard Needlepaw complain about it often enough. But was it worth fighting about? Surely warriors had a code for a reason. Otherwise they'd be nothing but rogues or loners.

"Silence!" Rowanstar leaped onto the low rock at the edge of the clearing and glowered at his Clan. His fur stood on end, and his eyes blazed in the twilight.

The Clan fell silent and watched their leader expectantly.

"Needlepaw." Rowanstar fixed his furious gaze on the silver apprentice. "You broke a rule and you will be punished. You will look after the elders. Clean their bedding, pull out their ticks, and hunt for them. They are your responsibility from now on."

Needlepaw returned his gaze, unruffled. "For how long?"

Rowanstar showed his teeth. "Until I say so."

"Okay." Needlepaw shrugged and turned away. She shouldered her way between her denmates and headed for the fresh-kill pile. Violetkit stared at her. How could she act so cool?

"Violetkit." Rowanstar's mew made her jump.

She stared at him, her heart in her throat.

"You shouldn't have left camp." The ShadowClan leader's mew was stern. His gaze flicked toward the nursery. Pinenose watched from outside. He beckoned the queen forward with a flick of his tail. "You should have been keeping a closer eye on her," he told the queen as she padded toward him.

She dipped her head. "I'm sorry."

"Don't let her out of your sight," Rowanstar warned.

Pinenose stopped beside Violetkit. "Couldn't Grassheart take care of her now?" she mewed hopefully. "Now that my own kits have left the nursery, I could return to warrior duties."

Violetkit tried to ignore the hurt jabbing her heart. She'd known for a long time that Pinenose had never been fond of her. *Of course she'd rather be hunting than watching me. I'm not her kit.* She smelled pine and fresh air in the queen's fur. Had she been out already?

Rowanstar scowled. "I know you miss patrolling and hunting, but it's Grassheart's first litter. She won't have the time to take care of another kit."

Violetkit lifted her muzzle defiantly. "I can take care of myself."

Rowanstar's hopped from the stone and padded closer. "If that were true, you wouldn't have left the camp today." He turned to Pinenose. "Look after her. Make sure she learns the warrior code. I don't want her turning out like *them*." He glowered at Sleekpaw and her denmates. "She's been spending far too much time with Needlepaw."

Pinenose lowered her gaze. "Okay," she grunted.

But Needlepaw is my only friend! Violetkit stared at Rowanstar, her heart as heavy as stone. *Now I'll have no one to talk to!* Anger sparking beneath her pelt, Violetkit padded to the nursery and squeezed inside. Grassheart's kits were squirming and mewling in their nest while Grassheart dozed. Violetkit scowled at them. They'd never know what it was like to lose a mother and a sister. Slinking into the shadows at the edge of the den, she curled up and buried her nose beneath her paw.

"Violetkit!" Needlepaw hissed across the clearing.

Violetkit looked up, blinking in the afternoon sunshine. She was tired after a morning spent playing with Grassheart's kits. Tawnypelt must have kept her word and spoken to her. As soon as she'd woken that morning, Grassheart had asked her to take Snakekit, Whorlkit, and Flowerkit outside to play. She'd enjoyed teaching them the rules of moss-ball and cat and mouse. For a while she'd felt less alone. But the kits were resting now, snuggled in their nest beside their mother, and Violetkit had nothing to do.

"Violetkit," Needlepaw called again.

Violetkit glanced toward Pinenose. The queen was picking irritably through the fresh-kill pile at the far end of the camp. Violetkit scrambled to her paws and hurried across the clearing.

Needlepaw was dragging a large bundle of bracken toward the elders' den. She let go as Violetkit reached her. "Dumb old cats," Needlepaw huffed. "They're always wanting something.

'Pull this tick, Needlepaw.' 'Bring me food, Needlepaw.'" Needlepaw mimicked their husky mews. "'I need new bedding, Needlepaw.'" She sat down wearily.

"Can I help?" Violetkit offered eagerly.

Needlepaw's eyes brightened. "Yes."

Violetkit leaned closer, preparing for orders. Would Needlepaw want her to look for moss around the camp? Or fetch prey from the fresh-kill pile?

Needlepaw leaned close and whispered in Violetkit's ear. "I need you to travel to the rogues' camp tonight."

"Me?" Violetkit blinked at her in surprise. "Are you coming too?"

"Of course not!" Needlepaw rolled her eyes. "How can I leave with every old fleabag in the Clan watching to make sure I stick to my stupid elder duties?"

Violetkit frowned. "Then why do I need to go?"

"I want you to give a message to Rain. I promised to meet him tonight, but I can't now, since I got caught with you."

Violetkit felt a prickle of guilt in her belly.

"So you'll go?" Needlepaw was staring at her imploringly.

Violetkit shifted her paws. "How can I? Pinenose will be watching me. And Grassheart."

"They'll be asleep by the time the moon's up," Needlepaw mewed. "They sleep like hedgehogs. Nothing will wake them until dawn."

Violetkit glanced at the nursery. Both queens *did* sleep heavily. The kits too. She probably could slip out of the nursery without anyone noticing. But she'd never been in the forest at night alone. What if she met a fox? And what if she was caught? Rowanstar would be mad. Fear sparked beneath her pelt.

Needlepaw seemed to read her mind. "You'll be fine. If a warrior patrol catches you, tell them I made you go. And keep an eye out for foxes and owls. Fox stench is easy to spot. Just stay away from it. Check the canopy for owls. Their eyes flash in the dark."

Owls? Violetkit shivered. She never wanted to see an owl again!

"You *have* to go!" Needlepaw looked desperate. "Rain will be expecting me, and if I don't turn up, he might not like me anymore."

Sympathy filled Violetkit's heart. Needlepaw was her only real friend in the Clan. She'd been so kind. No one else had taken her to see Twigkit. "Okay," she agreed.

Needlepaw's eyes brightened at once. "Thanks! You must reach their camp before moonhigh."

An owl screeched. Violetkit glanced nervously up through the dark canopy, looking for eyes flashing in the shadows. But this deep into the pine forest, there was hardly a glimpse of light between the closely packed trees. Her heart leaped into her throat as the owl sounded again. She felt sure it had been following her since she crossed the last ditch.

Pelt bushed, she padded onward, fear pushing exhaustion away.

She'd crept from the warm moss beside Pinenose as soon

as she was sure that the two queens and the kits were asleep. Gentle snores had filled the nursery as she squeezed through the entrance. She'd stiffened as she hit the chilly night air, her heart thumping as she'd crept through the dirtplace tunnel. Alone in the forest, she'd felt like prey. Now she was close to the edge of ShadowClan territory. The rogues' camp was near. Even in the dark she remembered the route, and she crawled under a bramble that still smelled of Needlepaw's scent from last time.

The trees thinned beyond the border where the land sloped up, and Violetkit trekked onward, comforted by the moonlight that began to light her path. At last pine gave way to alder and beech and stars sparkled reassuringly between the bare branches. She strained to see ahead, glimpsing the rowan bushes that marked the edge of the rogues' camp. *I made it!*

As pride surged through her, a screech sounded above. She jerked her head up and glimpsed the massive silhouette of an owl. It swooped toward her so fast she froze in panic. Claws glinted as the owl stalled in midair, twisting its wings as it dropped toward her. She felt a rush of air, then pain as talons dug into her fur.

A cat's yowl pierced the night. Feathers whipped her ears. The owl's grip loosened as something slammed into it, knocking it away.

She glimpsed gray fur, and silver. Rain and Roach reared and dragged the owl to the ground.

"Run!" Rain screeched as he grappled against the owl's powerful wings.

Violetkit couldn't move. Her heart nearly burst as she watched Roach leap onto the owl's back and sink his teeth into its thick plumage. The owl flapped wildly, its wings thumping against the ground as it threw him off. It wrenched free of Rain and struggled into the air, screeching as it beat the air and flapped up between the branches.

Rain turned on her, panting. "I said *run!*"

Violetkit shrank away, trembling as he glared at her.

"Be gentle!" Raven bounded from between the rowan bushes and slithered to a halt beside Violetkit. "She must be terrified." She curled her tail around Violetkit, searching her gaze. "Where's Needlepaw?"

Rain stiffened. "Did the owl get her?"

Violetkit shook her head, struggling to find her voice. "Sh-she couldn't come," she stammered. "That's why I'm here. She sent me to tell you."

"You came through the woods alone?" Raven looked shocked.

"So?" Rain was unimpressed. "I thought Clan cats could do anything. A little forest walk in the night isn't hard."

"She's barely three moons old." Raven crouched close to Violetkit, pressing her warm flank close.

I'm trembling. Violetkit realized she was shaking like trapped prey.

Roach nudged Rain, his eyes glinting. "Needlepaw couldn't make it, Rain. She must have better things to do." He sounded as though he was teasing his campmate.

"She doesn't," Violetkit mewed quickly. "She got in trouble

and has to stay in camp and look after the elders."

Flame slunk from the rowan bushes, her orange pelt pale in the moonlight. "Ain't that sweet," she drawled mockingly, her voice light now that her terrible whitecough had passed—and, with it, her kindness. "Needlepaw has to look after the old cats."

"She'll come as soon as she can," Violetkit promised.

Raven touched her muzzle to Violetkit's head. "I'm sure she will."

Violetkit felt a wave of gratitude for Raven's kindness. For the first time since leaving the nursery, she felt safe. "I guess I'd better go home." She glanced at the sky, hoping the rogues had scared the owl off for good.

Paw steps sounded in the shadows behind a beech. "You mustn't leave now." Darktail padded from the darkness, his eyes round with concern. "It's too dangerous for you to travel alone."

"But I have to be back in the nursery by dawn." Violetkit's heart skipped a beat. What if Pinenose woke and found her gone?

Darktail padded past her, weaving around his campmates. "Don't worry, little one. We'll have you home by then." He exchanged glances with Rain. "You must be tired and hungry. Nettle!" He called into the shadows.

The brown tabby padded out, a rabbit hanging from his jaws. Silt followed, carrying a squirrel.

"We'll share our catch with you and you can sleep." Darktail stopped in front of Violetkit and leaned so close that his breath washed her muzzle. It smelled of blood.

She blinked at him uneasily. She didn't want to stay, but she didn't want to walk home by herself either. "Could you take me home now?" she asked hopefully.

Raven purred softly beside her. "You must be exhausted, my dear." She glanced at Darktail, whose gaze was unreadable. "Eat with us and rest for a while. Then we'll take you home."

Violetkit woke up. Her heart lurched as she saw pale dawn light seeping between the trees. She sat up, the bracken rustling around her. Raven had made her a bed to rest in after they'd shared the rabbit. She'd lined it with moss, and it had been so warm and soft that Violetkit couldn't resist closing her eyes for a moment and dozing for a little while before the rogues took her home.

"It's dawn!" She glanced around her. The rogues sprawled in their nests. They'd fallen asleep too! She leaped from the bracken and crossed the small hollow in the hillside where they had made their camp. She stopped beside Raven. "Wake up." She poked the she-cat with a paw.

Raven jerked away, baring her teeth. "Who is it?" she snarled.

Violetkit jumped back, shocked. "It's me! We fell asleep. I'm meant be back at camp."

Raven's gaze softened quickly. "Oh, you poor thing," she mewed. She got to her paws and stretched. "Darktail." She called softly to the rogue leader, who was still snoring in his nest.

His tail twitched.

"Darktail," Raven called again. "It's time we took Violetkit back to her camp."

Darktail lifted his head and stared at her blearily. "Is it that time already?"

"I thought you were going to take me home last night," Violetkit ventured uneasily.

"I guess the fine prey Nettle and Silt caught for us made us sleepier than we expected." Darktail sat up. "Rain! Roach! Wake up!" He called to the sleeping toms. "We're taking Violetkit home."

Violetkit watched anxiously as the rogues yawned and stretched. She could see the fiery tip of the sun beyond the forest now. The Clan would be waking. What would Pinenose say when she found her gone? She began to pace.

Darktail nodded to Rain and Roach. "You two can come with me. The rest of you stay here."

Violetkit glanced at Raven. She wanted the kind she-cat to come with them. But she wasn't going to argue with Darktail. He seemed friendly, but there was a darkness that never left his gaze, and it scared her.

"Come on." The rogue leader headed from the camp. Violetkit followed, Rain and Roach at her heels.

The sun was up by the time they reached the bramble wall of the ShadowClan camp. Mist swirled between the trees. Violetkit pricked her ears as they neared, her heart sinking as she heard the sounds of the Clan preparing to start their day.

"Needlepaw!" Kinkfur mewed huskily. "Tell Leafpool I need mouse bile. I've found another tick near my tail."

"Tawnypelt and Stonewing." Crowfrost's order sounded through the chilly air. "You'll each lead a hunting party. And make sure your apprentices catch something worth eating this time. Crow-food doesn't count."

"Yarrowpaw! Strikepaw!" Wasptail sounded cross. "You should be out of your nests by now. Crowfrost is organizing the patrols."

Darktail's ears pricked. He stopped at the entrance. "Patrols? Apprentices?" He looked intrigued. "It's awfully regimented here, isn't it? You must not have a lot of freedom."

Violetkit didn't answer. She was straining to hear if anyone was looking for her. Perhaps she'd been lucky. Perhaps Pinenose and Grassheart hadn't noticed she was missing. She blinked at Darktail. "Thanks for bringing me home." Her gaze flitted to Roach and Rain. "And thanks for saving me from the owl." She turned, heading for the dirtplace tunnel so she could slip into camp unnoticed.

"Wait." Darktail's mew sent a chill through her pelt.

"What?" She faced him uneasily.

"I want to make sure you don't get into trouble." Darktail was eyeing the camp entrance.

"It's okay." Foreboding tightened Violetkit's belly. What was he planning? "I'll be fine."

But Darktail was already ducking through the entrance tunnel.

Rain nudged Violetkit after him. "Go on," he encouraged.

"We might as well see you safely into camp."

Heart pounding, Violetkit followed Darktail through the tunnel. Rain and Roach followed.

As they emerged into the camp, Violetkit felt the eyes of the Clan flash toward her. She wanted to run and hide. What would Rowanstar say? She'd brought rogues into the camp.

Darktail marched across the clearing, tail high.

Hisses sounded around him. Stonewing arched his back. Spikefur and Snowbird burst from the warriors' den, their eyes wide with shock.

Crowfrost pushed through the warriors that were gathered around him. "What are you doing here?" He met Darktail in the clearing.

Darktail signaled to Rain and Roach with a flick of his tail. They stopped a few paw steps behind. Violetkit halted between them, her pelt lifting along her spine. "I found this kit wandering in the woods," he told Crowfrost. "I thought I should bring her home. It's dangerous out there."

Spikefur lunged at him, but Darktail batted him away with a swift swipe of his paw.

"Is that the gratitude you show to a cat who has returned a lost Clanmate?" The rogue leader sounded hurt.

"Violetkit!" Pinenose burst form the nursery, her pelt bristling. "Are you okay? Did they harm you?"

Violetkit stared at the queen. "They looked after me," she whispered hoarsely.

"What were you doing out in the forest?" Pinenose demanded, her fear sharpening to anger.

Needlepaw hurried from the elders' den. "Violetkit. There you are. Did you get lost trying to find the dirtplace again?"

Violetkit blinked at her, confused. What had happened to the plan for Violetpaw to say that Needlepaw had sent her out?

But she is trying to cover for me, in a way, Violetkit thought. *Maybe she's just changed her mind about how.*

Kinkfur snorted. "Who gets lost finding the dirtplace? You only have to follow your nose."

Spikefur hissed, glowering at Darktail. "Why are we talking about the dirtplace? There are strangers in our camp."

"Worse than strangers." Dawnpelt fell in beside Spikefur, flexing her claws. *"Rogues."*

"What are you doing in our camp?" Rowanstar's growl cut through the angry murmuring of his Clanmates. The ShadowClan leader strode across the clearing and stopped a whisker away from Darktail.

"I brought your kit home." Darktail nodded toward Violetkit.

Violetkit shrank beneath her pelt as Rowanstar's gaze flicked toward her.

Darktail went on. "I don't understand why you're being so unfriendly." He blinked at Rowanstar with round eyes. "We were just trying to help your Clan."

Rowanstar narrowed his eyes. "Like you helped WindClan?"

Darktail returned his gaze innocently. "We were just defending ourselves. We have the right to do that, surely?"

"Rogues have no right to be on Clan territory!" Spikefur snarled.

Sleekpaw padded into the clearing. "Why not?"

Her Clanmates jerked their gazes toward her.

"Why *not*?" Tawnypelt's fur spiked. "I can't believe you would ask that. They're not Clan cats."

Yarrowpaw padded to Sleekpaw's side. "If they weren't on our territory, they couldn't have rescued Violetkit."

Sleekpaw blinked at her leader. "And what would your precious StarClan have said if something had happened to their *special* cat?"

"Be quiet!" Rowanstar glared at the yellow apprentice.

Darktail glanced at Rain and Roach. "I think we should leave," he meowed calmly. "We seem to be causing an argument."

He turned toward the entrance.

"Wait!" Rowanstar lifted his chin. "We're grateful you returned Violetkit to us. But you don't belong here."

Rain and Roach exchanged amused glances.

"A patrol will make sure you leave our land," Rowanstar went on. "Tawnypelt, Spikefur, and Dawnpelt." He nodded to his warriors. "Go with them and make sure they cross the border."

Tawnypelt nodded.

"Can I come with you?" Needlepaw hurried toward her mentor hopefully.

Tawnypelt curled her lip. "You're looking after the elders, remember?"

Violetkit saw anger flash in Needlepaw's eyes. Then she saw the silver apprentice's gaze dart toward Rain. Rain blinked at her, then looked away. He turned and followed Darktail and Roach as they headed for the entrance.

Tawnypelt, Dawnpelt, and Spikefur hurried after them.

Belly hollow with dread, Violetkit turned to face Rowanstar. The ShadowClan leader stared at her, exasperation glittering in his gaze. Hanging her head, Violetkit prepared for her punishment.

CHAPTER 9

❧

Fluffing her fur out against the cold, Twigkit followed Alderpaw through the moonlit forest. They were going to meet Violetkit and Needlepaw. It had been over half a moon since they'd met, and she longed to see her sister. She could tell Violetkit how she'd heard their mother's voice and smelled her scent when she'd nearly drowned. Perhaps Violetkit still remembered what their mother had smelled and sounded like. As Twigkit followed Alderpaw up a leaf-strewn rise, she tried to ignore the shame worming in her belly. "Do you think Bramblestar's still mad at me for falling in the lake?"

Alderpaw stopped beside a clump of frost-shriveled ferns. "He wasn't mad at you. He was just worried."

"The other cats think I've got feathers in my head." Twigkit remembered the water pressing against her muzzle. She'd been so afraid. "I wanted to prove to them I was special, but I just proved I'm a mouse-brain."

Since she fell into the lake, Leafkit and Honeykit had been teasing her constantly.

Did you want to be a RiverClan cat?

Perhaps she wants to be a fish.

160

They teased her the same way they teased each other—they were not trying to be cruel at all.

But it had still hurt.

Alderpaw leaped onto a log, which was blocking the path, and waited for Twigkit to scramble up beside him. "Jayfeather fell in the lake when he was a kit too," he told her.

She blinked at him, surprised. "Really?"

Alderpaw purred. "He left camp, just like you, trying to prove he was special."

"But he *was* special. He was one of the Three." Hope fluttered in Twigkit's chest like a moth.

"And you are special too."

Alderpaw's words warmed her. She couldn't wait to tell Leafkit and Honeykit that she was just like Jayfeather. She knew from nursery tales that Jayfeather had helped save the Clans from the Dark Forest cats. She swallowed. *Will I have to do that?*

An owl shrieked far away. Twigkit moved closer to Alderpaw, suddenly aware of how huge the forest seemed at night and how deep the shadows were. She peered into them. "Do you think the Dark Forest cats will ever come back?" she asked Alderpaw.

His eyes widened in surprise. "What makes you ask that?"

"If I'm special like Jayfeather, maybe I'm supposed to fight them too."

Alderpaw whisked his tail. "The Dark Forest cats won't dare return here." He leaped from the log and trotted along a trail between brambles.

Twigkit hurried after him. "Did your prophecy say what I'm supposed to do?"

"No." Alderpaw kept his gaze ahead. "It just said we must find what was in the shadows and it would help clear the sky."

Twigkit frowned thoughtfully. "Do you think I'm supposed to make the sun shine?"

Alderpaw purred. "Even StarClan can't do that."

"But they can make clouds cover the moon if the Clans argue during a Gathering." Twigkit wondered suddenly how powerful StarClan really was. If they could make clouds cover the moon, why did they need forest cats to help with their prophecies?

"Hurry up." Alderpaw quickened his pace. He seemed as excited as Twigkit about the meeting. "We're nearly there."

As they neared the ShadowClan border, he broke into a run. Twigkit hared after him, the cold air burning her lungs. She caught up as he reached the clearing where they'd met the two ShadowClan cats last time.

Alderpaw was skirting the edge, sniffing the tree roots hopefully.

"Can you smell them?" Twigkit scanned the shadows, hoping to see Violetkit's splotchy white fur glowing in the moonlight. "Are you sure we're meant to meet them *here*?"

"That's what Needlepaw said when I saw her at the border the other day." Alderpaw leaned forward.

Twigkit glanced through the branches. The moon was high. Why weren't they here? Worry prickled through her pelt. "Perhaps that owl caught them."

"Needlepaw could chase off an owl." Alderpaw was still straining to see across the border.

"What about a fox?" Twigkit began to pace. "Maybe the rogues attacked the ShadowClan camp. What if Violetkit's been hurt?"

"It's more likely that they couldn't sneak out of camp without being noticed." Alderpaw reasoned. "I'm sure nothing bad has happened."

"But what if you're wrong?" Twigkit's heart quickened. Surely her sister would find a way to meet her. As fear made her thoughts spin, paw steps sounded beyond the border. Her heart leaped. "Violetkit?"

"Who's that?" A gruff mew sounded beyond the brambles crowding the scent line.

Alarmed, Twigkit hurried to Alderpaw's side and pressed against him.

"It's just me," he called. "Alderpaw."

Twigkit could feel his fur spiking anxiously.

A ShadowClan warrior padded from behind the brambles. It was a broad-shouldered tabby tom. A gray tabby she-cat and a white tom followed him.

"Hi, Tigerheart." Alderpaw dipped his head to the tom. "Cloverfoot, Rippletail."

Twigkit tasted the air. She hadn't met these ShadowClan warriors before. Alderpaw must know them from Gatherings.

Tigerheart was scanning the shadows behind them. "Is Dovewing with you?"

"No." Alderpaw sounded surprised at his question.

Tigerheart shrugged. Was that disappointment in his gaze? "What are you doing here?"

"Gathering herbs," Alderpaw answered a little too quickly.

"At night?" Rippletail padded into the clearing, ears twitching.

"Some herbs are best gathered after dusk," Alderpaw told him.

Rippletail looked at Twigkit. "Does ThunderClan often send kits out of camp at night to help medicine cats with their duties?"

Cloverfoot padded around them. "Isn't that a bit dangerous?"

"She was worried about her littermate," Alderpaw told the tabby she-cat. "I said she could come in case we bumped into a ShadowClan patrol."

Twigkit was impressed by his story. She almost believed it herself.

"We're lucky we met you," Alderpaw went on. "Is Violetkit okay?"

"Of course." Tigerheart pushed between his Clanmates. "Why shouldn't she be?"

Twigkit lifted her chin. "I was worried the rogues might hurt her."

Tigerheart flexed his claws. "She has ShadowClan to protect her."

"Besides," Rippletail added, "the rogues are no threat."

Alderpaw stared at the young warrior. "They killed Furzepelt."

Rippletail huffed. "WindClan started that fight."

Alderpaw stared at the ShadowClan tom, surprise showing in his face.

Twigkit edged forward. "You'll protect her, though, won't you?" Didn't ShadowClan realize how dangerous the rogues were?

"Of course we will," Tigerheart growled. "It would be easier if she didn't keep sneaking out of camp with Needlepaw."

Alderpaw blinked. "She's been sneaking out of camp?"

Twigkit frowned, confused. She hadn't seen her sister for over half a moon. Where had Violetkit been going?

"Tawnypelt caught them the other night," Tigerheart told Alderpaw. "Rowanstar's put Needlepaw on elder duty and told Pinenose not to take her eyes off Violetkit for a moment."

Twigkit felt a flicker of relief. At least she knew why her sister hadn't come to the meeting. But then her heart sank. That meant that she wouldn't see her littermate tonight after all! She realized with a jolt that Tigerheart was staring at her.

"Why can't you and Violetkit stay in camp like normal kits?" he asked bluntly. "Clan kits are asleep in their nests by moonhigh."

Twigkit whipped her tail indignantly. "*We're* special," she told him.

Tigerheart snorted. "Let's wait and see about that." He turned, nodding to his patrol. Then he leaned toward to Alderpaw. "I hope you find the herbs you're looking for. But I think you should get Twigkit home. It's going to be a cold night, and her pelt is still only kit fluff."

Alderpaw dipped his head. "I will," he promised. "She'll sleep well now that she knows her sister is safe." He glanced at Twigkit as Tigerheart led his Clanmates back onto Shadow-Clan territory and disappeared into the darkness.

"That was close," Alderpaw whispered. "It's probably a good thing Needlepaw and Violetkit couldn't come. We'd have been in trouble if the patrol had found us together."

Twigkit gazed at him sadly. "I guess." How long would it be before she got another chance to see Violetkit?

Alderpaw must have seen the sadness in her gaze. He touched his muzzle to her head. "Let's go home. I'll speak to Needlepaw as soon as I can and arrange another meeting."

"What if Violetkit can never get away?" Twigkit followed Alderpaw as he headed back along the trail.

"I'm sure she will," Alderpaw promised.

"Perhaps it would be better if no one thought we were special." Twigkit sighed. "Then we could have stayed together." She stopped, a sudden thought piercing her like a thorn. "What if we're *not* special? Rowanstar will have taken her away for nothing!"

Alderpaw turned, his eyes round with sympathy. "Of course you're special," he reassured her.

Twigkit lashed her tail determinedly. "I'm going to be. Otherwise there's no point. I'm going to grow up big and strong and be important just like you."

Alderpaw's whiskers twitched. "I'm not very important."

"But you will be," Twigkit insisted. "Once you're a medicine cat like Jayfeather." She puffed out her chest. "I'm going to be a medicine cat too. I know about herbs already, and I know I'll be good at it. And I won't be a grumpy medicine cat like Jayfeather. I'll be a nice one like you and Leafpool."

Alderpaw's gaze glistened fondly. "I'm touched that you want to be like me. But you're young. Don't decide on your future yet. Your paws will walk wherever they must go. And you may change your mind about becoming a medicine cat."

"But I want to be important," Twigkit insisted.

"You will be," Alderpaw draped his tail over her spine and guided her forward. "But there are other ways to be important in a Clan. Look at Bramblestar and Squirrelflight. Or Gray-stripe and Millie. All cats find their own places in the Clan. And one day you'll find yours."

Twigkit padded closer, her pelt brushing his. "Do you really think so?"

Alderpaw wrapped his tail tighter around her. "I'm certain."

CHAPTER 10

Crouching miserably beside the nursery, Violetkit stared across the camp. Clouds covered the sun, and a damp wind rattled the brambles. She shivered. Beside her, Pinenose swallowed the last morsel of mouse and sat up. "I'm going inside. Bad weather's coming." She glanced at Violetkit. "You'd better come with me."

Violetkit's heart sank. "Can I just finish this?" She pawed her half-eaten shrew closer. She wasn't hungry, but she wanted to stay outside a while longer. Being stuck in camp was boring, but being inside the nursery was worse. Especially when Grassheart's kits were asleep and she wasn't allowed to make a sound.

"Okay," Pinenose agreed. "But don't be long."

As the queen disappeared into the bramble den, Violetkit pretended to take another mouthful of shrew. Since the rogues had brought her back, Pinenose had watched her like a hawk. Violetkit felt a prickle of resentment toward Darktail. Why had he marched right into the camp? She knew the Clan blamed her for leading enemies into their home. The older warriors eyed her as if she were a traitor. But weirdly, the younger warriors and apprentices had begun to greet her as they passed, interest glittering in their gaze as though they had just noticed she existed. Yarrowpaw had even stopped and asked what the rogues were like, but Pinenose had shooed the apprentice away. "How would Violetkit know?" the queen had snapped. "They just found her in the woods. They didn't make friends with her."

As her thoughts wandered, Violetkit gazed across the clearing. Leafpool and Puddlepaw were rolling herbs into bundles outside the medicine den. Crowfrost was sharing a thrush with Dawnpelt. Berryheart and Rippletail lounged outside the warriors' den, half-asleep as the wind rippled their fur. Tawnypelt, Tigerheart, and Spikefur sheltered from the wind beside the great stone, while Rowanstar sat outside his den, watching the camp through half-closed eyes.

Violetkit looked toward the elders' den. Was Needlepaw there? She hadn't seen her friend all morning. Perhaps Kinkfur had sent her to fetch fresh bracken for her bedding again.

Loneliness gnawed at Violetkit's belly. She looked hopefully toward Yarrowpaw and Beepaw. They were practicing battle moves at the edge of the clearing while Sleekpaw lay in the long grass and watched. Perhaps they would teach her how to fight. That had to be more interesting than sitting in the nursery with Pinenose. She tried to catch their eye, but they didn't notice her. She blinked at Juniperpaw. The black tom was trotting toward the entrance after his mentor, Stonewing. He didn't look her way. Perhaps Strikepaw would speak to her. But the tabby tom was nodding unenthusiastically as

Wasptail demonstrated a hunting stance in the clearing. He yawned wearily as Wasptail crouched close to the ground.

Suddenly a hiss sounded beside the entrance. Violetkit jerked her gaze toward the bramble tunnel. Stonewing stood, back arched, his pelt spiked. Strikepaw crouched beside him, growling. Their gaze was fixed on a tom padding into camp.

Rain.

Violetkit recognized the gray tom at once. She got to her paws, her pelt rippling nervously along her spine. What was he doing here?

A plump pigeon hung from his jaws. Behind him, Raven and Flame squeezed through the tunnel. They each carried prey. Violetkit smelled the warm fragrance of blood.

Crowfrost lifted his head sharply, baring his teeth as he saw the rogues. He hurried across the clearing to meet them. "What are you doing here?" His ears were flat as he stopped in front of Rain.

Leafpool poked her head from the medicine den, her eyes rounding with surprise.

Rowanstar bounded from his den and skidded to a halt beside his deputy. "I told you to leave our territory!" he told the rogues.

Rain laid the pigeon in front of the ShadowClan leader. "We brought you these offerings." He dipped his head as Flame placed a young rabbit beside the pigeon and Raven dropped a fat thrush on top. It was fine prey.

Crowfrost stared at the heap warily. Rowanstar flexed his claws.

"We want to join your Clan," Rain meowed before either cat could speak.

"Join ShadowClan?" Rowanstar stared at the rogue, eyes widening.

Tawnypelt, Tigerheart, and Spikefur padded from the shelter of the great stone. Leafpool moved closer to Puddlepaw. The other apprentices lined up at the edge of the clearing, their eyes sparkling with interest.

Needlepaw! Violetkit suddenly realized that her friend was among her denmates. She blinked. Where had she been?

Rain crouched submissively in front of Rowanstar and gazed hopefully at the Clan leader.

Rowanstar glared at him. "Did you think you could bribe your way in with prey you caught on *our* land?"

Crowfrost hissed. "No cat hunts in ShadowClan territory except ShadowClan."

Rain crouched lower. "I'm sorry. We didn't realize." He glanced at his campmates, who both dipped their heads humbly. "Forgive us," he went on. "If we have offended you, we will leave."

As he turned, Rowanstar leaned forward. "Wait."

Rain faced the leader, a faint glow lighting his eyes.

"Where in our territory did you find such good prey?" Curiosity softened Rowanstar's mew.

"We are lucky when it comes to hunting," Rain told him. "Perhaps we can bring some of that luck to your Clan."

"No." Crowfrost stepped forward, his black-and-white pelt bristling. "Take your prey and leave!" He glared at Rowanstar.

"We can't accept prey from cats who attacked another Clan!"

"Why not?" Needlepaw demanded.

Violetkit stiffened as her friend padded forward.

"Is WindClan our *friend* now?" Needlepaw looked around her Clanmates. "I thought ShadowClan stood alone. The only truce we recognize is the truce of the Gathering. Why deny ourselves prey on WindClan's behalf?"

Sleekpaw and Strikepaw were nodding.

So was Berryheart. The young black-and-white she-cat lashed her tail. "Would WindClan do the same for us?"

Sleekpaw joined Needlepaw. "WindClan has never brought us prey. Nor has ThunderClan or RiverClan. But we're supposed to feel loyal to them. Why?"

Violetkit frowned. If the Clans weren't meant to stick together, did that make Twigkit her enemy? Anxiety prickled in her fur.

"Why?" Rowanstar repeated Sleekpaw's question, his eyes widening with surprise. "Because they are Clanborn like us. They follow the warrior code."

"These are rogues!" Crowfrost puffed out his chest. "They have no code."

"We could learn," Rain mewed softly.

Rowanstar stared at him. "Why should we believe you?"

Rain glanced around the camp. "We see how you live," he meowed. "How you thrive. We want to be like you."

Tigerheart marched forward, his eyes glittering with outrage. "Then go and start your own Clan, on your own land!"

Rowanstar drew himself up. "I've had you escorted from

our land before. Today you will be escorted again." He nodded sharply to Tigerheart, Spikefur, and Tawnypelt. "Next time we find you on ShadowClan territory, you will feel the sharpness of our claws."

The rogues glanced at one another. Violetkit searched their gaze for some sign of fear, but they showed only calm acceptance.

Rain blinked at Rowanstar. "We will respect your wishes."

Rowanstar stiffened. "You have no choice."

Rain flashed him an amused look before turning away and letting Tawnypelt lead the way out of camp.

Violetkit swallowed. She realized that her heart was beating hard. Needlepaw had taken a risk speaking out for the rogues. Why had she done it? Wasn't her Clan more important than her new rogue friends?

As the patrol disappeared through the bramble tunnel, Needlepaw crossed the clearing.

Violetkit's breath caught in her throat as Needlepaw stopped in front of Rowanstar.

She kicked the prey toward him. "What are you going to do with this?" she snarled. "Throw it out with the rogues?"

Rowanstar's eyes widened with shock. "ShadowClan catches its own prey."

"We'd catch more if we had Clanmates like them." Needlepaw flicked her tail toward the entrance. "Why didn't you let them join?"

Dawnpelt padded from the edge of the clearing. "They're not Clanborn."

"Neither is Violetkit," Needlepaw retorted. "But you let her join. And what did she offer the Clan but another mouth to feed?"

Violetkit's heart lurched. Was that truly what Needlepaw believed? *I thought you were my friend!*

Tigerheart looked at the silver apprentice. "You're the one who brought her back from Alderpaw's quest," he pointed out. "You made such a big deal about her being part of the prophecy that Rowanstar *had* to take her."

Dawnpelt flicked her tail. "She *is* part of the prophecy. One day Violetkit may clear the skies."

"You don't even know what that means!" Needlepaw's pelt bristled along her spine. "You turned away three strong hunters. Why?"

Tawnypelt padded forward, her stern gaze raking Needlepaw. "That's enough!" she snapped.

"It's *not* enough!" Strikepaw marched forward and stopped beside Needlepaw. "We have a chance to make ShadowClan powerful again."

Yarrowpaw whisked her tail. "Aren't you tired of agreeing with everything ThunderClan suggests? Don't you wish we could hunt where we please instead of where the other Clans tell us we can hunt?"

Rowanstar flexed his claws. "Do you want *war* with the other Clans?"

Strikepaw flattened his ears. "We want to choose our own path, not follow the path of other Clans."

"What you want doesn't matter!" Rowanstar hissed. "*I* am ShadowClan's leader. *I* decide what's best. Taking in strange cats who have proved they are dangerous is not good for any Clan."

"Not for weak Clans like WindClan or RiverClan," Strikepaw snarled. "But we are ShadowClan. With cats like those, we could rule the whole lake!"

"You are young and foolish." Rowanstar struggled to calm his mew. "You don't understand the pain and loss that battle brings. I have been too soft with you." His gaze flicked around the other apprentices. "With *all* of you. I've let small rules be broken." He caught Juniperpaw's eye. "Don't think I don't smell the prey blood on your breath when you return from hunting. What you catch is for the fresh-kill pile, not your own belly." He lifted his chin, yowling across the camp. "From now on, the warrior code will be followed. StarClan is watching us. Respect for our ancestors will guide our paws."

Violetkit watched Needlepaw, wishing she'd drop her gaze and back away.

Instead the silver she-cat glared at the ShadowClan leader. "You want us to obey a bunch of dead cats!" She nodded toward the pines looming over the camp. "Look at the living world. It has everything we need. We can push our territory as far as we like and take whatever we want. Who cares what StarClan thinks? Their lives are over. It's our turn to live."

Behind her, Beepaw, Juniperpaw, and Sleekpaw yowled in agreement.

Dawnpelt and Crowfrost stared at them in horror, as though they couldn't believe that their own kits would turn on their Clan.

Rowanstar met Needlepaw's gaze coolly. "You can live according to our rules."

"Never." Needlepaw lashed her tail. "I'm sick of living in a Clan that only cares about peace. The rogues would have made us strong. But, if you don't want them to join us, *I'm* going to join *them*!"

Violetkit flinched. *What?*

Around her, pelts spiked.

"Traitor!" Crowfrost glared at Needlepaw.

Tawnypelt seemed frozen with shock. "Have you gone crazy?" Her mew faltered as she spoke.

Stonewing and Ratscar flattened their ears. Snowbird and Dawnpelt exchanged looks, their eyes wide.

Violetkit swallowed back alarm. Surely Needlepaw didn't mean it? She watched in disbelief as Needlepaw marched toward the entrance.

"I'm going with her," Juniperpaw growled. "Nobody's going to tell me what prey I can eat ever again."

"I'm going too!" Sleekpaw turned and padded after Needlepaw.

As murmurs of disbelief rippled around the Clan, Rowanstar stared after the apprentices, astonishment flashing in his wide amber gaze. "If you leave the Clan, you become our enemy!" he yowled.

Violetkit stared as Needlepaw padded past her. "Don't go!"

Her heart twisted with grief. Needlepaw was her only friend in the Clan. And yet she'd said that Violetkit was just another mouth to feed. *Was I wrong to trust her?*

Needlepaw paused and met Violetkit's gaze. "You're coming with me."

"I am?" Shock flashed through Violetkit. She felt limp with relief. *She is my friend!*

"You're not staying here with these kittypets." Needlepaw whisked Violetkit forward with her tail. She glanced back at Rowanstar. "I'm taking the kit because *I* found her."

"You can't!" Leafpool hurried forward. "She belongs to the Clans. StarClan needs her to be here."

"*I* found her," Needlepaw repeated. "If she's special, she can be special anywhere."

Rowanstar flicked his tail angrily. "Take her!" he called to Needlepaw. "You did ShadowClan no favors by finding her. There's been nothing but trouble since she arrived. We're better off without her. And without you!"

Violetkit felt numb. She stumbled after Needlepaw, Sleekpaw and Juniperpaw flanking her. Her thoughts whirled. Was it true? Had she brought only trouble to ShadowClan? Overwhelmed, she followed Needlepaw through the entrance tunnel. As it closed around her, she glanced back and saw the familiar dens. She was leaving another home. Was she making the right choice?

Her eye caught Rowanstar's. His gaze was as hard as ice.

It's not a choice. Despair washed through her pelt. *I'm not wanted here. I never truly was.*

CHAPTER 11

Overhead, the full moon lit a crow-black sky. In the chilly island clearing, Alderpaw fidgeted beside Jayfeather.

"Can't you sit still?" Jayfeather grunted.

It was the Gathering. Cats milled in the clearing in front of them, their pelts shining in the moonlight. Bramblestar padded between them, greeting old allies. Onestar was already sitting in the great oak, staring at the Clan cats through narrowed eyes.

Mistystar chatted with the deputies lined up at the foot of the tree. She purred as Squirrelflight nodded toward a group of apprentices, happily showing off battle moves to one another at the edge of the clearing. Alderpaw wished he were with them, sharing Clan gossip. Did he have to sit here, being solemn and serious with Kestrelflight, Mothwing, and Willowshine, just because he was a medicine-cat apprentice? If he was going to be an apprentice longer than any other cat, couldn't he at least have fun?

He glanced at Sparkpelt. It was her first Gathering as a warrior, and she sat beside Cherryfall, her chest puffed out proudly. Her green eyes sparkled as she gazed at the other cats. Bramblestar padded to her side and touched his muzzle fondly to her head. Alderpaw ignored the prickle of envy in his pelt. He was proud of Sparkpelt too.

He glanced at the long grass at the edge of the clearing, tasting the air for ShadowClan scent. They were late. He leaned forward eagerly. Would Needlepaw come? If she was still being punished for letting Violetkit leave the camp, she might not be allowed to attend the Gathering this time. His tail flicked anxiously. He'd promised to take news home to Twigkit about Violetkit. If he couldn't ask Needlepaw, perhaps Sleekpaw would tell him.

Alderpaw stiffened as Mintfur jerked his gaze toward the edge of the clearing. Alderpaw pricked his ears as the River-Clan tom's nose twitched. Paws scrabbled over the tree-bridge, beyond the stretch of grass. Pebbles cracked. The Shadow-Clan cats were coming.

The cats in the clearing turned their heads one by one as the grass rustled and ShadowClan padded out.

Alderpaw frowned. They looked battle-worn. Rowan-star had a cut above his eye. Crowfrost's pelt showed signs of scratches. Wasptail was limping. Who had they been fighting? He looked for Needlepaw, his heart sinking when he saw she wasn't with them. Sleekpaw wasn't there either. Perhaps Yarrowpaw or Strikepaw would be able to tell him about Violetkit.

Leafpool!

The medicine cat slid from the long grass.

Of course! He could ask her! Alderpaw hurried to meet her

as she headed for the group of medicine cats. As he neared, he saw that her eyes were dark with worry. Puddlepaw padded behind her, tail down. "Has something happened?" he asked as he reached them.

Leafpool lowered her gaze and padded past him. "Rowanstar will share the news."

"Is Violetkit okay?" Anxiety flashed through Alderpaw's fur.

"She was well the last time I saw her." Leafpool sat beside Mothwing. She glanced at Alderpaw, then looked away.

The last time she saw her? Alderpaw stared at her, confused. "What do you mean?"

Jayfeather shooed him back to his place with a flick of his tail. "Sit down and be quiet," he ordered. "It's not Leafpool's duty to share ShadowClan's news." His blind gaze flashed toward the gathered cats.

As the ShadowClan warriors and apprentices slid among them, Rowanstar strode to the great oak and climbed onto the branch beside Onestar. Onestar shot him a hostile glance and shifted away.

Bramblestar left Sparkpelt and hurried to the oak as Mistystar heaved herself stiffly up the trunk and took her place beside Rowanstar. The murmuring of the cats quieted as Bramblestar sat down and gazed toward them.

"We have good weather," he observed, his gaze flicking toward the wide starry sky. "StarClan has blessed us."

Rowanstar grunted dismissively. "ThunderClan cats

always think they are blessed, even when they're half-starved in leaf-bare."

"It is not leaf-bare yet," Mistystar reminded them. "We must be glad that prey is still running and the snows are not yet here."

"Prey is always running in RiverClan," Onestar sneered. "Or should I say *swimming*."

"Not if the river freezes," Mistystar corrected him.

Alderpaw whisked his tail over the ground. Why were the leaders so prickly tonight?

Rowanstar stood and raised his tail. "ShadowClan has two new warriors," he announced. "Strikestone and Yarrowleaf."

"Strikestone!"

"Yarrowleaf!"

The Clans cheered the names of ShadowClan's new warriors. Their voices rang through the brittle night air.

Mistystar raised her voice over them. "RiverClan has new warriors too. Shadepelt and Foxnose!"

Bramblestar called out. "And Sparkpaw is now Sparkpelt!"

"Shadepelt!"

"Foxnose!"

"Sparkpelt!"

Sparkpelt glanced around the cheering cats, her pelt fluffing with excitement.

"Sparkpelt!" Alderpaw raised his voice, making sure she could hear him celebrating her warrior name.

She caught his eye, her green gaze lighting up with

happiness. Pride swelled in his chest, and he called her name louder.

Beside him, Jayfeather remained silent.

Alderpaw nudged him. "Even medicine cats are allowed to cheer," he hissed in his mentor's ear.

Jayfeather grunted. "Why should I cheer? More warriors means more wounds and more work for me."

Alderpaw glanced at Leafpool, expecting her to chide Jayfeather for being so gloomy, but Leafpool was chanting, her expression blank as though her thoughts were elsewhere. His cheer died in his throat as he gazed across the cheering cats. *Shouldn't Sleekpaw be receiving her warrior name? And Juniperpaw?* They were Strikestone's littermates. Had they failed their assessments? He scanned the crowd, looking for them, but there was no sign of the two apprentices. Alderpaw shifted uneasily and looked toward Rowanstar as the Clans fell silent.

Rowanstar gazed out gravely at the Clans. "The rogues that attacked Onestar's patrol are living on the edge of our territory, near our border with ThunderClan."

Shocked murmurs rippled through the gathered cats.

"Why don't you chase them off?" Brackenfur called.

Breezepelt showed his teeth. "They're murderers!"

Crowfeather lifted his muzzle. "We should join forces and drive them away."

Rowanstar spoke over them. "They asked to join ShadowClan. They came with gifts of prey, but I turned them away."

"How dare they?" Oatclaw lashed his tail.

Sparkpelt flattened her ears. "They could never be Clan cats!"

"*I turned them away!*" Rowanstar repeated, the fur prickling along his spine. His glare silenced the angry cats. "But some of our apprentices have chosen to join them."

Alderpaw braced himself for louder cries, but the Clans stared at the ShadowClan leader in shocked silence as Rowanstar went on.

"They took Violetkit with them."

Mistystar jerked her muzzle toward him. "The kit from the prophecy?"

Rowanstar nodded.

Bramblestar flattened his ears. "You *let* them take her?"

Rowanstar scowled. "We were wrong about the prophecy, Bramblestar. Violetkit is just an ordinary kit. Twigkit is probably ordinary too. And Needlepaw found her. Why shouldn't she take her?"

Why shouldn't she take her? Alderpaw froze. Had Needlepaw left to join the rogues? His mouth grew dry. Surely not. Needlepaw liked to break rules. But she'd never betray her Clan.

Bramblestar was growling, his angry gaze fixed on Rowanstar. "You let a vulnerable kit be taken away to join a group of *rogues*? What were you thinking? I should have known Violetkit would never be safe in ShadowClan. If you didn't believe she was part of the prophecy, why did you take her in the first place? We could have kept her."

"We have to get her back!" Mothwing called.

"How will we clear the sky with her gone?" Mintfur yowled.

Squirrelflight flicked her tail angrily. "Let the sky take care of itself for now. A *kit* has been taken from her Clan! We must rescue her."

The clearing rang with mews of agreement, but Alderpaw hardly heard them. *What will I tell Twigkit?* He'd brought Violetkit to the Clans. And now she was in the paws of vicious rogues. Guilt scorched his pelt. *Twigkit will never forgive me. She'll be heartbroken.* Alderpaw swallowed back panic. *We'll get her back. We have to. I'll tell Twigkit that everything will be okay.* He hoped it was true.

Fur brushed his flank as Leafpool slid in beside him. "I'm sorry I couldn't tell you," she murmured. "It was Rowanstar's news to share. But I'm sure Needlepaw will look after her. She is very fond of Violetkit. Whatever happens, Needlepaw will protect her."

Alderpaw met her gaze, trembling. "But Needlepaw is only an apprentice. What can she do against a gang of rogues?"

His heart lurched as Leafpool stared back at him wordlessly. He wanted her to reassure him.

Bramblestar's yowl cut through the anxious chattering of the gathered cats. "What are you going to do about this, Rowanstar?" He glared at the ShadowClan leader.

Rowanstar's tail twitched. "We attacked them last night," he reported. "We hoped that when they saw us fighting for them, our apprentices would come back to us."

Alderpaw's heart lurched as he saw panic in the ginger tom's gaze. He'd never seen a leader *frightened* before.

"But they didn't." Rowanstar's mew was trembling. "In fact, one more apprentice and two of our warriors joined them and fought against us."

"Who?" Onestar demanded. The WindClan leader was bristling with rage.

"Beepaw, Berryheart, and Cloverfoot." Rowanstar stared at his paws.

Onestar thrust his muzzle close to the ShadowClan leader. "How dare you call yourself a leader? You can't even control your own Clan!"

"They'll come back." Rowanstar's mew was thick with emotion. "They're young and wrongheaded. But they'll realize their mistake and come back."

"Perhaps you're right." Bramblestar's mew softened.

Alderpaw saw pity in his father's eyes as he gazed at the broken ShadowClan leader.

Onestar showed his teeth. "Meanwhile, we have rogues on the edge of Clan territory. If they steal Clanmates, you can be sure they'll steal prey."

Mistystar glared at the WindClan leader. "They're as far from your borders as they can be. There's no need for you to worry about your precious rabbits."

Onestar hissed at her contemptuously. "Or you to defend your *fish*."

"This affects us all!" Bramblestar yowled. "They have Violetkit, and she is part of the prophecy."

"So *you* say," Rowanstar muttered, unconvinced.

Mistystar ignored the ShadowClan leader and faced

Bramblestar. "We can't risk trying to rescue her. She's a kit. They could easily kill her if we attack their camp."

"Then we must wait," Bramblestar decided.

Onestar's hackles lifted. "So we're going to do nothing?" He stared at Bramblestar in disbelief. "These cats killed my Clanmate."

And took one of your lives, Alderpaw thought darkly. *And drove SkyClan from the gorge.* He couldn't help feeling that Onestar was right to want to do more to fight the rogues.

"We should attack now and drive them as far from the lake as we can," Onestar went on.

Rowanstar's eyes rounded with fear. "I don't want to fight my Clanmates, even if they've made a terrible decision. They still might change their minds and return to the Clan."

"I understand." Bramblestar met Rowanstar's gaze sympathetically. "And we mustn't risk Violetkit's life by attacking."

Onestar growled, his eyes flashing in the moonlight. "Then we have no more to say." He leaped from the great oak and stalked across the clearing, signaling to his Clanmates with an angry flick of his tail.

Harespring hurried away from the other deputies and fell in beside his leader. Their Clanmates quickly followed, pushing their way through the gathered cats. Moonlight glittered on their pelts as they headed into the long grass and disappeared.

Alderpaw looked at Bramblestar. *What now?*

"The meeting is over," the ThunderClan leader called, jumping down from the tree.

Alderpaw's pads seemed frozen to the ground. Was that it? They were going to live beside the rogues as though they were just another Clan? Had Bramblestar forgotten that these cats had driven SkyClan from their home? What if they were planning to do the same here?

As the rest of the cats headed for the tree-bridge, his throat tightened. He didn't want to follow. Going home meant telling Twigkit that her sister was with the rogues.

CHAPTER 12

"Keep your hindquarters low," Ivypool ordered.

Twigpaw lowered herself farther, her gaze fixed on the leaf ahead.

Newleaf sunshine dappled the forest floor. Buds lit the trees in a green haze. Four moons had passed since Violetkit's disappearance. In the half-moon since becoming an apprentice, Twigpaw had worked hard to impress her new mentor. She wanted to be as good as Larkpaw, Leafpaw, and Honeypaw. They were already learning battle moves, while she was practicing hunting moves on leaves. But they had been made apprentices three moons ago, when snow had covered the forest floor and ice had frozen the rivers and streams.

"Keep your tail still," Ivypool reminded her.

Twigpaw pressed her tail flat against the soft earth. She could smell prey-scents drifting between the trees, and she longed to be hunting a real mouse.

"Judge the distance," Ivypool told her. "And when you are sure, jump."

Twigpaw narrowed her eyes, sensing the space between herself and the leaf. Her hindquarters twitched. Excitement pulsed beneath her pelt. Pushing off with her hind paws, she leaped.

She landed, skidding on the leaf. It shot along the slippery ground. Her forepaws shot along with it, and she thumped, chest first, onto the ground.

Ivypool padded to her side, purring. "Your leap was the perfect distance. Unfortunately, you hadn't prepared for your prey to try to escape." She gently nudged Twigpaw up and flicked a scrap of leaf litter from the apprentice's shoulders with a paw. "Landing on balanced paws is the most important skill you will learn. It's vital for hunting and fighting."

Twigpaw shook out her pelt, embarrassed. "I didn't realize the ground was so wet." She glanced at the muddy streak her landing had smeared across the forest floor.

"Next time you'll remember to think about where you're landing. Landing on mud, stone, or leaf litter all require different techniques. But you did well. Your concentration is excellent and you learn fast. Lilyheart will be pleased when I tell her."

Twigpaw purred proudly. "Am I learning as quickly as Larkpaw?" She knew that Larkpaw was a great hunter already. Lilyheart often boasted how he carried prey home to her every day.

"It's not a competition," Ivypool told her gently. "You must learn at your own speed."

"But I want to prove I'm *special*." Moons later, Rosepetal's words still haunted her. *Twigkit does seem pretty ordinary. And until she learns to hunt, she's another belly for the Clan to fill.* She stared desperately at Ivypool. "I *have* to be the best."

"That's not true," Ivypool soothed.

"But if I'm not, why am I here?"

Ivypool's gaze shone sympathetically. "You've never truly felt part of the Clan, have you?" She didn't wait for Twigpaw to answer. "I hope that one day you will."

Twigpaw dropped her gaze guiltily. "You make me sound disloyal."

"No," Ivypool purred fondly. "I can see that you are as loyal as any Clanborn cat. But you have grown up away from your true kin. That must have been hard." Her eyes brightened encouragingly. "Still, Lilyheart is very proud of you, and if your real mother could see what's become of you, I'm sure she'd be proud of you too. What a shame Squirrelflight's patrol never found her."

Twigpaw frowned, puzzled. "Squirrelflight's patrol?" What was Ivypool talking about? Had Squirrelflight led a patrol to search for her mother? Why didn't anyone ever speak about it? Her heart fluttered like a bird in her chest. Perhaps they'd found her mother's body and wanted to protect her from knowing. She blinked at Ivypool. "Did they find any trace at all?"

"Only the nest where Alderpaw had found you. It was abandoned."

"Nothing else?"

Ivypool shifted her paws nervously. "I don't really know. No one talked about it afterward."

Fear spread down Twigpaw's spine. What was the Clan

hiding from her? *I have to know!* Twigpaw glanced up the rise that led toward camp. *Alderpaw!* He'd be honest with her, even if it were bad news. "Can we go back to the hollow now?" She had to speak with Alderpaw.

Ivypool's tail whisked over the damp leaf litter. "I didn't mean to upset you."

"It's all right." Twigpaw's thoughts were whirling. "I just need to get back to camp."

"Okay." Ivypool watched her anxiously.

Twigpaw hardly noticed her glistening gaze. She was already climbing the rise and heading for the gorse barrier. She ducked through the tunnel and hurried into camp. Her thoughts raced ahead of her. Alderpaw would be in the medicine den. What would he say? Did he know about her mother? As she bounded across the clearing, Graystripe called from the fallen beech.

"What's the hurry, Twigpaw?"

"Is something wrong?" Briarlight was beside the fresh-kill pile, sharing a mouse with Fernsong.

"I need to speak with Alderpaw!" Twigpaw burst through the trailing brambles into the medicine den.

Jayfeather snorted but didn't look up from the moss he was soaking in the water, which pooled beside the rock wall of the den. "I thought Alderpaw had lost his shadow once you'd been made an apprentice." He shook water from his paws. "For a shadow, you make a lot of noise."

Alderpaw was picking stale moss out of Briarlight's nest. He turned as Twigpaw scrambled to a halt beside him.

"Did Squirrelflight's patrol find my mother?" she demanded bluntly.

He blinked at her, confusion clouding his gaze. "Squirrelflight's patrol?"

"The one Bramblestar sent to look for my mother moons ago!" Frustration churned in Twigpaw's belly. It turned to fear as she saw alarm flash in his eyes. He *knew* something!

"Let's talk about this in private." His gaze darted guiltily toward Jayfeather.

"Don't worry about me," Jayfeather mewed sarcastically. "Stay as long as you like. It is only my medicine den, after all."

Twigpaw ignored the medicine cat. "You have to tell me," she begged Alderpaw. "Did they find my mother?"

Alderpaw nudged her toward the entrance. "Come outside."

Why? He must have something terrible to tell me! Suddenly light-headed, Twigpaw followed him through the trailing brambles.

Alderpaw guided her into the fern hollow beside the den. Out of sight of their Clanmates, he met her gaze. "We don't know what happened to your mother," he whispered.

She stared at him blankly. "Why hide here to tell me that?"

Alderpaw seemed to squirm beneath his pelt. Why was he being so weird?

"You can tell me if she's dead," she pressed. "I'd rather know than spend my life wondering."

"I *can't* tell you." Alderpaw stared at her. "I don't know."

"So the patrol *didn't* find her?" Twigpaw demanded.

Alderpaw looked away. "The patrol wasn't looking for *her,*" he mumbled.

"What?" Twigpaw could hardly believe her ears. What was he talking about? "Squirrelflight led a patrol to search for my mother. That's what Ivypool told me."

Alderpaw shook his head. "That wasn't who they were searching for."

"Not my *mother?* Then why does Ivypool think that?" Twigpaw stared at him, anger surging in her chest as he looked back at her, not replying. "Did they *ever* look for her?"

Alderpaw stared at the ground guiltily. "No." His mew was barely a whisper.

"Never?" Heat seared her pelt as she watched Alderpaw struggling for words.

"They were looking for something else," he mumbled at last.

"Why does Ivypool think they were looking for my mother?"

"The *whole Clan* believed they were looking for your mother." Alderpaw was still avoiding her gaze. "They still do."

"What *were* they searching for?" Twigpaw tried to think of something more important than her mother.

Alderpaw looked at her hopelessly. "I can't tell you."

"Why not?" *I thought you told me everything! I trusted you!* She curled her claws into the ground.

"It's Clan business."

Twigpaw's pelt spiked. "So I'm not to know because I'm not part of the Clan!"

"Of course you are!" Alderpaw's gaze rounded guiltily. "That's not what I meant. Only a few cats know where the patrol went. It's a secret I can't share with you."

Twigpaw hesitated, unsure whether to be hurt that he was keeping secrets from her or comforted that she wasn't alone in being lied to. Irritation sparked through her pelt. "Why *didn't* Bramblestar send out a patrol to look for my mother?"

Sadness darkened Alderpaw's gaze. "He didn't think there was any point."

"Didn't he care what had happened to her?" Twigpaw's heart twisted.

"I'm sure he did. But . . . A mother doesn't abandon kits who are too young to take care of themselves unless . . ." Alderpaw's mew trailed away.

"Unless . . . unless she's *dead*?" Twigpaw lashed her tail. "That's what you were going to say, isn't it?" She tried to push the thought away, but it nagged at her. It would explain why she'd left them. *But we can't be sure.* Until they checked, there was still the tiniest, sweetest chance she was still alive. She glared defiantly at Alderpaw. "Maybe something happened to stop her coming back. She might have returned and found us gone. She might be wondering where we went. She might still be looking for us!" She thrust her muzzle close to Alderpaw's. "If you hadn't taken us, Violetkit and I might still be with her!"

Before Alderpaw could answer, Twigpaw pushed her way

from the ferns and strode out of camp. She wouldn't be in this dumb Clan if it weren't for Alderpaw. She'd be with her sister. And her sister wouldn't be with a gang of rogues. Burning with rage, she followed the trail that headed toward the ShadowClan border. She hadn't seen Violetkit since Needlepaw had taken her from ShadowClan. But she was going to see her now. She was going to find her and tell her what she'd discovered.

Twigpaw had heard the Clan gossip, and words swirled in her thoughts as she pushed past the undergrowth. *The rogues live beyond ShadowClan territory, near the border with ThunderClan.* She headed that way now. *I must speak with Violetkit.* She had to tell her that the Clan cats had lied to her. *What if our mother came back for us?*

Birds called to one another overhead, warning and serenading, preparing their nests. The sun, glittering through the budding branches, dappled Twigpaw's back with gentle warmth. She hardly felt it. She veered from the track as she neared the border and shadowed the scent line deeper into the forest, where the ground began to rise. She had never been this far before—even on her first day as an apprentice, when Ivypool had shown her ThunderClan's territory. She'd felt so proud that day, knowing that this was her land and that one day she'd be patrolling it, keeping it safe for kits and elders.

Who's keeping my mother safe? She lifted her chin defiantly and pressed on. The ground grew softer beneath her paws, turning to mud as the trees thinned. She reached the ThunderClan scent line and crossed it, her heart quickening as she set paw outside Clan territory.

The rogues must be near. She could smell strange scents. Tensing, she scanned the undergrowth. Darktail's gang seemed more like ghosts than real cats. They never came to Gatherings, and they lived on the outskirts of the territory, occasionally glimpsed in the shadows by patrols. The Clan whispered about them in hushed mews, as though speaking of Dark Forest cats.

Her pelt pricked with unease as she headed away from the sun, trekking closer to the edge of ShadowClan's land. Opening her mouth, she tasted the air for scents, smelling the newleaf tang of fresh leaves and mud. The ground turned to grass beneath her paws, sloping steeper. Beech and alder grew here. Rowan bushes crowded between the trunks. She slowed, aware that she could already be on rogue territory, and ducked closer to the bushes.

A pelt moved ahead, and she stopped, her heart lurching. A tom was carrying prey upslope. Twigpaw froze and watched as he padded between two rows of ferns and disappeared from view.

"Spying?"

A mew behind her made her spin. Her heart in her throat, she blinked at the young she-cat who was staring at her accusingly. She sniffed and smelled the unfamiliar scent of rogue.

"What are you doing here?" the she-cat demanded. The black splotches on her white pelt rippled as her hackles lifted.

"Violetkit?" Relief surged through Twigpaw. Violetkit

looked well. The rogues clearly hadn't harmed her. Twigpaw stared, hardly able to believe that this sleek young cat was her sister. Muscle showed beneath her pelt. Her paws had grown wide, sharp claw-tips showing beneath the fur. Twigpaw hesitated as Violetkit stared back. Was that *suspicion* in her gaze? "It's me, Twigpaw."

Violetkit narrowed her eyes. "I'm Violet*paw* now."

Twigkit blinked at her. *Isn't she pleased to see me?* "I came to find you."

"Why now?" Violetpaw's gaze didn't betray anything.

"I found something out. All the other cats in ThunderClan were told that they sent out a patrol to look for our mother, but they didn't. It was a lie. They never checked to see if she came back for us." The words tumbled from Twigpaw, leaving her breathless.

Violetpaw shrugged. "Are you really surprised?"

"But they *should* have!" Shock pulsed through Twigpaw. What had happened to her littermate? Had her time with the rogues made her cruel? "Alderpaw lied to me. I thought he was my friend. Everyone believed that Bramblestar sent a search party to look for our mother. But he didn't. Alderpaw said the patrol was looking for something else." Twigpaw guessed she wasn't making sense, but she needed her sister to understand how she felt. No one in the Clan did. Violetpaw was the only one who might.

Violetpaw blinked at her, still showing no sign of emotion.

Twigkit's eyes widened. "Don't *you* care either?"

"I always thought our mother was dead." Violetpaw

frowned. Twigpaw could see that she was thinking. "Why else would she leave us?"

"What if she came back after Alderpaw took us?"

Violetpaw tipped her head. "She'd have found we were gone."

"But she might be looking for us!" Twigpaw willed her sister to feel what she was feeling.

"After all this time?" Violetpaw looked unconvinced.

"Don't you want to find her?" Frustration welled in Twigpaw's throat.

The bracken behind Violetpaw swished. "Find who?" Needlepaw padded out.

Violetpaw jerked her muzzle round, her pelt pricking guiltily. "Hi, Needletail."

Needletail. The ShadowClan apprentice must have given herself a warrior name after leaving her Clan.

She stopped beside Violetpaw. "Find *who?*" she repeated, her ears flattening.

Twigpaw lifted her chin. "Our mother," she mewed, ignoring the fear rippling through her pelt. Needletail had grown. Her body was long and sleek, her tail thick and glossy. And there was threat in her gaze. "I think she might be alive and searching for us. I want Violetpaw to help me look for her."

"Why?" Needletail leaned close, her eyes narrowing. "She has a family here with the rogues." Her gaze flicked to Violetpaw. "Don't you?"

"Yes," Violetpaw answered quickly. "The rogues are my kin now. They're way nicer to me than ShadowClan used to be.

And Needletail is like a sister."

Hurt jabbed Twigpaw's belly. *But I'm your sister! I've been worrying about you for moons.* Had Violetkit forgotten they were littermates? "So you won't help me find her?" She felt suddenly weary. Her anger at Alderpaw seemed to drain into the ground.

Violetpaw stared at Twigpaw, her gaze softening a little. "I can't just leave my campmates. They've fed me and protected me. It would be wrong to leave with you."

Needletail's tail twitched. "Darktail takes loyalty very seriously." Her mew was a growl.

Instinctively, Twigpaw backed away.

Violetpaw blinked at her sister. "I'm sorry, Twigpaw. I can't help you. You should go home."

"Yeah, *Clan* cat," Needletail sneered. "Go home where it's safe." She glanced upslope, as though watching for rogues.

Twigpaw's belly tightened. What if the rogues found her here? Needletail clearly wasn't going to defend her.

"Come on, Violetpaw." Needletail headed into the bracken. "Our campmates will be expecting us"

"I'm sorry." Violetpaw blinked at Twigpaw, then held her gaze for a moment before turning away.

Twigpaw watched the bracken swallow her sister. She stood, frozen, her heart empty. Alderpaw thought her mother was dead. Violetpaw didn't seem to care if she was alive. She suddenly felt foolish. She'd created such a scene. And no cat was interested.

She glanced toward the forest. It looked green under the

pale blue sky. The sun shone, and she knew that beyond the trees the lake would be glittering.

Perhaps finding her mother *was* a dumb idea. Even if she was still alive, she might have new kits by now. What would she care about two kits she'd abandoned moons ago? Wearily Twigpaw turned her paws toward home and padded down the slope.

CHAPTER 13

❧

Violetpaw glanced over her shoulder, trying to catch a final glimpse of Twigpaw through the bracken. But the young stems blocked her view. Doubt tugged in her belly. *Should I have gone with her? She is my littermate, after all.*

"Hurry up!" Needletail flicked her tail as they broke from the bracken and reached the smooth stretch of grass that led toward camp. "The hunting patrols will be back soon, and I'm hungry."

Patrols! Violetpaw huffed quietly to herself. The rogues' idea of a patrol was nothing like ShadowClan's. Darktail would suddenly decide prey was needed and send cats to hunt, reminding them as they left to mark the group's ever-changing borders. There was no sense of the organization and routine she'd been used to in ShadowClan.

Perhaps they'll learn eventually. Violetpaw quickened her step. She had hardly recognized her sister. Twigpaw looked so different. And she seemed so *ThunderClan.* Violetpaw suddenly understood what Needletail, Beenose, and the other former ShadowClan cats meant when they joked about ThunderClan acting as though they were better than every other Clan. Had

Twigpaw really expected Violetpaw to abandon her campmates to go on some mouse-brained mission to find their dead mother? Violetpaw's pelt pricked irritably. *Twigpaw only comes to see me when she wants something. She hasn't tried to find me in the four moons since I left. Hasn't she been worried about me?* She huffed to herself. *She thinks her needs are more important than anyone else's.* Besides, what made her think their mother was alive? *Of course she's dead. Why else would she have left them? Twigpaw thinks she's so smart. Typical ThunderClan,* Violetpaw huffed to herself crossly.

Needletail glanced at her. "What are you growling about?"

Violetpaw shook out her pelt. "Nothing." She didn't want to complain about Twigpaw to Needletail. Twigpaw was annoying, but she was kin. Although *Needletail* felt more like her kin now. *But what about the others?* Violetpaw wondered if she would ever feel as close to her other campmates as she did to Needletail. Raven wasn't as kind as she had been before Violetpaw had joined the group. *None* of the rogues were. And the ShadowClan cats who had joined them had as little patience for her now as they'd had when she'd lived with them in ShadowClan.

But I have Needletail, Violetpaw comforted herself. *She's all I need.*

Paw steps thrummed the ground. Violetpaw followed Needletail's gaze as her mentor looked toward the camp. Rain and Sleekwhisker bounded toward them, each carrying a mouse. They skidded to a halt beside Needletail and Violetpaw.

"You're running!" Needletail blinked at them in surprise. "Is a fox chasing you?"

Sleekwhisker dropped her mouse. "Why shouldn't we run? We were worried our campmates might be hungry." She flashed Rain an amused look. "Weren't we?"

Rain purred. "Sure."

Needletail scowled jealously at Sleekwhisker and pushed between the two cats.

Violetpaw didn't believe either of them. She could see flattened fur on Sleekwhisker's flank where she had been lying down. More than once, Violetpaw and Needletail had caught Sleekwhisker dozing in the newleaf sunshine. Rain too. Neither of them seemed to think hunting was very important these days.

Needletail glanced at the mice, clearly unimpressed. "That's not going to feed us all. Let's hope Cloverfoot and Roach got a better catch. I'm starving."

Sleekwhisker whisked her tail crossly. "What did *you* catch?"

"We weren't *supposed* to be hunting." Needletail lifted her chin. "I was teaching Violetpaw some new fighting moves."

Sleekwhisker stared witheringly at Violetpaw. "I don't know why you bother training her. We don't live in a Clan anymore. Let her learn to fight and hunt the way rogues learn—by experience. Or isn't she smart enough?"

Needletail showed her teeth. "Violetpaw is going to be a *warrior*, not a rogue."

Rain stiffened. "Are you thinking of going back to ShadowClan?"

"Of course not!" Needletail snorted. "But warriors fight better than rogues."

Rain's whiskers twitched. "Tell that to *Onestar.*"

Needletail tipped her head. "But he wasn't fighting just any rogue." Her mew softened flirtatiously. "He was fighting *you.*"

Rain's eyes sparkled. "So you think I fight like a warrior?" He padded around Needletail, brushing against her.

"Better," Needletail answered, purring.

Sleekwhisker rolled her eyes. "Can you two stop acting like a pair of mouse-brains? I want to get this prey back to camp before it gets stiff."

Violetpaw's ears twitched. *You want to get it back before Clover-foot's patrol so you can hide it at the bottom of the fresh-kill pile.* It was a meager catch, even for Sleekwhisker and Rain. Darktail had begun to notice and complain. At least Silt and Beenose wouldn't want to eat. They were sick with some illness that had stolen their appetite.

She saw Rain catch Needletail's eye. "Perhaps *we* should go hunting tomorrow," he mewed silkily. "Just the two of us."

Violetpaw frowned crossly. She wasn't going to make it easy for Rain to steal her friend. "Needletail promised to show me how to stalk rabbits tomorrow."

Needletail dragged her gaze from Rain's. "She's right." Was that regret in her mew?

Sleekwhisker picked up her mouse and headed for the camp. Rain grabbed his mouse and followed, glancing over his shoulder at Needletail. Violetpaw hurried ahead of her mentor to block his view.

As they padded into camp, Cloverfoot turned her head. The gray tabby was standing beside a plump rabbit and a thrush.

"You're back." Sleekwhisker sounded surprised as she dropped her mouse onto the fresh-kill pile.

Cloverfoot sniffed. "Of course. Catching this didn't take long."

Juniperclaw was washing leaf litter from his pelt. He looked up. "Prey is running well."

"We've been back for ages." Roach yawned. The silver tom was lounging nearby.

Rain dropped his mouse beside Sleekwhisker's. "How are Silt and Beenose?" He glanced toward the drooping rowan bush where the sick cats were sheltering.

The branches trembled and Nettle nosed his way out, looking worried. He answered Rain's question. "They're worse. Beenose keeps coughing, and Silt's fever is rising."

Nettle was the closest the rogues had to a medicine cat. But the brown tabby only knew a few herbs. He'd tried them all on the sick cats, but nothing had made them better.

Rain shrugged. "Oh, well." He sniffed the rabbit hungrily. "More prey for us."

"Wait!" A sharp growl sounded outside camp.

Violetpaw tensed as she recognized Darktail's mew.

The rogue leader padded from the long grass edging the camp. His menacing gaze fixed on Rain. "You're getting nothing from the fresh-kill pile today."

Rain's hackles lifted. "No cat tells me I can't eat."

"You want to eat?" Darktail padded slowly toward him. "Go catch something worth eating." He stopped beside the fresh-kill pile and hooked up a mouse with his claw. "This is kit food."

Violetpaw glanced nervously at Needletail. There was a threat in Darktail's mew, and Rain was eyeing him challengingly. The gray tom had been standing up to the rogue leader more and more often. Yesterday he'd refused to go on patrol. "Are they going to fight?" she whispered.

"Hush." Needletail didn't look at Violetpaw. Her gaze was on Rain. Her eyes sparkled eagerly as the long-furred tom stepped closer to Darktail.

"The prey I catch isn't good enough for you?" Rain growled.

The rogue leader lashed his tail. "You've been bringing less and less back to camp." He dropped the mouse. "This is the most pitiful offering yet."

Rain's eyes narrowed to slits. "Have you been counting what I catch?"

"Of course I have," Darktail hissed. "I'm the leader of this group. I make sure every cat pulls his weight."

"You sound like a Clan cat," Rain sneered.

"So?" Darktail lifted his chin. "They live well."

"If you like rules!" Rain flexed his claws.

"Rules will keep our bellies full." Darktail spoke slowly, his vicious gaze not moving from Rain.

"Is that why we came here?" Rain hissed. "To hide behind bushes and hunt prey no one else wants?" He flicked his tail toward ShadowClan's pine forest, stretching far behind them.

"We live on a tiny piece of land when there's a whole territory right there for the taking."

Cold fear ran along Violetpaw's spine. Did Rain want the rogues to drive ShadowClan from their land? Why? There was enough prey here, and over the past four moons Darktail had seemed happy to leave ShadowClan in peace. She thought of Pinenose and Rowanstar, Puddlepaw and Grassheart. *Grassheart's kits!* Was he threatening *them*?

"We don't need the pine forest yet!" Darktail snapped. "For now we've got everything we need and we don't have to fight for it. We won't be taking over anyone's territory until *I* say so."

Rain flattened his ears. "You've grown soft." A growl sounded in his mew as he crouched threateningly.

Darktail's eyes flashed. With a yowl, he flung himself at Rain. Rain reared and caught him, staggering back as the full force of the muscular tom hit him. Digging in his claws, Rain rolled onto his spine and thrashed viciously at Darktail's belly with his hind paws. Violetpaw leaped back, her heart pounding, as the two cats rolled, screeching, across the clearing. She'd seen the rogues fight each other before, but today there was a viciousness in their yowls that set her fur on end.

Needletail darted around them, her gaze fixed on Rain, her pelt rippling as though thrilled by the fight.

"Watch out!" Violetpaw yelped a warning as Darktail struggled free and swung a paw wildly through the air.

Needletail dodged it as it sliced past her and caught Rain hard on the cheek, drawing blood.

Scrabbling to his paws, Rain ducked a second blow and lunged at Darktail's forepaws. Knocking them from under him, he sent the rogue leader crashing onto his belly. Rain reared and slammed his paws hard onto Darktail's spine.

The rogue leader rolled clear with a snarl. He sprang to his paws, his gaze flaming. Baring his teeth, he leaped at Rain. Violetpaw gasped as she saw the rogue leader sink his teeth into Rain's neck.

With a grunt, the long-furred tom collapsed. Darktail let out a low yowl as he pressed Rain to the ground, his teeth still in the gray tom's neck.

Rain jerked beneath him, his breath gurgling in his throat.

"Let him go!" Needletail's panicked cry split the air. "You'll kill him."

Violetpaw's breath caught in her throat as Rain fell still beneath the rogue leader. Only when Rain slumped in defeat did Darktail let go. Fear surged beneath Violetpaw's pelt as Darktail backed away. Was this how it would always be in the rogue camp? Bloody fights over leadership? She glanced warily around at the other rogues. Would any of them challenge Darktail?

Needletail dropped down beside Rain. "Are you okay?" Terror lit her gaze.

Rain grunted. The fur at his neck shone with blood. Rasping, Rain staggered to his paws and faced Darktail.

Darktail scowled. "Who's the leader?"

Rain glared at him. "You are," he growled.

Violetpaw was trembling.

"Don't challenge me again," Darktail hissed softly. The tip of his tail twitched menacingly behind him.

Rain stared at him, anger showing in his gaze. "I won't."

"No, you won't." Without warning, Darktail lashed out, as fast as a snake. His claws raked Rain's eye before the tom could close it.

Violetpaw's belly heaved as blood welled around the socket. Rain staggered backward, ears flat with shock. He let out an agonized yowl before collapsing to the ground.

Needletail hunched over him. "You've blinded him!" she shrieked at Darktail.

Darktail curled his lip. "I only half blinded him," he growled. "A half-blind cat threatens no one." He padded to the fresh-kill pile and grabbed the plump rabbit between his jaws, then carried it to the edge of the clearing and began to eat.

Violetpaw stared at Rain, horror scorching though her as she saw his face. She'd seen fights here before, but none this cruel. His cheek was ripped and his eye was closed and oozing blood. Nausea swept over her, and she raced from the camp. Skidding to a halt behind an alder, she vomited, her body convulsing with shock.

Hunched in her nest, Violetpaw stared through the darkness. The camp was quiet except for Rain's moans and Needletail's soothing mews as she nursed him the best she could. Nettle had been racing in and out of camp all evening with herbs. Now he crouched outside the patch of long grass where Rain and Needletail were huddled together.

Violetpaw watched Nettle's eyes slowly close as sleep over-whelmed him. Darktail's snores echoed across the camp. No moon lit the clearing, and clouds covered the sky. The other cats were curled in their nests. There was still prey on the pile. Darktail had been the only cat to eat. The others had slunk to the edges of the camp in silence. Violetpaw wondered if they were as shocked as she was by the brutality of their campmates. She wondered if the ShadowClan cats regretted leaving their Clan now. Perhaps ShadowClan did have too many rules, but the cats looked after one another. They would never *blind* one another!

Violetpaw knew she had to leave. She could not live like this, in a group ruled by fear and claws. But where could she go? Her heart fluttered anxiously as she imagined life as a loner. Perhaps she could ask Rowanstar to take her in, or Bramblestar. Perhaps some of the Clan cats still believed she was part of the prophecy and would welcome her back. She just knew she couldn't stay here. These cats were too unpre-dictable. What if she said something wrong? Or failed to bring home enough prey? How long would it be before Darktail or one of the other rogues turned on *her*?

She could hear Needletail murmuring beyond the long grass. Needletail had been growing closer and closer to Rain. *She won't leave him. Especially not now.* And if they *did* become mates, would Needletail still have time for Violetpaw? *I'd be alone here.*

Quietly Violetpaw got to her paws and climbed from her nest. Heart pounding in her ears, she tiptoed across the clearing. She paused beside Nettle, who was snoring gently now, and strained to see past him through the grass but could make out nothing but shadow. She wanted to tell Needletail she was leaving, and to thank her. But she didn't dare risk being caught.

"Don't worry, Rain. It'll hurt less soon."

She listened to the soft murmur of her friend. This would be the first time in moons she'd be without her. *Good-bye, Needletail.* Her heart aching, she turned away and headed out of camp.

The scent of pine and moss filled her nose as dawn broke and early newleaf sunshine seeped into ShadowClan territory. Violetpaw crouched beneath a bramble a tree-length from the camp wall. A juicy rabbit lay beside her. Would it be enough?

Rowanstar had turned Darktail away when he had come bringing a gift of prey. And he'd told Needletail to take her. *You did ShadowClan no favors by finding her. There's been nothing but trouble since she arrived. We're better off without her.* His words still rang in her head, as they had in the moons since she'd left. Was she wasting her time even trying to come back? Perhaps she should head straight for ThunderClan territory and beg Bramblestar to take her in. Twigpaw would support her, wouldn't she?

Her heart quickened with fear. What if no Clan wanted

her? What if they saw her as trouble: just an extra mouth to feed? The rogues would never forgive her for leaving. She'd be a loner.

"Who's there?"

Tawnypelt's mew took her by surprise. A tortoiseshell muzzle pushed through the brambles, and Violetpaw found herself staring into the warrior's green eyes. "Violetkit?" She blinked.

"I'm Violetpaw now," Violetpaw mewed uncertainly. She'd had no naming ceremony. Needletail had decided it was time she began her training. Did that mean she wasn't a proper 'paw?

Tawnypelt backed out. "Come out here." She sounded stern.

Nervously Violetpaw grabbed the rabbit between her jaws and crept out.

Spikefur and Tigerheart stared at her from behind Tawnypelt.

"Are you *hunting* on our land?" Tawnypelt stared at her, shocked.

Violetpaw dropped the rabbit. "I caught it before I crossed the border." She wasn't going to make the same mistake as Darktail.

"Why did you come here?" Tawnypelt demanded.

Violetpaw could see confusion and anger in the tortoiseshell's gaze. "I want to come back to ShadowClan." She stared at her paws, her mew hardly more than a whisper.

Spikefur growled. "You *chose* to leave. You no longer have a place here."

"Rowanstar *told* Needletail to take me." Violetpaw lifted her gaze, forcing herself to be brave. "I know I was never really wanted here. But I was hoping I could *make* a place for myself."

Spikefur glared at her. "As what? The Clan traitor?"

"Hush!" Tawnypelt turned on her Clanmate. "She wasn't the only one who left."

"They're all traitors!" Spikefur hissed.

Tigerheart pushed in front of the angry tom. "Violetpaw was only a kit when she left. And Rowanstar *did* tell Needletail to take her. She can't be held responsible for her decision."

Tawnypelt was looking at the rabbit. "Did you catch that yourself?"

"Yes," Violetpaw told her meekly.

Spikefur nudged Tigerheart away. "She may have brought others with her!"

Violetpaw puffed out her chest. "I came here by myself! The others don't even know I'm gone."

Tawnypelt poked the rabbit with a paw. "It's a good-sized catch. I can see you're not a kit anymore." She nodded toward the camp. "Come on. We'll let Rowanstar decide what to do with you."

Rowanstar was resting beside the great rock at the edge of the clearing as Tawnypelt, Spikefur, and Tigerheart escorted Violetpaw into camp. Tigerheart carried the rabbit. As they crossed the clearing, Violetpaw ignored the stares of the ShadowClan cats. She heard Kinkfur whispering to Oakfur outside the elders' den but couldn't make out her words. Pinenose watched her from the warriors' den. Violetpaw avoided the she-cat's gaze, shame pricking through her fur. She guessed that Pinenose wasn't thinking anything good about her. Stonewing and Wasptail looked up from washing as she passed the warriors' den. Dawnpelt was rummaging through the fresh-kill pile, picking at last night's leftovers. Violetpaw glanced toward the nursery, hoping to catch a glimpse of Whorlkit, Snakekit, and Flowerkit. Perhaps they were apprentices by now. But the nursery was silent, lit by the early morning sunshine.

Rowanstar scrambled to his paws as he saw her. Violetpaw tensed, straining to read his gaze. Was that relief in his green eyes?

"I knew you'd all come back!" His gaze flicked hopefully past her toward the entrance.

"It's just Violetpaw." Tawnypelt stopped in front of the ShadowClan leader. "She came alone."

Rowanstar's eyes narrowed suspiciously. "Is she spying?"

Tigerheart dropped the rabbit at his paws. "She wants to rejoin the Clan. She brought this as a gift."

Rowanstar frowned. "Just like those rogues."

"I'm not a rogue!" Violetpaw flicked her tail. Why did Clan cats have to call everyone names? Anger surged through her. Did no cat want her? She'd spent her life being passed around by other cats. First Alderpaw had taken her from her mother's nest. Then Rowanstar had snatched her from ThunderClan. Then Needletail had taken her to the rogues. This was the first time she'd had any choice in the matter, and she was choosing to join ShadowClan. They were *lucky*! "I know I'm not a Clan cat now, but I *want* to be. I've decided to come *here*. But I can always go to ThunderClan."

Worry flashed in Rowanstar's gaze. "No."

"Why?" She met his gaze, surprised at her own boldness.

"We need you here." The ShadowClan leader looked suddenly weary. "Perhaps if you come back, the others will too."

"That's their decision." Violetpaw was unconvinced. "Don't take me as bait to catch the others. Take me because you want a Clanmate."

Spikefur growled under his breath. "Don't believe her, Rowanstar. The rogues may have sent her. It could be a plot."

Violetpaw scowled at the tom. "Do you really think they'd send *me* if they wanted to infiltrate the Clan? I'm the last cat ShadowClan wants. I'm not even Clanborn."

Tawnypelt's flank brushed hers. "Rowanstar, I think we should take her back. It was brave of her to leave the rogues and risk coming here."

Tigerheart nodded. "She may not be Clanborn, but she has the courage of a Clan cat." He blinked at her warmly.

Surprise pricked through Violetpaw's pelt. Was it really going to be this easy? She stared at Rowanstar, her heart beating fast.

Rowanstar hesitated, glancing around the camp. Then he dipped his head. "Very well. We need all the warriors we can get right now. I welcome you back to ShadowClan as a Clanmate." He looked toward the fresh-kill pile. "Dawnpelt! You will be Violetpaw's mentor."

Dawnpelt padded toward Violetpaw, her nose wrinkling as she approached. "Okay," she agreed. "But I'm not training her until she's washed off that filthy rogue stench."

Violetpaw hardly heard her. She didn't care what she smelled like. Joy flooded her belly. She was going to be a Clan cat again. A *real* apprentice!

CHAPTER 14

Now that she'd been accepted back into ShadowClan, Violetpaw was determined to show what a helpful cat she'd become. She rose early each day to fetch fresh bedding for the elders before Dawnpelt took her out for training. She was always last to take prey from the pile at the end of a long day's hunting. When Dawnpelt was busy, she would help Puddleshine gather herbs. The last time she'd seen him, Puddleshine had still been an apprentice, but he'd been given his full medicine-cat name when Leafpool had returned to ThunderClan. Violetpaw liked helping him. He was always friendly, although he seemed anxious in his role as the Clan's medicine cat, and a little overwhelmed by the daily worries of keeping his Clan healthy.

Her time with the rogues had made her a good hunter, and Dawnpelt was impressed with her skills. Violetpaw didn't dare explain that Needletail had trained her. She hardly mentioned Needletail or the others, even when her Clanmates asked about them. Rowanstar had pressed her for information about the rogues, but Violetpaw had refused to answer in any detail, saying only that as long as Darktail was leader, they were no threat to the Clan. She'd heard Darktail say that he had no wish to take over ShadowClan territory, and she hoped it was true. Eventually Rowanstar stopped asking. The whole Clan stopped asking, and she knew that she had earned their grudging respect for refusing to betray her former campmates. She'd even overheard Kinkfur talking to Ratscar one evening as she'd padded wearily to her den. "If she won't betray them, then she won't betray us."

Of course, some of her Clanmates didn't trust her yet. Snowbird and Scorchfur watched her through narrowed eyes. Spikefur barely spoke to her. Pinenose acknowledged her with polite nods but kept her distance. At least Yarrowleaf and Strikestone were friendly enough, content to share prey with her at the end of the day.

She missed Needletail, and guilt jabbed her belly every time she thought of her friend. Keeping busy helped her not think about what she'd left behind. It also stopped her wondering about Twigpaw and their mother. Could Twigpaw be right? Could their mother still be alive? Perhaps she should have gone with Twigpaw when she'd asked. Violetpaw pushed the questions away and made herself busy each time they popped into her thoughts.

Today rain dripped through the canopy as she woke. She heard it from inside the cozy apprentices' den and fluffed out her fur before nosing her way into the clearing. The rest of the Clan was still sleeping as she padded quietly across camp. Weak dawn light hardly showed through the clouds. As she tried to think of a sheltered patch of bracken where she could gather dry stems for the elders' bedding, Puddleshine padded from the medicine den.

Worry clouded his gaze.

"What's wrong?" Violetpaw hurried toward him, her paws squelching over the muddy ground. She glanced past him toward the medicine-den entrance. She knew Wasptail and Oakfur were inside, sick with a mysterious illness. "Are they worse?"

"I don't know what to do." Puddleshine paced, oblivious to the rain soaking his fur. "I've tried every herb I know. I thought it was greencough, but catmint hasn't helped. Tansy eases their breathing for a while, but their fever is getting worse, and nothing seems to help."

"Can I help?" Violetpaw offered. "I can fetch more herbs—"

"Didn't you hear me? *Herbs aren't working!*" Puddleshine stared at her, panic glittering in his gaze. "I don't know what to do."

"Speak to Rowanstar," Violetpaw urged, wishing she had something better to suggest. "Perhaps he's seen the illness before. He might know what Littlecloud used to do."

Puddleshine blinked at her gratefully and headed for the leader's den.

Violetpaw followed, shaking rain from her pelt.

"Rowanstar!" Puddleshine called softly through the entrance.

A husky growl sounded from the shadows. "Who is it?"

"It's me, Puddleshine." The young medicine cat stepped back as Rowanstar slid from his den.

The ShadowClan leader's eyes were bleary with sleep. His fur was unkempt, and he stared listlessly at Puddleshine. "What do you want?"

"I don't know how to cure Wasptail and Oakfur," Puddleshine confessed. "I've tried everything I know, but none of it works."

"I thought they had greencough," Rowanstar grunted. "Give them catmint."

"Catmint isn't working. It must be another illness. One I don't know." Puddleshine looked frantic.

Rowanstar's pelt prickled irritably along his spine. "You're the medicine cat," he growled. "Why are you asking me?"

Violetpaw padded closer. "He thought you might have seen the illness before," she told him. "He hoped you'd know what to do."

"Littlecloud took care of sickness." Rowanstar blinked at her crossly.

"Perhaps we should ask a more experienced medicine cat," Violetpaw ventured. "Perhaps Leafpool could come and help again. I can go and fetch her now—"

"No!" Rowanstar's eyes flashed with anger. "We're not asking ThunderClan for help."

"But she trained me!" Puddleshine argued. "You didn't mind asking for help *then*."

"I had no choice," Rowanstar growled.

"We have no choice now," Puddleshine pressed. "We can't let Wasptail and Oakfur get sicker. Oakfur is old. I don't know if he can survive much longer. And what if the sickness spreads? I *have* to know what to do."

"Try other herbs." Rowanstar fluffed out his pelt against the hardening rain. He turned and slunk back into the shelter of his den.

Puddleshine stared after him, eyes round. "I've tried everything I know," he mewed thickly.

"I could slip out of camp now and fetch Leafpool anyway," Violetpaw mewed softly.

"No." Puddleshine shook his head. "Rowanstar would be angry."

"But you need help!"

Puddleshine gazed at her wearily. "I'll just keep giving them the herbs I've got and hope that they improve." He wandered away, lost in thought. "Perhaps if I mix tansy, coltsfoot, and borage . . ."

His voice trailed away as he neared his den.

Violetpaw stared after him, wondering how to help. *I'll suggest to Dawnpelt that we spend the day gathering herbs.*

Dawnpelt agreed, and through the wet morning she and Violetpaw gathered bundles of tansy, coltsfoot, and borage. Puddleshine had shown them sprigs from the store in his den, and soon Violetpaw could trace the scent of them from several fox-lengths away.

At sunhigh they headed back to camp, their jaws filled with herbs. Violetpaw felt dizzy from the heady fragrances as she padded through the entrance tunnel. She blinked through the rain. Scorchfur, Crowfrost, and Tawnypelt were gathered at the entrance to Rowanstar's den, Tigerheart hurrying to join them. Violetpaw could tell by their rippling pelts that something was wrong.

She glanced at Dawnpelt. Her mentor's eyes flashed with worry. She must have seen them too. Together they raced across camp.

Violetpaw dropped her bundle of herbs as Tawnypelt turned and stared at her, alarmed. "What's happened?"

"Rowanstar's not well." Tawnypelt's eyes glittered with worry. She glanced at the mouse at her paws. "I took him some prey but he won't wake up. He must be really sick."

Hoarse coughing sounded from inside the den.

Scorchfur backed away. "He sounds like Wasptail and Oakfur did."

Crowfrost straightened, his gaze hardening. "Fetch Puddleshine," he told Violetpaw.

Violetpaw turned and raced for the medicine den. She burst in, gagging as the stench of sickness swept over her. Wasptail and Oakfur wheezed in their nests, their fur matted, their muzzles dripping.

Puddleshine was dozing beside a pile of herbs. He jerked his head up and blinked at her. "I was just taking a nap," he mumbled.

Violetpaw stiffened with alarm. "Are you sick too?"

Puddleshine scrambled to his paws. "No. Just tired."

"You've been working hard," Violetpaw sympathized. "But we need you. Rowanstar is—" She stopped. Puddleshine was staring at her as though he hardly saw her. Stars seemed to sparkle in his faraway gaze. She tipped her head, anxious. Perhaps he *was* sick? "Are you sure you're okay?"

Puddleshine blinked, his attention flashing to her. "I'm fine!" He pushed past her eagerly.

She followed him into the clearing, surprise sparking through her fur. What was wrong with the medicine cat? Why was he acting so strangely?

"Crowfrost!" Puddleshine slid to a halt in front of the deputy, his pelt glittering as rain caught in his fur. "I had a dream!" He sounded jubilant. "StarClan has finally shared dreams with me!"

Crowfrost stared at the young tom, his ears flicking. "What was it?"

"The sickness is called yellowcough. Runningnose came and led me to StarClan's hunting grounds. He told me what to do." Puddleshine spoke fast. "There's an herb called lungwort. It grows on the moor. Its leaves will cure our Clanmates."

Crowfrost lifted his tail. "Did he show you what it looks like?"

"Yes!" Puddleshine nodded excitedly.

"Good." Crowfrost glanced toward Rowanstar's den. "Our leader is sick."

Puddleshine ducked inside, darting out a few moments later. He glanced around his Clanmates, his gaze clouded with worry. "Do any of you know what tansy looks like?"

"I do." Dawnpelt nodded toward the bundle of herbs at her paws. "And coltsfoot and borage."

"Of course!" Puddleshine mewed, as though only just

remembering he'd shown her what they looked like earlier that morning. "Chew equal parts into a thick pulp and try to get Rowanstar to swallow it. It won't cure him, but it will help his symptoms until I can get back with the lungwort." Puddleshine turned toward the entrance.

"Wait!" Crowfrost blinked through the rain at the medicine cat. "You're needed here."

"I'm the only one who knows what lungwort looks like." Puddleshine stared at the deputy.

Crowfrost hesitated, then nodded toward Tigerheart. "Go with him. You too, Scorchfur."

Violetpaw stiffened in surprise as Crowfrost's gaze flicked to her. "And you."

Joy fizzed in her paws. Crowfrost trusted her enough to send her on this important mission!

Scorchfur frowned. "Tawnypelt should come instead of *her*." He scowled at Violetpaw. "*Tawnypelt* can be trusted."

Crowfrost scowled. "So can Violetpaw!"

Scorchfur grunted.

"Hurry!" Puddleshine headed for the entrance. "We mustn't waste time."

Crowfrost flicked his tail toward the medicine cat. "Go with him."

Violetpaw bounded across the wet clearing, Tigerheart at her tail. Scorchfur raced past her, kicking up mud as he passed, and ducked out of camp.

As Violetpaw followed them, Tigerheart called from behind. "I'll lead! I know the quickest route." He pulled past Violetpaw, Scorchfur, and Puddleshine, heading for the ditches. As he reached each one, he leaped it in turn. Violetpaw raced behind, one eye on Puddleshine as she cleared the gashes in the forest floor. The medicine cat was nimble, making the jumps with ease. As the ground smoothed ahead, she glimpsed light. They were nearing the edge of the forest.

Tigerheart broke from the trees first. Violetpaw followed, narrowing her eyes against the driving rain as she left the shelter of the pines. She dodged a bramble, her paws slithering on the wet grass as she hurried toward the lake.

She could see the Twoleg halfbridge reaching into the water. Beyond it, a stretch of meadow led to the lower slopes of the moor.

"Tigerheart!" A loud yowl sounded from behind the patrol.

Violetpaw looked back. A ThunderClan cat was calling from the border. She could just make out the shape on the shore. *Dovewing.* Another cat was with her. She strained to see. *Twigpaw!* Her heart leaped. Did her sister know she'd left the rogues and returned to ShadowClan? *Has she come here to see me?* She thought, with a pang of guilt, about their last meeting, when she'd refused to help Twigpaw search for their mother. Had Twigpaw gone alone? Had she found her?

Dovewing paced the scent line, staring eagerly at the ShadowClan patrol. Did they have news? Violetpaw turned to Tigerheart. The tabby tom was still charging toward the WindClan border. He couldn't have heard Dovewing's call. "Wait!" she yowled.

Tigerheart pulled up and turned to stare at her. "What?"

"Twigpaw and Dovewing!" She jerked her muzzle toward the ThunderClan cats.

Scorchfur and Puddleshine stopped.

"So what?" Scorchfur's wet pelt bristled.

Tigerheart seemed to be avoiding looking toward the ThunderClan cats. "We don't have time. Let them wait until the next Gathering to chat."

Violetpaw itched with frustration. She wanted to speak with Twigpaw.

Puddleshine whisked his tail. "We should warn them about the illness," he mewed. "It spreads quickly. They should know."

Violetpaw's heart leaped as the medicine cat bounded toward the ThunderClan border. Growling impatiently, Tigerheart raced after him.

Scorchfur rolled his eyes. "Medicine cats have no sense."

Violetpaw hardly heard him. She chased after Tigerheart, wind streaming though her fur.

"Warn Leafpool." Puddleshine was already talking to Dovewing by the time she caught up. The young medicine cat's eyes glowed with pride. "But tell her I know which herb cures it. Tell her I had a dream from StarClan!"

Twigpaw stared at her paws, a tail-length behind Dovewing. *Look at me!* Desperately Violetpaw tried to catch her sister's eye. *Did you look for our mother?* Twigpaw was acting as though Violetpaw wasn't there. Was she still angry? Or perhaps she was ashamed she hadn't found their mother. *It's okay. I knew there wasn't much chance. I'm sorry I didn't help you.* She swallowed back the words, her paws hot with frustration.

Dovewing was eyeing Tigerheart. "Thanks for sharing this with us. It was good of you to stop."

Tigerheart fluffed out his fur. "It was Puddleshine's idea, not mine."

Dovewing returned his gaze coolly. "We thought it was strange to see a ShadowClan patrol heading toward Wind-Clan territory. We thought something might be wrong."

"Well, there is, and now you know." Tigerheart turned away brusquely.

"Twigpaw?" Violetpaw twitched her ears hopefully, but Twigpaw carried on staring at her paws, her tail flicking restlessly. She clearly wasn't going to talk.

"Come on, Violetpaw!" Tigerheart's urgent mew called her away.

Violetpaw threw a last pleading glance at Twigpaw. "I'm sorry," she murmured before turning to race after the others.

Tigerheart and Puddleshine had already reached Scorchfur and were heading for the WindClan border. She glanced over her shoulder.

Twigpaw was staring after her.

Hope flickered in Violetpaw's chest. If Twigpaw was watching her, she *must* care. *We'll talk soon!* She hoped she'd be able to keep her silent promise; there was so much to talk about, but there was no time to worry about it now. Scorchfur had already leaped over the stream that cut between ShadowClan land and the moor. She pushed harder against the wet grass, closing the gap. Her lungs were burning as she caught up to the patrol.

The grass felt coarser as brambles gave way to heather, which grew thicker and thicker as the slope steepened. Wind whipped the rain harder against Violetpaw's pelt. She was relieved as the heather closed around them and she found herself chasing Scorchfur through a narrow gap, rough stems closing in on either side. The trail twisted one way, then the other. She breathed in the sweet scent of peat and a sour smell she didn't recognize. She'd never been on the moor before.

Suddenly the heather opened onto a wide stretch of grass. Gorse swayed on one side, and above she saw the top of the moor, arched like a spine against the glowering sky.

Tigerheart slowed, Scorchfur beside him. Puddleshine eased his pace and glanced across the slope as though scanning for lungwort.

"Can you see any?" Violetpaw pulled up beside him.

"Hush!" Tigerheart's hiss made her jump. The tabby tom had halted and was staring at a bank of heather ahead. It rocked in the wind. Violetpaw narrowed her eyes, suddenly wary. Tigerheart was tasting the air. "WindClan cats," he warned.

Scorchfur shifted beside her.

Violetpaw blinked at Tigerheart. "They'll understand why we came, won't they?"

"Of course they will." As Puddleshine padded forward, his

ears pricked eagerly, three WindClan warriors emerged from the heather.

Violetpaw stiffened. Hostility shone in their eyes. The largest tom's hackles were up. Puddleshine halted and glanced nervously at Tigerheart.

"Don't worry." The ShadowClan tom stepped in front of the medicine cat and faced the WindClan patrol.

"What are you doing here?" The dark gray tom flattened his ears threateningly.

"Hi, Crowfeather." Tigerheart stood his ground and mewed briskly. "We've come on an herb-gathering mission. It's urgent."

A black tom with amber eyes padded closer, showing his teeth.

"Wait, Breezepelt," Crowfeather cautioned.

"Wait for what?" hissed the third tom. His tabby fur was plastered to his lithe frame by the rain. "We should chase them off our land."

"Not yet, Leaftail." Crowfeather padded closer and stopped a muzzle-length from Tigerheart. "First we're going to take them to Onestar so they can explain themselves to him." Spite glittered in his gaze.

Tigerheart lifted his chin. "I'll be happy to talk to Onestar. I'm sure he'll understand why we came."

Crowfeather and Leaftail exchanged glances. Was that amusement in their eyes? Violetpaw suddenly felt cold.

Puddleshine seemed unaware of the menace in the air.

He blinked at the WindClan warriors. "Are we going to your camp?" His eyes lit up. "Good! I need to speak with Kestrelflight."

Crowfeather's whiskers twitched. "I doubt you'll be doing much talking," he meowed darkly.

Violetpaw's belly tightened with foreboding as the WindClan warriors flanked them and began to guide them along the slopes. They crossed the moor until she saw a dip surrounded by gorse. Crowfeather led them to a gap in the thick green wall and ducked through it. Violetpaw followed Scorchfur and Tigerheart, Puddleshine at her tail.

The tunnel opened onto a wide stretch of grass. Heather clustered at the edges, backed by thick gorse. Small, sleek cats slid from dens and stared at them as the patrol marched them across the clearing. Their eyes sparkled nervously. Violetpaw's heart quickened. Tension hung in the air as though thunder was coming. She padded closer to Puddleshine, comforted by the touch of his flank against hers.

Onestar was sitting on a wide, flat rock at the end of the clearing.

His gaze sharpened as he saw them. He leaped onto the grass and stood motionless as they approached.

Violetpaw blinked at him, her throat tightening. Was this how the rogues had felt when they'd first entered the ShadowClan camp? She doubted they'd been as scared. Rowanstar was stern, but his gaze had never been as icy as Onestar's.

Her fear intensified when the WindClan leader looked

right at her, nostrils flaring. "What is *she* doing on my territory?"

Crowfeather looked confused he stopped in front of Onestar. "Er—we caught them inside our border."

Fury flashed in Onestar's eyes, turning ice into fire in a moment. He lashed his tail in her direction. "This one is a *rogue*. She lived among the same cats who killed Furzepelt!"

Violetpaw stiffened with fear.

The WindClan leader's pelt spiked along his spine. "How dare you?" he hissed. "Get her off my territory before I take my revenge!"

Tigerheart stepped backward, and Violetpaw saw the two warriors' claws curl into the grass as though preparing for a fight. She tried to back up as well, but hit a wall of tawny fur, thick with WindClan scent. Cats padded closer on every side. The gorse hemmed them in. Her paws trembled. They were trapped.

"Hear me out. Violetpaw is a ShadowClan cat now. She poses no threat," Tigerheart said in a steady voice.

Onestar snarled. "Make it quick."

Tigerheart glanced at Puddleshine, whose gaze was frozen on Onestar. Violetpaw could smell his fear. Tigerheart said quickly, "Three of our Clanmates are ill with a sickness we've never seen before. StarClan sent Puddleshine a dream telling him which herb would cure it. They told him that he must gather it on the moor."

Onestar narrowed his eyes to slits. "I don't care what

StarClan told him. No ShadowClan cat crosses onto Wind-Clan land."

Tigerheart's tail twitched and Violetpaw guessed he was angry, but he replied calmly. "We mean no harm. But we can't let our Clanmates die."

Onestar snorted. "And yet you shelter rogues who killed *my* Clanmate." He glared again at Violetpaw.

Scorchfur bristled. "Violetpaw is one of us! We're not sheltering them!"

Onestar thrust his muzzle close to the dark gray warrior. "Even if she is loyal to ShadowClan . . . you let the others live at the edge of your territory, despite the fact that they are murderers. Half your apprentices left to join them. It just proves what I've always thought: ShadowClan cats are no better than rogues. You will not gather herbs on my land."

Violetpaw could hardly believe the rage in the WindClan leader's mew. What was wrong with him? Was he really going to let Clan cats die just because of the rogues? Weren't leaders meant to be wise?

She saw movement at the corner of her vision and saw Kestrelflight approach. "Surely Puddleshine can gather herbs?" The WindClan medicine cat blinked nervously at his leader. "The Clans have always allowed medicine cats to gather herbs when lives are at stake."

Onestar turned on him. "No!"

"But our Clanmates need—"

Onestar cut Kestrelflight off with a hiss. "They will gather no herbs here." His malicious gaze flicked back to Tigerheart. "Get off my land."

Tigerheart returned his gaze without moving.

"Go!" Onestar screeched. "Head for the border and don't stop. The moment you leave the camp, I'm sending a patrol after you. If they catch up with you, they'll tear the pelts from your backs."

Tigerheart shifted his paws. "Please," he pleaded softly.

Violetpaw stared at the warrior in surprise. He was begging. He must care for his Clan more than his own pride.

"Leave!" Onestar's yowl rang around the camp.

Tigerheart turned, signaling with his tail for the patrol to follow.

Violetpaw hurried after him as he headed for the entrance. She could feel Puddleshine crowding her heels and smell his fear. As they emerged from the entrance, Tigerheart broke into a run. "Keep up!" he called over his shoulder. "Onestar is out of his mind. The sooner we get out of here the better." As he raced away from the WindClan camp, Violetpaw charged after him. Scorchfur dropped back and fell in behind. Violetpaw felt a rush of gratitude to the tom. She knew that he was placing himself between her and the WindClan patrol that would soon be on their tails. Perhaps he was beginning to accept her at last.

CHAPTER 15

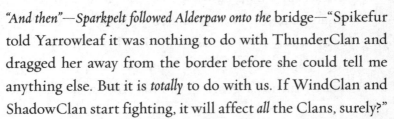

"And then"—Sparkpelt followed Alderpaw onto the bridge—"Spikefur told Yarrowleaf it was nothing to do with ThunderClan and dragged her away from the border before she could tell me anything else. But it is *totally* to do with us. If WindClan and ShadowClan start fighting, it will affect *all* the Clans, surely?"

"I guess." Alderpaw padded over the damp bark, trying not to look into the dark water swirling below. "But Yarrowleaf might just have been spreading gossip. You can't be sure it was true." Sparkpelt had been chattering about the spat between ShadowClan and WindClan since they'd crossed the River-Clan border.

The full moon lit the lake. The trees on the island glowed, their buds pale in its light. He wondered if WindClan and ShadowClan were already waiting at the Gathering and glanced up to check for stray clouds. Would the two Clans be able to keep the truce? Or would StarClan cover the moon with clouds to keep the battling Clans apart? What if they fought anyway? Alderpaw's mouth grew dry.

He jumped onto the beach, pebbles crunching beneath his paws. "I can't believe Onestar would drive away a medicine cat asking for herbs." He waited as Sparkpelt jumped down beside him.

"Of course he would," Sparkpelt mewed. "Everyone knows he's been as crazy as a cuckoo since he lost that life."

Alderpaw frowned. Losing a life did seem to have made the WindClan leader burn with a strange fury. But enough for him to deny help to sick cats?

Sparkpelt brushed past him. "Hurry up. I can't wait to see what will happen." She headed into the long grass.

Bramblestar and Squirrelflight were ahead, leading Brightheart, Cloudtail, and Berrynose toward the clearing with Leafpool. Alderpaw glanced over his shoulder. Molewhisker was coaxing Honeypaw onto the tree-bridge. "I'll be right behind you," he promised his apprentice. "If you slip, I'll grab your scruff."

Larkpaw and Leafpaw jostled on the far shore, staring eagerly at the tree-bridge.

Rosepetal nudged them away. "Let your sister cross first."

"Honeypaw's scared of water!" Larkpaw teased.

Rosepetal glared at her apprentice sternly. "Sometimes being afraid is smart."

Leafpaw snorted. "Warriors aren't meant to be afraid of anything."

Bumblestripe nudged her playfully. "I'll remind you of that next time we smell a fox while we're out training."

Leafpaw puffed out her chest. "I wasn't being afraid," she sniffed. "I was being smart."

Bumblestripe and Rosepetal swapped bemused glances.

Behind them Poppyfrost, Graystripe, and Millie waited patiently, while Twigpaw hung back with Ivypool and Dovewing.

"Alderpaw!" Sparkpelt called from the long grass. "Come on! WindClan is already here. I can smell them."

Alderpaw nosed his way into the dew-soaked grass, following her trail. He opened his mouth, tasting for scents. There was no sign of ShadowClan. He padded into the clearing. Brightheart and Cloudtail were already sharing tongues with Minnowtail and Mallownose. The RiverClan cats were looking sleek again after the long leaf-bare. The fish must be teeming in the river once more.

WindClan cats skirted the clearing, keeping their distance. They glanced anxiously at one another and then at the other Clan cats. Alderpaw's pelt prickled with foreboding. He scanned the clearing for Onestar.

The WindClan leader was pacing beneath the great oak, his pelt rippling along his spine. As ThunderClan arrived, his gaze flashed toward the long grass, sharp with suspicion as though he was waiting for an ambush. He flinched as Leafpaw, Honeypaw, and Larkpaw raced into the clearing.

"Nightpaw! Breezepaw!" Leafpaw greeted the RiverClan apprentices with a purr and hurried to join them. Larkpaw and Honeypaw followed.

Fernpaw and Brindlepaw, the WindClan apprentices, eyed them eagerly but didn't move from their mentors' side.

As Sparkpelt headed toward a group of RiverClan warriors, Alderpaw followed Leafpool toward the great oak.

Jayfeather had stayed in camp, complaining that if he wanted to spend the night listening to cats bicker, he could sit in the elders' den. "It's going to be a weird Gathering," Alderpaw murmured softly as he stopped beside her.

She followed his gaze toward Onestar. "Tensions are high."

"Has this happened before?" Alderpaw asked.

Leafpool sat down. "Clans have always fought."

"But has a Clan ever refused to help others treat their sick?" Alderpaw blinked at her earnestly.

"It's been known to happen," she admitted.

"Did they ever let cats *die*?" Alderpaw shifted his paws uneasily.

"Warriors and medicine cats think differently," Leafpool sighed.

"Why?" Alderpaw was puzzled. It didn't make sense. If the Clans helped one another, then no one needed to suffer.

"Only StarClan knows." Leafpool gazed across the clearing and changed the subject. "Is Twigpaw okay?" She was watching the young she-cat, who was sitting alone beside a clump of ferns.

"I don't know." Alderpaw followed her gaze, his belly pricking with guilt. Twigpaw had hardly spoken to him since he'd told her that Bramblestar had never sent a search patrol to look for her mother. Even though he shared the apprentices' den with her, she would leave her nest by the time he woke and would be curled asleep—or pretending to be asleep—when he settled down for the night. During the day they were both busy with training, but he noticed how she always took her prey to the far side of the clearing and avoided his gaze when they passed in camp.

"Is she upset about something?" Leafpool pressed.

Alderpaw couldn't explain. Leafpool, like the rest of the Clan, believed that the search party had been looking for Twigpaw's mother. She didn't know about SkyClan. He shrugged. "I'm not sure."

"Ivypool says she works hard." Leafpool frowned. "She must be committed to the Clan. Perhaps she still misses her sister."

"Perhaps."

Leafpool wrapped her tail over her paws. "She must be happy to know that Violetpaw is back with ShadowClan. She'll be safer away from those rogues."

"I guess." Alderpaw wished he knew *what* she felt. When Dovewing had returned to camp with the news, he'd hurried to congratulate Twigpaw. But Twigpaw had only shrugged and turned away.

The Clan cats were beginning to glance toward the long grass, shifting impatiently. There was still no sign of Shadow-Clan. The round white moon was crossing behind the great oak. Had ShadowClan decided not to come?

Bramblestar crossed the clearing, nodding to Mistystar as he passed her. The RiverClan leader followed him to the oak and climbed the trunk after him. As they settled on the low-est branch, Onestar leaped up beside them and took his place, glowering at the cats as they clustered below. Squirrelflight followed Harespring and Reedwhisker to the deputies' spot among the roots. Kestrelflight, Mothwing, and Willowshine sat down beside Leafpool.

"Let's begin," Bramblestar called.

Mistystar shifted beside him. "Should we wait a little longer for ShadowClan?"

"They can join in when they arrive." There was impatience in Bramblestar's mew. He lifted his gaze to the gathered cats. "I have important news, and if ShadowClan isn't here to share it, then I must. Violetpaw, one of StarClan's chosen kits, has returned to ShadowClan."

The RiverClan cats lifted their gaze happily, ears pricking.

Mistystar blinked at Bramblestar. "Did ShadowClan rescue her?"

"She returned because she wanted to," Bramblestar told her.

Onestar's eyes flashed with anger. "So she claims, and ShadowClan is fool enough to believe her. What about the other ShadowClan traitors?"

"As far as I know, they are still with the rogues," Bramblestar meowed.

Uneasy murmurs rippled through the cats below him.

The ThunderClan leader ignored them. "But Violetpaw is back. StarClan's prophecy is safe once more."

Crowfeather called from the crowd. "Are we sure the prophecy is safe? StarClan hasn't confirmed that Violetpaw and Twigpaw are part of it."

Mistystar flicked her tail. "They haven't told us they're not."

Minnowtail called from among the other RiverClan warriors. "What else could the prophecy mean? The kits are the only things we've found in the shadows."

It could mean SkyClan. Alderpaw swallowed back frustration. *Embrace what you find in the shadows, for only they can clear the sky.* The *sky* had to refer to SkyClan. Even though StarClan hadn't shared with him for moons, he felt sure that SkyClan was crucial to the prophecy. He glanced toward Twigpaw, who was sitting beside Ivypool, her round eyes fixed on the leaders. Of course Twigpaw and Violetpaw might be part of it too, but surely StarClan would not let SkyClan simply disappear. And yet how could the four Clans have a serious conversation about the prophecy when hardly any cat knew about the missing Clan?

Onestar stepped to the edge of the branch, his ears twitching angrily. "Why are we wasting time when there are important matters to discuss?" He glared at the Clans. "A few days ago, a ShadowClan patrol invaded our land—with one of the former rogues!"

Dovewing jerked her head up. "It wasn't an invasion! I saw the patrol. It was Puddleshine and Violetpaw, who is a ShadowClan apprentice now. They wanted herbs, not a battle!"

"Then why send two warriors with them?" Onestar scowled at her. "Why send a cat who has aligned herself with those who killed *my* warrior?"

Bramblestar snorted. "Two warriors and an apprentice don't make an invasion."

Onestar lashed his tail. "They were *ShadowClan!*" he hissed. "For all we know, that apprentice was scouting for her rogue friends."

"Traitors!" Emberfoot yowled.

"Rogue lovers!" Crowfeather hissed.

Oatclaw flattened his ears. "ShadowClan has forgotten what it is to be a Clan."

Harespring leaped onto an oak root, his pelt bushed. "Half their apprentices live with the rogues."

Onestar nodded approvingly at his deputy. "They don't even come to Gatherings anymore."

Leafpool padded to the front of the crowd and glared up at the WindClan leader. "Stop yowling about ShadowClan's mistakes and think about your own!"

Onestar's eyes narrowed to slits. He leaned down toward the ThunderClan medicine cat, hissing, "I have made no mistakes."

"You denied a valuable herb to a Clan in need!" Leafpool hissed back.

As she spoke, the grass at the edge of the clearing rustled. Crowfrost was leading his Clan into the clearing. They streamed around the other cats, eyes flashing watchfully in the moonlight. Crowfrost pushed through the crowd and climbed into the great oak. He sat in Rowanstar's place. "Rowanstar has the sickness that has stricken our Clan. I will take his place tonight."

Bramblestar and Mistystar dipped their heads to the

ShadowClan deputy as, below them, cats shifted to make room for his Clanmates. Puddleshine sat down beside Willowshine and Mothwing.

A low growl rumbled in Onestar's throat.

Crowfrost ignored it. "Rowanstar would be well by now if Onestar had allowed us to gather herbs on his land."

Onestar showed his teeth. "Gather your precious herb somewhere else. No ShadowClan cat will ever set paw on WindClan land again."

Mothwing blinked up at Crowfrost. "What is this herb?"

"Lungwort," Crowfrost told her. "StarClan shared dreams with Puddleshine. Runningnose told him that the sickness is called yellowcough and that lungwort is the only cure."

"Puddleshine had a dream from StarClan!" Willowshine's eyes lit up. "Then he *is* truly a medicine cat."

Mothwing shifted stiffly beside her.

Willowshine jerked her nose toward her former mentor, guilt flashing in her gaze. "Of course that's not the most important part of being a medicine cat," she mewed quickly.

Alderpaw felt a stab of sympathy for Mothwing. "But he is ShadowClan's only medicine cat," he murmured. "It will be better for them that he can speak with StarClan."

Mothwing looked at Puddleshine. "What does the herb look like?"

"It has dark green leaves specked with gray," he told her. "I would show you if I could find some. But Runningnose told me it only grows on the moor."

Mothwing turned to Onestar. "May I pick the herb on your land? I'm not a ShadowClan cat."

Alderpaw leaned forward. Mothwing's idea was a good one.

Onestar curled his claws into the oak bark. "Not if the herb is for ShadowClan," he snarled.

Crowfrost's pelt bushed. "Two of our elders are sick. They can't last much longer without the herb," he snapped at Onestar. "Are you determined to see innocent cats die?"

"No ShadowClan cat is innocent," Onestar spat. "You are all sheltering the rogues."

Crowfrost flattened his ears. "They live *outside* our territory!"

"How can we be sure?" Onestar thrust his muzzle close to Crowfrost's. "You took Violetpaw back. Can you be sure of her loyalty? And now you're the Clan with a sickness you've never seen before. Perhaps the rogues brought it into your Clan."

Crowfrost held his gaze, hackles rising. "Violetpaw is one of us. The rogues are not living with our Clan."

"But your Clanmates are living with the rogues!" As Onestar spat back, yowls of agreement rose among the WindClan cats. RiverClan shifted uneasily, while ThunderClan exchanged anxious glances.

Fear spiked through Alderpaw's pelt. The leaders mustn't fight over this. Fighting wouldn't cure any cat. "Kestrelflight?" He stared at the WindClan medicine cat. "Surely you won't let Clan cats die?"

Panic sharpened the mottled gray tom's gaze. He glanced at Onestar, who was glowering at him, ears flat. "I can't betray my Clan," he mewed hoarsely.

Mothwing touched Alderpaw's shoulder with her tail softly. "It's not fair to ask that of him."

"Of course it's fair. He's a medicine cat, not a warrior!" Leafpool bristled beside them. "What's not fair is asking innocent cats to die because of one cat's stubbornness!" She turned her furious gaze on Onestar.

Onestar stared at her coldly. "If ShadowClan drives the rogues away, they can have the herb." Without waiting for a response, he leaped from the oak and pushed his way through the gathered cats. His Clanmates joined him, and they stalked away through the grass, pelts spiking.

"I'm sorry."

Kestrelflight's whisper made Alderpaw jump. The Wind-Clan medicine cat was murmuring in Puddleshine's ear. Before Puddleshine could respond, the WindClan medicine cat hurried away to join his Clanmates.

Bramblestar's tail drooped over the edge of the branch as he watched WindClan leave.

Mistystar glanced at the sky. Clouds were trailing across the moon. She turned to Crowfrost. "I will send patrols to search RiverClan territory for this herb," she offered. "But if StarClan has said it is only on the moor, I don't have much hope of finding it."

Crowfrost dipped his head gratefully as the RiverClan leader jumped down from the branch.

Alderpaw blinked at Puddleshine as ThunderClan headed for the tree-bridge. "Congratulations on your dream."

"Thank you." Puddleshine dipped his head. "I just wish Runningnose had told me something that had helped us instead of making things worse." He hurried away, following Crowfrost and Tawnypelt into the shadows. Mistystar had already led her Clanmates into the long grass. The clearing was nearly empty.

Alderpaw padded to the foot of the great oak and waited for his father to jump down. "Could you send a secret patrol to gather lungwort in WindClan's territory?" he mewed as Bramblestar landed behind him.

Bramblestar padded wearily past him. "And what would happen when Onestar found out?"

Alderpaw hurried after him. "Who cares about Onestar?" Frustration rippled through his pelt. "Sick cats will die unless we help them."

"Then ShadowClan must deal with the rogues," Bramblestar meowed simply.

Alderpaw blinked eagerly. "We could help them!"

"It's not our battle."

"It's everyone's battle! These are the rogues who drove SkyClan away."

"So?" Bramblestar's shoulders sagged.

"Don't you care about SkyClan?" Why was his father giving up so easily? "They may be part of the prophecy!"

Bramblestar faced him in the deserted clearing. "SkyClan is gone," he meowed. "The sooner you accept that, the better."

Alderpaw watched his father walk away, shock pulsing in his paws. Did Bramblestar really believe that? He glanced at the sky. *StarClan! Would you really let SkyClan disappear without giving us a chance to save them?*

CHAPTER 16

Twigpaw paced the edge of the clearing, her pelt fizzing with excitement. The dawn patrol had already left, and the sun promised warmth as it lifted over the misty forest. Ivypool was in the medicine den, asking Jayfeather for traveling herbs. They would leave soon.

She could still hardly believe that Ivypool had suggested they search for her mother. At the Gathering last night, Twigpaw had barely heard the Clans bickering. She was tired of their dumb arguments. All any cat seemed to care about was prophecies and rogues. No one cared that her mother might be out there somewhere, searching for her lost kits.

And then, on the trek back from the island, Ivypool had asked her what was worrying her. "Your mind hasn't been on your training for a half-moon," she'd mewed softly.

Twigpaw had hesitated about confiding in her. Would her mentor think it was selfish to still be worrying about her mother after the Clan had done so much for her? But Ivypool had understood.

"Every cat needs kin," Ivypool had said. "One day I hope the Clan will feel like your kin. But if you need to find out about your mother, I'll help you." The silver-and-white she-cat had suggested they set out first thing in the morning. Bramblestar had agreed reluctantly, after Ivypool had promised they'd be careful.

Now, as she waited to leave, she listened to Squirrelflight giving orders below the Highledge. "Check for rogue scent near the ShadowClan border." She nodded to Cloudtail and Thornclaw. "Poppyfrost and Berrynose can go with you."

"Can I go too?" Fernsong blinked at her eagerly. "I haven't been on a border patrol for days."

Squirrelflight shook her head. "I want you to travel with Ivypool and Twigpaw. Will you go?"

"On their mission to find Twigpaw's mother?" Fernsong glanced across the clearing at Twigpaw, his eyes sparkling. "Of course!"

Twigpaw felt a surge of happiness. Fernsong was coming with them! This was turning into a real Clan mission. Just like the one Bramblestar should have sent in the first place.

Squirrelflight frowned. "It's a long journey," she warned Fernsong. "I want everyone back safely."

Cloudtail flicked his tail. "Is there any point in traveling so far? Surely there'll be no trace of Twigpaw's mother now. It's been so long."

Ivypool padded from the medicine den as he spoke. She glared at the white warrior. "Twigpaw has hope. It's a risk, but what if she's right? We have to look."

Poppyfrost tipped her head thoughtfully. "But if Squirrelflight's search party didn't find her, how do you hope to?"

Ivypool fluffed out her fur. The hollow was chilly where the sun hadn't yet reached it. "Twigpaw might notice something Squirrelflight's party didn't."

Twigpaw felt a surge of gratitude toward her mentor. She was glad there was one cat in the Clan who believed in her. She scowled at the medicine den. She still resented Alderpaw for his part in lying about the quest to find her mother.

The brambles at the entrance twitched. Alderpaw padded out, a bundle of herbs in his jaws. He crossed the clearing and dropped them in front of Twigpaw. "Jayfeather says you and Ivypool have to eat all of them." He separated the pile into two.

"Fernsong's coming with us," Twigpaw told him. "He'll need herbs too."

"Fernsong?" Ivypool joined them, surprise lighting her eyes. "I thought we were going alone."

"Squirrelflight just asked him," Twigpaw told her happily. "You don't mind, do you? It'll be like a real mission."

"Of course I don't mind." Ivypool glanced warmly at Fernsong as he headed toward them.

Alderpaw frowned. "It'll be dangerous."

Twigpaw sniffed. "You made the journey when you were younger than me."

"Yes." Alderpaw looked thoughtful. Then his gaze brightened. "I should come with you!"

Twigpaw stared at him. "Why? You think my mother's dead." Did he just want to come so he could say *I told you so*? Or did he want to justify stealing her from her nest before her mother could return? She pushed the thoughts away. Alderpaw wouldn't do that.

"I know where the nest was." As he gazed hopefully at Ivypool, hope trembled along Twigpaw's spine. He was right! He could lead them straight to it. Why hadn't she thought of it before?

Ivypool blinked at him. "It would be great to have you show us the way."

Fernsong stopped beside her. "When are we leaving?"

"As soon as you and Alderpaw have gotten some traveling herbs from Jayfeather," Ivypool told him. "We'll have to make sure he's all right with Alderpaw joining us, too."

"Alderpaw's coming too?" Fernsong purred. "Great!" He headed for the medicine den, Alderpaw on his heels.

Ivypool caught Twigpaw's eye. Her gaze was somber. Unease pricked Twigpaw's belly. "You know we may not find anything, right?" Ivypool warned.

Twigpaw swallowed. "Yes." *But at least I'll know I tried,* she thought. *I'll know* somebody *tried.* She reached down and lapped up the leaves, wrinkling her nose as their bitterness shriveled her tongue.

Ivypool shuddered and licked her lips, finishing her pile. "Well, we'll have plenty of energy."

Fernsong and Alderpaw hurried from the nursery. Alderpaw looked pleased. "Jayfeather says it's all right for me to go."

Fernsong's pelt was prickling. "Traveling herbs are the worst!" He stuck out his tongue.

Ivypool purred and nudged him toward the entrance.

"Hopefully they'll give you enough strength to protect us. That *is* why you're coming, isn't it?" There was a tease in her mew.

Fernsong looked at her, whiskers twitching. "I was hoping you'd protect me."

"If you're nice to me, I might," Ivypool purred.

The warriors headed for the entrance, their pelts brushing amiably.

Twigpaw followed, feeling awkward beside Alderpaw. It had been so long since they'd spoken properly; it would be weird traveling with him.

"How long will it take to get there?" she asked, avoiding his gaze.

"We should reach the Thunderpath tomorrow if we keep moving."

Twigpaw felt suddenly daunted. "Will we have to travel all night?"

"We'll find somewhere to rest tonight." Alderpaw ducked through the entrance. "And if we wake early, we'll be there before sunhigh tomorrow."

Twigpaw followed. Half excited, half anxious, she followed Alderpaw up the rise that led toward the lake. The ground squelched beneath her paws. Newleaf warmth was slowly softening the forest. Green buds clung in a haze to the trees, and beyond them stretched a pale blue sky.

"I hope we find her, Twigpaw." Alderpaw's mew was gentle as he waited for her to catch up.

She blinked at him and saw warmth in his eyes. *He really*

means it. The anger that had sat like ice in her belly for a half-moon began to melt. "So do I."

Twigpaw's paws ached as she followed Fernsong and Ivypool from the trees. Since yesterday they'd crossed hills and meadows, tracked rivers, and skirted Twoleg nests. They'd slept through the coldest part of the night in a sheltered hollow. Now, at last, they were close. She winced as bright sunlight bathed her face.

Alderpaw stopped beside her and nodded toward the bottom of the long slope in front of them. A wide Thunderpath cut through the valley, snaking along the bottom like a stinking river. "We found you down there."

"Near the Thunderpath?" Twigpaw blinked. She'd never seen a Thunderpath before—not that she could remember, anyway. The noise and smell made her shrink back. Monsters roared along it, the sun flashing on their shiny pelts.

"Yes." Alderpaw frowned.

Ivypool and Fernsong paced the top of the slope, their pelts twitching nervously. "Should we go down there?"

"Of course!" Twigpaw flattened her ears against the sound of the Thunderpath and padded forward. "I want to see the nest." She'd heard how Alderpaw and Needletail had plucked her and Violetpaw from a nest hidden in the shadows. Perhaps some trace of her mother's scent lingered there, a trace they could track.

Ivypool hesitated.

Fernsong looked at her. "We've come this far," he meowed.

"We might as well go all the way."

"But the monsters." Ivypool stared at them nervously. "What if they leave the path?"

Fernsong whisked his tail. "They never leave the path," he meowed. "Monsters may be big and loud, but they are bee-brained."

Twigpaw flicked her tail. Warriors weren't supposed to be scared. She hurried forward, her heart quickening as she scanned the slope for some sign of a nest.

Alderpaw hurried to catch up to her. "We have to go underneath it."

"Underneath?" Twigpaw looked at him, shocked.

"There's a tunnel. It's not very—" The sound of the monsters drowned his mew.

Twigpaw could feel their heat as they neared. She raised her voice. "Where's the entrance?"

Alderpaw scanned the edge of the Thunderpath, frowning for a moment. Then he nodded toward a small shadowy hollow where the side of the Thunderpath dropped into a ditch. "There it is."

Excitement surged in Twigpaw's belly. She broke into a run. Ignoring the acrid wind from the monsters, which tore through her fur, she leaped into the ditch. Pebbles lined it, jabbing her paws. She hurried along it until she reached the shadowy hollow. A huge monster screamed past. She screwed up her eyes as grit sprayed her.

Alderpaw landed beside her. Leaning over her, he shielded her as another monster streaked past.

Paw steps crunched behind them. Ivypool and Fernsong were hurrying along the ditch toward them.

"Is this it?" Ivypool blinked at the hole in the side of the ditch. Smooth, dark sticks crisscrossed it.

Twigpaw peered between them. The scent of dank stone and sour water filled her nose. She sniffed nervously, straining to see through the darkness. As her eyes grew accustomed to the gloom, she could see twigs littering the bottom of the tunnel. Water pooled there, gleaming as it stretched into the distance. Pale light showed at the far end. Something skittered there. A rat?

Alderpaw crouched close beside her. "Are you okay?"

"Yes." Twigpaw swallowed. She realized that her pelt was bristling as she struggled to remember this place. Was this really where her mother had left them? Sadness twisted her heart. What a terrible place for a nursery. She thought of the bramble den back at camp, where countless queens had raised litters in warmth and safety. What had driven her mother to this? She stuck her head between the sticks and squeezed through them.

Foul-smelling water soaked her paws. The skittering paw steps sounded again, echoing along the stone walls of the tunnel. Picking her way among the debris, Twigpaw sniffed. She tried desperately to smell some trace of her mother through the stench, but nothing remained except the scent of monsters and rats.

Alderpaw squeezed after her, while Fernsong and Ivypool

crouched at the opening, their eyes wide as they peered through.

"The nest must have been washed away," Alderpaw guessed.

Twigpaw blinked at him through the darkness. Sorrow tugged at her heart. "Why did she leave us here?"

"Surely she had no choice." Alderpaw's eyes glinted in the shadows.

Twigpaw glanced around. "I see why you took us now." Suddenly she understood that Alderpaw couldn't have left her and Violetpaw here. If cold or hunger hadn't killed them, rats might have. But hope still pricked her heart. "I wonder where she went."

Without waiting for a response, she pushed past Alderpaw and slid back through the crisscrossed sticks. Flattening her ears against the monsters' roars, she glanced along the ditch. She tried to imagine what her mother had been thinking when she left the nest. *She must have gone looking for food.* Had she gotten lost? Had she forgotten her way back to the tunnel? Twigpaw nosed past Ivypool and Fernsong and headed along the ditch. She climbed onto the slope and toward a swath of long grass. Mice would be there, right? Her mother might have followed this path, guessing the same.

"Twigpaw!" Ivypool called after her.

Twigpaw glanced back.

The silver-and-white she-cat was hurrying after her, Fernsong and Alderpaw on her heels. "Wait for us." She caught up to her, puffing.

"I have to figure out where my mother went," Twigpaw mewed urgently.

Ivypool gazed at her sympathetically. "But it was moons ago, Twigpaw. You can't hope to find a trace of her."

Fernsong stopped beside her. "The leaf-bare snows would have washed any scents away."

Twigpaw stared at them, panic opening like a whirlpool in her belly. White fur caught her eye. She glanced past them. A cat was on the Thunderpath! It sat, motionless, in the middle as monsters thundered past it. "Look!"

Ivypool snapped her head around, following her gaze.

"What in StarClan!" Fernsong's mouth gaped open as he saw the stranded cat.

"Why isn't she trying to run away?"

Twigpaw hardly heard Ivypool's gasp. She hared down the slope. "We have to save her!"

She tore toward the Thunderpath, desperation driving her on. What if that was her mother? She leaped over the ditch, her paws hitting the Thunderpath as a monster howled past, a tail-length from her nose. Her gaze flicked across the stretch of gray stone. If she could dodge the monsters, she could reach the cat and guide her to safety. Her thoughts whirled. Blood pounded in her ears. She glanced back and forth, searching for a gap to race through.

Suddenly claws gripped her pelt. Her paws scratched over the stone as someone jerked her backward. Teeth sank into her scruff as the ditch opened below her and Ivypool hauled her down into its shelter.

"What in StarClan do you think you're doing?" Ivypool stared at her.

Fernsong landed beside them, his pelt bushed. "Do you want to get yourself killed?"

"What about the cat?" Twigpaw wailed above the monsters.

She reared onto her hind legs, peering over the edge. A bright red monster, far bigger than the rest, pounded toward the helpless cat. "Run!" The shriek tore from Twigpaw's throat. But the cat didn't move. Horror shrilled though Twigpaw as the red monster hurtled over it. She stared in disbelief as the cat disappeared.

"They killed her." Her words caught in her throat.

Ivypool hopped onto the edge of the Thunderpath and stared across it. Twigpaw jumped up beside her, her heart pounding as she scanned the stone for blood. But there was none. All that was left of the cat was white fluff, tossed in the wake of the monsters like thistledown.

Twigpaw stared at it. "That cat wasn't real." Her murmur was swept away as another monster tore past.

Ivypool nudged her down into the ditch. "It must have been some Twoleg trick," she meowed as they landed with a crunch on the pebbles.

Fernsong blinked at them. "Let's get out of here."

Twigpaw stared at him, hardly hearing. She felt frozen. That could have been her mother. Realization swept over her like an icy wind. How could her mother still be alive? She'd had kits to feed. She'd had to hunt. She would have had to cross the Thunderpath countless times. She was probably hit, like that lifeless ball of fluff, by a monster. Why else would she have not returned to their nest? Certainty sat in Twigpaw's belly like a stone. Her mother was dead.

"Come on." Alderpaw's soft mew sounded in her ear. She felt his warm muzzle nudging her forward. Numbly, she let him guide her out of the ditch and back up the slope.

She was dimly aware of Ivypool and Fernsong moving beside them. Her heart ached with every paw step, and then shadow swallowed her. She blinked, realizing they were among the trees once more.

She met Alderpaw's gaze. "I know she's dead now," she murmured hoarsely. "Let's go home."

CHAPTER 17

Violetpaw rolled over in her nest, half waking as fur brushed the door of the den. Through a mist of sleep, she wondered if she'd slept late and Dawnpelt had come to wake her. She half opened her eyes and, seeing it was still dark, decided that she must have dreamed it.

She let sleep drag her into blackness once more.

"Violetpaw."

A hiss beside her ear made her leap to her paws. "Who is it?" Shock pulsed through her as she smelled unfamiliar scent. This wasn't a ShadowClan cat. She could make out the shape of a young she-cat in the gloom.

"It's me," the voice hissed again. "Twigpaw."

Violetpaw froze. "What in StarClan are you doing here?"

"I had to see you."

Violetpaw looked around, alarm spiking her pelt. Thank StarClan Whorlkit, Flowerkit, and Snakekit hadn't been made apprentices yet. She had the den to herself. "You can't be here!" she whispered anxiously. "If someone finds you, we'll both be in trouble." Her Clan was just starting to accept her. She couldn't be found with a ThunderClan cat. She nudged Twigpaw toward the entrance, her nose wrinkling as she smelled ThunderClan scent on her sister's pelt.

"But I have to talk to you!" Twigpaw dug her paws in.

Violetpaw shoved her harder. "Not *here*!" She bundled Twigpaw from the den and hurried toward the shadow at the edge of the clearing. "This way!" Her gaze darted nervously around the camp. Snores sounded from the dens. Nothing moved apart from Twigpaw, pale in the moonlight. "Hurry!" Violetpaw led the way quickly and quietly to the dirtplace tunnel.

She turned. Twigpaw wasn't following. Her sister stood beside the camp wall, her eyes flashing in the darkness. "What are you doing?" Violetpaw demanded. Did Twigpaw *want* to get into trouble?

"I went to find our mother," Twigpaw hissed. "She's gone. She's dead. You were right."

Violetpaw stared at her. "Of course she's dead. Why else would she have abandoned us? Did you come just to tell me that?"

She saw pain glitter in Twigpaw's eyes. Frustration welled in her chest. What did Twigpaw want from her? "I'm sorry! But don't expect me to be surprised." She glanced nervously around the camp. The stench of ThunderClan cat was bound to wake someone soon. "Look," she growled, "I know you're upset, but you've got to get out of here."

"Don't you care?" Twigpaw stared at her, still not moving.

Violetpaw's pelt spiked. Were her dumb sister's paws rooted to the ground? "What difference does it make?" she reasoned.

"We're not kits anymore. We're apprentices. We're going to be warriors. We have homes and Clanmates."

"But we don't have kin," Twigpaw whispered. "Only each other. We have to stick together."

Twigpaw was making even less sense. "You want to join ShadowClan?"

"Of course not," Twigpaw snapped. "I just wanted to see you. I wanted to know that you're here for me."

Violetpaw narrowed her eyes, bewildered. "Of course I'm *here* for you. But *you're* in ThunderClan."

Paw steps brushed the earth nearby. "Who's there?"

Violetpaw's heart leaped into her throat as she recognized her mentor's mew.

Dawnpelt was skirting the camp wall, making her way from the warriors' den. Her cream pelt glowed in the moonlight.

"Quick!" Violetpaw motioned Twigpaw toward the dirtplace tunnel with a flick of her nose. But Twigpaw was staring at Dawnpelt, her eyes wide with fear. Violetpaw pressed back a growl. Was Twigpaw totally mouse-brained? Did she really think she could stand arguing in another Clan's camp without being noticed?

Violetpaw hurried toward Dawnpelt. "Hi," she mewed, trying to sound innocent. Perhaps Dawnpelt hadn't noticed Twigpaw.

But Dawnpelt looked past her, her ears flattening. "I smell ThunderClan," she growled. "Who's there?" She pushed past Violetpaw and padded toward Twigpaw.

"It's just me." Twigpaw's mew sounded small. "I had to see

Violetpaw. It wasn't her fault. I sneaked in and woke her up. She was trying to get rid of me." She shot a reproachful look at Violetpaw.

Violetpaw rolled her eyes. What else did she expect? Her Clanmates had been right all along: ThunderClan cats *were* frog-brained.

Dawnpelt paced around Twigpaw, her hackles lifting. "Did you come to spy on us?"

"No!" Twigpaw sounded offended. "I told you. I had to speak with Violetpaw."

"What about?" Dawnpelt stopped a whisker from her nose and glared at her.

"About our mother," Twigpaw told her. "She's dead."

Dawnpelt flashed a look at Violetpaw. "Is that *news?*"

Violetpaw padded forward, sighing. "It's news to Twigpaw." She stopped beside her mentor, feeling a sudden wave of pity for her littermate. "She was hoping our mother was still alive."

Dawnpelt sniffed Twigpaw warily. "What changed your mind?"

"I went searching for her." Twigpaw sounded forlorn. "I saw the Thunderpath where she'd made our nest. When I saw the monsters, I knew one of them must have killed her."

"Give her a break," Violetpaw mewed softly. "She didn't mean any harm."

Dawnpelt narrowed her eyes thoughtfully. "She can't just come here every time she wants to tell you something."

"It was something important!" Twigpaw lifted her chin.

"*You* thought it was important," Dawnpelt growled. "That doesn't mean everyone agrees. You're as arrogant as your Clanmates."

Don't criticize my sister! Violetpaw glared at Dawnpelt. "Just let her go home. No one need ever know she came."

A voice sounded from the clearing. "It's a bit late for that."

Violetpaw stiffened. Tawnypelt was staring at them, the fur spiking along her spine. Scorchfur and Yarrowleaf padded sleepily from the warriors' den. Snowbird and Tigerheart followed. Kinkfur peeked from the elders' den. Whorlkit and Flowerkit tumbled out of the nursery, their eyes widening as they saw Twigpaw.

"Invasion!" Whorlkit dashed across the clearing, yowling loudly.

Grassheart darted from her den, panic lighting her eyes. She wrapped her tail around Flowerkit and stared at Whorlkit as he hared around the clearing, his fur fluffed out excitedly.

Violetpaw shrank inside her pelt as Crowfrost padded sleepily from his den.

"What's happened?" He blinked in the moonlight, his gaze widening as it reached Twigpaw.

Dawnpelt lifted her tail. "A ThunderClan apprentice has found her way into our camp."

"Twigpaw." Crowfrost looked relieved as he saw Twigpaw standing alone in the clearing. He put out a paw to stop Whorlkit as the young tom hared toward him. "Go back to your mother," he ordered. As Whorlkit trudged reluctantly toward Grassheart, Crowfrost turned back to Dawnpelt. "Is it just Twigpaw?"

Dawnpelt nodded. "She wanted to speak with Violetpaw."

Crowfrost's gaze flashed warily to Violetpaw. "Why?"

Dawnpelt shook her head wearily. "Some nonsense about their mother. Nothing important."

Violetpaw saw Twigpaw draw herself up indignantly. She guessed Twigpaw was about to tell the ShadowClan deputy that her mother was *very* important. "I'm sorry," Violetpaw butted in quickly. "It won't happen again. Twigpaw made a mistake, that's all."

Scorchfur let out a low growl. "How do we know Violetpaw didn't invite her here?" he snarled. "Perhaps she's planning to invite the rogues here next."

"That's not fair!" Violetpaw lashed her tail. She'd worked hard to be accepted. How could they distrust her so easily?

Twigpaw stepped forward, puffing out her chest. "My sister would never betray anyone like that!"

Scorchfur scowled at the ThunderClan apprentice. "And yet you're here."

Crowfrost padded heavily across the clearing. "Clearly, these young cats have made a mistake. But there's no harm done." He looked sternly at Twigpaw. "You can't come here to visit your sister, understand? If you need to speak to her, wait for a Gathering. You may be kin, but you live in different Clans now."

Twigpaw blinked at him anxiously. "But what if it's important?"

"Then speak to Bramblestar about it," he told her. "He'll know the proper way to behave."

Twigpaw hung her head. "I'm sorry," she murmured.

Twigpaw's sadness touched Violetpaw's heart. She blinked sympathetically at her sister. Twigpaw hadn't meant any harm.

Crowfrost beckoned to Snowbird and Tigerheart with a flick of his tail. "Take this apprentice back to her Clan. Speak to Bramblestar and make sure he doesn't let it happen again."

Tigerheart nodded and headed toward Twigpaw. Snowbird followed at his heels.

"Wait!" Scorchfur's growl made Violetpaw jump.

Scorchfur padded across the clearing and stopped beside Crowfrost. "We have sick cats in our Clan," he meowed. His gaze was sly.

Crowfrost narrowed his eyes. "Yes?"

"And we need WindClan to let us have the herb."

Violetpaw's paws prickled nervously as Scorchfur went on. What was the old fleabag up to?

"But WindClan won't help us." Scorchfur looked around his Clanmates meaningfully. "None of the Clans will help us. But perhaps we could use this opportunity to *persuade* them to help us."

Dawnpelt looked confused. "How?"

Crowfrost's gaze sharpened. "You mean we could persuade *ThunderClan* to help us." He glanced pointedly at Twigpaw.

Violetpaw stepped forward, anxiety rippling thorough her fur. "What are you talking about?" Was Twigpaw in danger?

Crowfrost must have seen her panic. "Don't worry. No one is going to hurt your sister. But she's going to stay with us a while so that we can reason with Bramblestar."

"A hostage?" Violetpaw gasped. "You're going to use her as a hostage?"

Tawnypelt shifted her paws. "It makes sense, Violetpaw. ThunderClan and WindClan have always had a special relationship. ThunderClan has saved WindClan more than once. If *we* can't persuade WindClan to give us the herb, perhaps ThunderClan can."

"Given the right incentive." Scorchfur's eyes lit with malice as he looked at Twigpaw.

Crowfrost flicked his tail. "I think Rowanstar would agree if he were well enough. No harm will come to Twigpaw while she's with us." He gazed around at his Clanmates. "She will be treated as one of our own. But she will remain here until WindClan gives us the lungwort."

Violetpaw stared at Twigpaw, her belly tightening as she saw fear flash in her sister's eyes. She hurried to stand beside her, letting her pelt brush Twigpaw's. "It's okay," she whispered. "I won't let anyone hurt you. If Crowfrost says you'll be safe, you'll be safe."

Twigpaw blinked at her gratefully.

"Take her to your den," Crowfrost told Violetpaw. He nodded to Tigerheart. "Stand guard outside until dawn; then Tawnypelt can take over. Twigpaw must not be left alone while she's with us." He gave a warning stare to his Clanmates. "She is our best chance of securing the cure for this sickness. I will send a patrol to speak with Bramblestar in the morning."

Ripples of agreement sounded around the clearing. Violetpaw nudged Twigpaw toward the apprentices' den. Twigpaw padded stiffly in front of her and ducked inside.

Violetpaw followed, relieved to be away from the eyes of her Clan. "I *said* you shouldn't have come here!" Irritation prickled through her pelt as she stared at her sister. She felt sorry for Twigpaw's predicament, but it *was* her own fault.

Twigpaw's shoulders drooped. "What will Bramblestar say when the ShadowClan patrol tells him what's happened? I'm such a mouse-brain."

She sounded so sad that Violetpaw's anger melted. She touched her nose to her sister's cheek. "You *are* a mouse-brain," she teased softly. "But your heart is in the right place."

Twigpaw leaned against her wearily.

"Come on." Violetpaw nosed her into her nest. "You must be tired. Let's get some rest."

Twigpaw climbed into the moss-lined bracken and sat down.

Violetpaw curled around her. "It'll be okay," she promised. "Perhaps this is the best way to get WindClan to help us. You're doing ShadowClan a favor. If WindClan gives us the herb and our Clanmates are cured, it will be because of you."

Twigpaw lifted her gaze toward Violetpaw's hopefully. "It will, won't it?"

Violetpaw purred. "I bet your Clanmates won't mind if

they know they're saving lives."

"Alderpaw will be pleased." Twigpaw slowly lay down beside her sister. "Jayfeather will think I'm a bee-brain, but he always has, so that won't be different."

"Get some sleep and try not to worry." Happiness suddenly infused Violetpaw's pelt. She'd never had the chance to comfort another cat before. It warmed her to feel Twigpaw relax beside her. She watched her sister yawn.

"I guess I am tired," Twigpaw mewed. "I haven't slept all night."

"Sleep now, then," Violetpaw urged gently. "Everything will look better in the morning. It always does."

As Twigpaw rested her nose on her paws, Violetpaw curled tighter around her. It felt good to share her nest with her littermate. Sensing the soft warmth of Twigpaw seeping through her pelt, she closed her eyes. Purring quietly, she let herself drift back into sleep.

CHAPTER 18

"Alderpaw!"

A hiss woke him. He jerked up his head, blinking in the
pale dawn light, which was seeping into the apprentices' den.
Leafpaw shifted in his nest but didn't wake. Larkpaw and
Honeypaw were still snoring.

Ivypool was standing beside his nest, her gaze sharp with
worry. "Have you seen Twigpaw?"

Alderpaw stared at her, still befuddled with sleep. "Not
since last night." He glanced toward her nest. It was empty.

"She was supposed to be coming on dawn patrol with me,"
Ivypool mewed urgently. "But I can't find her anywhere."

"Have you checked the dirtplace?" Alderpaw kept his voice
low.

"Of course I've checked the dirtplace." Ivypool looked
exasperated. "I've checked all around camp. She's not here."

Alderpaw was awake now. Panic flashed through his pelt.
Twigpaw had been quiet on the trek back from the Thunderpath. He knew she must be devastated. She'd been so full of
hope. But he'd thought returning to camp and sharing prey
with her Clanmates would make her feel better. He looked

269

anxiously at Ivypool. "You don't think she's done anything dumb, do you?"

Ivypool huffed impatiently. "What? Like thrown herself in the lake again?"

Alderpaw scrambled from his nest. "She's probably just gone for a walk, to think about things."

"She's an apprentice," Ivypool snapped. "She's meant to be on the dawn patrol. She can think about things later." Alderpaw could see beyond the exasperation in Ivypool's eyes. The silver-and-white she-cat looked worried. "She's too young to be out in the forest alone." Ivypool began to pace. "What if a fox attacks her? She's only learned basic battle moves. She may have been gone all night. I should have kept a closer eye on her. I knew she was upset after our journey."

"It's not your fault." Alderpaw tried to press back the guilt welling in his own chest. He shared a den with Twigpaw. He should have been more alert. He should have noticed her leave. He shook out his pelt. "Worrying won't find her." He headed out of the den. "Does Squirrelflight know she's missing? We should tell her before she's finished organizing the patrols. Someone needs to look for Twigpaw."

Bramblestar was on the Highledge. Below him, Thunder-Clan warriors milled around Squirrelflight.

Brackenfur, Whitewing, and Cinderheart were already padding toward the entrance, clearly heading out on patrol.

"There's a mouse nest near the birch trees." Whitewing's eyes shone eagerly.

"Let's stalk squirrels first," Cinderheart suggested. "They'll still be sleepy and slow."

Rosepetal trotted toward Alderpaw. "Is Larkpaw awake?"

"Not yet." Alderpaw didn't stop.

"Apprentices!" Rosepetal huffed. "They're always the last ones up."

As she headed away, grumbling, Alderpaw pushed between Blossomfall and Bumblestripe. He caught Squirrelflight's eye. She was putting together another patrol.

"Cherryfall and Sparkpelt, you can—"

Alderpaw cut in. "Twigpaw is missing."

Squirrelflight jerked her muzzle toward him. "For how long?"

Ivypool caught up. "We don't know. I think she slipped out of camp in the night."

"You've checked all the dens?" Squirrelflight looked up at Bramblestar, beckoning him with a flick of her tail.

"Yes," Ivypool reported. "And the dirtplace and around the outside of the camp. There's no sign of her."

"Any scents?" Squirrelflight moved aside as Bramblestar leaped down the rock tumble and stopped beside her.

"I can't trace any," Ivypool told her.

"What's happened?" Bramblestar frowned.

"Twigpaw is missing," Squirrelflight told him.

Blossomfall stepped forward. "It rained just before dawn. She must have left before then; the rain has washed away her scents."

Bramblestar's gaze flicked to the thorn barrier. "Has anyone come into camp?"

Alderpaw's heart quickened. Did he think someone had come and taken Twigpaw? *No.* He pushed the thought away. Twigpaw had been upset. "It's more likely she's gone because she wanted to go," he told Bramblestar. "She was pretty upset about not finding her mother."

Squirrelflight's tail twitched irritably. "She's probably wandering through the woods feeling sorry for herself."

Ivypool bristled. "And I suppose you never did that when you were young?"

Squirrelflight met the silver-and-white she-cat's eyes, her gaze softening. "I'm sorry. You're right. She must be upset." She nodded to Blossomfall. "Will you lead a patrol to search the lakeshore, Blossomfall? Lionblaze." She turned to the golden tom. "Take two warriors toward the ShadowClan border. Ivypool can take Stormcloud and Hollytuft to the WindClan border."

Alderpaw felt a glimmer of relief. It felt good to be doing something. "Can I join a search patrol?" he asked.

Bramblestar shook his head. "You'll be more use here, getting on with your medicine-cat duties."

As he spoke, Jayfeather padded from the medicine den. His blind gaze scanned the clearing. "Alderpaw?"

Alderpaw's shoulders drooped. Jayfeather must be able to read minds. There was no way the grumpy medicine cat would let him roam the forest when he could be counting poppy seeds or rolling herb bundles. He slouched toward the medicine den. "I'm coming."

"We'll find her!" Ivypool called after him.

He glanced back at her. "Thanks."

Jayfeather shooed him into the medicine den. "What's the fuss about? Has one of the apprentices forgotten how to hunt?"

Alderpaw ignored the medicine cat's sarcasm. He padded past Briarlight, sleeping in her nest, and reached into the medicine store. "Twigpaw is missing." He pulled out a jumble of leaves and began to sort them into piles.

Leafpool was dipping leaves into the water collecting beside the rocky wall of the den and laying them out to dry. "Missing?" She stopped and blinked at Alderpaw.

"Let's hope she hasn't gone swimming again," Jayfeather grunted.

Why did everyone keep saying that? Alderpaw turned on him, anger sparking though his pelt. "Don't you care about anyone except yourself?"

Jayfeather stiffened, his blue eyes fixing on Alderpaw as though he saw him as clearly as an ordinary cat would. "Of course I do!" he snapped. "I can sense every cat's feelings in the camp. From their mew, from the way they walk, from the swishing of their tails. The noise of it never stops. If I took every feeling seriously, I'd never be able to focus on my work."

Alderpaw stared at him, shocked. Was Jayfeather really that sensitive to his Clanmates' moods? "Did you know Twigpaw was upset?"

"She trudged into camp yesterday like there was a badger

sitting on her shoulders," Jayfeather replied. "Of course I knew she was upset. But I didn't know she was going to run off in the middle of the night. I can't read thoughts."

Alderpaw turned back to the herbs. "Do you think she'll be okay?"

"I'm sure she'll be back soon," Leafpool reassured him.

"Fresh air and exercise will do her good," Jayfeather mewed briskly. "She'll probably come home once she's caught some prey. Twigpaw's the sort of cat who can't enjoy fresh-kill unless she's sharing it with her Clanmates."

Alderpaw glanced at him, surprised. Had Jayfeather actually said something kind about Twigpaw?

Briarlight stretched in her nest, waking. She yawned. "Is the sun up already?"

"It'll be above the hollow." Jayfeather padded toward Alderpaw and swept the herbs away from him. "I'll sort these. You can help Briarlight with her exercises."

Relief shimmered through Alderpaw's pelt. Helping Briarlight would be more distracting than sorting dry old herbs.

"Is something wrong?" Briarlight frowned as he approached her nest.

Alderpaw didn't try to hide the worry that was making his fur twitch. "Twigpaw is missing." He hooked his paws under Briarlight's and helped her stretch them.

"For how long?" Briarlight rolled her shoulders to extend her stretch.

"She disappeared in the night."

"Are there any signs of a struggle?" Briarlight's eyes sparkled with worry.

"No." Alderpaw moved to her hind legs and grasped one between his paws. Pulling it, he worked the weak muscles. "There's no sign a fox has taken her. Or scents of strange cats. I think she decided to leave on her own."

Briarlight jerked her gaze toward him. "Do you think she's gone for good?"

"I don't know." Alderpaw didn't want to think about it. And yet Briarlight's words jabbed his heart. Could the realization that her mother was dead have made Twigpaw rethink her place in the Clan? Surely it would have made her understand that the Clan was her only family now. His belly tightened. *Or it made her think that she doesn't truly belong anywhere.* He grabbed Briarlight's other hind paw and began working it back and forth. As he felt the stiffness in her muscles ease, Jayfeather cleared his throat.

"She'd be a fool to turn her back on her Clan now," he grunted. "And Twigpaw is not a fool."

Alderpaw prickled with irritation. "You've called her one often enough." Perhaps if Jayfeather hadn't been so hostile toward Twigpaw, she'd have felt more at home in the Clan.

"I call everyone a fool." Jayfeather placed a fresh bundle of herbs with the others. "Twigpaw wouldn't have wanted me to tiptoe around her like she was a newborn kit."

How do you know? As Alderpaw moved Briarlight's leg back and forth, a yowl of surprise sounded from the clearing.

He dropped Briarlight's leg and pricked his ears.

Jayfeather was already tasting the air. "ShadowClan cats."

"In our camp?" Alderpaw's heart lurched. He headed for the entrance and barged through the brambles.

Foreboding gripped him as he saw Crowfrost, Scorchfur, and Tawnypelt in the clearing. Did they have news of Twigpaw?

Lionblaze, Dovewing, and Bumblestripe flanked them. Graystripe stood outside the elders' den with Millie, while Larkpaw, Leafpaw, and Honeypaw whispered excitedly beside the fresh-kill pile. Rosepetal and Molewhisker paced the edge of the camp, their hackles high.

Bramblestar was already hurrying to meet them. "Why have you come?" His eyes blazed as he stopped in front of Crowfrost.

Lionblaze stepped forward. "They were waiting beside the border. They approached us as soon as we neared. They want to speak with you."

Crowfrost dipped his head. "We thought you'd like to know that Twigpaw is safe."

Alderpaw darted forward. "Where is she? What happened to her?"

Crowfrost didn't take his eyes from the ThunderClan leader. "We found her in our camp in the middle of the night." His tail twitched. Alderpaw suspected that the ShadowClan deputy was enjoying this. "Does ThunderClan teach its apprentices to invade other Clans' camps while they're sleeping?"

Bramblestar narrowed his eyes. "Of course not," he snapped. "I don't know what she was doing there."

Alderpaw hurried to his father's side. "She probably went to see Violetpaw. She was upset about her mother. She probably just wanted to talk—"

Crowfrost spoke over him. "Do none of your apprentices have manners, Bramblestar? Or is it usual for ThunderClan warriors to take advice from the youngest cats in the Clan? Perhaps you should check the nursery in case a kit has anything to say." His mew dripped with sarcasm.

Graystripe snorted. "Don't lecture us on our younger cats," he growled. "At least they don't abandon their Clan to fight for rogues."

Crowfrost's hackles lifted. But he ignored the Thunder-Clan elder and went on. "Twigpaw will be staying with us for a while."

Shock pulsed through Alderpaw. Had Twigpaw decided she'd rather live in her sister's Clan?

Bramblestar flicked his tail. "I don't believe it. No Thunder-Clan cat would choose ShadowClan over ThunderClan." His gaze instantly flicked to Tawnypelt and flashed with guilt.

Tawnypelt blinked at him slowly. "Yes, they would." Bramblestar's sister had chosen to live in ShadowClan moons ago.

Bramblestar shifted his paws, clearly ruffled. "That was different. Our father was in ShadowClan."

Tawnypelt's pelt smoothed along her spine. "Twigpaw's sister is in ShadowClan," she reminded Bramblestar. "But that is not why she is staying with us."

Scorchfur curled his lip. "We're keeping her with us until you agree to help us."

Alderpaw glanced at his father, fear tightening his belly. *Twigpaw!*

Bramblestar bristled. "You're holding an apprentice hostage!" Outrage filled his mew.

"She's our guest," Crowfrost told him smoothly. "And she will be well cared for."

Bramblestar's gaze hardened. "What *help* do you want?"

Tawnypelt exchanged glances with Crowfrost. Alderpaw saw a question in her gaze. Crowfrost nodded, and Tawnypelt padded forward. "Our Clanmates are sick. Wasptail and Oakfur are fighting for their lives. Kinkfur has come down with the same sickness. Rowanstar is so ill that Puddleshine dares not leave his side. And now Yarrowleaf and Snakekit are sick."

"A kit?" Squirrelflight stepped from the shadow of the Highledge.

Tawnypelt blinked at her. "The sickness is spreading through the Clan, and we can't cure it."

"Not without lungwort." Crowfrost stared at Bramblestar. "But you heard Onestar. He won't let us gather it."

Bramblestar's gaze flitted away from the ShadowClan leader uneasily. "How do you think we can help?"

"Onestar is not angry with you," Crowfrost meowed. "ThunderClan has always had a closer relationship with WindClan than we have. You might be able to persuade him to share the herb."

Tawnypelt's eyes rounded pleadingly. "You could tell him you need it for your own Clan."

"I will not lie." Bramblestar lifted his chin.

Tawnypelt stared at him. "But will you help us?"

Squirrelflight padded to her mate's side. "We can't let elders and kits die, even if they are not from our Clan."

Bramblestar lowered his voice as he answered her. "What makes you think Onestar will let us have the herb?"

"Surely we must try?" Squirrelflight pressed.

Molewhisker crossed the clearing, his brown-and-cream pelt bristling. "Why should we help ShadowClan? They're holding one of our Clanmates hostage!"

Crowfrost narrowed his eyes ominously. "That's *exactly* why you should help us."

Alderpaw stared at the ShadowClan deputy in alarm. "Will you harm her if we don't help?"

Crowfrost curled his claws into the earth. "She will stay with us until we get the herb."

That's not an answer! Alderpaw wanted to rake the Shadow-Clan's deputy's muzzle. How dare he threaten an apprentice! A growl rumbled in his throat.

"Hush, Alderpaw." Bramblestar silenced him. He met Crowfrost's gaze grimly. "We will discuss your offer and send word when we have decided."

Crowfrost dipped his head. "Very well."

"Are you going to let them bully us?" Molewhisker stared in surprise at the ThunderClan leader.

Bramblestar ignored him. "You should go now," he told

Crowfrost. "Dovewing and Bumblestripe will escort you back to your border." He nodded to the two warriors.

A chill seeped beneath Alderpaw's pelt as he watched the ShadowClan patrol head for the entrance.

Molewhisker padded to Bramblestar, his tail lashing. "We should attack their camp and rescue Twigpaw."

Rosepetal joined her denmate, eyes glittering with rage. "It will be easy to get her back. Half their Clan is sick and the other half has joined the rogues!"

Graystripe crossed the clearing. "And if we get Twigpaw back, what then?" He stopped in front of Bramblestar. "ShadowClan will still need the herb."

Bramblestar blinked at the elder. "Is that our problem?"

Squirrelflight stiffened. "Of course it is! A sick kit is every Clan's problem."

Bramblestar's gaze darkened. "And what if WindClan still refuses to help when we ask?"

Alderpaw watched the warriors gaze at one another, worry worming in his belly. Twigpaw must be terrified. She was being held hostage in a strange Clan. "We have to do something!" he blurted.

Bramblestar gazed at him solemnly. "We will," he promised. "But first we have to decide what." He turned and leaped up the rock tumble, signaling with a flick of his tail for Squirrelflight to follow.

Breath quickening, Alderpaw watched them disappear into his den. What would they decide?

Alderpaw padded into camp, thyme dangling from his jaws. He'd been pleased to find it this early in newleaf, but his thoughts were still on Twigpaw. He'd spent all morning wondering if he could find an excuse to visit Puddleshine in the ShadowClan camp. He might get a chance to talk to her.

Bramblestar stood in the clearing, Squirrelflight, Jayfeather, and Leafpool beside him. He looked up as Alderpaw reached the edge. "You're back!" The ThunderClan leader sounded pleased.

Alderpaw headed toward them and laid the thyme on the ground. They were looking at him expectantly. Did they have news about Twigpaw? "What's happened?"

"We have a plan." Squirrelflight told him.

Alderpaw leaned closer, his heart quickening.

Bramblestar met his gaze. "I want you and Leafpool to travel to WindClan and speak with Kestrelflight and, if possible, Onestar."

Alderpaw's mouth dried. He glanced at Jayfeather. He could understand why Bramblestar would entrust the mission to medicine cats. It would seem less confrontational. But surely Jayfeather would be a better choice. "Why me?"

Jayfeather grunted. "Apparently, you're less likely to offend anyone." He sounded prickly, as though Bramblestar's decision had irritated him.

Leafpool blinked at Alderpaw. "This is a mission that requires tact and politeness." Her gaze flashed toward Jayfeather.

The blind medicine cat huffed. "I don't know why we don't

just travel to the moor and *take* some of this lungwort."

Bramblestar stared at him. "We want to settle this peacefully, not make it worse."

"Besides," Leafpool interjected gently, "we don't know what it looks like."

"It's dark green with gray spotted leaves. How hard can it be to find?" Jayfeather grunted.

"Bramblestar has made his decision," Leafpool meowed firmly. "Alderpaw is coming with me. We will speak with Kestrelflight and see if there's any chance of getting our paws on this herb."

Alderpaw shifted nervously. "What if WindClan is angry that we crossed their border?"

"That's why I'm sending medicine cats," Bramblestar explained. "Even Onestar can't object to that."

Squirrelflight's gaze darkened. "I wouldn't be so sure. He's been getting more unreasonable every moon."

"Will he listen to us?" Alderpaw asked nervously.

"I don't know," Leafpool confessed. "That's why we need to speak with Kestrelflight first. If we can get his support, perhaps he can persuade Onestar to see reason. We have to try. Not just for Twigpaw's sake, but for Puddleshine's sake too." Her eyes glittered with worry. Alderpaw suddenly realized that she must be concerned about her former apprentice coping alone with the illness that was raging through ShadowClan.

Alderpaw lifted his chin. "When do we leave?"

"The sooner the better," Bramblestar meowed. "I want

Twigpaw home as soon as possible."

"Can we leave now?" Alderpaw whipped his tail.

"I'm ready if you are," Leafpool told him.

Nodding good-bye to their Clanmates, they headed out of camp and followed the trail to the WindClan border, as though traveling to the Moonpool. But instead of following the stream uphill, they leaped over it and crossed onto the moor. Heather crowded around them as they climbed the slope. Gorse rose ahead, its yellow buds bright in the afternoon sunshine.

Alderpaw glanced around nervously. "Should we stop and wait for a WindClan patrol to find us?" he asked Leafpool.

"Let's find them." She ducked into a swath of heather.

Alderpaw followed. The peaty earth felt soft underpaw, and the prickly fronds scraped his pelt. As they emerged at the far side, Alderpaw glimpsed the pale gray-and-white pelt of Gorsetail across a stretch of grass. Emberfoot was with her.

Leafpool halted and lifted her tail. "Hi!" she called across the slope.

The WindClan cats jerked their heads around and stared, anger sparking in their gazes.

Alderpaw moved closer to Leafpool, his heart pounding.

"Don't worry," she whispered. "We're medicine cats, remember?"

She held her tail high as the WindClan cats bounded across the hillside to meet them.

Emberfoot reached them first, his pelt bristling. "What are you doing on our territory?"

Leafpool met his gaze, unflinching. "We need to speak with Kestrelflight."

Gorsetail caught up. "What about?"

Leafpool sniffed. "It's medicine-cat business."

Alderpaw blinked at her admiringly. Wasn't she afraid? Gorsetail's and Emberfoot's ears were flat. Mistrust glittered in their eyes.

Leafpool lifted her chin. "Are you going to take us to him or do we have to find our own way?"

Gorsetail's ears twitched. "We'll take you," she growled grudgingly.

Leafpool brushed against Alderpaw as the WindClan cats turned and headed up the slope. "Stick close to me," she whispered.

Alderpaw's heartbeat thundered in his ears as he followed Gorsetail and Emberfoot into the WindClan camp. Although it was tucked into a dip in the hillside, the wide, grassy clearing felt exposed. Wind whipped over the encircling gorse and tugged at Alderpaw's fur.

WindClan cats stared from the long grass rippling at the edges of the camp, surprise glinting in their eyes. Breezepelt strode toward them, chest puffed out indignantly. "What are they doing here?"

"They want to speak with Kestrelflight," Emberfoot told him.

Breezepelt narrowed his eyes.

Nearby, Nightcloud's gaze flicked nervously toward a den entrance at the head of the clearing. Was that Onestar's den?

Gorsetail stopped. She nodded toward an opening in the gorse wall of the camp. "He's in there."

Leafpool dipped her head and ducked inside.

Alderpaw followed her quickly, relieved to be out of the wind and hidden from the curious gazes of the WindClan cats.

Kestrelflight was tearing borage leaves into strips and rolling them into tight bundles. He looked up as Leafpool and Alderpaw entered. "What are you doing here?" Surprise edged his mew.

Leafpool whisked her tail. "One medicine cat may visit another, surely?"

Kestrelflight glanced nervously toward the den entrance. "Does Onestar know you're here?"

"He probably does by now," Leafpool answered matter-of-factly.

Alderpaw looked over his shoulder, half expecting the WindClan leader to barge angrily into the den.

"He won't be pleased," Kestrelflight warned.

"We're not ShadowClan cats," Leafpool pointed out.

"Onestar doesn't trust any cat these days," Kestrelflight lowered his voice. "Not even his own Clanmates."

Leafpool's eyes rounded. "Why not?"

Kestrelflight looked at his paws, not answering.

"Surely losing a life can't have affected him so badly?" Leafpool's ears twitched impatiently. "Have the rogues done something else to unsettle him?"

Kestrelflight bristled defensively. "Wasn't killing Furzepelt and bringing sickness to the lake enough?"

Leafpool stiffened. "Is the sickness here?"

"Not yet." Kestrelflight's eye shone with worry. "But what if it comes?"

Leafpool shrugged. "If Puddleshine's dream is correct, you have the cure growing right here on your territory."

Kestrelflight padded past her to the entrance and peered out as though checking to see if anyone was listening. "Is that why you're here?" he whispered, turning back to Leafpool.

Alderpaw's heart quickened. Would the WindClan medicine cat agree to help them?

Leafpool met his gaze. "ShadowClan is holding Twigpaw hostage. They won't return her to us until we persuade Onestar to give them lungwort."

Kestrelflight's eyes widened. "Did they kidnap her?"

Leafpool sighed. "The silly young cat decided to visit her sister in the middle of the night. They caught her in their camp."

Alderpaw puffed out his fur. "She was upset about her mother," he mewed defensively.

Leafpool blinked at him. "Let's not worry about why she did it. The situation is that she is ShadowClan's hostage until we give them lungwort."

Kestrelflight frowned. "I wish I could help."

"Then help!" Leafpool urged.

"I can't go against Onestar's wishes." Kestrelflight argued.

"Cats are dying!" Leafpool thrust her muzzle closer to his.

"You're a medicine cat. How can you sit back and let that happen?"

"Onestar blames ShadowClan for Furzepelt's death and for losing a life," Kestrelflight lowered his gaze.

"You know that's nonsense!" Leafpool exclaimed.

Alderpaw could hardly believe his ears. "The rogues killed Furzepelt, not ShadowClan!"

"But ShadowClan hasn't retaliated," Kestrelflight argued. "Onestar thinks ShadowClan is defending the rogues."

"What else can they do?" Leafpool's tail whisked over the sandy floor of the den. "So many of their apprentices left to live with the rogues. Would Onestar attack his own cats?"

"He would if they betrayed their Clan," Kestrelflight answered grimly.

Leafpool flexed her claws. "This isn't getting us anywhere. Why should we care who attacks who? We're medicine cats. Our duty is to heal. We need lungwort, not just to bring Twigpaw home, but because ShadowClan cats will die without it."

She was staring deep into Kestrelflight's eyes. Alderpaw willed the WindClan medicine cat to agree.

Kestrelflight's pelt prickled uneasily. "You will have to ask Onestar."

Dread dropped like a stone in Alderpaw's belly. He didn't want to face the angry WindClan leader. He'd seen him raging at the Gatherings. And if Onestar's own Clanmates feared him, how would he react to unwelcome visitors?

"Come on." Kestrelflight slipped past them and nosed his way out of the den.

Alderpaw blinked nervously at Leafpool. "Do you think we'll be able to persuade him?"

"We have to try." Leafpool followed Kestrelflight into the clearing.

Belly hollow with fear, Alderpaw hurried after her.

Onestar was pacing the head of the clearing as Alderpaw emerged from the gorse den. The WindClan leader's furious gaze tracked Leafpool and Kestrelflight as they approached him.

Alderpaw trailed behind, his paws as heavy as stone.

Onestar curled his lip, his gaze flashing toward Alderpaw. "You've brought Bramblestar's kit," he snarled. "Was Bramblestar too mouse-hearted to come himself?"

Outrage surged in Alderpaw's chest. "Nothing scares Bramblestar!"

"Perhaps he's just too proud." Scorn laced Onestar's mew. "I assume you've come to beg for lungwort. Has ShadowClan been whining in his ear?"

Alderpaw faced the WindClan leader, trying to stop his paws from shaking. "ShadowClan is holding Twigpaw hostage until you give them the lungwort."

He felt Leafpool's warning gaze flashed toward him. Had he said too much?

Onestar drew himself up, eyes blazing. "Typical Shadow-Clan. If they can't get what they want fairly, they resort to sly tricks."

"They've promised not to hurt her," Alderpaw blurted, hoping to smooth over his mistake. He didn't want to make Onestar hate ShadowClan more.

Onestar sniffed. "Then why are you worried? Let her stay with them. She has a sister in their Clan, doesn't she? Perhaps she'll enjoy living there."

Leafpool stepped forward. "Twigpaw is not the issue. We miss her, of course, but if Rowanstar has promised not to hurt her, he will not hurt her. He will keep his promise."

Onestar's ears flattened. "Just as he's kept his promise to the rogues."

Alderpaw's tail twitched with anger. Onestar was being so unreasonable! "He's promised nothing to the rogues!"

"Then why are they still here?" Onestar glared at Alderpaw.

Alderpaw groped desperately for a reply, but the WindClan leader went on.

"ShadowClan allowed them to stay near their territory." His mew rose to an angry yowl. "They paid for this foolishness by losing some of their best apprentices. When the so-called 'special' kit returned, they took her back in, and now she lives among them—giving who knows what information to her rogue friends! They are weak and foolish! They deserve no help. They don't even deserve the name of Clan cats. They are no more than rogues themselves. Let them keep Twigpaw. Let them die of sickness. I will not be tricked or bullied into helping them. They deserve everything StarClan has brought upon them."

Alderpaw stared into Onestar's wild, blazing eyes. Fear ran beneath his pelt like icy water. He glanced at Leafpool. She was staring in disbelief at the WindClan leader.

"Come on," she mewed loudly to Alderpaw. "We're wasting our time here." She shot a last pleading look at Kestrelflight, but the WindClan medicine cat had backed away, his gaze on his paws as though shame washed his pelt.

Leafpool turned and headed for the camp entrance.

Alderpaw hurried after her, his pelt burning as he felt Onestar's intense gaze on it. "What are we going to do?" he whispered desperately.

CHAPTER 19

Pale sunshine streamed through the gaps in the walls as Twigpaw paced the ShadowClan apprentices' den. The scent of pinesap was making her queasy. She missed the musty smell of the ThunderClan camp.

Violetpaw watched her, anxiously. "Won't you come outside?"

"I don't want to." Anxiety prickled in Twigpaw's belly. This wasn't her Clan. She didn't know any of the cats. And she felt foolish for having come here and gotten caught. "I just want to stay inside." She'd spent yesterday hiding in the apprentices' den while Violetpaw went training with Dawnpelt. She had been relieved when Violetpaw had returned, although the ShadowClan cats had kept her well-fed. Fresh-kill had been left at the entrance of the den, as well as moss soaked with water to quench her thirst. But Birchpaw and Lionpaw, who shared the den, had only come there to sleep and had hardly acknowledged her presence. She'd been relieved when they'd left their nest this morning and headed into the clearing.

Violetpaw tipped her head impatiently. "You can't stay here forever."

Twigpaw stiffened. "I hope I won't be here forever!"

Violetpaw ignored her. "Dawnpelt said I was excused from training today so I could spend time with you. She's worried about you. She says young cats need exercise. It's newleaf, and the forest is filled with prey-scent."

"All I can smell is pinesap," Twigpaw growled. "Besides, Crowfrost would never let me roam the forest. I could hear warriors outside the den all last night. He's keeping me under guard."

Violetpaw blinked at her apologetically. "I know it's not nice for you to be held here. But let's make the best of it."

Paw steps pattered outside. "Grassheart says ThunderClan cats can climb trees," Whorlkit mewed.

"She told *me* that if kits misbehave, they throw them in the lake." There was a tremor in Flowerkit's mew.

Whorlkit snorted. "Don't be frog-brained! You're too old to believe nursery tales. We're going to be apprentices in less than a moon."

"What if she smells funny?" Flowerkit fretted.

"Hold your breath." The entrance rustled as Whorlkit barged in. "We've come to see you." He blinked at Twigpaw. "Is that okay?"

"I guess." Twigpaw stared uncertainly at the gray-and-white tom.

A pair of eyes blinked in the gap behind him. "Is she there?" Flowerkit squeaked.

"Of course she's here!" Whorlkit rolled his eyes. "Where else would she be?"

A silver she-kit crept in. Her eyes widened as she saw Twig-paw. "You look like a normal cat today!"

"What did you *think* I'd look like?" She glared at Flowerkit.

Flowerkit looked thoughtful. "Last night, in the moon-light, you looked like a fox."

Violetpaw's whiskers twitched. "Your head is full of fluff!"

"It's not!" Flowerkit retorted. "Scorchfur and Ratscar say all ThunderClan cats are just foxes in cat pelts."

Twigpaw flicked her tail irritably. "Scorchfur and Ratscar are a pair of old gossips."

Flowerkit spluttered with amusement. "Can I tell them you said that?"

"No!" Alarm spiked through Twigpaw's pelt.

Whorlkit was still staring at her. "Is it true that you're spe-cial?"

Twigpaw exchanged glances with her sister. She hadn't thought about being special for ages. She'd been too busy try-ing to be the best Clan cat she could be.

When Twigpaw didn't answer, Violetpaw answered for her. "Only StarClan knows if we're special or not, and they're not telling." She trotted to the den entrance and peeked out. "What are you doing here, anyway?"

"We're bored," Whorlkit complained.

"Grassheart spends all her time with Snakekit," Flowerkit mewed sadly.

"She's sick," Whorlkit told Twigpaw.

Flowerkit shifted her paws. "I hope she gets better in time for our naming ceremony," she whimpered.

Twigpaw felt a sudden wave of sympathy for the two kits. "Would you like us to play with you?" she suggested. "We could teach you some hunting moves."

Whorlkit's eyes brightened. "That'd be great."

Twigpaw crouched, starting to show him a stalking position, but Whorlkit blinked at her.

"There's not enough space here. We'll have to go outside," he mewed.

"Outside?" Twigpaw stared at him, her heart lurching.

"Good idea!" Violetpaw nudged her toward the entrance. "Come on, Twigpaw. Let's go outside."

Reluctantly, Twigpaw let Violetpaw nose her out of the den. Flowerkit and Whorlkit pushed past them and raced into the clearing.

Twigpaw hesitated at the edge. Early morning light broke through the thick canopy, splashing puddles of sunshine over the camp.

Tawnypelt stood at the head of the clearing. ShadowClan warriors paced restlessly around her while Tigerheart listened intently a few tail-lengths away. "Snowbird and Pinenose have both come down with the sickness," Tawnypelt told them. "There's not enough room in the medicine den, so Crowfrost is helping to move them all to the warriors' den."

"We've noticed," Stonewing grumbled.

Tawnypelt ignored him. "Until they're well, you can make your nests in the elders' den."

"Oh, great." Strikestone rolled his eyes. "We'll never be able to sleep! Ratscar snores like a badger."

"You'll have to try." Tawnypelt sounded impatient. "You'll each have to make two hunting trips today. Tigerheart, can you mentor Lionpaw until Snowbird is well again?"

Tigerheart nodded. "I'll take her hunting with me."

"Good." Tawnypelt turned to Scorchfur. "Can you concentrate your training on hunting too? I want the fresh-kill pile well-stocked." She glanced at the shriveled mouse and limp thrush left over from yesterday's hunt, then blinked at Dawnpelt. "Will you take Violetpaw hunting?"

"I promised that she could spend the morning with her sister," Dawnpelt told her.

Tawnypelt's gaze flitted toward Twigpaw. She looked relieved. "Our visitor is finally out of her den." Twigpaw blinked with surprise as Tawnypelt dipped her head in greeting. "Help yourself to prey if you're hungry," she called across the clearing.

"Th-thank you." Twigpaw stammered.

Violetpaw brushed against her. "I told you. ShadowClan isn't as bad as ThunderClan says."

As she spoke, Mistcloud and Rippletail barged past her, knocking the kits out of the way as they swaggered across the clearing.

"Hey!" Whorlkit shouted after them indignantly. "Watch out!"

The warriors ignored him.

"You're late for the morning meeting," Tawnypelt snapped.

"So?" Rippletail flicked his tail.

"I need every cat out hunting today," Tawnypelt told him.

Mistcloud puffed out her pelt. "But we spent yesterday hunting. Can't we patrol borders instead?"

"Borders will have to wait," Tawnypelt told her. "We have too many sick cats to worry about."

Rippletail stopped in front of her and rubbed his nose with a paw. "Sick cats don't eat. Why do we need to catch so much prey?"

Mistcloud mewed in agreement. "We only need to catch half as much prey as—"

A yelp cut her short. At the fresh-kill pile, Birchpaw and Lionpaw were tugging the thrush between them, snarling at each other, their jaws tightly clamped into the bird's flesh.

Tawnypelt growled at them. "Can't you just share it?"

Birchpaw threw her a look of disdain and yanked the thrush from his denmate.

Lionpaw glared at him as he carried the bird away.

Twigpaw leaned closer to her sister. "In ThunderClan, apprentices aren't allowed to eat until they've caught prey for their Clan."

Violetpaw shrugged. "It's just leftovers from last night."

Twigpaw's pelt pricked with surprise. She knew ShadowClan wasn't ThunderClan, but she'd assumed they all followed the same warrior code.

As Twigpaw wondered how two Clans could be so different, Lionpaw hissed at her brother. With a growl she raced after him and leaped onto his back. Knocking the thrush from his paws, she began pummeling him with her hind legs.

"Her claws are unsheathed!" Twigpaw stared in shock as

she saw Birchpaw's fur fly. He struggled to free himself, yowling in pain. Twigpaw turned to the older cats, waiting for one to race across the clearing and separate the fighting cats.

Mistcloud sat down and began washing her belly.

Tawnypelt went on with her orders as though nothing was happening. "Tigerheart." She nodded to the dark tabby tom. "Hunt around the ditches. There are bound to be mouse nests around there."

Twigpaw couldn't stay quiet. "Aren't you going to stop them?"

Birchpaw had twisted free and turned on his sister. Slamming his paws onto her shoulders, he held her chin to the earth while he raked his claws along her flank. She wailed with pain.

Scorchfur met Twigpaw's gaze coolly. "They started it," he meowed. "Let them finish it."

"But they might hurt each other!" Twigpaw gasped.

Mistcloud looked up. "If they do, it's their own fault."

Twigpaw raced toward the fighting cats. "Stop!" Hooking her claws into Birchpaw's scruff, she hauled him away from his sister.

His eyes flashed with rage. He swung out at her and raked her muzzle. Surprised, she staggered, pain scorching through her. Lionpaw jumped to her paws and swiped at her, hissing. Alarm spiraled into Twigpaw's chest as both apprentices turned on her. She batted them away, trying not to hurt them.

"Stop!" Tawnypelt's yowl cut across the clearing. The she-cat bounded toward them, barging into the fight and pushing the ShadowClan apprentices away. "Crowfrost promised that she wouldn't be hurt."

As Twigpaw backed away, Violetpaw rushed to her side. "You should have just let them fight it out."

Twigpaw stared at her sister, trembling. "Is this *normal?*"

Violetpaw met her gaze, puzzled. "Isn't ThunderClan like this?"

"No!" Twigpaw could hardly believe her ears. She glanced around the clearing at the unruffled warriors and the scratched and bleeding apprentices. None of them seemed shocked by what had happened. Whorlkit and Flowerkit were watching, their eyes bright with excitement.

"Why did you stop them?" Whorlkit hurried to Twigpaw's side.

Flowerkit joined him. "Now we won't know who would have won."

Twigpaw felt sick. *I want to go home!* She suddenly felt a surge of anxiety for Violetpaw. *She grew up here. Is she like this too? No wonder she joined the rogues!* As her thoughts swirled, the entrance to the warriors' den trembled and Puddleshine stumbled out.

The medicine cat's eyes were clouded with exhaustion.

"How are the sick cats?" Tawnypelt padded toward him.

"I'm doing the best I can," Puddleshine glanced back at the den. "I need more tansy and borage."

"Lionpaw and Birchpaw can gather some for you," Tawnypelt told him.

Lionpaw huffed. "Do we have to? Herb gathering is boring."

She seemed unruffled by her fight.

"Yes, you do," Tawnypelt told her sternly. "Dawnpelt can go with you to make sure you don't get distracted."

"We'll go when we've finished eating," Lionpaw told the tortoiseshell. She leaned down and took a bite from the thrush, which was covered in dirt from the fight.

Birchpaw rubbed a streak of blood from his muzzle and settled beside her to eat.

Twigpaw stared at them. Why had they fought over the thrush if they were going to share it anyway? And how could they eat when their sick Clanmates needed herbs? "I can help." She hurried to Puddleshine's side. "I used to help Alderpaw. I know what borage and tansy look like. I can gather some now if you like."

"No." Tawnypelt's gaze flashed toward her. "You're not to leave camp."

"Then let me do something else to help." Twigpaw looked pleadingly at Puddleshine. His fur was dull and his ribs were showing through his pelt. He clearly hadn't slept or eaten properly in days. "I'll fetch you some food." Twigpaw hurried to the fresh-kill pile and grabbed the shriveled mouse. She carried it back to Puddleshine and dropped it at his paws. "Eat this. I'll check on the sick cats."

Puddleshine stared at her gratefully. "Oakfur needs water."

"I can do that," Twigpaw told him.

"Kinkfur too." He crouched stiffly and began gnawing at the mouse. "There's moss at the back of the warriors' den, but it needs soaking."

Twigpaw beckoned Violetpaw with a jerk of her nose. "Come and help."

Tawnypelt was staring at her in surprise. "This is very kind of you."

Twigpaw blinked at her. "Since I have to stay here, I might as well be useful." Flicking her tail, she padded into the warriors' den.

A sour stench hit her as she padded into the gloom.

Violetpaw followed her in. "Ewww."

"Ignore the smell." Twigpaw had spent enough time in ThunderClan's medicine den to recognize the scent of sickness. But she'd never smelled it this strongly before. She crouched beside the nest closest to the entrance. An old tom lay as limp as prey, his fur matted, on the stinking moss. "Who's this?" Twigpaw whispered to Violetpaw.

"It's Oakfur," Violetpaw told her. "One of our elders." She moved on to the next nest. "This is Kinkfur." A ragged she-cat lolled restlessly in a filthy nest.

A few nests away, a black she-cat lifted her head weakly. "My throat hurts."

Violetpaw blinked at her. "We're going to fetch you water, Pinenose. It'll help." She padded between other nests, where cats lay moaning, and stopped beside a small nest near the back to the den. A young queen crouched beside it, gazing anxiously at a she-kit squirming on the damp bracken.

"Hi, Grassheart," Violetpaw mewed softly. "How's Snakekit?"

Grassheart blinked at her, her eyes glittering. "I've never seen her this ill."

Snakekit moaned, and Grassheart ran a soothing paw along her flank.

Twigpaw shivered. These cats were *really* sick! Suddenly she understood the desperation that had driven Crowfrost to keep her here. ShadowClan needed lungwort badly. Anger surged beneath her pelt. If only Onestar could see the suffering he was causing by his stubbornness!

She faced Violetpaw. "Where do you soak moss?"

"There's a puddle beside the elders' den," Violetpaw told her.

"Good." Padding to the back of the den, Twigpaw spotted the pile of moss Puddleshine had mentioned. She grabbed a thick wad between her jaws and headed out of the den.

Violetpaw followed, carrying more. They passed Birchpaw and Lionpaw as they bounded out of camp behind Scorchfur and Tigerheart. Violetpaw slipped ahead and led Twigpaw to the puddle. The water was clear, pooled in a hollow lined with bracken. Twigpaw dropped her moss in. "One we've made sure every cat has water, we can gather fresh bedding." She glanced around the camp, relieved to see bracken crowding one corner.

Violetpaw blinked at her. "How do you know what to do?" She sounded impressed.

"I used to hang out in the medicine den," Twigpaw explained. "I guess I learned a lot." She leaned down and plucked the dripping moss from the puddle, then hurried back toward the den.

As Violetpaw carried moss to Pinenose's nest, Twigpaw crouched beside Oakfur. The old tom's eyes were closed. She nosed the wet moss closer to his cheek. "Can you lap just a little?" she coaxed.

Oakfur grunted, not opening his eyes. Lifting the moss between her teeth, Twigpaw held it to the tom's lips, pressing it gently so that water ran into his mouth. Oakfur twitched and coughed, and then he swallowed.

Violetpaw looked at her from Pinenose's nest. "She won't drink." Worry darkened her gaze.

"It hurts to swallow," the black she-cat rasped.

"Let me try." Twigpaw crossed the den and nudged Violet-paw aside. "Can you fetch water for Kinkfur and the others, please?"

Violetpaw nodded quickly and headed for the entrance, pausing only to snatch the moss from Oakfur's nest.

"I know it hurts, but you need to drink." Twigpaw held the dripping moss against the queen's mouth. Pinenose's eyes flickered open as the moisture dripped along her jaws. She parted her lips and swallowed, coughing. Then she drew back, her eyes opening fully. She stared at Twigpaw. "Violetpaw?" she mewed hazily. "Is that you?"

"I'm her sister," Twigpaw told her gently.

"You're Lionpaw? My kit?" Pinenose looked confused. Her gaze darted anxiously around the clearing. "Where are Pud-dleshine and Birchpaw? I want you all near me."

"Puddleshine is eating," Twigpaw told her gently.

"What about Birchpaw?" Panic flashed in the queen's glassy gaze.

"Is he your kit too?"

"Yes." Pinenose pushed herself weakly to her paws. "Is he okay? He's not sick, is he?"

"He's fine," Twigpaw soothed, easing Pinenose back onto her belly.

"What about you, Lionpaw?" Pinenose blinked at her. "Are *you* sick?"

"No." Twigpaw wondered whether to tell Pinenose that she wasn't Lionpaw. But Pinenose was staring at her so desperately that she hesitated. She couldn't remember anyone looking at her like that before.

"I want Birchpaw," Pinenose rasped. "I want him here. With you and Puddleshine."

"He's out training."

"But I need him." Desperation filled Pinenose's eyes.

"I'm here." Twigpaw's throat tightened. Did Lionpaw realize how much her mother loved her?

"Pinenose?" Puddleshine padded into the den.

Pinenose's gaze softened, as though just seeing another of her kits eased her pain.

Twigpaw moved aside as Pinenose crouched in her place. "We're giving all the cats water," she told him. "Then we'll fetch fresh bracken for their nests."

Puddleshine blinked at her wearily. "They need more herbs."

"Have you got any?" Twigpaw scanned the den.

Puddleshine nodded to a pile of shredded leaves. "There's tansy, coltsfoot, and borage." Tiredness slurred his words. "I need to chew it into a pulp so that they can swallow it."

"I can do that," Twigpaw told him.

Puddleshine stared at her. "You're not a medicine cat."

"I used to help Jayfeather and Alderpaw." Twigpaw padded to the herbs. "You need to rest. You'll be no help to your Clanmates if you collapse from exhaustion."

Puddleshine's tail drooped. "I might close my eyes for a moment." He rested his chin on his mother's nest. Pinenose relaxed beside him, her wheezing breath ruffling his fur.

As Puddleshine's eyes slowly closed and his breath deepened into sleep, Twigpaw crouched over the herb pile. She took a mouthful as she'd seen Alderpaw do and began chewing the leaves to a pulp.

Violetpaw trotted into the den, dripping moss dangling from her jaws.

Twigpaw nodded toward the sleeping medicine cat, hoping Violetpaw wouldn't wake him. Violetpaw blinked at Puddleshine, her gaze softening as she saw him. She placed the wet moss beside Oakfur and hurried to Twigpaw's side. "What are you doing?" she whispered.

"I'm giving herbs to the sick cats while Puddleshine rests." Twigpaw padded to Oakfur's nest and spat pulp onto her paw. As she smeared it around the sick tom's lips, she felt his rough tongue graze her pad. He was licking the herbs. "When you've given the others water, can you gather bracken so that we can make them clean nests?"

"Of course." Violetpaw headed out of the den.

Twigpaw watched her leave, relief washing her pelt. Violetpaw did want to help her Clanmates. Growing up here hadn't made her like Birchpaw and Lionpaw. In fact, she hardly seemed like a ShadowClan cat at all.

Stiff with tiredness, Twigpaw curled into the nest beside Violetpaw. Birchpaw and Lionpaw had fallen asleep ages ago, their bellies full of the prey the sick cats couldn't eat. Her sister sat up, washing.

"I'm too tired to wash," Twigpaw whispered.

"I want to get the stench of herbs out of my fur," Violetpaw answered between licks.

Twigpaw had already cleaned the pulp from her paws, although the taste lingered in her mouth despite the two shrews she'd gulped down at sunset. Worry still wormed in her belly. Oakfur was so sick. Snakekit too. And the others were fighting hard against the illness. What if one of them died during the night?

At least Puddleshine was rested now. He'd slept the day away while she and Violetpaw had tended to the sick cats. It was Pinenose who had finally roused him. She'd woken, her eyes a little brighter, and broken into a purr when she'd found him still sleeping beside her nest.

A thorn seemed to jab Twigpaw's heart as she remembered

the fondness in the she-cat's gaze. "Do you think our mother loved us as much as Pinenose loves Puddleshine, Birchpaw, and Lionpaw?"

Violetpaw stopped washing. "I've never thought about it."

Twigpaw frowned. "Why not?" She wondered why Violetpaw seemed so detached.

Violetpaw lowered the paw she'd been licking. "I suppose I just assumed that since she was gone, there was no point thinking about her."

"But didn't you miss her?"

"I had Pinenose."

"But Pinenose didn't ask for you today," Twigpaw pointed out softly. "She only asked for her *own* kits." She searched Violetpaw's gaze for a reaction, but Violetpaw seemed unmoved. Pity swamped her. When had Violetpaw stopped expecting to be loved?

"I guess I decided that Pinenose was better than nothing," Violetpaw mewed simply.

Twigpaw gazed wistfully into space. She'd had Lilyheart, at least. The ThunderClan queen had been fond of her, and kind. But Twigpaw had always been aware that they weren't real kin. "Just imagine if there was a cat who loved us as much as Pinenose loves *her* kits."

"Oh, Twigpaw." Sympathy flooded Violetpaw's gaze. "You always want to be close to some cat."

"Don't you?" Twigpaw frowned, puzzled.

"I guess I just didn't think it was possible." She touched her muzzle to Twigpaw's cheek. "But I'm glad I've got a sister."

Affection swelled Twigpaw's heart. "So am I." She met Violetpaw's gaze. "I guess being here has given us a chance to get to know each other again." She searched Violetpaw's gaze, hoping that her sister felt the same way.

Violetpaw's eyes clouded. She purred and snuggled down beside Twigpaw. "Let's never forget we have each other. We're kin, and that's stronger than being Clanmates or denmates. We'll always be close. Nothing will ever change that."

"Do you promise?" Anxiety pricked Twigpaw's belly.

"I promise."

CHAPTER 20

❧

Two sunups later, Violetpaw opened her eyes and blinked through the darkness. Voices in the clearing had woken her. Her breath warmed her paws as she listened.

A growl made her stiffen.

She jerked up her head as a snarl rang through the night air. "Twigpaw! Wake up!" She prodded Twigpaw sharply.

Twigpaw lifted her muzzle, her eyes hardly opening. "What?" Her mew was slurred with sleep.

"Listen!" Violetpaw strained her ears.

"You can't come in here!" Scorchfur's growl sounded beyond the den walls.

"We have come to take our Clanmate home!" Bramblestar's mew cut across the growling of ShadowClan warriors.

Twigpaw opened her eyes wide. "Bramblestar!"

Birchpaw and Lionpaw were stirring in their nests.

"What's all that noise?" Birchpaw sounded half-asleep.

Violetpaw's heart lurched. "Quick!" She nosed Twigpaw from the nest. "Let's hide."

Twigpaw dug her paws deep into the bracken, refusing to be pushed. "Hide? Why? He's come to rescue me."

Violetpaw hardly heard her. "We can tunnel under the brambles at the back of the den and slip out past the dirtplace. If we run fast, we can hide so deep in the forest they'll never be able to find us!"

Twigpaw stared at her. "But I want to be found."

Violetpaw froze. "What?" She didn't understand. Twigpaw had said she wanted to be close to her. They'd talked about being sisters—how that was more important than anything. *You made me trust you!* "You promised we'd always be close."

Squirrelflight's growl sounded outside. "We're staying until you give her back."

"Get out!" Dawnpelt's hiss was hard with rage.

"Give us Twigpaw!"

Lionblaze! Violetpaw recognized the ThunderClan tom's mew with a start. ThunderClan had brought its strongest warriors. Panic swirled in her mind. "Come hide with me!" she pleaded.

Twigpaw stared at her, her eyes glittering with guilt. "I can't," she mewed. "I have to go back to my Clan."

Birchpaw jerked his head. He glared at Twigpaw. "You're not going anywhere!" With a hiss, he leaped from his nest and slammed into her.

"No!" Shock jolted through Violetpaw. "Don't hurt her!"

The pale brown tom had knocked Twigpaw to the ground and was holding her there.

Violetpaw sank her teeth into his scruff and, with a grunt, dragged him off.

Twigpaw scrambled free and shot from the den.

Birchpaw turned on Violetpaw, snarling.

Lionpaw jumped from her nest. "What's happening?"

"ThunderClan has come to take Twigpaw!" Before her denmates could move, Violetpaw pushed past them and followed Twigpaw out of the den.

ThunderClan cats bunched near the entrance, pelts bristling. Violetpaw recognized Bramblestar, Squirrelflight, Lionblaze, Cloudtail, and Blossomfall among them. Their eyes flashed in the moonlight, glancing at her briefly before their gaze flicked toward the other ShadowClan cats. Did they remember her? She'd been part of their Clan once.

"Twigpaw!" Violetpaw's heart twisted in her chest as she saw her sister race toward them.

Rippletail lunged at her, but Twigpaw escaped his grasp and zigzagged between Sparrowtail and Mistcloud. She ducked past Scorchfur and Spikefur, who were facing the Thunder-Clan invaders, their backs arched.

Violetpaw stared in dismay as Twigpaw flung herself against Squirrelflight and nestled beside her. "You can't leave!" she wailed.

Twigpaw stared at her from among her Clanmates. "I can't stay."

Why not? Fury surged through Violetpaw. Why had Twigpaw begged to stay close if she was just going to leave? She padded forward, her pelt bristling as Scorchfur lined up beside Mistcloud, Sparrowtail, and Rippletail. Lionpaw and Birchpaw charged to join them.

Tigerheart strode from the shadows and faced the

ThunderClan cats. "Do you really think we're going to let you take her without a fight?"

Bramblestar's eyes flashed with scorn. "The fight wouldn't last long."

Violetpaw shuddered. He was right. With so many ShadowClan cats sick, and so many of the Clan's young cats with the rogues, ShadowClan's warriors were outnumbered in their own camp.

"Let them go." Crowfrost's mew was hoarse as he padded heavily from his den. He pushed between his Clanmates and faced Bramblestar. "You can take her."

Scorchfur stared at the ShadowClan deputy, his pelt spiking. "What are you doing?"

"We've held ThunderClan's apprentice long enough," Crowfrost growled. "It seemed like a good plan at the start, but now it feels wrong. There is sickness here. We should return her before she gets ill, too. Why should Twigpaw suffer for us?"

"She wasn't suffering!" Violetpaw cried out desperately.

Scorchfur ignored her. He snarled at Crowfrost. "How else are we going to get the lungwort?"

Spikefur stood beside his denmate. "Our Clanmates are dying!"

"ThunderClan knows that," Crowfrost told the dark brown tom. "WindClan knows that too. If they want to let innocent cats die, then it is for StarClan to judge them, not us. ShadowClan cats are *true* warriors." He turned his accusing gaze on Bramblestar.

Bramblestar's eyes rounded guiltily. "We tried," he meowed. "We sent Leafpool and Alderpaw to plead with Onestar. But Onestar is determined to make you suffer."

Crowfrost curled his lip. "And you're going to let him."

Uncertainty darkened Bramblestar's gaze. He glanced at Squirrelflight. His warriors shifted around him uneasily. "Let's go," he meowed at last.

Violetpaw stared helplessly at Twigpaw. *We treated you kindly! You helped Puddleshine!* Surely her sister must feel some connection with ShadowClan now? "Why can't you stay?" she mewed plaintively.

Twigpaw looked confused. "ThunderClan is my *Clan*."

But I'm your kin. Violetpaw's heart dropped like a stone as the ThunderClan cats began to back through the tunnel. She watched Twigpaw as shadow swallowed her. *She's gone.*

Tigerheart turned on Crowfrost, his eyes blazing. "How could you?"

Spikefur lashed his tail. "You've let our only hope disappear."

Crowfrost stared at them, his gaze clouded. "I couldn't risk a young cat's life any longer. What if she got sick here and died?"

"It would have made ThunderClan understand our suffering," Spikefur snapped.

"We should have fought to keep her!" Scorchfur faced him, ears flat.

"A battle wouldn't have stopped them." Crowfrost sounded weary. "And even if we'd managed to keep Twigpaw, do you really think ThunderClan could make Onestar change his mind?"

Spikefur curled his lip. "You're a coward!" he snarled.

Scorchfur puffed out his chest. "Rowanstar would never have let her go."

"Rowanstar may not live through the sickness," Crowfrost reminded him gravely.

"He has nine lives," Scorchfur retorted.

"And he's losing them one by one."

Violetpaw's gasped at Crowfrost's words. Was it true? Were their leader's lives really slipping away?

Spikefur thrust his muzzle close to Crowfrost. "Let's hope he doesn't die," he hissed. "Because you're no leader."

Dawnpelt hurried to Crowfrost's side. "That's not true."

Tawnypelt joined her. "Crowfrost made the right decision. Twigpaw was spending too much time with the sick cats. She might have become ill too. What would StarClan think if she died because of us? And Onestar is determined to make us suffer. You *know* that. Holding Twigpaw here wasn't going to change anything."

Spikefur growled. "Now we'll never know." He turned his tail on Crowfrost and stalked across the clearing. Scorchfur followed, Birchpaw and Lionpaw at his heels. Rippletail and Mistcloud glanced nervously at each other before following the disgruntled cats. Tigerheart padded toward the shadows, his pelt rippling uneasily.

Tawnypelt blinked at Crowfrost. "You made the right decision."

Dawnpelt nudged him toward his den. "It's just a few ruf-fled pelts, that's all. They'll be smooth again by the morning."

A few ruffled pelts. Violetpaw watched her Clan melt into the shadows, her heart aching. Twigpaw was gone. She'd *chosen* to go. Sorrow clouded Violetpaw's eyes. *Why did I ever let myself believe that she truly loved me?*

Violetpaw pressed dripping moss to Kinkfur's mouth, just as Twigpaw had taught her. The den felt stuffy, warmed by the bright newleaf sun. Outside, sunshine sliced across the clearing.

After Twigpaw had left, Violetpaw hadn't been able to go back to sleep. Instead she'd come to help Puddleshine. At least here the stench of sickness blocked out the lingering scent of Twigpaw.

Kinkfur wheezed, pushing the moss away as a spasm of coughing gripped her. The old she-cat jerked weakly in her nest, helpless against the seizure. Fear sparked through Vio-letpaw's pelt. "Puddleshine!" She jerked her muzzle toward the medicine cat. He was leaning over Snakekit, gently dab-bing green pulp around her jaws.

He turned sharply as Violetpaw called. His gaze flicked to Kinkfur, still twitching in her nest. The coughing gave way to a rattling wheeze. She seemed no more than fur and bones, shaken by a cruel wind. "Fetch thyme!" Puddleshine ordered.

Violetpaw stared at him. "I don't know what it looks like!"

"It has woody stems and small leaves—" Puddleshine stopped as Kinkfur fell limp.

Violetpaw stiffened with panic. "I'll go and look."

"There's no need." Puddleshine's mew was desolate. He stared at the old she-cat, his eyes misting.

"She's dead?" Violetpaw felt cold. Kinkfur was lying still, as though she was sleeping. "Perhaps the sickness has gone away and she's just resting." Kinkfur couldn't be dead.

Gently Puddleshine touched Kinkfur's flank with his paw. "She's with StarClan now."

"No!" Shock sparked through Violetpaw's fur as she suddenly saw the stillness of death. She looked like prey. Overwhelmed, Violetpaw bolted for the entrance. She raced across the clearing, ignoring the surprised stares of her Clanmates.

"Where are you going?" Dawnpelt's mew rang across the clearing.

Violetpaw didn't answer. She raced through the entrance tunnel and burst from the camp. Gulping the pine-scented air outside, she tried to fight the waves of grief washing over her. Her Clanmates were *dying*. Twigpaw was gone. There was no one in the Clan she could talk to. Not *really* talk to. For a moment she wondered where Needletail was. Needletail would know what to say. She'd flick her tail carelessly and tell Violetpaw not to worry. She'd say that Kinkfur would be happier lying in the warm sunshine of StarClan's hunting grounds than coughing in a stuffy nest She'd tell her that she didn't need Twigpaw because she had *her*.

I should have stayed with her. Violetpaw had tried not to think of her friend since she'd rejoined ShadowClan. She'd tried not to worry how Needletail might be getting along with the rogues and had kept her thoughts focused on the present. She'd tried to put her Clanmates first. Now, with a stab of grief, Violetpaw realized that Needletail had *never* abandoned her. When she'd left, she'd taken Violetpaw with her. *I abandoned* her. Guilt pricked through Violetpaw's pelt.

She headed away from camp.

"Where are you going?" Dawnpelt padded from the camp and called after her.

Violetpaw looked over her shoulder. "Kinkfur died," she meowed bluntly. "I need to get some fresh air."

Dawnpelt stared at her, shock sparking in her gaze. "She's dead?"

"Yes." Violetpaw turned away and headed between the trees. She heard Dawnpelt's fur brush the brambles as the cream-colored she-cat hurried back into camp.

Paws heavy, Violetpaw walked on. The forest floor was warm where the sun reached it and chilly where shadows lingered. Pushing all thoughts from her mind, Violetpaw found herself wandering toward her old territory—the land held by the rogues. *Do I want to see Needletail?* Violetpaw couldn't decide. She wanted Needletail to comfort her, like she had when Violetpaw was a kit. But she knew that Needletail was unlikely to treat her kindly if she ever ran into her again.

As Violetpaw felt her chest sink in regret, she heard a familiar voice.

"Well, well." Needletail slid out from behind a pine and blocked her path. "Look who we have here."

Violetpaw's heart leaped. "Needletail!" Her old friend's fur looked glossy. Muscles rippled over her shoulders. Violetpaw broke into a purr.

Needletail scowled and looked over her shoulder. Rain followed her onto the path and stopped beside her. His injured eye was gone. Pale fur covered the space where it had once been. His remaining eye flitted coldly over Violetpaw.

Violetpaw felt an icy chill settle in her belly. Needletail didn't look pleased to see her. "I'm sorry I left like I did," she mewed hurriedly. "I just didn't know what else to do."

Needletail narrowed her eyes. "So you ran away in the night."

"I wasn't running away." Violetpaw pushed back guilt. "I just didn't feel like I belonged there anymore."

Was that *hurt* sharpening Needletail's gaze? Violetpaw leaned closer. "I'm really sorry. I should have talked to you. But . . ." Her mew trailed away as she glanced at Rain. Were Needletail and Rain mates now? Perhaps she'd chosen the right time to leave. Maybe Needletail didn't have room for friends in her life anymore.

She realized that Needletail was staring at her, malice shimmering in her green gaze. There was no hurt there now, only threat. Violetpaw backed away. "H-how are the others?" she asked nervously.

"What do you care?" Needletail hissed. "You're a Shadow-Clan cat now. That *is* where you went, isn't it?" She sniffed Violetpaw's pelt. "You *smell* like a Clan cat."

Violetpaw suddenly felt very small.

"Why did you go back?" Needletail's question sounded more like an accusation.

Violetpaw glanced at Rain again, staring at his lost eye.

Rain's whiskers twitched with amusement. "I think she was scared someone would spoil her pretty face."

"Coward, eh?" Needletail stepped closer.

Violetpaw flinched. "I belong in a Clan," she mewed quietly.

"Traitor!" Needletail's ears flattened.

You *betrayed* your *Clan!* Violetpaw wished she had the courage to say it. Needletail had been *born* in ShadowClan. They were her kin. *They only took me in because of the prophecy.* But Rain and Needletail were staring at her malevolently. "Every cat has to find their own path."

Needletail snorted. "You even sound like a Clan cat!"

"It's where I belong." Violetpaw was determined to appear brave, even though her heart was pounding.

Needletail backed away, her eyes glittering. "So you let me wake up alone, wondering where you'd gone!"

Violetpaw hesitated. *That is sadness!* Was the sleek silver she-cat truly hurt that Violetpaw had left her? "I couldn't stay," she mewed helplessly.

Needletail showed her teeth. "We could take you back with us now. I'm sure Darktail would be delighted to have his *special* Clan cat back."

"I don't want to go back to the rogues!" Violetpaw tried to stop her paws from trembling.

"Who says you get a choice?" Needletail hissed.

Violetpaw stared at her pleadingly. "I'm sorry, Needletail. I just want to go home."

Needletail glanced at Rain. "What do you think?" she asked. "Should we take her back to camp with us?"

Rain stared at Violetpaw, his gaze betraying nothing.

Violetpaw's breath stopped in her throat. She glanced around the forest, looking for some escape. Perhaps if she bolted for the brambles beyond the ditch, she'd be able to lose them in the tangled branches. Or she could just head back the way she'd come. She was light on her paws. She might be able to outrun them.

"Well?" Needletail pressed. "Should we take her?"

"No."

Rain's mew washed Violetpaw like a cool breeze. She let out a breath as he went on.

"We don't want cats who don't want us. Besides, she's too soft." He sniffed. "There's still kit fluff behind her ears."

As her shoulders loosened, he glared at her. "But I'm sure we'll be seeing you again."

Fear jabbed her belly. As he stalked away with Needletail, Violetpaw realized she was shaking. She backed away, then turned and raced for camp.

Damp air settled over the clearing as the sun sank behind the trees. Violetpaw crouched at the edge of camp, a half-eaten mouse beside her. Her Clanmates moved quietly around the body lying in the middle. Kinkfur had been carried from the den and placed there, her paws tucked neatly beneath her.

Tawnypelt and Dawnpelt had smoothed her fur. Mistcloud, Sparrowtail, and Ratscar had gathered pinecones and early primrose and laid them around her body. Now they sat in the twilight, ready to begin the vigil.

Violetpaw watched them, her thoughts jumbled. Twigpaw had left; Kinkfur had died; Needletail was no longer her friend. *Did I think she would be, after I left her like that?* She couldn't forget the flash of pain in Needletail's gaze as she'd spoken about waking up and finding Violetpaw gone.

Crowfrost padded from his den. He moved stiffly, like an elder. His fur was unkempt. Violetpaw sat up, unease tugging in her belly. Was he just grieving? Or was something else wrong? He stopped beside Kinkfur's body and beckoned his Clanmates closer with a flick of his tail.

Violetpaw crossed the clearing and stopped beside Lionpaw and Birchpaw. Puddleshine blinked at her from the other side of Kinkfur's body. Scorchfur and Spikefur sat together, their gazes dark.

"Kinkfur was a loyal ShadowClan cat for many moons before I was born." Crowfrost's mew was hoarse. "And she remained loyal and kind to the end. She fought beside us against the Dark Forest cats. She was at the front of every battle. She defended her Clanmates as though she were defending her own kits."

As the ShadowClan deputy went on, Spikefur narrowed his eyes, watching him as though watching prey.

"StarClan will welcome her. She has many friends there, and a kit, Dewkit, and long days of endless hunting lie ahead of her." He dipped his head. "She will be remembered."

Ratscar leaned down to grasp a primrose between his teeth. He lifted it and laid it on Kinkfur's body. Kinkfur's surviving kits, Mistcloud and Sparrowtail, leaned close, touching their noses to her pelt one last time. As Ratscar settled down beside his old friend, Crowfrost began coughing.

His Clanmates turned to watch as Crowfrost crouched, his body jerking. His rasping coughs echoed in the evening air. Violetpaw stiffened. For the first time she saw that his gaze was glassy with fever. Fear spiked through her chest as Puddleshine hurried to the deputy's side.

"Fetch tansy!" Puddleshine called.

No cat moved.

The ShadowClan deputy was ill. No one was left to lead.

Violetpaw felt weak with dread. Was sickness going to destroy the Clan?

CHAPTER 21

Catching his breath, Alderpaw paused on the last rocky slope that led to the Moonpool. His pads burned from the climb. Leafpool leaped ahead of him. Jayfeather stopped at his tail.

"Hurry up," the blind medicine cat grunted. "The moon won't stay up all night."

Still Alderpaw hesitated. A warrior was standing on the rim of the hollow, looking down at them. Alderpaw couldn't make out who it was, but he caught the scent of WindClan. "It looks like Kestrelflight brought an escort again," he told Jayfeather.

"It's Harespring." Jayfeather pushed past Alderpaw.

"How do you know?" Alderpaw clambered after him.

"I've smelled his scent all the way along the trail," Jayfeather puffed. "I wonder why Kestrelflight only came with one warrior this time."

"Perhaps Onestar thinks that his deputy is as good as two ordinary warriors," Alderpaw guessed.

"Perhaps." Jayfeather sounded unconvinced. He nodded to Harespring as he reached the top, and padded past him.

Alderpaw followed, glancing nervously at the WindClan

deputy, who watched them, betraying no expression. After his trip to the WindClan camp with Leafpool, he didn't trust any of WindClan. Perhaps they all shared Onestar's rage and paranoia.

He padded down the dimpled stone path. The Moonpool shone at the bottom. The half-moon's reflection was rippling in the wind, which spiraled down between the sheltering cliffs. It ruffled Alderpaw's fur, but he didn't feel cold. New-leaf had finally loosened the stone grip of leaf-bare. The night air was fragrant with scents.

Willowshine was sitting beside Mothwing and Puddleshine, but as the ShadowClan medicine cat spotted Leafpool, he hurried forward.

"How's Twigpaw?" he asked as she reached the pool.

"She's fine." Leafpool dipped her head politely.

In the days since the ThunderClan patrol had brought her home, Twigpaw had been quiet, her thoughts drifting easily. When Alderpaw had asked her about her time with Shadow-Clan, she'd told him that they'd treated her well but she was glad she didn't have to live in such a disorganized Clan. Sadness had tinged her gaze as she'd said it, and, when he'd pressed her, she'd admitted that even though she didn't miss ShadowClan, she wished she could still be with Violetpaw.

"It felt good to have kin close by," she had murmured.

Alderpaw had touched his nose to her cheek, wishing there was something he could say to comfort her.

In the hollow, Puddleshine's eyes flashed with gratitude. "Twigpaw was amazing."

Alderpaw blinked at him as he reached the pool. What had Twigpaw done that had impressed the medicine cat so much? "Amazing?"

"She helped me with the sick cats," Puddleshine explained. "She knew which herbs to give and how to make even the sickest cats swallow them."

Jayfeather grunted. "I suppose all that time she spent getting under my paws wasn't entirely wasted."

Alderpaw ignored the grumpy medicine cat, relishing the pride warming his belly. "Twigpaw loves to help."

Leafpool leaned forward anxiously. "How are the sick cats?"

The glow faded from Puddleshine's gaze. Alderpaw suddenly noticed how weary he looked, his pelt dull and unwashed, his tail drooping. "Kinkfur died a few days ago," he mewed.

Kestrelflight shifted his paws uneasily, avoiding the ShadowClan medicine cat's gaze. Had he known about Kinkfur's death before the meeting? Did he feel responsible?

Puddleshine went on. "No cat has shown signs of improvement. Snakekit is just fur and bones, and Rowanstar's lives are ebbing away." He lowered his voice, one eye on Harespring, still standing at the top of the hollow. "And now Crowfrost has been taken ill."

Alderpaw saw Leafpool swap anxious looks with Kestrelflight. His heart lurched. ShadowClan had no leader now. They would be more vulnerable than ever.

Mothwing padded forward. "We've scoured RiverClan

territory for lungwort, but we've found nothing that fits your description."

Willowshine pricked her ears. "We wondered if birch sap might help. There's a young tree near the river. The bark is soft enough to score into. We can gather sap and bring it to you if you like. Its sweetness will give the sick cats energy when they can't eat."

Jayfeather tipped his head curiously. "Birch sap? Does it cure coughs?"

"We don't know yet. We've only just discovered it," Willowshine told him. "But it won't do any harm. It might be worth trying until Onestar changes his mind."

Alderpaw's belly tightened. From what he'd seen of the WindClan leader, Onestar was never going to change his mind. His thoughts quickened. *And if he doesn't? How many ShadowClan cats will die?* Would there be any cat left? Anger surged through him. "Why don't the Clans join together and *make* Onestar give ShadowClan the herb?"

Kestrelflight's fur rippled uneasily.

Leafpool blinked at Alderpaw, clearly surprised by the anger in his mew.

Puddleshine's ears twitched. "If only it were that easy."

"It *is* that easy!" Alderpaw's pelt bristled. "We need to stand up to Onestar."

Leafpool's tail swished over the stone. "You're right, Alderpaw. But we need the support of our leaders. I'm not sure they are ready to start a war over this yet."

Alderpaw growled. "They should be! Don't they care that ShadowClan is dying? Aren't *all* cats' lives important?"

Kestrelflight glanced at Harespring. He nodded to the warrior, who turned and disappeared over the edge of the rim. "I think I have a more peaceful solution."

The medicine cats swung their heads toward him.

Alderpaw's heart leaped into this throat. "What?"

Kestrelflight padded to the pool. "I need to share with StarClan before I tell you. I need to know that what I want to do is right."

Alderpaw watched the WindClan medicine cat crouch at the edge of the pool and touch his nose to the water. Curiosity gnawed in his belly. "What do you think he means?" he blinked at Leafpool.

"Let's share with StarClan," she mewed softly. "And then he can tell us."

Alderpaw followed Leafpool as the cats fanned out around the pool. Mothwing lay down by the pool to wait. Closing his eyes, Alderpaw crouched and touched his nose to the water.

Sun-drenched meadows opened in front of him. A warm breeze ruffled his pelt. The stone beneath his paws turned to soft grass, tickling where the wind set it rippling against his fur.

A broad-faced gray she-cat padded toward him, stars sparkling in her thick, long fur. She purred as she neared. Alderpaw dipped his head, wondering who she was.

"I am Yellowfang." She stopped in front of him.

Yellowfang. Alderpaw had heard stories of the brave she-cat who had killed her own son to save her Clan. He blinked at her, his heart quickening. "Have you come to tell me if Twig-paw and Violetpaw are what we were meant to find in the shadows?" He'd come to the pool with the same question burning in his thoughts every half-moon.

Yellowfang's whiskers twitched with amusement. "Haven't you wondered whether finding out for yourselves might be part of the prophecy?"

Alderpaw leaned forward eagerly. "Does that mean they are?"

Yellowfang gazed at him steadily. "It means I'm not telling you."

Alderpaw frowned, frustration pricking through his fur.

Yellowfang purred louder. "I'd forgotten the impatience of youth." She padded around him, letting her thick tail trail across his flank. "I came only to praise you for speaking out."

"When?" Alderpaw met her gaze, puzzled.

"Just now. With the other medicine cats." She stood still. "I wondered at first if you had what it takes to be a medicine cat, but now that I see that you are willing to say what you believe, I trust that StarClan made the right choice after all."

After all? Alderpaw frowned. "Didn't you choose me?"

"StarClan does not always speak with one voice."

Alderpaw remembered many dreamless moons. "Some-times you don't speak at all."

"Would you rather we guided your every paw step?" Yellowfang tipped her head. "Wouldn't you rather walk your own path?"

"I guess." Alderpaw glanced past her, wondering if any other StarClan cats were here. "But there are some paths that are too hard to walk alone. And we can't see some paths at all." He thought of the missing Clan. "You never mention Sky-Clan. Do you know where they are?"

Yellowfang blinked at him, giving nothing away. Alderpaw flexed his claws irritably. "Then what about ShadowClan?" He thought of Onestar and ShadowClan and the dying cats. "Why tell Puddleshine where to find lungwort without telling Onestar to let him gather it?"

"What lesson would any cat learn from that?" Yellowfang began to fade, her pelt growing translucent in the bright sunshine.

"Don't go!" Alderpaw wanted to ask how he could help save ShadowClan. But Yellowfang was hardly more than a shimmering heat haze above the grass.

"Speak out for what you believe." Her mew whisked away on the breeze.

Alderpaw opened his eyes, blinking to adjust to the gloom of the hollow. The other cats were getting to their paws.

Leafpool fluffed her fur out against the night air. "Did you share with StarClan?" she asked him.

"Yellowfang told me to speak out for what I believe," Alderpaw whispered.

Leafpool glanced at Jayfeather, amusement flashing in her gaze. "That might not go down too well in the medicine den."

Kestrelflight whisked his tail. Excitement was burning in his eyes. "I spoke to them!" he mewed. "I know what to do.

Follow me!" He bounded up the dimpled path to the rim of the hollow. "Harespring! It's okay. StarClan says it's okay!"

Startled, Alderpaw hurried after the WindClan medicine cat. "*What's* okay?"

Mothwing, Willowshine, Jayfeather, and Leafpool followed.

Puddleshine hurried at their heels. "What's happening?"

Kestrelflight was already jumping down the steep rocks after Harespring. The WindClan cats' pelts were spiked. Alderpaw smelled fear-scent. They were scared! What of? Heart quickening anxiously, he scrambled down after them, relieved when they reached a flatter part of the stream.

"It was Harespring's idea," Kestrelflight told him as he caught up to the WindClan medicine cat. "He insisted on being the only warrior to escort me tonight and told me about it on the way. I wasn't sure. That's why I had to ask StarClan."

Alderpaw's thoughts swam. What was Kestrelflight talking about?

The WindClan cat glanced over his shoulder toward the other medicine cats. "Hurry!" He beckoned them on with a flick of his tail and hurried after Harespring.

"Where are we going?" Alderpaw fought for breath as he raced to keep up with the WindClan cats.

"To the moor." Kestrelflight nodded to where the heather-covered slopes reached down to the stream. Harespring was already crossing the border onto WindClan territory.

As Kestrelflight followed him, Alderpaw hesitated at the scent line. "Onestar won't want us on his territory."

Leafpool and Puddleshine caught up to them. They blinked at Kestrelflight and Harespring, puzzled. The WindClan cats had stopped and were staring at them expectantly.

"Follow me!" The wind whipped Harespring's call toward them. "But hurry! We have to be quick."

"We're going to show you where the lungwort is," Kestrelflight told them. "You can gather as much as you want."

"What about Onestar?" Alderpaw stared at him.

"Onestar doesn't know." Harespring flicked his tail impatiently. "He can't know. He's wrong to let cats die. The *rogues* harmed us, not ShadowClan. ShadowClan shouldn't have to pay for other cats' cruelty."

Jayfeather, Mothwing, and Willowshine reached the border.

"What's going on?" Jayfeather puffed.

"Harespring and Kestrelflight are going to let us gather lungwort. It was Harespring's idea." Alderpaw nodded toward the WindClan deputy, impressed by his compassion and sense of duty to the Clan cats beyond his borders. His pelt bristled with excitement, but as he gazed across the heather-pelted slope, fear hollowed his belly. What if a WindClan patrol found them? He pushed the thought away. *Who cares?* ShadowClan needed the herb. And StarClan had given its permission.

Puddleshine had already crossed the scent line and was following Harespring, who was weaving between the heather bushes.

Alderpaw hurried after them, Kestrelflight at his side. "Is it far?"

"It's just over the next rise," Kestrelflight purred.

The chill that comes before dawn was seeping through the forest, spreading deep into Alderpaw's bones by the time he reached the ThunderClan camp. Leafpool carried the lungwort she'd gathered to the medicine den, nodding good night to Alderpaw as she went.

Jayfeather paused in the empty clearing. Around them, gentle snores sounded from the shadowy dens.

"Puddleshine still has a long night ahead of him," he mewed softly to Alderpaw.

"I wish I could have gone with him to help give the herbs to the sick cats." Alderpaw's heart ached with the hope that Puddleshine had gathered the herb soon enough to save his Clanmates.

"There's been enough sneaking around tonight," Jayfeather murmured.

"I hope Harespring and Kestrelflight don't get into trouble." Alderpaw fluffed out his fur against the chill.

"Hopefully, Onestar won't find out," Jayfeather mewed. "But if he does, he'd be mouse-brained to turn on his deputy and his medicine cat. He needs their support, especially if he's being as unreasonable with his Clanmates as he is with the rest of us."

Alderpaw's thoughts flitted back to the fearful glances of

the WindClan warriors as they'd watched their leader rage against Leafpool. "At least we may have saved some lives tonight."

"And we have our own stock of the herb in case the sickness ever reaches our forest." Jayfeather shifted his paws.

Alderpaw pressed back a shiver. Tiredness dragged at his bones, and he longed to head to his warm nest. But Jayfeather seemed to have something on his mind, so he waited in the dark clearing with him until, at last, the ThunderClan medicine cat spoke.

"Well done, speaking up tonight." His blind blue gaze flashed in the moonlight. "I wondered when you'd finally find your tongue."

"I've spoken up before—"

Jayfeather cut him off. "Talking back to an old badger like me is not the same as standing up for what you believe to cats from other Clans. I was proud of you."

Alderpaw blinked, wondering if he was imagining Jayfeather's words. Perhaps he *had* gone to his nest. Perhaps this was a dream.

Jayfeather turned and headed for his den. "I think you may be ready to become a full medicine cat."

Alderpaw watched him go, too stunned to speak. Was it true? Was he going to get his full medicine cat name soon? *Alderpatch. Alderleaf. Alderblaze.* Possible names flitted through his mind as he headed for the apprentices' den. Suddenly he hardly felt the cold. Warmth seeped through his pelt as he imagined the other medicine cats cheering his new name.

He'd felt self-conscious being the only apprentice, especially when Puddleshine had been named after only two moons of training. Happily, he ducked into the den and climbed into his nest. *Perhaps I will be a great medicine cat after all.*

CHAPTER 22

Violetpaw tore another small morsel from the sparrow and laid it on the edge of Snowbird's nest. The white she-cat was recovering well. In the half-moon since Puddleshine had returned to camp with the lungwort, the sickness that had gripped ShadowClan had slowly eased. But the stench of death still lingered in the ShadowClan camp. Wasptail had died the night after Kinkfur, and, more troubling, Crowfrost had been too ill to respond to the herb and had died a few days later. Shadow-Clan had lost its deputy.

As Snowbird leaned forward and lapped up the scrap of sparrow flesh, Violetpaw glanced at Dawnpelt. Her mentor's gaze was empty as she gently washed Oakfur's pelt. It had been hard enough for Dawnpelt to lose Sleekwhisker and Juniperclaw to the rogues. But the death of her mate, Crowfrost, had been devastating. And yet Dawnpelt had carried on with her duties without complaining. Violetpaw wished that some of her other Clanmates could do the same. Mistcloud and Sparrowtail had hardly hunted since Kinkfur's death. Violetpaw had heard them muttering about Crowfrost, even as he lay dying, blaming him for letting Twigpaw go. Had they convinced ThunderClan to help by keeping Twigpaw, they might have gotten the herb sooner and not lost their deputy.

Mouse-brains! Violetpaw ripped away another piece of sparrow flesh and laid it in front of Snowbird. Puddleshine had managed to gather the herb without a hostage.

Yarrowleaf snored gently in her nest, while Puddleshine leaned over Pinenose, listening to her breathing, his ear pressed against her ribs. Snowbird, Oakfur, Yarrowleaf, and Pinenose were the last four cats recovering from the sickness. In a few days they'd all be well, and the den would be cleared out to make way for fresh nests. The bramble shelter could become the warriors' den once more. And with Rowanstar well enough to resume his role as leader, Violetpaw hoped that ShadowClan would start to feel more organized. Rowanstar was still weak, but he had made Tigerheart his new deputy and given Whorlpaw, Snakepaw, and Flowerpaw their apprentice names. The nursery was empty now, and Grassheart had returned to her warrior duties.

Snakepaw had recovered quickly from the sickness once Puddleshine had administered the lungwort. Violetpaw could glimpse the honey-colored tabby now, lying in a strip of sunshine beside the clearing while Whorlpaw and Flowerpaw practiced stalking in the long grass behind her.

"How are they?" Scorchfur's urgent question made Violetpaw jump. She turned and saw the dark gray tom swagger into the den, a frown in his eyes. He must have come to check on Snowbird and Yarrowleaf.

Puddleshine turned to face the tom. "Snowbird's breathing

is much better," he reported. "And Yarrowleaf is well enough to leave her nest when she feels rested."

Yarrowleaf opened her eyes. "Hi, Scorchfur." She greeted her father weakly.

Scorchfur glowered at Puddleshine. "She doesn't seem much better."

"She's just tired. A long sleep will—"

Scorchfur didn't let the medicine cat finish his sentence. "She wouldn't have gotten sick at all if Rowanstar had acted sooner. And she'd have had the lungwort quicker if Crowfrost hadn't given away our hostage."

Puddleshine blinked at the tom. "That's not true. Bramble-star said that Onestar refused to cooperate even when he knew we had Twigpaw."

"And why would Bramblestar tell us the truth? It was *his* apprentice we held." Scorchfur scowled at him.

Snowbird swallowed another morsel of sparrow. "Go easy on him, Scorchfur. Puddleshine has been a lifesaver. More would have died without him."

Scorchfur grunted. "And no cat would have died if we'd had stronger leaders."

Violetpaw narrowed her eyes. Who in the camp could have been stronger than Rowanstar and Crowfrost? The tom seemed determined to be dissatisfied. Perhaps he had been hoping to take Tigerheart's place as deputy, and he was only expressing his resentment.

Lionpaw broke into her thoughts. The young she-cat stuck

her head through the den entrance. "How's Pinenose?" She blinked at her mother anxiously.

Puddleshine padded toward his littermate. "She's much better today."

Spikefur's mew sounded outside. "She'll get well quicker if you stop pestering her, Lionpaw."

"I'm not pestering—"

"Spikefur!" Pinenose called eagerly to her mate.

The tom squeezed past Lionpaw and padded to her nest. "Has Puddleshine been taking good care of you?"

"Of course." Her gaze flitted to Puddleshine. "I'm very proud of him. He practically saved the Clan single-pawed."

Lionpaw huffed at the entrance. "I wish he'd told us he was going to gather lungwort. Birchpaw and I could have helped." Was that envy in Lionpaw's mew?

"There wasn't time to ask for help," Puddleshine told his littermate. "If I hadn't gathered it then, I couldn't have gathered it at all."

"What made Onestar change his mind?" Scorchfur looked at Puddleshine, eyes glittering with suspicion.

"Maybe StarClan sent him a message," Puddleshine answered vaguely. He hadn't told any cat exactly how he'd gotten his paws on the lungwort, and, clearly, he wasn't going to share the information now.

Scorchfur grunted and stalked from the den. Spikefur touched his muzzle fondly to Pinenose's head, then followed.

Dawnpelt blinked at Violetpaw. "You must be hungry."

They'd been helping Puddleshine with the sick cats since dawn. "Let's go and see if there's anything left on the fresh-kill pile."

Violetpaw left the sparrow beside Snowbird and nodded to Puddleshine. "Should I bring you something to eat?"

Puddleshine shook his head. "I'll fetch something when I'm done here."

The medicine cat looked skinnier than ever. Dawnpelt must have noticed too.

"You need to take care of yourself," the cream she-cat warned him. "If you collapse, there's no one else to take care of the Clan."

Puddleshine dipped his head to her. "I won't be long," he promised.

Violetpaw followed Dawnpelt to the fresh-kill pile. A vole and a lizard were left over from yesterday's catch.

Dawnpelt glanced around the camp. "Haven't the hunting patrols been out yet?" The morning sun was lifting about the treetops. Mistcloud and Sparrowtail sat beside the flat rock, eyes half-closed. Scorchfur and Spikefur were murmuring to each other at the far end of the clearing.

Tawnypelt was gazing expectantly toward Rowanstar's den. Wasn't the ShadowClan leader up yet? And where was Tigerheart?

Strikestone padded toward Dawnpelt. He greeted his mother with a purr. "I hope Tigerheart organizes the hunting patrols soon." He glanced at the vole and lizard. "I'm hungry for *fresh* prey."

Dawnpelt tossed the stale vole toward Violetpaw and pulled the lizard closer. "Why hasn't Tigerheart organized the patrols?"

"Rowanstar called him into his den," Strikestone told her. "Maybe they're deciding who's fit to hunt."

"Let's hope they don't spend too long talking. Hungry bellies make grumpy cats." She leaned down and tore the head off the lizard and began chewing it.

Violetpaw shuddered. She'd never liked lizards, although her Clanmates happily gobbled them down as though they were a delicacy.

She sniffed the vole. It still smelled stale, but she suddenly realized how hungry she was and bit into it. As its musky flavor bathed her tongue, she saw Strikestone turn his head toward Rowanstar's den. Rowanstar and Tigerheart appeared at the entrance and padded out toward their Clanmates.

Tawnypelt turned to face them at once. But Rippletail, eyes glinting with disdain, crossed the clearing and murmured something in Spikefur's ear. The dark brown tom curled his lip, his icy gaze on Rowanstar.

The vole seemed to turn dry in Violetpaw's mouth. What were the warriors saying? Nothing pleasant, by the look of it.

Tigerheart padded to the head of the clearing, Rowanstar at his side. "We've been discussing the hunting patrols," he called, his eyes flitting around the Clan. "Our Clanmates are recovering and have good appetites, but some are not yet fit to hunt. This means that the rest of us must hunt harder than ever. I want the fresh-kill pile full by this evening."

Scorchfur and Spikefur exchanged glances.

Tigerheart went on. "Spikefur, take Lionpaw, Mistcloud, Whorlpaw, and Rippletail to the ditches and hunt there. Scorchfur, take Birchpaw, Grassheart, Flowerpaw, and Sparrowtail to the lake to hunt. Dawnpelt, take Violetpaw, Tawnypelt, and Strikestone to the alder grove near the border. There will be good hunting there now that it's newleaf, but watch out for the rogues."

Dawnpelt straightened, swallowing the last of her lizard, and nodded to the deputy.

Spikefur stared at Tigerheart. "Where will you and Rowanstar be hunting?"

"Rowanstar needs to rest," Tigerheart told him. "He's still recovering from his illness."

"He looks fine to me," Spikefur looked the leader up and down scornfully.

Rowanstar's eyes flashed. "I will hunt," he mewed hoarsely, "if the Clan needs it."

Scorchfur nodded toward the den where the remaining sick cats lay. "The Clan needs it," he growled.

Worry darkened Tigerheart's gaze. "You shouldn't risk your health," he mewed to Rowanstar.

Rowanstar met his deputy's gaze. "I must show my Clan I am still strong."

Spikefur snorted. "It's a bit late for that." Flicking his tail sharply, he headed out of camp, his patrol hurrying after him.

Violetpaw watched him go, her pelt rippling with unease. Even ShadowClan's warriors were showing no respect for their leader now. She glanced toward Dawnpelt, hoping for reassurance, but her mentor was already following the other patrols out of camp. *I came back here because I wanted to live by the warrior code.* But right now she felt as though ShadowClan had forgotten the one thing that made them warriors: they seemed to have forgotten loyalty.

She followed Dawnpelt. *Perhaps tonight's Gathering will remind them what it is to be a true Clan.*

Violetpaw draped the last piece of dried moss inside the freshly woven bracken nest and sat back on her haunches to admire her work. Outside, the full moon was rising, so bright that it lit the camp and shafts of moonlight speared the elders' den.

Ratscar nodded approvingly at the new nest. "Oakfur will be pleased with it."

"Puddleshine says he can return to the elders' den tomorrow," Violetpaw told him. "I wanted him to be comfortable." She glanced at Ratscar's shabby nest. "I can make you a fresh nest tomorrow if you like."

A purr rasped in Ratscar's throat. "That would be great." His gaze flitted to the third nest in the den, now stale and cold. "It's going to be quiet in here without Kinkfur," he murmured sadly. "Oakfur isn't much of a talker."

"ShadowClan!" Rowanstar's call sounded outside the den.

Blinking at Ratscar, Violetpaw hurried out. *Let Rowanstar choose me to go to the Gathering.* She wondered if she'd see Twigpaw, then pushed the thought away. *Why would I want to see her?*

Anger flashed beneath her pelt. *She left me.*

Tawnypelt and Tigerheart were already standing expectantly in front of Rowanstar. At the edge of the clearing, Strikestone plucked at the grass eagerly, the remains of the fresh-kill he'd been eating beside him. Dawnpelt crossed the camp, heading toward Rowanstar, her tail high.

Violetpaw hurried to join her mentor, her paws prickling with excitement as Rowanstar began to call the names of the cats who would travel with him to the island. "Tawnypelt, Tigerheart, Violetpaw." *He chose me!* Violetpaw purred as she reached Dawnpelt.

"Puddleshine!" The medicine cat was already crossing the clearing as Rowanstar called his name.

"Dawnpelt, Strikestone, Spikefur, Mistcloud, Whorlpaw, Sparrowtail, Flowerpaw."

Violetpaw glanced over her shoulder, scanning the clearing for the young apprentices. Their first Gathering! Flowerpaw was hurrying toward Rowanstar, her eyes shining. Whorlpaw followed at her heels.

Violetpaw's purr faltered as she caught sight of Spikefur. He was hanging back at the edge of the clearing, his shoulders stiff. Mistcloud stood beside him. The warriors' eyes were dark. Why weren't they hurrying to join the others?

"Scorchfur, Sparrowtail." Rowanstar went on, apparently unaware that some of the cats he had named weren't moving from their place.

Scorchfur glowered at the ShadowClan leader. "We're not

coming." His yowl cut across the moonlit camp like a claw slicing through the darkness.

Tigerheart and Tawnypelt jerked their muzzles toward the dark gray tom. Dawnpelt turned to face him.

Violetpaw stared in disbelief as Spikefur, Sparrowtail, Mistcloud, and Rippletail padded to join Scorchfur. They glared malevolently at Rowanstar.

Scorchfur lashed his tail. "Why should we meet with the Clans who refused to help us?"

Spikefur hissed. "They were prepared to let us die!"

Rowanstar pushed between Tawnypelt and Tigerheart, stopping short of the rebellious warriors. "I am the leader of ShadowClan, and I say we're going."

Scorchfur huffed. "Where were you when Crowfrost handed our hostage over to ThunderClan without a fight?"

"Holding an apprentice hostage wasn't going to change anything," Rowanstar retorted. Tawnypelt had told the ShadowClan leader what had happened while he was ill. "Sickness is no excuse for a Clan to act like rogues."

"And how do rogues act?" Spikefur stepped forward. "Do they withhold herbs while innocent cats die? Or is that just *Clan* cats?"

Mistcloud's ears twitched. "Onestar behaved badly and the other Clans let him. We are not like them. We don't want to be like them."

Rowanstar's eyes rounded sympathetically. "If you want to air your grievances, come to the Gathering. Speak with the other Clans. Perhaps we can make them see that they've treated us badly."

"Words didn't work before," Scorchfur snarled. "Why should they work now?"

"I'll speak to them for you." Rowanstar's tone was conciliatory. "You can stay here and I will report back what they said."

Scorchfur narrowed his eyes to threatening slits. "If you go to the Gathering, don't bother coming back," he hissed. "ShadowClan doesn't need a leader as weak as you."

As he spoke, Spikefur turned toward the entrance to the camp.

Violetpaw's heart lurched as she saw shadowy figures streaming into the clearing. She tasted rogue scent, and as the shapes moved into the moonlight, she recognized Darktail, Rain, Raven, and the rest of their campmates. Violetpaw felt sick. Needletail was with them, and Sleekwhisker and Cloverfoot. Every cat from the rogue camp was here except Beenose. Had she left them? Had the sickness killed her?

Violetpaw pressed against Dawnpelt, ashamed of her trembling paws. *What are they doing here? Why have they come?*

Spikefur padded to greet the rogues, dipping his head to Darktail before turning back to Rowanstar. "We need new leadership," he growled. "*Strong* leadership."

Rowanstar's eyes sparked with fury. He glared at Spikefur, and then his gaze flitted angrily around the rebellious cats before resting finally on Darktail. "Are you suggesting that we give our Clan over to rogues?" His mew was icy.

Violetpaw saw the muscles rippling across Rowanstar's shoulders. His ribs still showed through his pelt from the illness, but as his hackles rose, she remembered what a fierce warrior he was.

He faced Darktail. "You will take this Clan over my dead body."

Delight sparked in Darktail's gaze. "That sounds fair."

The rogue leader flung himself at Rowanstar.

Violetpaw gasped.

Rowanstar reared, but the force of Darktail's attack pushed him back. Rowanstar's hind legs trembled as he dug his paws into the earth and braced himself against the snarling rogue. Eyes flashing, Darktail turned his head and bit into the ShadowClan leader's neck.

Rowanstar grunted, twisting beneath Darktail as he tried to shake him off. But the ShadowClan leader must have lost his balance. With a jerk, Darktail flipped him onto his side, jaws still gripping his neck.

Help him! Violetpaw stared at her Clanmates. They drew closer, their eyes wide with shock. *Why doesn't someone help?* Her gaze flitted from the Clan cats to the rogues. *Needletail, where are you?* But as soon as she spotted her friend, she knew she would not stop the attack. Needletail was watching the attack with excitement—just like the rest of the rogues.

Rowanstar hissed, struggling free from Darktail's grip. He turned on the rogue leader, but Darktail was quicker. He dived beneath Rowanstar's belly and heaved him off his paws. As

Rowanstar fell, Darktail lashed out, slicing the ShadowClan leader's muzzle. Blood splashed across the clearing, shining darkly in the moonlight.

Tigerheart snarled and leaped at the rogue leader.

At last! Violetpaw leaned forward, blood roaring in her ears.

Tawnypelt hurled herself after Tigerheart, and together they shoved Darktail away from Rowanstar. Batting at him with vicious blows, they drove him back toward his campmates.

Tigerheart glanced at Tawnypelt, and together they began stalking toward the glowering rogues, snarling. But then, suddenly, Tigerheart looked around and seemed to realize that he and Tawnypelt were the only cats moving to defend their leader. "Wait," he hissed to Tawnypelt, looking around the camp. She dropped onto all four paws, narrowing her eyes as she glared at the invading cats.

The rest of ShadowClan watched, unmoving.

Tigerheart and Tawnypelt looked at each other, uneasy acceptance flashing in their eyes, and then slowly backed away.

What was wrong with the others? Violetpaw stared at them in disbelief. Did they truly all want a rogue leader instead of Rowanstar?

She glanced at Rowanstar as he staggered to his paws. Blood welled on his muzzle and darkened his neck fur. As he backed toward Dawnpelt, Violetpaw could see that he was trembling. Dawnpelt pressed against his flank to steady him. Tigerheart and Tawnypelt joined them, bunching close together like cornered mice.

Violetpaw blinked at the huddled group of her Clanmates, feeling sick. "What do we do?" she breathed, one eye on the rogues.

Rowanstar looked at her, pain showing in his eyes. "We go to the Gathering." He padded forward, lifting his chin. Tigerheart and Tawnypelt followed. Violetpaw started after them, Dawnpelt at her side.

Spikefur curled his lip. "If you go," he reminded the ShadowClan leader, "don't come back."

"Puddleshine!" Rowanstar beckoned to the medicine cat with a flick of his tail. "Come with us."

Puddleshine hurried after him.

"Wait." Spikefur blocked his son's path. "You can't leave. Your Clan needs you."

Puddleshine halted, his pelt ruffling. He glanced toward the den where the sick cats lay, then around at his Clanmates and the rogues.

Spikefur went on. "ShadowClan can't be without a medicine cat again. What if Pinenose relapses? Would you ever forgive yourself if your mother died because you left?" He leaned closer to Puddleshine. "If *any* of your Clanmates died?"

Puddleshine's eyes glittered with uncertainty.

Rowanstar paused and looked at the young medicine cat. "I will understand if you decide to stay," he meowed grimly.

Puddleshine dropped his gaze. "I can't leave," he murmured. "I have sworn to protect my Clanmates."

As he turned and retreated to the medicine cat den, Sleekwhisker padded forward and fixed her gaze on Dawnpelt.

"Didn't you miss me and Juniperclaw?"

Violetpaw felt Dawnpelt stiffen beside her, but her mentor could hardly meet her kit's gaze. "You betrayed your Clan," she mumbled.

"But we've come to help them. And you." Sleekwhisker's eyes glittered in the moonlight. "Now that Crowfrost is dead, we're all you have."

Dawnpelt puffed out her chest. "I still have Strikestone." But as she glanced at the young tom, he backed away. "Are you staying?" She sounded like she could hardly believe it.

"Where else can I go?" Strikestone murmured. "Where can *you* go? This is our home."

Dawnpelt hesitated.

"You can't stay!" Violetpaw stared at her desperately, but she could see resignation in her mentor's gaze.

"He's right," Dawnpelt whispered. "I can't leave every single one of my kits. And this is the only home I've known. How can I leave?" She blinked apologetically at Rowanstar, her father, and then Tawnypelt and Tigerheart.

The ShadowClan leader turned away, dismay darkening his eyes. Lifting his tail, he barged between the rogues and ducked through the tunnel. Tigerheart and Tawnypelt followed him, their pelts spiking.

Violetpaw glanced at Needletail, who was watching Rowanstar's retreat with satisfaction. *It's like I don't even know her,* Violetpaw thought. But then she swallowed hard. *Except I do.* Hadn't Needletail always questioned all the rules of the

Clan? It was what had always scared Violetpaw about her—
and thrilled her.

Violetpaw tore her eyes from Needletail and headed after
her Clanmates.

"Wait!" Needletail's mew sounded in her ear as she passed.
The silver she-cat's scent washed over her. "Where are you
going? I thought you'd stay. Please don't leave me again!"

Violetpaw met Needletail's pleading gaze. Even as her
paws tingled with eagerness to leave, the fact that Needletail
wanted her to stay warmed a place deep inside her. "You don't
need me. You have plenty of friends here." Her gaze flashed to
Rain. "And you have him."

"But they're not my kin, not like you are." Needletail stared
at her anxiously.

My kin. She'd felt the same way about Needletail. Guilt
surged through Violetpaw. Needletail had been the only cat
in ShadowClan who had always been kind to her, and she had
repaid her by abandoning her without a word. Could she leave
her again? Was that fair?

"Please stay," Needletail begged. "We can make Shadow-
Clan the Clan it used to be, before you came. A great Clan.
A brave Clan. You'll be proud to be part of it." She looked
around the rogues. "These are cats who understand what
it's like not to belong. They will be as loyal to you as I have
been. We're like kin now. Can you say that about any other cat
you've known?"

Grief clawed at Violetpaw's heart as she remembered

how ThunderClan had let Rowanstar take her from her sister without lifting a paw to stop him, and how Twigpaw had walked away from her to return to her Clanmates. Needletail was right. She was the closest thing Violetpaw had ever known to *real* kin.

She blinked at Needletail. "Okay," she mewed. "I'll stay."

As Needletail purred and pressed her muzzle to Violetpaw's cheek, Violetpaw breathed in her scent. It felt good. She turned her back on the entrance through which Rowanstar, Tigerheart, and Tawnypelt had disappeared and gazed at her new Clan.

CHAPTER 23

Twigpaw shifted her paws nervously. Countless scents washed over her, and the chatter of voices wasn't helping to calm her anxiety. Would Violetpaw come to the Gathering? Guilt still pricked her belly each time she remembered leaving the ShadowClan camp, Violetpaw staring desperately after her.

Beside her, Wavepaw looked around. The RiverClan apprentice's eyes were wide as she, Nightpaw, and Breezepaw took in the scene. "It's our first Gathering."

Honeypaw sniffed. "I've been to plenty."

Wavepaw's sister shifted closer as Brindlepaw and Fernpaw padded toward them. "I didn't realize there'd be so many cats here," she breathed.

"Don't worry, Cypresspaw." Wavepaw nuzzled his sister's ear. "There's a truce, remember? We're safe here."

"Hello!" Brindlepaw stopped and blinked at Wavepaw. "You're new, right?"

Wavepaw nodded.

Honeypaw barged in front of him.

"*I* met them first," Honeypaw boasted.

"So?" Brindlepaw glared at her.

Twigpaw swiveled her ears toward the long grass, hoping to hear paws hurrying toward the clearing. WindClan, ThunderClan, and RiverClan were here. But where was ShadowClan? Were they going to be late again?

Bramblestar and Mistystar were talking at the foot of the great oak. Onestar was already seated on the branch above them. His gaze was cast down, as though he was avoiding the eyes of the other Clans. Twigpaw wondered if he felt guilty for having withheld lungwort from ShadowClan.

Is that why they weren't here? Were too many cats sick? The worry that had been nagging in Twigpaw's belly since she'd left the ShadowClan camp suddenly hardened. What if Violetpaw was sick? She tried to push the thought away, but then she pictured her sister looking after her Clanmates in the medicine den. She could have easily caught the illness. Twigpaw remembered grimly how sick the cats had been. Had Oakfur died? Or Wasptail? Or the others? *What about Violetpaw?*

Guilt surged through Twigpaw's pelt as she remembered the hurt in her sister's eyes when she'd left. *I had to go! You are my kin, but ThunderClan is my home!* She'd hoped for a chance to explain to Violetpaw that they would always be sisters even if they lived in different Clans, but what if she never got that chance?

She glanced at Alderpaw, who sat between Leafpool and Jayfeather. Would he go check on ShadowClan if they didn't show up at the Gathering? Perhaps he'd let her go with him.

Honeypaw's mew broke into Twigpaw's thoughts.

"Wavepaw says that RiverClan kits learn to swim before they become 'paws."

"No way!" Brindlepaw exclaimed. "Don't they drown?"

Wavepaw snorted with amusement. "RiverClan cats are born to swim."

Brindlepaw's eyes widened. "I hate getting my fur wet."

Twigpaw gazed at them distractedly. She was only half listening. Her thoughts were still on her sister.

Honeypaw blinked at the RiverClan apprentices. "I've never even *stood* in a river."

Wavepaw shrugged. "You should try it," she mewed. "Rivers are fun. And fish taste delicious."

Cypresspaw looked shyly at Honeypaw. "We can teach you to swim if you like."

Honeypaw shuddered. "No, thanks!"

Wavepaw's eyes sparkled with mischief. "Are you scared?" He nodded toward the trees. Beyond them, the lake glittered in the moonlight.

Honeypaw fluffed out her fur. "Of course not. But it's too cold."

"No it's not!" Wavepaw headed through the crowd toward the trees. "Come on."

Honeypaw followed.

"You can't!" Alarm jerked Twigpaw from her thoughts. She hurried after them. "The Gathering's going to start in a moment."

Honeypaw stared at her. "But ShadowClan isn't even here yet."

As she spoke, Onestar's mew rang across the clearing. "I'm tired of waiting. Let's start the meeting."

Mistystar and Bramblestar exchanged glances and scrambled up the oak, taking their places beside the WindClan leader.

Bramblestar's gaze flicked toward the long grass, as though he was hoping that ShadowClan might appear. Then he blinked down at the Clans as the cats drew closer. "Newleaf has brought more prey and fine weather. ThunderClan has thrived." He turned to Mistystar, dipping his head.

"Prey is running well in RiverClan. And, as you see, we have two new apprentices, Wavepaw and Cypresspaw."

The two young cats shifted self-consciously as the Clans turned to look at them.

As Onestar leaned forward, ready to address the gathered cats, the long grass rustled.

Twigpaw jerked her gaze toward it, her heart skipping a best. *ShadowClan?* Would Violetpaw be with them? She watched Rowanstar pad into the clearing. As Tawnypelt and Tigerheart followed, she strained to see others behind them, but no cat followed the three ShadowClan warriors.

Pelts ruffled anxiously around Twigpaw as Rowanstar stopped at the edge of the crowd and looked up at Bramblestar. "We come alone," he meowed curtly.

Twigpaw saw tufts of fur sticking from his pelt. Blood had dried on his muzzle. He'd been fighting! Her gaze flitted to Tawnypelt and Tigerheart. They looked unharmed. What had happened to the ShadowClan leader?

Bramblestar shifted on the branch, beckoning Rowanstar to his place beside the others. As the ShadowClan leader wove between the Clans, Bramblestar called to him. "You have recovered from the sickness." Relief glowed in his moonlit gaze.

Rowanstar leaped onto the low branch and stood beside him. "The whole Clan has recovered."

Mistystar looked surprised. "Then why haven't you brought them?" Her gaze flicked to Tawnypelt and Tigerheart, who had pushed their way to the front.

Rowanstar lifted his chin. "They wouldn't join us." His gaze flashed angrily around the Clans. "They believe you betrayed them by allowing Onestar to withhold the herb we needed so desperately."

Onestar growled. "You recovered, didn't you? You never really needed it!"

Rowanstar snarled at the WindClan leader. "We only recovered because Harespring and Kestrelflight have more compassion than you! They gave us the herb!"

Shocked murmurs rippled through the crowd. Twigpaw stretched to see over the heads of the bigger cats. Kestrelflight seemed to shrink beneath his pelt. Harespring stared impassively at the gathered cats, betraying nothing. Twigpaw's pelt prickled with curiosity. Why had Alderpaw dropped his gaze? Why was Jayfeather puffing out his chest? Had they known about this? Clearly Onestar hadn't.

The WindClan leader's eyes sparked with rage. He glared down at Harespring. "Is this true?"

His deputy looked up steadily. "I could not let a Clan die."

Kestrelflight padded forward. "I consulted StarClan," he mewed. "They told me that it was the right thing to do."

Onestar's fur lifted along his spine. He dragged his astonished gaze from his medicine cat to Rowanstar, but before he could speak, the ShadowClan leader flicked his tail. "You were right about the rogues, though, Onestar."

Onestar stared at him.

"We should have driven them from the edge of our territory moons ago." Rowanstar's shoulders drooped. His anger over the herb seemed to drain from him. Suddenly he looked old, his pelt dull in the moonlight, his ribs showing where the sickness had ravaged him. "They have taken over my Clan."

"What do you mean?" Bramblestar padded along the branch, thrusting his muzzle close as shocked mews rang from the crowd.

Rowanstar met the ThunderClan leader's gaze. "Before we left for the Gathering, the rogues entered our camp."

Mistystar stiffened. "Was there a battle? Are many hurt?"

"There was no battle." Shame glittered in Rowanstar's gaze. "My Clan chose them over me."

"They *chose* them?" Bramblestar sounded puzzled. "What do you mean?"

"They said that any ShadowClan cat who came here tonight would not be allowed to return to the Clan."

Twigpaw stared at the ShadowClan cats in confusion. *But where is Violetpaw? She couldn't have decided to stay among the rogues— could she?* Twigpaw felt cold as she watched Rowanstar's paws tremble beneath him. He no longer looked like a leader. He looked like a hungry, frightened loner.

Onestar curled his lip. "I always said that ShadowClan was no better than rogues."

Rowanstar glared at him, energy sparking though his pelt suddenly. "That's not true! They have just made a mistake!"

Tigerheart called out from below. "The real ShadowClan cats will come to their senses before long and drive the invaders out!"

Tawnypelt stood beside her son, her chin high. "The sickness scared them. They are like frightened kits looking for someone strong to protect them!"

Onestar's tail flicked ominously. "And why didn't they look to Rowanstar? Isn't he strong?"

Rowanstar paws suddenly steadied on the branch. He lifted his head, his shoulders squaring. "I have been sick. Crowfrost has died. For days ShadowClan had no leadership, thanks to you. If you'd given us the herb earlier, this might never have happened."

Murmurs of agreement sounded around Twigpaw. She turned her head, seeing RiverClan and ThunderClan cats nodding. Even some of the WindClan cats were staring accusingly at their leader.

"What's done is done." Bramblestar's mew was calm. "For now Rowanstar, Tawnypelt, and Tigerheart will be welcome in ThunderClan. They can stay until their Clanmates realize their mistake."

Tawnypelt hissed miserably. "*If* they realize their mistake."

Bramblestar blinked at her sympathetically. "I know you feel betrayed. But it takes more than sickness and rogues to destroy the bonds of Clanship."

Onestar grunted. "Not in ShadowClan."

Rowanstar turned on the WindClan leader, teeth bared. Twigpaw's heart lurched. Was he going to attack Onestar? Her breath caught in her throat, but the ginger tom hesitated, then backed away. He turned to Bramblestar. "Thank you for your offer. We will be honored to stay with ThunderClan."

Honeypaw snorted beside Twigpaw. "Oh, great," she huffed sarcastically. "ShadowClan cats in our camp."

Twigpaw hardly heard her denmate. *But where is Violetpaw?* Why had she decided to stay with the rogues? What if they were holding her against her will? Was she in danger? Panic gripped Twigpaw's heart with stone claws.

"Are you okay?" Honeypaw stared at her bristling pelt.

"My sister," Twigpaw whispered hoarsely. "She's with the rogues." Her paws itched to race to the ShadowClan camp. She had to speak with Violetpaw. She had to know she was okay.

Paws pattered behind Twigpaw as Ivypool caught up to her the next day. They were approaching the border of ShadowClan, and Ivypool was hesitating. "You're really worried, aren't you?"

"Imagine if it was Dovewing!" Twigpaw snapped.

Ivypool didn't reply, but she stayed in step with Twigpaw.

"All I want to do is check that she's okay." Twigpaw felt hot.

She didn't like being so disrespectful, but this was important.

"What if ShadowClan takes you prisoner again?" Ivypool pointed out. "There's no Crowfrost around this time to let you go."

Twigpaw padded on, pressing back the fear churning in her belly. "It's just a risk I'll have to take. You can go back to camp. I don't mind going by myself."

Ivypool's ears twitched uneasily. "I'm not letting you cross the border alone."

Twigpaw glanced at Ivypool. "Maybe you can just wait there for me while I slip across." She didn't want to get her mentor into trouble.

"I'm not letting you out of my sight." Ivypool fell quiet for a few moments as they scrambled down a steep slope and leaped over a stream. On the far side, Twigpaw paused to catch her breath.

Ivypool stopped beside her. "Having ShadowClan cats in our camp is strange. I'm not sure I like it."

"I guess." Twigpaw headed toward the border once more.

Ivypool fell in beside her. "Two leaders *and* two deputies in one camp is just way too many. Did you see Tigerheart and Squirrelflight getting into it this morning about which to send out first, the border or the hunting patrols? I thought Squirrelflight was going to attack him. It was like a rabbit had just given her hunting advice. And Rowanstar!" Ivypool rolled her eyes. "He follows Bramblestar around like a shadow, giving 'tips.'"

"They seem all right," Twigpaw said with a flick of her tail.

"Anyway, they'll be gone soon, we hope."

"I guess." Ivypool didn't sound convinced. "I'd like to see them all go home soon. Especially Tigerheart."

Twigpaw looked at her mentor, surprised. "Why?"

Ivypool didn't return her gaze. "I'm not sure it's good for Dovewing to have him around the camp."

"Why not?" Twigpaw frowned, puzzled. "He doesn't seem so bad." She remembered the prickliness between the two warriors when they'd met in the forest.

"If only." Ivypool lowered her voice. "You know what it feels like to worry about your littermate, don't you? I mean, that's why we're here."

Twigpaw looked at her in surprise. "Of course."

Ivypool flicked her ear. "Well, this is a secret, so you mustn't tell, but Tigerheart and Dovewing used to have feelings for each other."

"*Feelings?*" Twigpaw took a moment to understand. "You mean they *liked* each other?"

"I think it was a bit more than *like*." Ivypool sounded disapproving. "But they're in different Clans, so it couldn't go anywhere. It's not good for things like that to be stirred up."

Twigpaw kept walking, her mind spinning. Dovewing and Tigerheart were in different Clans . . . just like her and Violetpaw. Couldn't Ivypool see that it was even worse to be separated from your kin? To not even be able to worry about her littermate properly, because she never knew what was going on?

The thought flitted away as ShadowClan scent touched her

nose. They were near the border. She could see the sprawling bramble that straddled the scent line. Slowing, she led Ivypool to the edge and crept along it. She peered around the end of the bramble and scanned the forest ahead. Where the oaks turned to pine, shadows closed in.

She narrowed her eyes, wondering where she'd find the quickest trail to the ShadowClan camp. Last time she'd come, she'd had the cover of darkness. Would her gray pelt camouflage her in daylight? Doubt tugged at her paws. Perhaps they should head home after all. Ivypool was right; if they were caught this time, Crowfrost and Rowanstar wouldn't be there to protect them. Only rogues.

Ferns shivered ahead. Paw steps scuffed the earth.

"Quick, hide!" Ivypool scuttled under the bramble and dragged Twigpaw after her.

Thorns snagged Twigpaw's pelt, and she screwed up her eyes as Ivypool pulled her deeper into the thicket.

She could hear two ShadowClan cats talking as they approached.

A she-cat was purring. "Darktail's not used to having to organize so many patrols. Did you see him this morning trying to decide who to send hunting? He looked like a confused badger."

Twigpaw stiffened. She recognized that mew. *Needletail.* She wriggled to the edge of the brambles and peered out.

The silver she-cat was walking beside a one-eyed tom, looking pleased with herself. "He should appoint a deputy to help him." She brushed close to the tom. "Someone like you."

The tom stopped and gazed at Needletail. "You remember what happened the last time I challenged Darktail for leadership."

"You won't be challenging him this time, Rain," Needletail murmured silkily. "You'll be offering to help him out."

Rain's whiskers twitched with amusement. "*You* should offer to be deputy," he meowed. "You'd be good at it."

As he leaned forward to nuzzle Needletail's cheek, Twigpaw hauled herself from beneath the brambles. Needletail cared about Violetpaw. She'd help, wouldn't she?

"Twigpaw!" Ivypool grabbed for her tail.

Twigpaw tugged it free from her mentor's paw and burst out in front of Needletail. She shook the prickles from her pelt. "Needletail. You have to help me!"

Needletail's eyes widened. "Twigpaw? What are you doing here?"

"I have to speak with Violetpaw."

"Violetpaw's in camp."

"But I have to know if she's okay." Twigpaw ignored the one-eyed tom, who was staring at her in surprise.

Ivypool slid from beneath the bramble and stood beside her. "We're sorry to intrude," she mewed apologetically. "But Twigpaw has been frantic about her sister. We just need to know she's okay and then we'll go."

"Of course she's okay!" Needletail bristled. "Do you think I'd let anything happen to her?"

"I have to talk to her." Twigpaw dug her paws into the leaf-strewn earth. Now that she'd come this far, she was determined to see Violetpaw for herself. What if Needletail was lying?

Needletail frowned. "I can't just go fetch her for you!"

Twigpaw stared at her pleadingly. "But you used to, remember? When we were kits. You and Alderpaw used to sneak us out so we could see each other. It's no different from that."

An impatient growl rumbled in Needletail's throat.

Twigpaw leaned closer. "If you're scared of Darktail, I understand. I'm happy to go to the camp myself."

Rain's gaze sharpened. "That would be brave."

Twigpaw shrugged. "I want to see my sister, that's all." *Please StarClan. Don't let them smell my fear-scent!*

Rain glanced at Needletail. "You'd better fetch her," he grunted. "This is the sort of cat who gets other cats into trouble." He scowled at Ivypool. "Are you her mentor?"

Ivypool lifted her muzzle. "Yes."

"You shouldn't have let her come here."

"That's like telling me I shouldn't let the wind blow through the forest. Some things you just can't argue with."

Needletail flicked her tail crossly. "Wait here." She turned and raced away.

Rain stayed where he was, staring at Twigpaw and Ivypool. He tipped his head. "How was the Gathering?" Amusement edged his mew. "Did the other Clans miss us?"

Ivypool's pelt ruffled. "Why would we miss rogues at a Gathering?"

"Didn't Rowanstar tell you?" Rain asked innocently. "We're ShadowClan now. We're just like you."

Ivypool flexed her claws. "No, you're not! You may have taken over ShadowClan's camp, but you're still rogues!"

Rain's whiskers twitched.

Twigpaw could see that he was enjoying irritating Ivypool. "Ignore him." She sat down, her gaze fixed on the forest where Needletail had disappeared.

Ivypool shifted uneasily beside her.

Rain stared at them, his gaze cold.

High above them, clouds stretched long paws over the pale blue sky. A breeze stirred the budding leaves. An age seemed to pass as they waited, but at last Twigpaw heard paw steps. She pricked her ears.

Familiar black-and-white fur flashed between the trunks. Violetpaw was running toward them, Needletail at her tail.

"Violetpaw!" Twigpaw rushed to meet her, startling Rain as she flashed past him. But she soon slithered to a halt, surprised at the anger in Violetpaw's eyes.

"Why in StarClan did you come here?" Violetpaw was glaring at her. "You could have gotten Needletail into trouble. Darktail asked her what she was doing back at camp. She had to lie."

Twigpaw blinked at her sister. Did Violetpaw care more about Needletail getting into trouble than about seeing her? "I could get into trouble too, you know," she snapped. "We're not *supposed* to be here. But I had to find out if you were safe."

"Of course I'm safe." Violetpaw glanced at Needletail. "I have friends here."

Irritation sparked beneath Twigpaw's pelt. She nudged

her sister aside and lowered her voice. "Are you really okay?" she hissed in Violetpaw's ear when they were out of range of Needletail. Perhaps Violetpaw was putting on a show for the rogues.

"Yes!" Violetpaw drew away.

Twigpaw kept her voice soft. "You can come back with me and Ivypool. You don't have to stay with the rogues. You can join ThunderClan, with me." She stared desperately into Violetpaw's amber eyes. This was their chance to be together again.

Violetpaw frowned. "Why should I? You didn't want to join ShadowClan to be with me."

"I didn't *want* to leave you! But I couldn't turn my tail on my Clanmates."

"Neither can I. Go back to your Clan and I'll go back to mine."

Twigpaw stared at her. "We're still sisters, right?"

Violetpaw blinked slowly. "I suppose." She glanced at Needletail again. "But we've each found our own Clan. We've each found where we belong."

Twigpaw stared at her. Was Violetpaw telling her they could never be together again?

A paw knocked Twigpaw aside. "Stop whispering!" Needletail pushed between them and glared at Twigpaw.

"It's okay," Violetpaw mewed. "We're done."

"Good." Needletail whisked her tail, still staring at Twigpaw. "Now leave."

Ivypool padded forward. "Is everything okay?"

Twigpaw nodded. "Everything's fine—"

Needletail lashed out, slicing Twigpaw's ear tip with a claw. "I said *leave!*"

Twigpaw flinched as pain seared through her.

"How dare you?" Ivypool hurled herself at Needletail. Hissing, she dragged Needletail to the ground, pummeling her belly with her hind paws. Needletail wriggled free, glowering at Ivypool. The smell of blood tainted the air as fur fluttered around them.

"Stop!" Panic flashed through Twigpaw. Rain was padding closer. "There's no need to fight."

Needletail and Rain circled them, eyes slitted and growls rumbling in their throats.

Violetpaw shoved Twigpaw away, her frightened gaze on the one-eyed tom. "Run! Get away from here before you get hurt!"

Ivypool nodded to Twigpaw. "Let's go."

Twigpaw ran. Her paws sent leaf litter flying as she hared around the bramble and crossed the scent line. She felt Ivypool's breath at her tail and heard Rain and Needletail chasing them. Pushing harder, she raced into ThunderClan territory. Ivypool pounded after her. Behind them, the sound of paw steps faded. She glanced back. Needletail and Rain were standing at the border, backs arched. Violetpaw stood beside them, watching with round, sad eyes.

Good-bye, Violetpaw. Twigpaw slowed, her lungs burning. Was that the last she'd see of her sister? Now that ShadowClan had turned rogue, could they ever meet again? She stumbled as her paws grew numb beneath her. Grief choked her. She and Violetpaw had chosen different Clans. Maybe their bond of kinship wasn't strong enough to survive their decision.

CHAPTER 24

♣

Alderpaw peered closer at Twigpaw's ear. The split in the tip had opened again, and he could smell fresh blood oozing from it. The sun had set, but the light of the half-moon, seeping through the medicine-den entrance, gave enough light to work by.

He reached for the herbs Jayfeather stored beside the pool for cats who came in with fresh cuts and scratches. The marigold would clear up any infection. "Remind me how you got this wound?" Alderpaw asked casually. He had asked Twigpaw when she'd first come to him, the day after the Gathering, when the nick in her ear was fresh. She'd just shrugged and told him it was a training accident.

She shrugged again now. "I can't remember. But I caught it again today on a bramble." Was she protecting her denmates? Had one of them been practicing their battle moves a little too roughly?

Worry wormed through his belly as he chewed marigold leaves to pulp. He couldn't help feeling that there was more to it than that. Twigpaw had been quiet since the ShadowClan rogues had cut ties with the other Clans. He spat pulp onto his paw. "Are you worried about Violetpaw?"

Twigpaw stared at the ground as he smeared it onto her ear. "I wish she weren't with the rogues."

"She has Needletail."

Alderpaw's words seemed to make Twigpaw's shoulders droop more.

"And Pinenose and Puddleshine." Alderpaw pressed on, determined to comfort her. But Twigpaw carried on staring at the ground.

"She grew up there," he reminded her. "ShadowClan is probably like family to her now."

Twigpaw looked at him, her gaze blank. "Are you finished?"

For a moment he wondered what she meant. Was she telling him to stop talking about Violetpaw and ShadowClan?

"My *ear*?" Twigpaw mewed when he didn't answer. "Are you finished treating my ear?"

"Y-yes." Alderpaw wondered if she'd been listening to a word he said.

"Thanks." She turned to leave.

"Twigpaw." He called after her. "You would tell me if something was really wrong, wouldn't you?"

She blinked at him, sadness glittering in her eyes. "Yes." Her mew was barely more than a whisper.

"Are you okay?"

Twigpaw hesitated, then dipped her head. "I'm okay," she promised. "Just a bit sad, that's all." She lifted her gaze, and he saw affection there.

Relief washed over him. The bond between them wasn't

broken. She just needed time to sort out whatever she was going through. "I'm always here if you need me," he told her.

"Thank you." Turning, she left the den.

"Alderpaw!" Jayfeather's mew sounded from the clearing.

Alderpaw hurried out, his paws still sticky with marigold pulp.

Jayfeather and Leafpool were waiting beside the entrance. Jayfeather turned his blind blue gaze toward the half-moon. "We don't want to be late for the meeting," he meowed gruffly. "Especially not tonight."

Excitement surged in Alderpaw's chest. He couldn't believe the time had finally come. As he hurried to join Jayfeather and Leafpool, Bramblestar padded across the clearing toward him.

"It's a big night for you." His father licked his ear affectionately.

Alderpaw blinked at him, suddenly nervous. "I hope I don't mess up the ceremony. What if I forget the words?"

"What do you have to say?"

"*I do.*"

Bramblestar purred. "I think you'll remember. I just wish I could be there to see you." Pride warmed his gaze.

So do I. Alderpaw half wished that his naming ceremony could happen in front of his Clanmates instead of at the Moonpool with the other medicine cats. He wanted to hear them cheer his name, just as they'd cheered Sparkpelt. But this was a StarClan ceremony, not a ThunderClan ceremony. It was right it should be held in their sacred place. Would they share with him afterward? He hoped so. He wanted to know if his ancestors were proud of him.

Squirrelflight paced the clearing a few tail-lengths away.

"Blossomfall, Berrynose, Sparkpelt, and Tawnypelt." She flicked her tail toward the warriors at the edge of the clearing. "I want you to come hunting with me."

Alderpaw blinked happily at his sister. Her eyes were bright, and she blinked back at him affectionately as Squirrelflight went on.

"We could do with a few more pieces of prey on the fresh-kill pile now that we have extra mouths to feed." Her gaze flicked toward Rowanstar and Tigerheart, who were sharing a pigeon beneath the Highledge.

Tigerheart leaped to his paws. "I'll hunt with you!" he offered eagerly.

Squirrelflight flicked her tail. "You stay here. Tawnypelt can help us."

Tawnypelt looked toward Rowanstar. "Is it okay if I hunt?"

Squirrelflight's hackles lifted. "You don't need to ask him!" she snapped. "*I* organize the hunting parties in Thunder-Clan."

Squirrelflight's pelt spiked angrily as Rowanstar nodded to Tawnypelt and the ShadowClan she-cat crossed the clearing.

As Blossomfall and Berrynose joined the patrol, the ThunderClan deputy glowered at them. "Do you need to ask Rowanstar's permission too?" She glanced pointedly at Tawnypelt. "Or are my orders enough?"

Blossomfall and Berrynose glanced at each other, confused.

Tawnypelt looked away, as though she hadn't heard the ThunderClan deputy's barbed reproach.

Alderpaw shifted his paws, unsettled by the discord the ShadowClan cats had sent rippling through the Clan. *They won't be here forever,* he told himself. He glanced at Tigerheart. The broad-shouldered tom's gaze was fixed on Dovewing again.

He always seemed to have one eye on the blue-eyed she-cat. Dovewing seemed unaware of it now, deep in conversation with Bumblestripe. But Tigerheart kept watching, his eyes narrowing as Bumblestripe moved closer to his Clanmate.

A shiver ran through Alderpaw's fur. *Do Dovewing and Tigerheart share some kind of history? The sooner these ShadowClan cats are gone, the better.*

"Hurry up." Leafpool's mew shook him from his thoughts. Jayfeather was already heading through the entrance tunnel.

"Good luck!" Sparkpelt called to him from beside Squirrelflight.

Squirrelflight gazed at him proudly. "We'll wait up for you!"

"Thanks!" Alderpaw ducked through the tunnel after Leafpool and Jayfeather, his heart quickening as he followed them toward the Moonpool.

"Do you think he's coming?" Kestrelflight's gaze was fixed on the rim of the hollow.

Alderpaw followed it, tasting the air for Puddleshine's scent. "I guess if the rogues didn't come to the Gathering, they won't let Puddleshine come here either."

Jayfeather flicked his tail. "He's not coming," he meowed.

Leafpool jerked her nose toward the blind medicine cat. "You know for sure?"

"No," Jayfeather mewed. "But I'm pretty certain. I'm also pretty certain that I don't want to sit here freezing my fur off all night. Let's get on with it."

For newleaf, the night was clear and cold. The crow-black sky sparkled with stars. Mothwing nodded her agreement, and the medicine cats drew into a circle around Alderpaw.

Alderpaw stiffened, his heart quickening. "Can't we wait a bit longer?" He wanted Puddleshine to see his naming ceremony. He had waited so long for it. "I want him here."

Jayfeather snorted. "You can want all you like. Shadow-Clan has made their choice and you can't change it."

Leafpool blinked at Alderpaw. "Puddleshine doesn't need to witness your naming ceremony to know what a good medicine cat you will be. He has always respected you."

Even though he's been saving lives while I've been rolling herb bundles. Alderpaw pushed away the prick of resentment, realizing that he wouldn't want to swap places with the ShadowClan medicine cat. He cleared his thoughts. He had worked hard, and he had earned this.

Jayfeather lifted his chin. "Let's begin."

Alderpaw faced him, excitement surging beneath his pelt. He was going to receive his medicine cat name at last!

"I, Jayfeather, medicine cat of ThunderClan, call upon my warrior ancestors to look down on this apprentice. He has trained hard to understand the ways of a medicine cat, and with your help he will serve his Clan for many moons." Jayfeather stared at Alderpaw. His blue gaze was so intense that Alderpaw felt as if the blind cat were looking straight into his thoughts. His paws felt hot against the chilly stone.

"Alderpaw has always had a natural connection with StarClan," Jayfeather went on. "You chose him, and you chose well. He is loyal, determined, and smart. He has compassion and strength, a rare combination. He will serve his Clan well."

Alderpaw's pelt pricked with surprise. Jayfeather was complimenting him! He could feel the gazes of the others burning his fur. Self-consciously he shifted his paws and straightened his spine. *I must behave like a medicine cat!*

Jayfeather went on. "Do you, Alderpaw, promise to uphold the ways of a medicine cat, to stand apart from rivalry between Clan and Clan, and to protect all cats equally, even at the cost of your life?"

Alderpaw blinked at him, his mouth dry. "I do."

"Then, by the powers of StarClan, I give you your true name as a medicine cat. Alderpaw, from this moment you will be known as Alderheart. StarClan honors your devotion and kindness, and we welcome you as a full medicine cat of ThunderClan." Jayfeather stepped forward and rested his muzzle on Alderpaw's head. "Well done," he breathed softly.

Alderpaw felt his mentor's warm breath swirl around his ears as he drew back. Pride warmed his pelt.

"Alderheart! Alderheart!" The other medicine cats called his name, their voices ringing around the stone sides of the hollow, spiraling up to the stars.

Jayfeather turned to the Moonpool. "Let us share with StarClan." He crouched and touched his nose to the water.

Leafpool caught Alderheart's eye as she padded toward the water. Pride glowed in her gaze. "Congratulations," she purred softly.

"Thanks." Alderheart ducked down beside her, his heart bursting with joy, and dipped his muzzle toward the pool.

At once, sunshine bathed him. Its warmth reached through his fur. He blinked at the brightness. He was back in the rolling meadows where he'd met Yellowfang. He padded forward, the soft grass brushing his paws. "Yellowfang?" He scanned the field hopefully. There was no sign of her, but at the edge of the field he saw the shapes of two cats sunning themselves in the low branches of a tree. He bounded toward them, his tail streaming behind him.

The light brown tabby she-cat and the pale gray tom didn't seem to see him. Sunshine glinted on their glossy pelts. The light brown tabby's tail draped over the branch as she blinked at the tom. The tom returned her gaze, his round eyes bright, his ears pricked. As Alderheart neared, he heard them murmuring quietly to each other. Skidding to a halt beneath the tree, he looked up. Should he call out? Should he tell them he was here? That he was a medicine cat now? As he lifted his face, leaves showered over him. They twirled in the breeze, brushing his face and whiskers. Five-pointed leaves.

Embrace what you find in the shadows, for only they can clear the sky.

The voice rang in his head.

It was the prophecy. StarClan was telling him again.

Heart pounding, Alderheart jerked his nose from the Moonpool. As the cold chill of the hollow closed around him once more, he blinked. The others were still sharing with StarClan. Only Mothwing watched him, from where she lay beside the pool.

Alderheart hardly saw her. His thoughts were spinning too fast. The leaves had five points! *Five points! Five Clans!* Suddenly he knew what the prophecy meant, more surely than he'd ever known before.

We need to find SkyClan!

A NEW WARRIORS
ADVENTURE HAS BEGUN

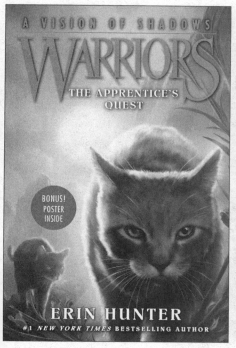

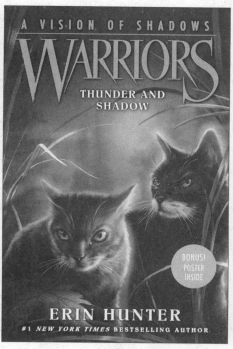

1   **2**

Alderpaw, son of Bramblestar and Squirrelflight,
must embark on a treacherous journey
to save the Clans from a mysterious threat.

HARPER
An Imprint of HarperCollinsPublishers

www.warriorcats.com

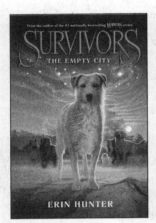

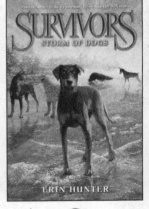